AN UNWELCOME QUEST

Also by Scott Meyer

MAGIC 2.0 SERIES

Off to Be the Wizard
Spell or High Water

A COLLECTION OF BASIC INSTRUCTIONS

Help Is on the Way
Made with 90% Recycled Art
The Curse of the Masking-Tape Mummy
Dignified Hedonism

SCOTT MEYER

47NORTH

Published by 47North, Seattle

www.apub.com

Amazon, the Amazon logo, and 47North are trademarks of Amazon.com, Inc., or its affiliates.

ISBN-13: 9781477821404

ISBN-10: 1477821406

Cover design by inkd

Library of Congress Control Number: 2014948928

Printed in the United States of America

The following is intended to be a fun, comedic sci-fi/fantasy novel. Any similarity between the events described and how reality actually works is purely coincidental.

PROLOGUE

It was a momentous day in Camelot. Not as momentous as the day a time-traveling computer enthusiast named Phillip showed up, called himself a wizard, and demonstrated the ability to do what appeared to be genuine magic. Not as momentous as the day another wizard calling himself Merlin talked the king into changing his oldest son's name to Arthur, and the city of London's name to Camelot. Certainly not as momentous as the day construction of the monstrously huge, gold-plated castle at the heart of Camelot had been completed.

All of these things were made possible by a computer file that Phillip, Merlin (or, as he was originally known, and would be known again one day, Jimmy), and all of the other wizards had found. The file proved that reality was merely an artificial construct controlled by a computer program. Manipulating this file allowed one to manipulate reality itself, travel in time, and create things that were, in a word, magical. Things like the initiation of a new wizard, which was the particular momentous event scheduled for this day.

What nobody knew was that this would also be the day that the wizards of Camelot first found reason to expel a wizard and exile him back to his own time. It was, as we've established, a momentous day.

Every wizard in Europe was gathered in the main ceremonial hall of the castle Camelot, eating good food that was bad for them, drinking very good drinks that were very bad for them, and generally enjoying themselves, because that was how the initiation ceremony worked. Besides, the powers they gained from their use of the computer file ensured that the food and drinks couldn't really hurt them, which made the party all the more enjoyable.

Twenty or so wizards sat around a table that would have filled any reasonably sized room, but which was almost lost in the vastness of the great hall. The hall was a cavernous expanse of polished marble and gold. The wizards all wore flowing robes and pointed hats. Most of them had staffs leaning against the table or lying on the floor behind them. A few had wands. Every group has its nonconformists. All of them, regardless of their personal magical-prop preference, were just finishing their meals.

"So, Gary, how'd you enjoy having an apprentice?" Phillip asked, before taking a swig of beer from his large earthenware stein.

Gary winced, which was funny, because that was exactly how most of the people who knew Gary had reacted when they heard it was his turn to train an apprentice.

"I dunno," Gary said. "It was cool, I guess."

Gary lapsed into a silence that begged those who heard it to ask for more detail. Phillip responded with a silence that invited Gary to keep talking.

"We, uh, we didn't really hit it off," Gary continued, shaking his head. He was a tall, spindly man with limp black hair and a limp black robe. When he shook his head, the ends of his hair waved like the tassels on the dress of a flapper dancing at a funeral.

Tyler asked, "What do you mean? Did you fight?"

Tyler and Jeff were the other two members of the contingent from the small town of Leadchurch. Tyler was one of the few black men who had ever found the file and used it to go to Medieval England instead of, say, ancient Morocco. Jeff was a slightly built man with black hair and a brilliant mind. He had been a successful engineer before finding the file. Jeff and Tyler were good friends with Phillip, and even better friends with Gary. They usually spent a great deal of time hanging around with Gary, because he was fun, and his place was something of a party house, or in his case, a party skull-shaped cave. They had deliberately kept their distance since Gary had been assigned his trainee.

"We didn't fight. Nothing like that," Gary said. He looked to the far end of the table. The trainee being initiated was sitting at the head of the table being lightly brainwashed by the chairman of the wizards, Merlin, as was also the custom. The Leadchurch wizards were sitting at the far end of the banquet table, and Phillip was taking periodic breaks from the conversation to glare at Merlin, his face a mask of loathing and scorn. Again, this was the custom.

"It's just . . ." Gary struggled, "our senses of humor didn't really mesh."

Jeff said, "So he didn't think you were funny. Big deal. Neither do I, most of the time."

"No," Gary said, "it's not that he didn't think I was funny. It's that he thought I was funny at the wrong times. If I said or did something I thought was funny, it would just confuse him, but occasionally I'd say something serious and it would make him laugh."

"For example?" Phillip asked.

"When I told him that we could make it so we didn't need air or water, but we couldn't figure out how to not feel like we need them, he thought that was the funniest thing ever. I told him it would be horrible, and he said, 'So we don't do it to ourselves. Just save it for someone else.' He even wrote up a quick macro, just to prove it could be done. It makes you invisible too. He called it *ghosting*."

"I can see how that would make you uncomfortable," Phillip said.

Gary said, "I know, right?"

"Well, I wouldn't worry," Tyler said. "It wouldn't work."

Phillip looked to the end of the table. Jimmy (everyone called him Merlin, but to Phillip he'd always be Jimmy, or that jackass Jimmy, if he was feeling particularly honest) was leaning toward the trainee, smiling broadly and chuckling as he said something Phillip was certain wasn't funny. The trainee had dark brown hair and a face that was mostly nose. He wore a brand new chocolate-brown robe. His staff, a varnished piece of wood as straight as a tent pole, topped with what appeared to be a red mushroom with white dots on the cap, leaned against the table. The trainee looked on impassively as that jackass Jimmy laughed out loud and slapped the trainee on the shoulder.

"What's his name again?" Phillip asked.

"Todd," Gary answered.

"Where's he from?"

"Phoenix, Arizona. 2005."

"Where'd he find the file?" Tyler asked.

"He never said," Gary answered with a shrug.

"What do you mean, 'He never said'?" Jeff asked.

"When I say 'He never said,' what I mean is that he, Todd, never said. I can't break it down any farther than that."

"Yeah," Jeff said, rolling his eyes. "I get that, but didn't you ask? How could you spend nearly a month training the guy and never ask?"

"I never said I didn't ask," Gary explained. "I didn't say I never asked. I didn't never ask. I never didn't ask."

"Are you saying that you asked?" Jeff asked.

Gary said, "I asked every day. I asked where he found the file. I asked why he'd come here. I asked if he'd gotten in trouble back in his time. Hell, I asked what he did for a living. All I ever got out of him was that he was from Phoenix, from the year 2005. After that, he'd change the subject. Eventually, I figured my job was to train him, not to write his biography."

Phillip looked back to the far end of the table. Todd was giggling. Jimmy looked confused and shared a look with his assistant, Eddie, who looked uncomfortable. Jimmy glanced down to Phillip's end of the table. Phillip quickly looked away. He didn't want Jimmy to see him looking. Phillip would be mortified if Jimmy thought that Phillip cared what Jimmy thought.

"What kind of things made him laugh?" Phillip asked.

Gary said, "Weird stuff. Things you wouldn't expect. I told him all about all the pranks you can pull on people using teleportation and conjuring spells, and he just sat there. Then I told him about the spells we aren't allowed to do, body modification, you know, the dangerous stuff. I dunno, I guess something about the way I described it just struck him funny."

Phillip looked back to the head of the table. Jimmy's assistant, Eddie, was talking. Like his boss, Eddie had adopted a fake name to live under as a wizard, but Phillip was willing to give him a pass. Eddie was the only Asian wizard in Europe, so he wore a red and gold robe and worked under the name "Wing Po, the mysterious wizard from the Orient." At this point in history, people didn't know how to react to "Eddie, the mysterious wizard from the Orient." They already had difficulty dealing with Eddie's thick New Jersey accent.

Eddie was smiling broadly, talking to Todd, the trainee, who was staring back at him, expressionless. Jimmy was looking at Phillip's end of the table, staring at Gary as if trying to get his attention. Jimmy gave up on Gary and looked directly at Phillip. There was something in Jimmy's expression that kept Phillip from looking away.

Phillip had felt a little unsettled. Jimmy looked uncomfortable. Phillip had never seen that before, and that made him feel a whole lot unsettled.

Phillip thought for a moment, then asked Gary, "Say, what's Todd doing for his macro?"

A macro is a sort of simple program, often used by computer experts to trigger a series of commands with one keystroke. Since the wizards of Camelot's powers were derived from computer code, they used macros to create complex magical effects designed to impress other wizards and freak out the locals.

"I dunno," Gary answered. "He wouldn't tell me anything. I figured I'd let him have his surprise. He seemed excited about it. I think it might be something kinda public. He asked a lot of questions about the locals."

Phillip returned his attention to the head of the table. Todd was laughing heartily at something. Both Jimmy and Eddie were looking at Phillip. Jimmy glanced at Todd, then back to Phillip, raising his eyebrows as if to ask a question. Phillip didn't know what the question was, and certainly didn't know the answer, so he shrugged, ending the three-way nonverbal conversation that had only really communicated the fact that none of them knew what was going on.

Jimmy frowned and said something to Todd, who stopped laughing and sat up straight. Jimmy stood and cleared his throat. Slowly, all of the wizards stopped talking.

Jimmy spread his arms wide, the gold trim on his jade-green robe glowing in the candlelight. He said, "Well, friends, I hope you've all enjoyed your meal." There were nods and a murmur of assent.

Phillip said, "I enjoyed it too," intimating that he was not Jimmy's friend. It wasn't a very good heckle, not up to Phillip's usual standards. For some reason, his heart wasn't in it.

Jimmy smirked and continued, a bit more confidently than before. Phillip's hostility had put him back on familiar footing. "As you all know, we are here to celebrate the arrival of a new wizard: Todd. He has been studying with Gary, and tomorrow he faces the trials."

They all smiled at this. Everyone at the table except Todd knew that the trials were a sham, and that the real test was already under way. After living and training with a wizard for a few weeks, the initiate spent the evening making dinner conversation with Jimmy; then he would be asked to say a few words and perform an original piece of magic: his macro. Most of the wizards' powers were derived from a shell program Jimmy and Phillip had written many years ago, which made manipulating the file that controlled reality easier and safer. The trainee's macro would usually consist of several of the effects already written into the shell strung together by a simple program, and would give the other wizards an idea of what kind of magic they could expect from the new wizard in the future. After all of that, everybody would reconvene without the trainee and take a vote. It was a formality. Until this night, nobody had ever been rejected. The next morning, they'd do everything they could to make the trainee nervous, let him in on the joke, then do everything they could to make the new wizard drunk.

Jimmy continued. "As is our custom, Todd will now say a few words; then he will show us all his macro."

Jimmy sat down. Todd took a deep breath, then stood and addressed the group. He was not a large man, nor was he good-looking. That said, it was difficult to take your eyes off him. Later, Phillip would decide it was his eyes. Something about his eyes drew your attention to them. It was difficult not to look at them, much like when talking to a police officer, it is difficult not to keep glancing at his gun.

"I am not a guy who makes friends easily," Todd began.

This was an excellent way to start. One didn't find oneself at this table without first stumbling across a very well hidden computer file, and that meant spending a lot of time poking around on computers. People don't often spend lots of time poking around computers at parties. Everyone listening could have said the same thing about himself. Heads silently nodded, almost involuntarily, at Todd's confession.

Todd continued. "Knowing what I know now, what we all know about how the world really works, I'm glad I didn't try."

All around the table, silently, heads stopped nodding. Several turned slightly to the side.

"Because now, I find myself here," Todd said, "with all of you. You've all been very kind, and made me feel so welcome."

This set the audience at ease. Phillip could feel the room relax.

Todd smiled. "I feel very much at home here, with you all. I can't imagine how terrible I would feel if you all turned on me, like all the others have." His mood seemed to darken, as did everyone else's.

"But I hope that doesn't happen," Todd said. "That would be unfortunate."

After a long silence, Jimmy stood, clapping his hands. "Right," he said, with strained good cheer. "And now, Todd, please show us your macro."

Todd instantly brightened. He left his spot at the head of the table and walked to the empty area off to the side. The half of the group sitting closest to him turned so as to easily watch the show. The hall was vast, a hundred feet tall and a hundred yards long. It was more than large enough for anything Todd may have had planned, but he stayed relatively close, only moving about twenty feet away from the table.

"I know," Todd said, "that most of you use your macro as kind of a greeting. You pull it out when you meet someone new to demonstrate your power. I hear that usually means lots of fire and smoke and flying around."

A wave of good-natured laughter rippled around the table, as if the group were collectively saying "Guilty as charged."

Todd smiled and laughed, but there was no mirth in it. It was the laugh of a man who heard your joke and thought it was funny that you were dumb enough to think he'd find it funny.

"That doesn't really demonstrate any power, does it?" Todd asked. "No. I mean, sure, it shows that you have power, but it doesn't show what that power is, you know? It proves nothing. It's like a really cool explosion. Sure, the fireball and the big noise get your attention, but really, it's the crater and the destroyed day-care center that leave an impression."

The wizards listening knew what his words meant but didn't know what to make of what he'd said.

Todd continued. "I'm doing something different. My macro doesn't hint at my power with something big and showy. It demonstrates it clearly with something small, but unmistakable." Todd waved his staff over the empty marble floor beside him and said, "Unray acromay."

Pig latin, Phillip thought. *Not a promising start.*

There was an explosion that created a bright flash, a hollow sound, and a smallish mushroom cloud of dingy smoke. When the cloud dissipated, Todd was standing next to a blue plastic tarp, which was obviously draped over a large human form.

Todd giggled and rubbed his hands together. He reached down and grabbed one corner of the tarp with his free hand and held his mushroom staff aloft with the other.

Todd said, "Guys, let me show you what real power looks like." He ripped off the tarp and threw it with a flourish. The tarp burst into flame the instant it left his hand. It distracted the wizards from Todd's presentation more than he had expected, because he accidentally threw it directly at them and because it burned much more slowly than he had anticipated. The flaming tarpaulin fluttered to a rest draped over the middle of the banquet table, several chairs, and two wizards who hadn't been quite fast enough to get out of the way. The wizards cursed and flailed until they were out of danger, watching as the tarp burned itself out in a few seconds; then everyone was able to turn their attention back to Todd.

A large man, a full head taller than Todd and easily twice as broad through the shoulders, stood motionless next to Todd, who looked sickeningly pleased with himself. Many of the wizards immediately jumped to the conclusion that Todd had created the image of a man and had gotten many of the basic dimensions wrong. The wizards from Leadchurch knew better. Leadchurch was too small a town for someone as large as Kludge to go unnoticed.

Kludge was the second-largest, second-strongest, and second-most-violent person in Leadchurch. The fact that the largest, strongest, and most violent person in town was a woman named Gert had led Kludge to become the angriest person in town by a comfortable margin.

Gary, who had very specifically told his trainee that non-wizards were not allowed at the banquet, asked, "What's he doing here, Todd?"

"Anything I want," Todd nearly squealed, "and only what I want. He's powerless to make a move until I make him move. I have complete control."

"So, if you don't make him move, he'll just stand there until he dies?" Phillip asked.

"He'll keep standing there after that. He's held in place by invisible force bands around several parts of his body. Even if he goes totally limp, he'll keep standing there at attention, but what fun is that?" Todd muttered something under his breath, reached into his hat, and pulled out an object Phillip had never seen. It was an oddly shaped chunk of plastic that had been dyed unconvincingly to look like metal. It had two small handles and was covered with switches, triggers, and buttons.

Jeff asked, "Is that a Nintendo Wavebird?"

"Yeah," Todd said. "Good eye. They've never really made a better controller." Todd flipped a switch and a small light glowed on the controller. He held it in both hands, his staff tucked under his arm. Todd looked at Kludge, giggled a bit, then pushed the control stick forward with his left thumb. Kludge lurched forward with his right foot, as if suddenly seized with the irresistible urge to stomp on a bug. He stood motionless for a moment; then his left foot whipped forward and stomped down with bone-jarring force. His right foot lurched forward again, followed by his left, and the cycle repeated so that he walked inexorably toward the wizards. After a few graceless steps his trajectory curved so that he walked in a circle around Todd. Each step was a powerful stomp, as if he were trying to crush the floor with his heels. From the waist up, however, Kludge remained motionless, as if his lower half were a vehicle upon which his upper body merely rode.

"I know the walk cycle needs a lot of work," Todd said as Kludge continued to orbit him, "but you have to admit, it's a good proof of concept. This isn't all either. I can control his arms too."

Todd's right thumb pushed a second, smaller joystick to the left, and both of Kludge's arms whipped instantly to Kludge's left as if he were dancing the world's most aggressive hula. Todd pushed the stick to the right, and Kludge's arms followed suit.

Todd rolled the stick around, and Kludge waved his arms over his head as he continued to stomp circles around Todd.

Todd said, "I can also make him turn his head," and instantly, Kludge's head wrenched to the left, then to the right, then back and forth as he continued to flail and stomp laps around his master.

"Stop him!" Phillip yelled. "Stop him right now!"

"I can do that too," Todd said. He lifted his fingers and thumbs from the controls, and Kludge came to an immediate halt. Todd looked at the dumbstruck faces of the other wizards. He turned to Jimmy and said, "Mr. Chairman, would you like a closer look?"

Jimmy came forward, as did Phillip, even though he was not invited. As they got close to the now-stationary Kludge, they could see that while he stood unnaturally still, his eyes were alive, blinking and rolling around frantically in his head.

Jimmy turned to Todd and asked, "Is he awake?"

"Yes," Todd answered.

Jimmy asked, "Why?"

Todd snorted. "I guess he's not tired."

"But I thought you said you have total control over him," Phillip sputtered.

"I do," Todd replied. "I have total control over his motions."

"But not his mind," Jimmy said.

Todd shrugged. "Okay, yeah, you got me. Yeah, I can't control his brain, but I'm pretty sure I know what he's thinking."

Phillip looked up at the large man's eyes, glaring down at him, and thought, *Yeah, I think I do too.*

Jimmy asked, "Can I talk to him?"

Todd said, "Knock yourself out."

Jimmy and Phillip exchanged a look; then Phillip asked, "Will he be able to answer?"

Todd smiled. "Sure."

Jimmy and Phillip exchanged another look; then Jimmy asked, "Will he answer with his words, or yours?"

Todd said, "He can't say anything on his own, but I can make him talk. Check this out."

Todd pressed a button, and Kludge's mouth stretched open to the very limits of what his jaw muscles could endure and snapped shut violently, slightly out of sync with the syllables as a recording of Todd imitating a deep, menacing voice said, "Hello, world! I am Todd's slave! Isn't that great?"

A wave of uncomfortable murmurs rose from the wizards. Phillip and Jimmy glanced at each other, fidgeting nervously. Phillip knew what he thought of Todd's handiwork, and he knew what he hoped Jimmy thought, but with Jimmy it was always difficult to know for sure. *Maybe I should say something. Speak my mind*, Phillip thought. *It'll reassure the others who know this is unacceptable, and maybe sway the few who are on the fence. I hope it's only a few of them who're on the fence, anyway.*

"Todd," Phillip said, "this is awful."

Todd looked irritated and said, "Wait, wait, I know what you're thinking. Look, the lip sync is off, and the big dummy's moving kinda clumsily, but you have to admit the potential. I haven't even shown you all he can do yet. Here, one second. Look at this."

Todd pressed some combination of buttons that went by too quickly for Phillip to catch them. Kludge's arms whipped up in front of him with his palms facing forward. His mouth whipped open and the mocking recording of Todd's voice cried, "Double high five!"

Phillip and Jimmy glanced at each other again. Jimmy shrugged and started to oblige, but Todd lifted a finger and said, "One sec."

After a moment, the recording said, "Come on, bro! Don't leave me hanging!" Kludge's eyes were closed now, as if he were trying to convince himself none of this was happening, but his mouth still followed the recording like a reluctant ventriloquist's dummy.

Jimmy shook his head, then lifted his arms over his head to slap Kludge's hands. Just as his hands made contact, Kludge's right arm swung down in a blindingly fast arc and punched Jimmy in the crotch so powerfully that it lifted Jimmy off his feet.

Jimmy staggered backward, fell to the ground, and rolled onto his back, doubled over in pain. Several wizards ran to his side to offer assistance. Phillip strolled to his side to look at him. Jimmy looked up at Phillip, and the look in his eye removed any doubt Phillip had felt about Jimmy's feelings regarding Todd's macro.

Phillip looked at Kludge, standing frozen in his crotch-punching pose. His eyes were still closed. Phillip saw a single tear rolling slowly down Kludge's cheek. Phillip's eyes went down to Kludge's hand. Obviously, Todd didn't have control of the fingers, and had been unable to force Kludge to make a fist, because at least two of Kludge's fingers were badly broken.

The next morning, Phillip was back in Leadchurch, standing in a small side room in the lead-covered house of worship that gave the town its name. He was looking down at the sleeping form of Kludge, who was lashed to a heavy oak table with thick leather straps. Three of the fingers of his right hand were tied to wooden sticks, and his arms and forehead were ringed with dark bruises. In a sense, Kludge had caused the bruises himself by struggling against Todd's force fields. Phillip suspected there were more, all over Kludge's body, but he wasn't going to look.

Phillip asked, "How is he?"

Bishop Galbraith, the gruff, crusty master of the lead church, said, "He's resting comfortably."

Phillip shook his head. "Those straps don't look very comfortable."

"Maybe not for him," Bishop Galbraith said, "but they make me more comfortable. If he weren't tied down, I wouldn't want to be anywhere near him when he wakes up and remembers whatever it is you all did to him."

"Of course. Please give my thanks to the sisters for tending to him. I want you to know that we all didn't do this to him, Your Excellency. It was one wizard's work."

The bishop held up a hand and said, "I'll trust you lot to take care of that. Don't lose too much sleep worrying about this oaf. This isn't nearly as bad as some of the things he's done to other people in his life. Some of the villagers might actually think better of wizards once word of this gets out. I'd just recommend you all avoid Kludge in the future. He's not apt to forgive and forget."

"Don't worry about that," Phillip said. "I can't imagine any of us would be lax enough to let him catch us off guard."

"And what about whichever of you heathens did this to him?"

"It was an apprentice."

The bishop whistled. "An apprentice did this? Who was his master? Who'd be irresponsible enough to let this happen right under his nose?"

Phillip said, "His master was the necromancer of Skull Gullet Cave."

"Ah," Galbraith said. "That makes sense. What do you intend to do to the apprentice?"

"We're going to make certain that he never hurts anybody ever again."

Bishop Galbraith said, "Aye, you hate to do it, but killing him is probably the only way."

"What? No. I'm sorry, you misunderstood. We're not going to kill him."

The bishop shook his head. "Well, I understand wanting to be merciful, but I'm pretty sure that even if you don't do the apprentice in, Kludge here will as soon as he's up and around, and he won't do as clean a job of it as you would." The bishop looked sideways at Phillip and smirked. "Or is that your plan? You get to be merciful, the apprentice gets justice, and Kludge gets his revenge. Phillip, I didn't think you were that clever."

Phillip said, "That's not our plan."

"Oh," Galbraith said. "Oh well. Good to know I was right."

"About me not being clever?" Phillip asked.

"Yes, Phillip," the bishop answered, a bit more slowly than Phillip thought necessary.

"Don't worry, Your Excellency. While you and the sisters were tending to Kludge's wounds, we spent the entire night planning how to deal with the man who did this. We're going to send him to a place where he'll be safe from Kludge, and everyone will be safe from him. We've made sure that he will never be able to return."

"What are you thinking? Some sort of dungeon?"

"Worse," Phillip said. "Far worse. I give you my word, he will spend the rest of his life in a place many would consider worse than death."

1.

Seven years in Florida, Todd thought. *Has it really been only seven years?*

Todd, like most Americans, had a very clear picture in his head of what life in Florida was like, a picture created entirely by commercials for theme parks and old episodes of *Miami Vice.* Again, like most Americans, his real-world experience of Florida had been quite different. For most people, this was because they lived in the real world, in which they needed food, had to work, and didn't drive an apparently bulletproof Ferrari. For Todd, it was because he had spent his entire time in Florida sitting in a private cell in a top-secret maximum-security federal prison.

Life in an air-conditioned cinderblock cage had shaped Todd's perceptions of the whole state. If asked to describe Florida in three words, he would have said, "Gray, chilly, and dry."

For most of his time in The Facility (that was the only name his prison had ever been given), he had been in solitary confinement, not because he had done anything particularly bad but because none of the other prisoners had done anything bad enough to deserve being put near him. It wasn't that his company was that unpleasant. It wasn't *just* that, anyway. It was mostly because, for reasons that very few people understood, no electronic device would work anywhere near him. No television.

No radio. No computers. Nothing. Being near Todd Douglas meant also having nothing to distract you from the fact that you were near Todd Douglas, and that, it was decided, was cruel and unusual punishment.

For years, Todd sat in his cage and rotted, his only entertainment coming from video game strategy guides he got through the prison library. He loved video games. Reading about them when he couldn't play them was torture, but it was slightly less torturous than not reading about them at all. Todd had been on the verge of losing all hope when out of nowhere, a Treasury agent named Murphy turned up with a note from Merlin. He was calling himself Jimmy now, but he was still one of the bastards who had stripped Todd of his powers and exiled him here in the present for no reason.

I didn't even do anything, he often thought. *I just made someone else do stuff.*

With that one note, Jimmy had done Todd three big favors.

He had told Todd that he was not alone. Others had suffered the same fate he had, and at least one of those exiled like him was one of the very wizards who had exiled Todd in the first place.

He showed Todd that it was possible to escape. That one could regain one's powers. It was possible. You just needed to find someone stupid enough to help you.

Lastly, by having the letter hand-delivered by one of the Treasury agents who was working with him, Jimmy had essentially introduced Todd to someone who was, in fact, stupid enough.

It hadn't surprised Todd when the agent and his partner turned up later with Merlin (a.k.a. Jimmy). They never said as much, but their silence on the subject, their need for Todd to help them find another iteration of the file, and their overabundance of caution where Todd was concerned sent the clear message that Jimmy had regained his powers and escaped.

Of course, in doing so, he had made it that much harder for Todd to trick them into giving him his freedom, but Todd knew that sooner or later an opportunity would present itself.

It was late. Agents Miller and Murphy had long since left for the day, back to the one-bedroom condo the Department of the Treasury had rented for them when it became clear that they were going to be in Florida indefinitely. Todd sat on his bed and reread a strategy guide for a game he had, of course, never played. The game was about a fortune hunter exploring exotic locales, seeing the world, having adventures, and making love to beautiful women. Todd closed his eyes and dreamed of a future where he could escape this prison and, if he was lucky, play that game.

Todd was so caught up in his fantasy, picturing the game console, feeling the controller in his hands, that at first he didn't hear the footsteps coming toward his cell. Usually, the way their search for the file worked was that one agent would stand near the cell and get directions from Todd while the other sat at a computer around the corner and out of range of Todd's magnetic field, following the directions and yelling back what he saw, but all of that happened during business hours. Once the agents left for the day, nobody bothered Todd except to deliver meals. Todd put his game guide down and sat up straight, wondering who his visitor would be. One of the agents? The warden, perhaps?

Todd was surprised when a guard he'd never met walked around the corner. The guard studied Todd and didn't seem impressed with what he saw. Finally, he said, "I know who you are."

"Really?" Todd asked.

"Yes," the guard replied. "You're Todd Douglas, the prisoner who's been assisting Agent Miller and Agent Murphy, and now you're going to help me."

"Really?" Todd asked.

"Yes," the guard replied, squinting at Todd in a way he probably thought looked shrewd. "I don't know what you've done, or how it helped them, but it did, and you're going to tell me all about it."

Todd stood, and stepped toward the bars of his prison cell. He leaned on the bars and said, "Really?"

"Yes," the guard said.

A long silence passed before the guard coughed, then continued. "See, when they first showed up, we all looked down at Miller and Murphy. Heck, we sorta felt sorry for them. Murphy, at least. They clearly had a crap detail, shipped out here from California, stuck talking to you all day every day. Their lives sucked." The guard saw the look on Todd's face and said, "Oh, uh, sorry. No offense intended."

"Really?" Todd asked.

The guard pressed on. "I'm just sayin', they seemed so beat down. Then, all the sudden they're on top of the world."

It was true. Using the skills that had helped Todd hack into the file to begin with, and the patterns Agents Miller and Murphy had found going over their notes from their time spent seeking out copies of the file with Jimmy, they had, just two days ago, found a fresh, undiscovered copy of the file. One that hadn't been locked down by those who were trying to keep the power of the file for themselves.

They'd spent their work time since exploring the file. Miller and Murphy seemed very excited and asked many questions, which Todd tried to answer, directing them to use his own entry as an example.

The guard said, "Some of the guys say they heard Miller and Murphy talking. They say they're setting up a new headquarters for their task force. Getting an office. Hiring up a staff. Setting up shop. Seems they found a way to use whatever you told them to get the Treasury Department to give them some real funding."

Todd smiled and asked, "Really?"

"Yes, really!" the guard shouted. "Really, okay?! Really!"

"Fine, okay. Sorry," Todd said. He immediately assumed that this story was a smoke screen. The Treasury Department was, by definition, tight with money. One of the simplest applications of the file was generating unlimited amounts of cash. It was far more likely that Miller and Murphy were using this new office and staff to somehow hide and launder the money they were generating with the file. They were probably telling themselves that they'd use the money to bankroll their efforts to fight crime, but sooner or later, they'd go mad with power. Everyone who found the file did.

Everyone but me, Todd thought. *They took access away from me before I ever got the chance.*

"So, what's any of this got to do with you?" Todd asked.

The guard said, "Look, the thing is, I hate this place."

Todd said, "It's a prison."

"Yeah, I know, but man, you don't understand. I really want out of here."

"It's a prison, and I'm a prisoner. I understand wanting out of here."

"Not like I do," the guard said.

"You may be right about that," Todd said, showing more restraint than he usually had.

"Then you'll help me?"

"Help you do what?" Todd sputtered. "Leave? I can't leave myself! You can! Start walking down the hall. If a door is in your way, open it. Keep going until you're outside. I don't understand what you're asking for here."

"I know that you're a prisoner and I'm a guard, but I'm just as trapped as you are."

"No, you're not! You go home every night!"

"Yes," the guard said, "but every morning, I have to come back. I have to leave my home, get in my car I pay for, and burn my gas driving myself here, to this prison, every day. You inmates never stop to think about how terrible that is for us guards, do you?"

"No," Todd said. "You're right. We don't."

"So you'll help me?"

Todd said, "I still don't get it. You hate your job. So what? How can I help you with that? You want a reference? 'Of all the guards who have watched me, he watched me the closest'?"

The guard smiled. "You're on the right track, actually. Look, you're right. I hate my job. The problem is, they aren't going to promote me. They've made that clear. But I can't get a job anywhere else because I work at a secret prison. I can't put it on my resume, can I? If I try to fill out a job application, it'll look like I've been unemployed for a decade."

"I can see how that could be a problem," Todd said.

"Yeah, but Miller and Murphy, they're setting up a new office. I figure they'll probably need some help, and they know me already, so why shouldn't I go work for them?"

"Have you mentioned this idea to them?" Todd asked.

"Yeah."

"And since you're talking to me, I guess it didn't go well."

"They said they'd consider it."

"Which usually means no."

"Yeah," the guard agreed, "but I figure if you tell me what you told them that got the Treasury Department so excited, I can use that to get a job. You know, impress them with my moxie."

"Or blackmail them with the threat of taking it to another agency, or the press."

The guard shrugged. "Yeah, maybe, depending on what it is and how reasonable they're willing to be."

"Fair enough," Todd said. "But why should I help you?"

The guard smiled. "Well, that's the thing. If you don't, that means I stay here, with you. Only, like you said, you're an inmate. I'm a guard. You can't really do much to make my life worse. I can do *lots* of things to make yours worse."

I've been in solitary confinement for seven years, Todd thought. *What's he gonna do to make that worse, mess with the air-conditioning?*

Todd did not say this. Instead, he feigned a look of fear and said, "I see your point." Todd knew that this was his chance. This man came here intent on pulling Todd's strings and making Todd dance. He didn't realize that the strings could be pulled the other direction. In many ways, the puppeteer got the short end of the stick. While the puppet does the dancing and gets the applause, the puppeteer does all of the real work.

"Okay, fine. But I can't tell you what it is. You won't believe it. I kinda have to show you," Todd said, pointing. "Go see if the computer is on."

The guard walked around the corner, out of Todd's sight.

Todd knew that at the end of a thirty-foot hallway, just inside a locked gate, there was a computer, a desk of some sort, and a chair. He listened as the guard walked to the end of the hall. After a few seconds of silence, the guard turned and walked back. When he reached Todd's cell, he said, "Yeah, it's on."

Todd expected this. Once they'd found the file, they'd all been terrified of not being able to get to it again. Murphy had documented every move they'd made so that he could repeat it without Todd's assistance, but he also left the computer on with the file open, just in case. Of course, there was the chance that someone would find the computer and mess with the file, but the computer was located behind several locked gates, inside a top-secret maximum security prison, by itself in a hall near an inmate that the guards actively avoided, so the risk was considered pretty slight.

"Good," Todd said. "What's on the screen?"

The guard went back to the corner, peered down the hall, and said, "A bunch of words and numbers."

"Yeah, Todd said, "okay, but what are they? Go look for my name. Todd Douglas. Scroll up a little if you have to, but don't change anything."

Miller and Murphy had been very interested in how someone's file entry related to their physical existence, but they'd been too cowardly to look at their own entries. It was far safer to poke around in Todd's. Now their cowardice was paying off for the last person they'd want to help, as cowardice usually does.

The guard nodded and walked around the corner. Todd searched his cell as quickly as he could without making noise, looking for a specific book. It was a strategy guide for a

role-playing game. He didn't have to search long. He opened to
the section of the book with the maps of the various levels and
locations in the game. The maps had lots of empty space around
the borders, and Todd had furiously scribbled notes there whenever Miller gave him a moment of privacy.

The guard shouted, "Found it."

Todd leapt to the corner of his cell closest the computer. It
only got him a few feet closer, but Todd was too excited for ratio-
nal thought. "Okay," He yelled, "is there a box anywhere on the
screen labeled 'search'?"

After a few agonizing seconds, the guard said, "Yeah. It's in
the upper right-hand corner. Is that right?"

"Yeah, yeah, good," Todd said. "I want you to take the block
of words and numbers that has my name in it, and I want you to
select the whole thing. You'll have to scroll through a few pages,
that's fine, but get the whole block highlighted, okay?"

The guard shouted back, "Will do."

Todd waited. He heard the guard curse, and his heart
stopped.

"What?!" Todd shouted. "What happened?!"

If the guard accidentally closed the program, they probably
wouldn't be able to get it back before morning. Murphy would
see it and know someone had tampered with the computer. At
this point, he and Miller might just decide they didn't need Todd
anymore, and then Todd would be screwed.

"Oh," the guard yelled, "I didn't get the whole thing highlighted. I stopped about half a line short. Here, I'll start over."

"No!" Todd said. "Don't! That's fine! That'll do. We're good.
We're good."

Once the file was found, Miller had abandoned his post at the corner of Todd's cell and stood over Murphy as they discussed their discovery. Todd had strained to hear their conversation and heard them discuss his cursed magnetic field. He gathered that it was modified in the same way that Jimmy's had been. He talked the guard through the process of finding, then modifying the magnetic field's properties.

There was the clacking of keys, then a long silence. Todd heard the guard stand up and walk back to the cell.

"Did you do it?" Todd asked, trying to hide his excitement.

The guard said, "Yeah. What did it do? What was supposed to happen?"

Todd said, "I dunno. Say, is that a digital watch?"

The guard said, "Yeah."

"What time is it?"

The guard looked at his watch and said, "Huh, that's weird."

Todd asked, "Is it broken?" and tried to hide his disappointment.

The guard said, "Yeah," and held his arm out so Todd could read the watch himself. "It's just flashing twelve."

Todd instantly shifted gears. He had been hiding disappointment, and now he was trying to hide his glee. Being near him before they'd reset his magnetic field had clearly rebooted the watch, but it was working now. The cheap digital watch's dull, gray screen uselessly flashing twelve was the most beautiful thing Todd had ever seen.

The guard obviously noticed what an important moment this was for Todd. "How long have you been in here? You've never seen a digital watch before?"

"No, I've seen plenty of digital watches," Todd said. "That's just a really nice one. It looks like it's made from really good, um, plastic."

The guard looked down at his watch with some pride. "Yeah, well, Casio knows what they're doing. Look, I did what you said, and nothing happened. Nothing I could see on the computer anyway. What was supposed to happen?"

Todd tried to think fast. "I can't say. They didn't tell me. I don't know what it's supposed to do. I just know that they wanted my help finding that file, and that they were planning to do what we just did."

The guard asked, "Why'd they need your help to find it?"

"Because I found it before."

"How'd they know that?"

"It's why I'm in prison," Todd said, thinking fast. "Look at me, do I look like a criminal to you? I found that file, and whatever it is, it was important enough for them to throw me in jail."

The guard was clearly puzzled and was trying to solve the puzzle by the time-honored method of frowning about it. Eventually he said, "Well, that's what you showed them, and it got them their funding and their fancy new office. Maybe if I just casually mention it to them that'll be enough to either impress them or spook them into giving me a job, even if I don't know what it means."

Todd said, "Maybe. But what if it doesn't? What if you did it wrong, somehow, and they ask you what was supposed to happen and you don't know?"

"I did what you told me to. Did you tell me to do it wrong?" the guard asked.

"Well," Todd said, a little too loud, "I mean, you were working from instructions I was giving you without seeing the computer. I may have gotten some part of it wrong. That's understandable, right? And if I did, you'll look like a chump."

"Yeah," the guard agreed.

"And we don't want that," Todd said. "You'd be stuck here, and you'd make my life miserable, like you said."

The guard said, "Yeah, I would."

"We can keep that from happening. Just let me go have a look at the computer."

The guard shook his head. "Oh, I don't think that's a good idea."

"But it is," Todd said. "Look, you're a trained federal prison guard, right? I'm just some guy who found the wrong file and ended up behind bars. It stands to reason that you're smarter than me, doesn't it? I mean, if you weren't, I wouldn't be your prisoner, would I? Besides, you'll be right there watching me the whole time."

One minute later, Todd was out of his cell, standing in front of a functioning computer with the file open and cued up to his entry. Todd moved Murphy's metal folding chair back away from the desk so he could stand over the keyboard. The guard stood beside him, looking quite worried, but not quite worried enough.

Todd said, "Okay. Watch carefully. All I'm going to do is look for a specific set of numbers."

Todd selected his data chunk and searched for his current longitude and latitude while the guard looked on.

Todd's hands hovered over the keyboard for a moment while he thought. He asked the guard, "Hey, do you know what direction north is?"

The guard pointed to the left. Todd pointed to the right, the front, and behind him while mumbling "South, east, west." He reached back down to the keyboard, made a small change, and vanished instantly.

The guard squinted at the empty space where Todd had been. He was still trying to process what he had just seen when he heard a sound directly behind him. The guard turned just in time to be hit in the face with a metal folding chair.

The guard lay unconscious on the floor and didn't hear Todd say, "Look at the bright side. They'll probably fire you."

2.

Centuries earlier, in Medieval England, it was movie night for the wizards, which was just as confusing as it sounds.

The wizards were all time travelers, and for many years, they had held to an unwritten rule to not speak too much about their own times. Any two of them could be from times that were up to three decades apart. It was thought that discussion of the changes in society, social mores, and the quality of the various casts of *Saturday Night Live* would only lead to unnecessary conflict. In fact, the wizards from the mid-1990s or later refused to discuss any movies at all for fear of letting slip any details of the *Star Wars* prequels or the fourth *Indiana Jones*, a group of works that the later wizards would only refer to by the collective title *The Unpleasantness*.

Later, of course, attitudes grew more lax. Wizards from earlier times wanted to play with more advanced hardware, and wizards from later times wanted to see the looks on their faces when they did, so the system slowly broke down.

Eventually, the wizards started sharing information freely, even arranging a film festival, during which all three *Star Wars* prequels and the fourth *Indiana Jones* movie were all screened back to back, in the name of getting it over with.

Since then, the wizards of Leadchurch had settled into a nice routine, holding a weekly movie night, taking turns subjecting each other to a double feature of their favorite films (mostly science fiction) and their favorite food (mostly pizza).

It was Phillip's turn to host the party, and the guests were having difficulty processing his first selection. As the credits rolled, Phillip stopped his massive Betamax machine and hit rewind.

"Well, that's *Colossus: The Forbin Project*. What do you think?" he asked his friends, who were scattered comfortably around his rec room, their wizard robes unbuttoned to show the T-shirts, jeans, and sneakers they always wore underneath, except for Roy, who was of a different generation. He wore slacks, loafers, and a short-sleeved button-down shirt, but then again, he also wore a trench coat instead of a robe, and he had the only wizard hat with a fedora brim. His staff was what billiards players refer to as a "bridge."

Martin stood up from the chrome and leather couch he had been sharing with Tyler and Jeff. He stretched his back and groaned, "I dunno. It was interesting, but I want to see the sequel before I pass judgment."

Phillip smiled. "There was no sequel."

Gary, who was slowly unfolding himself after two hours of sitting cross-legged on the floor, asked, "What do you mean, no sequel? Didn't it do well enough to get a second movie made?"

Roy shook his head. He was the oldest man in the room in terms of physical age, because he was in his early fifties, and because he was from the year 1973. He also was an aerospace engineer by training and exuded a demeanor of terse, dependable authority. "See, kids, back in Phil's and my day, if you made a good movie, you took that success and made a different movie, not the same movie over again."

Phillip was the second-oldest man in the room. He was in his early forties, from the mid-1980s, and exuded an air of foppish, fallible authority. He smiled broadly and said, "Actually, that was your day. In my day they had started doing the endless sequel thing. This movie was from before, and I don't think there was ever any plan for a sequel."

"But it ended with a cliffhanger," Tyler said.

"No, it didn't," Phillip explained. "That was the end of the story."

"But," Tyler sputtered, "the supercomputer, whatcha-call-it, Colossus, had completely taken over the world."

"Yes," Phillip agreed.

"What? What kind of movie is that?" Tyler asked, indignant.

Phillip chuckled. "A seventies movie. The central message of science fiction was that we were all doomed."

Jeff snorted. "The message of the seventies was that we were all doomed." Jeff was from a time later in the future than anyone else in the room, but he and Roy had hit it off, and Roy had taken Jeff on a field trip to the early 1970s. Jeff returned badly shaken and refused to even discuss going back.

"Indeed!" Phillip said.

"And people paid to see these movies?" Jeff asked.

Phillip said, "Yeah. All the time. That was one of the first films my dad ever took me to see. It's why I went into computer science."

"So you could prevent computers from taking over?" Martin asked.

"That, or be on the winning side when they did," Phillip answered.

Tyler stood and picked up his staff from the floor. He asked, "Well, is the next movie going to be more positive?"

Phillip said, "We'll see." He smiled broadly, which meant that the answer was almost certainly no.

Tyler groaned and said, "I'm gonna go to the bathroom." Then he teleported away. One of the chief advantages of no-cost teleportation was that you never had to use a strange bathroom again.

Martin muttered something about getting some fresh air and stepped outside.

The bottom floor of Phillip's shop was where he read his crystal ball, made fake potions, and in general acted *wizardly*. The top floor was a chrome and plastic salute to bachelorhood in the mid-1980s, right down to the white Pontiac Fiero that was displayed like a coveted piece of art. In front of the Fiero there were two large doors that led to a deck that could also serve as a bridge for the Fiero to drive onto the hill behind the shop. Martin stepped out onto the deck, and suddenly he was back in the year 1153. Wood buildings with thatched roofs rested in darkness beneath a sky unspoiled by artificial light.

Martin was a typical young man from the year 2012 and couldn't have looked more out of place. The only nod to his surroundings was his wizard robe, but it was covered with silver sequins and did not help. He took a lungful of the clean, cool air. Predictably, after a moment, Phillip joined him.

They stood in silence for a moment; then Phillip said, "It's a shame Gwen couldn't come tonight."

"It is," Martin agreed.

"I'm glad you're here, though," Phillip added.

Martin said, "Thanks."

Phillip looked at Martin and asked, "Why couldn't Gwen make it?"

Martin said, "Because she knew I was going to be here."

"Ah."

A long silence passed in which Phillip tried to think of what to say, and Martin hoped intensely that Phillip wouldn't say anything. Instead, Phillip asked, "How long have you two been dating now?"

"Three years," Martin answered.

"Yeah," Phillip said. "I guess it has been. Ever since Atlantis, right?"

"Yup," Martin answered.

"Have you considered maybe moving your relationship to the next level?" Phillip asked.

"Yes, I have."

"And have you discussed it?"

"Yes, with you, several times."

"How about with Gwen?"

Martin said, "Yes."

"I see," Phillip said. "And have you come to an agreement?"

"Yes. We agree that we shouldn't move forward until she feels ready."

"Ah," Phillip said, nodding.

A silent moment passed; then Phillip said, "It'll work out, Martin."

"You're sure of that?"

"Oh yeah," Phillip said. "I mean, there are only three ways this can play out. Either she'll come around, you'll decide you're fine with the situation as it is, or the two of you will break up. Any of those qualify as it having worked out."

"That's not very reassuring," Martin said.

"I don't know. Looks to me like a two-out-of-three chance of being happy. Those aren't bad odds."

Martin asked, "How are things with you and Brit?"

Phillip answered, "Great! Things are really going well."

"Why isn't she here?"

Phillip smiled. "She never comes to these things, Martin. You know that. She thinks it's important that we both have friends and interests outside of our relationship."

"But, you two are solid?" Martin pressed further.

"Yeah," Phillip said. "She seems happy, and I know I am."

Martin said, "Good. I'm happy for you." Phillip could hear genuine emotion in Martin's voice as he said it. Phillip was a bit amused that the emotion didn't sound like happiness.

Phillip went back inside. Martin followed. Tyler had returned, and he, Jeff, and Gary were now completely filling the couch. Roy sat in one of the two easy chairs, and since it was Phillip's place, that meant that Martin had lost the game of musical chairs. He chose to stand at the periphery of the seating area until the next movie began. He didn't mind sitting on the floor, but that didn't mean he was in a hurry to start.

Tyler dug a pen and a notepad out of his pocket and quickly scribbled something down.

"Whatcha writing?" Jeff asked.

"Oh, uh, nothing," Tyler stammered, hiding the notepad away from Jeff. "Just an idea."

"What is it? Another fantasy novel?" Jeff asked.

"No," Tyler said, "I'm thinking of getting away from fantasy for a while. It's just an idea that occurred to me. It's probably nothing."

"Come on," Jeff pressed him. "What is it?"

Tyler shook his head. "I'd really rather not say, at least until I've had more time to flesh the idea out."

Jeff said, "That's okay. You don't have to tell us your idea. Martin will."

Tyler looked away from Jeff and saw that Martin had crept up beside him and read the note over his shoulder. Tyler snapped the notebook shut, but it was too late.

Martin said, "He wrote, 'Inspiring tale of a rock star who loses his hearing. Title: *I Can't Hear You.*'"

Jeff said, "Hey, that's not bad."

"Yeah," Gary agreed. "I've seen movies with worse stories. Just tonight, in fact."

Phillip pressed a button on the front of the surprisingly large VCR that was attached to his surprisingly small television. A metal and plastic cradle rose smoothly out of the top of the machine on complex and fragile-looking scissor-action arms. Phillip removed one rattling black plastic tape from the cradle and slid another into its place before firmly pressing the cradle back into the top of the machine with a loud mechanical click.

Phillip turned to face the group, rubbing his hands together in anticipation.

"Okay," he said, "who's ready for the next movie?"

Tyler asked, "Does this one have a happy ending?"

Phillip shrugged theatrically. "Depends what you mean by a happy ending."

Gary asked, "Do the good guys win?"

"That depends on what you mean by winning."

Jeff said, "Getting what they want."

Phillip thought for a moment, then said, "Ah, then no. The good guys don't win."

The three wizards on the couch groaned.

Phillip said, "Look, it's a science fiction movie that was huge in its day, but I suspect you haven't seen it. It can't have aged very well. They made a few sequels to it, so you'll all like that, and it has one of the most shocking endings you'll ever see."

That got their attention, particularly Gary's. "Okay," Gary asked. "What's it called?"

Phillip said, "*Planet of the Apes*."

The three on the couch exploded in an even louder chorus of groans.

"What?" Phillip asked. "You've heard of it?"

"Yeah," Martin said. "They remade it. A couple of times now."

Jeff said, "Actually, first they reimagined it. Then they rebooted it."

Roy scowled and asked, "Jeez, doesn't anybody in the future have any ideas of their own?"

Martin said, "We have plenty of ideas. It's just that most of them involve stuff that already exists."

"But why not make something new?" Roy asked.

Martin answered, "I think they'd rather make money."

Phillip said, "Okay, okay. Fine. You don't want to watch the *Planet of the Apes*. That's not a problem. I have another movie here that I know you haven't seen. It's called *The Wicker Man*."

Martin sighed and looked to Jeff, who was from a time after Martin's, and would be aware of the remake. Martin and Jeff had barely made eye contact when Jeff, Tyler, and Gary all disappeared.

"Huh," Martin said. "I know the remake wasn't that good,

but just taking off seems like an overreaction." He turned to look at Phillip and found him gone as well.

"What the hell just happened?" Roy asked, rising from his seat.

Martin said, "They disappeared."

Roy said, "Well, I knew that."

"Then why'd you ask?" Martin replied.

3.

Gary, Jeff, and Tyler materialized. Because the couch upon which they had been sitting did not materialize with them, they immediately fell to the ground. Because they had not expected to teleport, they wallowed around on the ground in confusion. Because they had been sitting next to each other on a couch, their confused wallowing resulted in a tangle of arms and legs, and a great deal of alarmed cursing.

Phillip materialized at the exact same moment as his three friends, but he had been standing before the teleportation, so he was in a better position to handle the surprise with dignity. He could tell that they were standing on stone, and that it was darker and colder than the night had been back home in Leadchurch.

Phillip pulled his open wizard robe shut, looked down at Gary, and asked, "What is this?"

Gary's love of practical jokes was legendary. Not his skill in executing them, just his love of them. Before discovering magic, his idea of a great joke was placing a flaming bag of dog poop on someone's doorstep. After discovering magic, he graduated to transporting the flaming bag of dog poop into the house. Thus, whenever something happened that was simultaneously inexplicable and not at all funny, all eyes turned to him.

Gary said, "I don't know. No idea." He, Tyler, and Jeff had got their bearings, and pulled themselves to their feet.

"Seriously," Phillip persisted. "What is this?"

Gary said, "I'm telling you, Phillip, I didn't do this."

"And I'm supposed to believe that?" Phillip asked.

"Did we land in anything nasty?" Gary countered. "No. Looks like we didn't. Does that sound like my style?"

Phillip had to admit, it didn't. "Then who did this? Any of you know?"

Tyler, in a low, angry tone, said, "Let's ask him." He pointed to the ground behind Phillip. Phillip turned and saw Jimmy, the one wizard who was trusted even less than Gary. Of course, Gary's greatest offense was pulling pranks on all of them. Jimmy had attempted to kill all of them, was exiled to the future, and after thirty years, fought and lied and tricked his way back. Now he was here, lying on the ground, wearing dark blue pajamas and holding a paperback copy of *Getting Things Done*.

"What is this?!" Phillip bellowed. Tyler, Jeff, and Gary moved to stand beside Phillip, and they all looked down at Jimmy, a unified front of accusation.

Jimmy sat up, coughing and gasping for air. He put the hand holding the book down to support himself and held up one finger of the other hand in an attempt to stave off their questions until he'd caught his breath.

Tyler growled, "Start explaining, Jimmy, and it'd better be good."

Jimmy waved his free hand and croaked, "My bed. It's, like, three feet high. When I materialized, I landed flat on my back. Knocked the wind out of me."

"Why'd you bring us here?" Phillip barked.

Jimmy chuckled, looked at what he was wearing, and said, "I wanted to show you all my pajamas. I'm really proud of them. Also, I was hoping you'd read my book to me. If you'd just do the part about managing multiple to-do lists, I think it'd really help me go to sleep."

Jeff said, "That's enough with the smart remarks."

Jimmy stood up, examining his clothes and his new surroundings. His white hair was a mess. He was still off balance but he moved with a speed that was impressive for a man who was physically in his sixties. He said, "I'm sorry, but I don't have anything else to offer you. Come on, guys. You can't honestly believe that I did this. Think about it. I'm still on permanent probation. You've only given me a few powers and you're monitoring me at all times. Even if I did want to harm any of you, which I don't, it'd be pointless. I might as well just exile myself."

The other wizards muttered grudging agreement, which was the closest thing to approval Jimmy got these days.

The five of them stood in confused, angry silence, peering into the darkness around them. As their eyes adjusted, they could see that the granite knob on which they stood was in fact the peak of a massive monolithic rock, somewhere high in the mountains. The silhouetted horizon looked like the teeth of a poorly made saw. Three sides of their rock ended abruptly in a fall that meant certain death. The fourth side narrowed into a precarious bridge leading to the dense pine woods that clung to the side of another large mountain.

After several seconds, the howling of the wind was drowned out by a mind-bendingly loud voice, which shouted, "Silence!"

The men covered their ears and fell to their knees. Even its echo was deafening. As the word reverberated over and over, Gary whimpered, "We were silent."

The voice repeated, "I said *silence!*" The sound was so intense the wizards actually felt it hit them, as if the sound had mass and weight. Again the voice echoed in the vast open space surrounding them. As the sound died in the distance, Phillip moaned, "You saying 'silence' is literally the loudest thing I've ever heard."

A light appeared in front of the wizards. It flickered and nearly disappeared; then it grew stronger. As their eyes adjusted, they could see that it was a flame, surrounded by a lantern, held by an old man with wild hair, eyes that were milky and white, and teeth that were not. His clothes looked well worn, but not well cleaned.

"Soon it will be dawn," the old man said, "and your quest will begin."

Jimmy removed his hands from his ears and asked, "I'm sorry, what did you say?"

"Aye," the old man replied. "You're going on a quest. A quest full of danger, and peril, and risk of life and limb."

Jeff said, "All that, huh?"

Gary shook his head. "Yeah, no thanks." Years of being nearly invulnerable had given the wizards a certain disrespect for threats that came from anyone but another wizard.

"First," the old man continued, "you'll brave the dangers of Cardhu Pass. If you survive, you'll make your way to the cursed Mines of Mortlach. There, you will seek out Blandoch, head of the mining guild."

Tyler said, "Um, no, pretty sure we won't."

"The miners will give you a sample of a mystical ore called dailuaine. You will take this splendid rock many miles, to the town of Bowmore, where it will be used to craft a weapon fit for use in the final battle."

"That's it?" Jeff asked. "That's the quest? That's like three things."

"Take a moment to prepare, adventurers, and be warned. On your journey, you will face death a thousand different ways," the old man continued, oblivious.

"Three different ways," Gary corrected.

"If that," Tyler added. "I mean, go to a mine, get a rock, and carry it to a town. None of that sounds dangerous."

"It does sound like a lot of work, though," Phillip said. He turned back to the old man. "I'm sorry, we're going to pass, thank you."

The old man was giving them a shrewd, appraising look, which dragged on a bit longer than necessary. Finally, he said, "I can see you are men of valor. Which of you shall lead his fellows on this quest?"

Jimmy said, "None of us, because we aren't doing it. I mean, I'm sorry, guys, I don't speak for everyone, but that's the impression I get. We definitely aren't doing it, right?"

The other men nodded, then waited to see how the old man would react to this. He continued looking over the group, as if judging their mettle. After a long moment, he said, "I can see you are men of valor. Which of you shall lead his fellows on this quest?"

"We said we aren't doing it," Phillip replied. He turned to the others and said, "Okay, now that that's out of the way, let's see about going home."

Jimmy said, "Well, that's going to be hard, since we got transported here without our staffs or our hats."

It was true. Phillip, Tyler, Gary, and Jeff had been enjoying a relaxed evening and had removed their hats and laid down their staves and Jeff's wand. Jimmy had clearly called it an evening early and had settled in for bed when he'd been pulled away. As far as Jimmy could tell, everything he had said was accurate. He couldn't figure out why the other men looked so pleased.

Jimmy asked, "What? What's funny?"

Jeff said, "You're the only one who needs to have the hat and staff to do magic anymore. We fixed that little weakness after you got the drop on us."

"Well, why didn't you include me?" Jimmy asked.

"Because you might try to get the drop on us again," Phillip replied.

Jimmy was chagrined, but it didn't last long, as their conversation was interrupted by the old man, who said, "I can see you are men of valor. Which of you shall lead his fellows on this quest?"

The wizards slowly turned to look at him. He was standing in the same spot. His arms were in the same position. The arm holding the lantern up showed no sign of fatigue. He just stood there, head moving slightly, as if he were studying the wizards, who had not changed one bit since he had started studying them several minutes earlier.

Tyler said, "I'm pretty sure he's not real."

Jeff said, "Yeah. He's computer-generated. They did some pretty sophisticated bump-mapping, but even in this light you can see the polygons if you look hard enough."

"It's like he's caught in a loop," Phillip muttered.

"Yeah," Jimmy agreed. "I think he's waiting for a response. Something he'll recognize."

A rock only slightly smaller than a softball arced heavily through the air and bounced off the old man's head. The rock fell to the ground with a dull thud, but the old man remained motionless, as if he had been hit with a Ping-Pong ball.

The wizards all turned to Gary, who was massaging his throwing arm. He said, "I wanted to see if he'd recognize that as a response."

Phillip said, "Fair enough. All right, fellows, what say we get out of here? Put a hand in, everyone." Phillip put his hand forward. Tyler, Jeff, and Gary placed their hands on Phillip's, making physical contact so that his spell would transport them as well. They looked at Jimmy, as if irritated that he was making them wait. Jimmy placed his hand on the pile. Phillip and Tyler looked at him as if irritated that they were having to touch him.

Phillip said, "Prenu min hejme," which made him smile, not only because it was the spell that would get them out of there, but because it was Esperanto for "Take me home," and was, as such, a Phil Collins reference.

Phillip's smile faded when they went nowhere. He tried his spell again; then the other wizards tried theirs. Attempts were made to fly and to create food or gold from thin air. Nothing worked. They were without their powers. Suddenly, the sheer cliffs that surrounded them looked more menacing; the narrow bridge leading to relative safety, more precarious; and the artificial old man standing silently, studying them, much more sinister.

"I can see you are men of valor," the old man said. "Which of you shall lead his fellows on this quest?"

Gary looked to Phillip and asked, "What should we do?"

The wizards all looked to Phillip, who thought for a moment, then said, "Well, we have two choices. We can be proactive, give him the input he wants, and see where this leads. Or, we can be passive. We don't do anything that he might construe as input. We just wait here and see what happens. Maybe in the meantime we'll think of something. You all know me. I think you'll all know which way I'm leaning."

The wizards sat down and settled in to do some serious waiting.

4.

Gwen was busy at her sewing machine. Whenever she and Martin were fighting, she would try to distract herself with her work. Lately, she had been getting a lot of work done.

She thought of designing and making clothes as her work, even though nobody paid her to do it. She didn't need them to. She was a wizard, or, as they were called in her home in Atlantis, a sorceress. She had access to unlimited funds, so she didn't need to earn money. She measured the success of her efforts in how many of her fellow sorceresses wanted her to make clothes for them, and by that measure she was quite successful indeed.

She finished a seam, then held the fabric up to the light to examine her work. It was nice and straight, not that it mattered. The fabric she was sewing had such a busy pattern that any minor mistakes she made would have been hidden. She looked at the pattern and frowned. She always made bold, exuberant garments when she and Martin were fighting. It was a sign of depression. When she was in a good mood, her tastes ran a little more Goth.

She reached for the next piece of fabric, and was about to start on the seam when the doorbell rang. Her frown deepened. It was nearly ten at night, and the only person who would show up at her door at this time of night would be Martin. That meant he probably wanted to make up, which was good, but they had only had their argument three hours ago. She wasn't quite ready to make nice yet. She put down her sewing and walked to the door.

When she opened it, she was not surprised to see Martin standing outside.

Martin said, "Gwen, we gotta talk."

Gwen replied, "I don't want to talk right now." She looked puzzled when she noticed that Martin was not alone. "You've got Roy with you."

Roy stood in the darkness several feet behind Martin, holding his billiards bridge, wearing the tan trench coat that he used as a wizard robe and the long, pointed wizard hat that he'd modified with the brim of a gray fedora. He looked like a grim film-noir version of Wee Willie Winkie. He'd look out of place anywhere, but standing next to Martin in his shiny silver wizard hat and robe on a balmy tropical evening in the glowing, mythical city of Atlantis, he seemed even more incongruous.

Martin said, "Yes. Roy is with me."

Gwen asked, "Why?"

Roy said, "In order to explain that, the boy would have to talk."

Martin asked, "Can we come in?"

She stood aside to let them enter.

She knew Roy. He and Jeff seemed close to inseparable. Gwen's relationship with Roy was awkward, which was an improvement; at first it had been downright uncomfortable. Part of it was probably generational. Sure, he looked much older than she did, but with time travelers that meant nothing. Mentally, she was much older than she looked, but they had been raised in very different times. Part of it was that he was military and she, very much, was not. Mostly, it was just that Roy always seemed to be on edge whenever Gwen was around. She couldn't relax in the company of someone who couldn't relax. The fact he often called her either "miss" or "young lady" hadn't helped much either. Since she appeared to be in her early twenties, and had a petite build and a cute brown pixie haircut, he had difficulty getting it into his head that mentally she was close to his age.

Martin stalked in silently. Roy removed his hat as he entered, exposing his thinning gray crew cut. He looked around the room, which looked more like the remnants section of a fabric store than a person's home. He said, "Hello, miss. It's good to see you again."

Gwen said, "Good to see you, Roy. Make yourself comfortable."

Roy thanked her, and continued to stand by the door, holding his hat. She turned her attention to Martin.

"So," she asked, "how was bad-movie night?"

"The first movie was slow and plodding, and ended with a tremendous bummer."

Gwen said, "Par for the course, then."

"Better than usual, actually," Martin said. "Then everyone vanished."

"Everyone in the movie disappeared?" Gwen asked.

Martin said, "No, the movie was over. We were about to start the second one and everyone but Roy and me just disappeared."

"I see," Gwen said. "Don't you think they're just messing with you?"

Martin rolled his eyes. "Gwen, Gary's involved. Of course we thought they were messing with us, but after half an hour of waiting around for the live skunk or whatever to materialize, we began to think something was up. Finally we went to my place and checked the file, and their coordinates make no sense. The longitude and latitude have been replaced with a line of code that calls out to some sort of secondary program."

"Did you try to pull them back?" Gwen asked.

"Yeah, but the file wouldn't let us. We couldn't change anything, and while we were trying, we noticed something else. Their settings have been reset. Wherever they are, they don't have their powers, and they can get hurt."

Martin could have predicted Gwen's thought. It had been the first thing to cross his mind when he'd found all of this out.

Gwen said, "Jimmy's finally made his move."

Roy said, "Maybe."

Martin said, "I think so."

Jimmy, as well as Phillip and Gwen, was one of the first wizards to show up in this time period, and he had been a problem from day one. Like all the worst problems, he didn't seem so bad at first. He was personable and always happy to help with whatever you were doing. Over time it became clear that he was also willing to take control of and credit for whatever you were doing, and that he was personable enough to make it stick. Eventually he wormed his way into a position of some power, both over the wizards and the normal citizens of Medieval England. He went mad with power and ended up accidentally killing a great many people and deliberately harming plenty of others.

As a punishment, the wizards cut off his access to the file that was the source of all their powers and exiled him to his own time, where he spent thirty years alone and destitute, struggling to make his way back. When he finally returned, he claimed to be remorseful and threw himself on the mercy of the other wizards, who let him stay, but on the condition that he submit to constant supervision. They did this partly because they wanted to believe that a person could redeem himself, but mostly because none of them trusted Jimmy, and they wanted to keep an eye on him. They hoped that if they kept him under surveillance, and controlled what powers he was allowed to use, they could prevent him from doing any real damage. Martin and Phillip in particular thought that eventually Jimmy would be a problem again.

It seemed that eventually was today.

"We pulled up Jimmy's entry in the file," Martin said. "Wherever the guys are, Jimmy's there too."

Roy said, "And?"

"And it looks like his settings have been reset too," Martin said, "but that doesn't mean anything."

"It means he's just as vulnerable as the others," Roy said.

"Or so it seems," Martin said. "But that might be what he wants us to think."

Roy frowned. "Kid, you're giving Jimmy an awful lot of credit."

Gwen said, "Roy, you weren't here when Jimmy tried to get rid of us. You don't know what he's capable of."

"You're right that I wasn't here," Roy said, "but I know full well what he's capable of. I know he didn't try to get rid of all of you. He tried to kill you. I know that if I had been there, he might not still be around to bother us today."

Martin started to object, but Roy stopped him with a raised finger and a change to a more conciliatory tone. "I'm not saying I'd have caught him any easier, just that if I'd been around when you were trying to decide what to do with him afterward, I would've argued against leaving him alive to stew in his own juices for thirty years."

"So you'd have killed him," Gwen said.

"Yes. I wouldn't have been happy about it, and I wouldn't have been in a hurry to do it myself, but yes. Sometimes you have a terrible situation, and you just have to deal with it. Right now, four of our friends, and maybe Jimmy, are in danger. We have to deal with that. Instead, we're just doing a lot of talking."

Gwen said, "We don't know for sure that they're in danger."

"No, Gwen," Martin said, gently. "Roy and I have been over this."

"At length," Roy muttered.

"Jimmy, or whoever did this, deliberately made it possible to hurt them. They didn't do that for no reason."

Gwen thought a moment, then said, "Yeah, you're right. We have to do something."

Martin said, "Agreed."

Roy said, "Finally."

Gwen said, "We should go talk to Brit."

"Good idea," Martin said, brightly, as Roy groaned.

5.

An hour later, the wizards were getting restless. Not answering the same question every thirty seconds will do that. The sun had come up, and the wizards could see their surroundings better. They stood on a tall chunk of craggy granite that fell away to fatal drops in all directions but one. The horizon was a random jumble of jagged gray mountains with patches of snow toward their peaks. The space between them and the horizon was filled with smaller peaks that were less snowcapped but every bit as jagged. The idea of attempting to travel through this landscape on foot strengthened their resolve to stay exactly where they were.

They also noticed that they were all uncomfortably cold. None of them had experienced that in quite some time. The modifications they had made to the file kept them comfortable regardless of the ambient temperature. If that modification had been rescinded, they couldn't help wondering which of their other changes had been undone.

As the sun rose, they were also able to get a better look at the old man. He remained motionless, except for slight head and mouth movements. He still held his lantern high, though now, in the light of day, its flame seemed weak and insubstantial. The man himself looked sickly and unnatural. His skin was a little too glossy, his movements a little too smooth.

Yet again, the old man said, "I can see you are men of valor. Which of you shall lead his fellows on this quest?"

Jeff said, "Look, guys, I think it's just going to keep saying that until we either give it an answer or starve to death."

Jimmy said, "We'd die of thirst, not starvation."

Tyler said, "You're right, 'cause I'd kill you and eat you first."

Jimmy smiled. "Tyler, that's the closest thing to a compliment you've said to me in a very long time."

Tyler started to reply, but Jeff interrupted. "Okay, look, we can sit here waiting for him to tire out, which I'm pretty sure isn't going to happen, or we can try something else, right?"

"Like what?" Phillip asked.

"How about if we start feeding him inputs he doesn't expect. Maybe we can force an error."

They waited for the old man to ask his question again. It seemed to take longer now that they were wanting it to happen. They were so focused that a couple of them were startled when the old man said, "I can see you are men of valor. Which of you shall lead his fellows on this quest?"

Phillip, speaking as clearly as he could, said, "Winston Churchill."

The old man froze for a moment, then said, "Can you please repeat that?"

"Winston Churchill," Phillip said.

The old man froze again, then said, "Can you please repeat that?"

Jimmy said, "James Kirk."

"Can you please repeat that?"

"James Kirk."

"Can you please repeat that?"

Tyler tried. "Jean-Luc Picard."

"Who's that?" Phillip asked.

"Can you please repeat that?" the old man asked.

Tyler shook his head. "Seriously, Phil, sometimes you just make me sad."

"Fine," a distant, hollow voice cried out, seemingly from all around them. "You bunch of jerks. You just aren't gonna take this seriously, are you?"

"Maybe we would," Phillip yelled, "if we knew who we were dealing with."

The voice said, "Heh, I doubt it."

In the empty space above the old man, a point of light appeared, expanding from nothing and cascading downward and outward until it formed a rectangle about ten feet wide and six feet high. The rectangle had a gray border, thin on the bottom and sides but thick on top. The upper-right corner of the border held pictograms of a line, a box, and an X. Inside the border was a head-and-shoulders image of a man. The area behind the man's right shoulder was dark. Behind his left shoulder, it was light. At first, Phillip thought this was meant to make some point, but then he realized that he was looking into someone's home. The dark area was a wall with wood paneling. The light area was the entryway to what looked like a kitchen. The man in the center of the frame had aged since they last saw him and had changed his hair. He was well into his late thirties and was wearing glasses and a headset with a microphone, but they still all recognized him immediately.

"Todd," Jeff said. "What is this?"

"Overdue," Todd answered. "You had to know you'd be dealing with me again. You can't really have thought you'd gotten rid of me."

"Yes," Phillip said. "We did! Because we had! We were rid of you, and I'm sure we still would be if Jimmy here hadn't sought you out."

Jimmy started to defend himself but was drowned out, surprisingly, by Todd defending him.

"Now, now, don't blame Jimmy. I'd have found a way out of prison eventually on my own; he just made it easier. Besides, it's not like I got out and immediately decided to come after you all."

"It isn't? Seems like it to me," Gary asked.

"No," Todd said. "See, guys, in prison, I had time to think. I spent a lot of time planning revenge, but then I remembered something I'd heard a long time ago. 'Living well is the best revenge.' So that's what I decided to do. I would get my revenge by ignoring you small-minded, backstabbing idiots and having a better life than any of you."

Phillip asked, "Then why are we here?"

"Don't jump ahead," Todd scolded. "When I got access to the file again, I jumped back in time to the late sixties and set up a false identity. Then I jumped to the mideighties and enrolled in Stanford. While I was there I networked. I learned a lot more about computers than I already knew, and I cheated on exams. Lots of exams. I graduated just in time to get hired on at a string of gaming companies. I let myself age naturally to a nice, respectable thirty-nine years old, then stopped it again, just to keep up appearances. Turns out you can hover at thirty-nine for quite a while before anybody notices. Anyway, for the last twenty years I've worked in the gaming industry, creating video games and amassing quite a personal fortune, all on the up-and-up. I've gained wisdom. I've matured. Also, I've spent most of my off time playing around with the file. Seeing what I could do."

Jeff asked, "What games have you worked on?"

Todd said, "Mostly shovel-ware and cheap games tied to super-hero movies. I didn't want to draw a lot of attention to myself."

"Well," Phillip said, "I must say, this is all great news, Todd. You turned away from violence. You made something of your-self. Clearly, you've evaded detection. You should be very proud of yourself."

"I am," Todd said.

"So, then, why are we here?" Phillip asked.

"Well, that's the thing. I was thinking about it, and I real-ized that while I'd gotten the best revenge, none of you knew about it, and really, what kind of revenge is it if the people you got revenge on have no idea you got revenge? It bugged me. So I decided to come back and tell you all how I got the best revenge."

"And now you have," Phillip said.

"Yes," Todd agreed. "And then I thought, while I'm going to be in contact with you all anyway, why not try the other kind of revenge too, just to compare."

"Ah. I see," Phillip said.

"Yes," Todd said. "I bet you do. So, look, you dummies already know you can't do magic to get out of this, and we all know you're going to get hungry and thirsty pretty soon. What you may not realize is that you're never going to get off that rock you're standing on until you answer the hermit's questions, so you'd better get to it."

"And what?" Gary asked. "You're just going to watch us run through your little maze for your amusement?"

Todd said, "Yeah, you've got the idea. It's not a little maze, though. It's a full-on epic quest, full of hardship, adversity, and danger."

"And you built it just to torture us?" Tyler asked.

"I designed it, but most of the actual work was done by interns. They thought they were working on a game. It's amazing. They'll do anything you ask if they think it'll get them a job as a real game designer. It's amazing what people will do for you if you just give them some false hope. They've really outdone themselves. I can't wait for you to see it. You'd better get a move on."

Todd's window disappeared.

The old man said, "I can see you are men of valor. Which of you shall lead his fellows on this quest?"

The wizards looked at each other, and Phillip said, "I suppose I will."

"Good," the old man said. "And who will be your second, should you fall?"

Phillip looked at the other wizards, trying to decide whom he'd want in charge if he weren't around. He would have chosen Tyler, but Tyler might kill Jimmy. If he chose Jimmy, Tyler would kill him, and Phillip would have thought he was right to do it. Gary was nearly as out of the question as Jimmy, so that left one choice.

"Jeff," Phillip said. "Jeff is my second."

The old man said, "Splendid, then tarry no further. Your quest awaits. Attain the ore, forge the weapon, and take it to the Chasm of Certain Doom, where you shall fulfill the prophecy, and reveal the identity of the chosen one, the man who will be free."

"Wait, what prophecy?" Tyler interrupted.

The old man, being a preprogrammed automaton, continued without noticing the interruption. "And so that you know what danger you face—"

AN UNWELCOME QUEST **63**

"Yeah, great. Danger. I've heard. What about this prophecy? What's the deal with that?"

The old man continued, unperturbed. "There will be a demonstration, so leave this place and seize your destiny, or else a coward's death will be yours."

"No, no," Tyler said, with just as much tenacity as the old man. "Don't change the subject. I want to hear about this prophecy."

Jeff leaned toward Tyler and said, "Man, it's just a recording."

"Yeah," Tyler said, "but we know Todd's listening, and he wrote this crap."

The old man stepped to the side with a flourish, motioned toward the narrow rock bridge to the forest, and froze as if about to speak. Above him, Todd's window winked back into existence. Todd looked irritated.

"You were talking over important dialog," Todd whined. "How are you supposed to understand what's going on if you don't pay attention?"

"Then make it worth paying attention to," Tyler yelled. "You don't lay out the entire quest for us, then just mention that there just happens to be a prophecy. You lead with the prophecy, man! Your hermit should have been all, 'It is written. Heroes will come. Might you be they?' Then you tell us what we have to do, and we might just be into it. You don't lead with 'This is gonna suck,' then expect us to be champing at the bit because you ended with 'Oh, by the way, prophecy!' That's just sloppy storytelling."

"Oh yeah," Todd said, "I remember now. You were trying to be a writer, weren't you?"

"Hey," Tyler yelled. "I'm published!"

"All of the worst books I ever read were published," Todd replied. "Look, he said that if you bring the mystical weapon to a certain place, the chosen one will be revealed. That's a prophecy, isn't it?"

"You didn't call it a prophecy before."

Todd said, "But it is one, and you'll find out more about it as you go, okay?"

"Well, I'm not sure I want to," Tyler said.

Todd looked dumfounded for a moment, then sputtered in frustration before finally saying, "You've interrupted the whole narrative flow here to insist that I haven't told you enough about something that now you say you don't care about. What sense does that make?"

"What I'm saying," Tyler explained, "is that you've created this fictional story for us to experience, but you have to give us a reason to care what happens, or else we won't bother to experience it."

Todd thought about this and smiled. "Okay. That's a fair point. I appreciate your note. I'll tell you what, I'm going to rewind a bit—you can listen to the old man this time and see where he's going. Then I'll check in with you and see if you're emotionally involved."

Todd's window disappeared. The old man, who had been frozen, statue-like, pointing the way across the rock bridge, suddenly lurched back to his original stance, holding his lantern high and blocking the path to the bridge.

The old man said, "Splendid, then tarry no further. Your quest awaits. Attain the ore, forge the weapon, and take it to the Chasm of Certain Doom, where you will fulfill the prophecy. And so that you know what danger you face, there will be a demonstration, so leave this place and seize your destiny, or else a coward's death will be yours." The old man stepped aside with a flourish and again motioned toward the narrow rock bridge that led off of the rocky crag and into the woods beyond.

The wizards waited for a moment, expecting the old man to say more, but instead they became aware of a distant rumbling noise. They felt the ground shake beneath them; at first it was merely a vibration, but it quickly grew to a steady shaking, strong enough to make them instinctively crouch to lower their centers of gravity. Cracks began to form in the rock beneath them. Without needing to discuss it, they all ran for the bridge, but the unsteady ground made them shamble like drunkards. The cracks grew with alarming speed, and one particularly large crack split the peak into two parts, the largest of which was still attached to the bridge, and the smallest of which held Jeff.

Jeff saw that his situation was dire. He ran to the edge of his island of rock, but in the time it took him to take three steps, the gap between him and his friends had grown too wide to jump. He managed to skid to a stop just before he fell into the crevasse. For a sickening moment he teetered, the toes of his sneakers hanging over the edge, unable to solidly catch his balance on the shifting surface. Finally, mercifully, his weight shifted backward, and he was able to stand with some dignity. His chunk of rock had shifted at least twenty-five feet away from the main body and somehow had sunk at least ten feet in the process. He looked up at the rest of his group. They were all standing at the edge, looking down at him. They reached for him, but clearly they could see that there was no longer any point.

Jeff felt his traction slip as the stone that was supporting his weight dropped several inches. He knew the next time it slipped, he'd be going all the way to the floor of the canyon. He couldn't fly. Todd had taken that power away. He couldn't teleport. Todd had taken that power away too. It hadn't really been explicitly spelled out, but Jeff was pretty sure Todd had given him back the power to be killed by falling from a great height.

Jeff looked up at his friends. As he felt the ground beneath him start to go, he said, "Crud."

The others watched helplessly as Jeff fell to the canyon floor, his gray wizard robe fluttering from around his neck and shoulders like a cape. They saw him hit the bottom. None of them held out any hope that he had survived.

The rest of the group scrambled desperately for the bridge to more stable land. As they ran and stumbled and pulled themselves along on all fours, the granite fell away behind them, driving them on in a blind panic.

Gary was the first to make it to the woods beyond the rock bridge. Phillip and Jimmy were close behind. Tyler was bringing up the rear, and with each step he took, the piece of ground directly behind him would fall into the abyss.

He was almost across the bridge, almost safe, when he suddenly said, "Wait a second," and stopped running. As he stopped, the wave of destruction that was pursuing him slowed and stopped as well. Tyler turned around and looked down at the void behind him. The air was still filled with a cataclysmic rumbling, but there was no sign of further destruction. Tyler took one large step backward, but since he had turned to look into the canyon, he moved closer to the others and safety. As his weight shifted, the stones that had been supporting his weight before immediately fell.

Tyler shook his head, disgusted. He turned and slowly strolled to the others, the bridge systematically disintegrating behind him until he reached solid ground. He picked up a pinecone and threw it back from where he had come. It flew in a predictable arc until it reached the empty space where the bridge had been, where it bounced. He muttered, "Lazy programming," his voice dripping with contempt.

"You mean it's still there?" Gary cried.

"The visible parameters were programmed separately from the physical," Tyler said. "The rocks that made up the bluff were massless shells. The shape of the bluff is still there."

Again Todd's chat window leapt out of the nothingness, and again he didn't look amused.

"It just had to look convincing enough to get you to run," Todd said. "Lazy or not, it did the job, but yeah, you're right. The mass of the plateau is still there, except the part Jeff was standing on, of course."

"What the hell was that?!" Phillip shouted.

Todd said nothing.

Phillip shouted, "Todd! We won't move another inch until you explain what just happened." They stood at the head of the trail, with a long trek through dark woods ahead of them and a sheer cliff behind them. None of the others made a sound, partly because they were stunned and partly because they wanted the question answered as well.

Finally, Todd said, "You want me to explain what just happened? Really? The rock crumbled and you ran. I don't see what's so difficult for you to get."

"What happened to Jeff?" Phillip demanded.

Todd said, "He fell."

"And what happened to him then?" Jimmy asked.

Todd leaned into the camera to emphasize his next statement. "He died."

Gary shook his head, saying, "But, okay, yeah, I get it, in the quest he died, but where is he? What happened to him? When will we see him again?"

Todd said, "He's at the bottom of the ravine, what's left of him. He really died. You'll see him again if you decide to climb down there and retrieve his corpse."

"You killed him?!" Phillip cried.

Todd chuckled. "In a way, you killed him, Phillip. When you named him your second in command, that's what made the game mark him for death. I suspected you'd pick him or Tyler, but didn't know for sure, so really, it's your fault that he's dead now."

"But I didn't know what I was choosing for!" Phillip said. "I thought it was in case we got split up or something. I had no idea I was choosing him to die!"

Todd shrugged. "Then I guess we'll have to share the blame."

Gary asked, "Why kill Jeff? Why kill any of us?"

Todd shook his head. "Guys, come on! What part of 'revenge' didn't you understand? You took the law into your own hands, sent me away to rot in a prison for the rest of my life, knowing that I'd had immortality and unlimited wealth in my hands before you all took it away. Now I'm back to get even, and you expect me to pitch underhand? You're all trapped in a deadly game that I have spent *years* dreaming up. Jeff died because I needed to kill someone at the outset so that you'd know what the stakes are."

"We're time travelers," Tyler said. "We'll figure out a way to get Jeff back."

Todd looked directly at Tyler. "If you survive to get your powers back, which Jeff didn't. You wanted a reason to be emotionally involved? Well, now you have one. You have to keep going, or you will be killed. If you fail to complete any of the challenges, you will be killed. If you get careless and make a mistake along the way, you will be killed."

"But you need to keep us alive to play this crappy game of yours out to the end," Tyler said.

"Eh, I dunno. Ideally, that'd be for the best, but really, if you all die miserably, then the game has served its purpose. I already know how it ends anyway. I made it. Besides, Tyler, just because I expect someone to make it to the end doesn't mean that I expect you to make it. The fact is, I really only wanted revenge on Phillip, Jimmy, and Gary. You and Jeff are here because I knew you were their friends. I figured watching you two die would spur them on."

"You're saying I'm expendable," Tyler said.

"The opposite," Todd explained. "If someone's expendable, you don't mind if they die. I expect you to die. I don't know if there's a word for that. Maybe 'sacrifice,' except that I won't be sorry when you're gone. By the way, a little way up the trail, you'll find a dead hunting party that you can loot for warm clothes and weapons. It's nothing fancy. Just some swords, shields, and animal skins. Should help you fight off the cold and the mountain wolves."

"What killed the hunting party?" Tyler asked.

Todd said, "Mountain wolves."

Jimmy said, "That doesn't speak well for the effectiveness of the weapons."

"No, it doesn't," Todd agreed, a little too enthusiastically.

"What if we refuse?" Phillip asked. "What if we just sit here and wait for you to give up?"

"You'll either freeze to death or be eaten by mountain wolves. I still get my revenge."

Phillip asked, "And what happens if we make it to the end of your quest?"

"To the Chasm of Certain Doom? You'll learn the identity of the chosen one. The man who will be free," Todd answered.

"One man," Phillip said.

"If any of you make it to the chasm at all," Todd said.

Jimmy said, "So the choice you're offering us is to not cooperate and be killed, or to cooperate and probably be killed."

"Yes," Todd answered.

"That's not a lot of incentive," Jimmy said.

Todd said, "It's enough."

6.

Gwen, Martin, and Roy materialized outside the door to Brit's quarters. They were in a long hallway carved from immaculate, opaque white glass, with a floor of textured nonslip white glass, and walls lined with doors made of off-white glass, for contrast.

"Yeesh," Roy said. "I'm inside, it's the middle of the night, and I feel like I need sunglasses. Which Brit is this we're visiting again?"

It was a wise question to ask. Brit was unique, in that there was more than one of her. If most people's lives form a straight line extending into the future, Brit's formed a loop. At this moment, past Brit and future Brit were sharing the same time and place, and they were doing so with all the grace of two siblings sharing the back seat on a long car trip. Brit the Elder was Brit the Younger's older self. She remembered everything that ever happened to Brit the Younger, and never let Brit the Younger forget it. Brit the Younger was Brit the Elder's younger self. She resented having to share her existence, and never let Brit the Elder forget it.

Gwen said, "This is Brit the Younger's place. She and Phillip are close. She'll want to know if he's in trouble." Neither Martin nor Roy needed to be told this. Phillip and Brit the Younger had been quite open about their relationship, and Brit had visited Leadchurch on more than one occasion. Really, Gwen made the statement not so much for their benefit as for her own. She wanted to reassure herself that they were doing the right thing. It was quite late at night. Brit would be asleep, and Gwen hated to wake her with bad news.

Gwen had barely rung the doorbell when the door swung open. Brit's housekeeper, Nik, opened the door. He looked well, as slim and as tan as ever. Nik had been seriously injured a few years ago but had made a full recovery, and now you'd never know anything had happened.

Nik was wearing a baggy white nightshirt instead of his usual uniform, but he smiled and said, "Ah, hello! Come in. They've been expecting you."

Brit's main room was as Martin remembered it: sleek, beautiful, and free from clutter. Everything in the room, like almost everything in Atlantis, was made of molecularly pure toughened glass, or for structural elements that needed the extra strength, diamond. One entire wall was a curved, seamless window with a view of the ocean outside. They were well below the surface, but at this time of night the only fish visible were the ones that came close enough to reflect the light from the apartment.

Brit the Elder and Brit the Younger sat on the couch looking identical, yet completely dissimilar. Brit the Elder looked as cool and crisp as fresh celery. She wore a simple white tunic and contrasting black slacks that matched the frames of her glasses. Her shoulder-length red hair was impeccably styled. Sitting next to her, Brit the Younger had on a baggy sweatshirt, shorts, and a pair of oversized wool socks. Her shoulder-length red hair looked a mess and her glasses were slightly askew. She clearly had just been pulled out of bed and was not happy about it.

Gwen said, "Oh, uh, we thought you'd be alone."

"Yeah," Brit the Younger said, "so did I. I'd settled in to read myself to sleep, and then she showed up, saying I was about to have company, but she wouldn't tell me who or why."

Brit the Elder patted the Younger on the knee and said, "It was important that you be awake to receive our visitors. Gwen, Martin, always a pleasure. It's good to see you again too, Roy."

Roy said, "I'm sorry, miss. I've met the other Brit a couple of times, but I don't believe we've . . . oh. Yeah. Right."

Brit the Elder said, "Mm hmm. Anyway, please make yourselves comfortable. We have important news to discuss."

Brit the Younger said, "This is my home. I'll play hostess, thanks."

Brit the Elder said, "Of course. I'm sorry. It's just hard because this used to be my place, back when I was you. In fact, I still have this couch. It's an antique now, of course."

Nik entered from the next room with a dining room chair that, while beautiful, looked far less comfortable than the other two available chairs. Roy insisted on taking it despite the fact that Nik had placed it closer to Gwen, and Gwen had already started to sit on it.

Once everyone was comfortable, Brit the Younger looked to Gwen and asked, "What's up?"

Brit the Elder said, "They're here to tell you that Phillip has been abducted."

Brit the Younger's eyes darted from Gwen's face to Martin's and back. "What? Is that true?"

"Yes," Brit the Elder said. "He and his friends Tyler, Jeff, and Gary. Oh, and Jimmy too."

"When?" Brit the Younger asked, still looking to Gwen and Martin.

Brit the Elder said, "A little over an hour ago. That's right, isn't it?"

Martin said, "Yeah, a little over."

"Who did this?" Brit the Younger asked.

"They don't know yet," Brit the Elder answered.

Martin said, "We think maybe Jimmy."

"But they don't know yet," Brit the Elder repeated.

Brit the Younger turned to glare at Brit the Elder. "Yet? So you know who did it."

"Yes."

"Who?"

Brit the Elder rolled her eyes. "Dear, you know I can't tell you about the future. You need to experience it for yourself, the way I did."

"But, you were just telling me about the future just now. I was asking them questions and you kept telling me how they were going to answer," Brit the Younger said without ever unclenching her teeth.

"No. See, they're here now, so by telling you what they were going to say I wasn't telling you about the future. I was telling you about the present."

Brit the Younger said, "Fine," but it didn't sound like she meant it. "Phillip's gone now. So, who has him?"

Brit the Elder shook her head. "See, that's the problem. Phillip's gone in the present, but you don't find out who took him until the future."

Brit the Younger pointedly looked away from Brit the Elder and back to Gwen. "Do you think Phillip's in danger?"

Brit the Elder said, "Don't be silly, dear. Of course he's in danger. His file settings have been restored to their defaults. He's in grave danger."

Brit the Younger closed her eyes, took a deep breath, then continued addressing Gwen. "Where is he? Do you know?"

Brit the Elder started to say something, but Brit the Younger held up a finger and said, "Shhh!" Brit the Elder pursed her lips but remained silent.

Gwen said, "Their location parameters have been replaced with a callout to an external program that we haven't been able to access yet. We don't know where they are, and any time we try to make a change to their file, it doesn't take. The external program is preventing us from tampering with anyone in its system."

Brit the Younger sat back and thought for a moment, then said, "So what do we do?"

Martin, Gwen, and Roy all looked at one another, but none of them spoke. Brit the Elder raised a hand and said, "If I may?"

"Go ahead," Brit the Younger sighed.

Brit the Elder cleared her throat. "Gwen would like to research the problem. She suspects that in time we might find the external program and nullify it. Roy, on the other hand, feels very strongly that Phillip and his friends are in danger right now, and that the best course is to reset all of your location settings to the callout for the external program so that you'll go wherever they are and help them."

Roy said, "Damn straight." Then he quickly glanced at both Brits and Gwen and said, "Pardon my French, ladies."

Gwen said, "Your French is fine, Roy, but your idea sounds really dangerous."

Brit the Younger said, "I agree. That's a terrible risk to take."

Roy explained, "Maybe, but so is sitting around studying the problem. Our buddies are being threatened. We have to act. Besides, whoever did this was expecting to only get the five people they took. They won't expect us. We'll have the advantage, especially if we still have our powers."

"But the program, whatever it is, seems to reset wizards to their defaults," Gwen said. "What makes you think you'll hold on to your powers?"

Brit the Elder said, "As I remember, Martin has an idea about that."

Roy smirked at Martin. Gwen glared at him. Martin said, "Um, well, I was thinking, what if I carried a copy of the Leadchurch shell program and the Atlantis Interface running on my smartphone? I mean, it's not like running the file itself, but both of those programs modify the file through a simplified interface, so I figure if we're running them on a machine that we take with us, it should counteract whatever the other program is doing."

Roy slapped Martin on the back. "Good idea, kid."

"Yes," Brit the Elder said. "It will be interesting for you to see if it works."

Brit the Younger said, "*Will?* You said *it will* be interesting. I suppose that means that we're going, doesn't it?"

Brit the Elder frowned. "I shouldn't have said that. I guess I've let the cat out of the bag. I might as well tell you. You'll try in vain to ferret out and neutralize this mysterious program, but after a day of intense effort and no progress you will decide to try Roy's foolhardy idea. I'll send you on your way. While you are wherever you're going, trying to save the three of them—"

"Five," Martin said. "Five of them are gone."

Brit the Elder smiled. "Sorry. My mistake. Anyway, while you're away the plan is that I stay here and continue to try to get access to that external program."

"That's the plan?" Brit the Younger asked.

"Yes."

"Tell me," Brit the Younger asked, "if you happen to remember that you fail to get access to the external program anyway, will you even try?"

Brit the Elder said, "I'm sorry, dear. That's a question about the future."

Roy said, "One good thing. Because she's still here to tell us this, we know we make it back in one piece."

Brit the Elder said, "To be more precise, you know that I do."

7.

The first morning of the quest was spent mostly in cold, miserable silence. Then, as predicted, they found the remains of another party that had been killed and devoured by wolves.

Gary, speaking to nobody in particular, said, "Look at all this gore. How much time did that turd spend just making this all look as realistic as he could?"

Tyler, who just happened to be standing closest to Phillip at the time, said, "Maybe no time. Maybe he just brought in some people and had the wolves eat them."

Gary gasped. "It's hard to believe he'd really do that."

Tyler asked, "What, kill someone just for effect?"

All four men spent the next several seconds not saying what they were thinking and trying their hardest not to think what they were thinking.

As they approached, the corpses faded out of existence, leaving behind pristine weapons, wineskins full of presumably potable water, and folded clothing items. The men picked through the loot with no enthusiasm.

The path was narrow, with a sheer drop on one side and a rock wall on the other. The ill-fated party had clearly been attacked by wolves from both sides. Stains on the wall and ground marked the place where they had gone down, but the leavings were scattered along the trail for dozens of feet in both directions. Furs, cloaks, bedrolls, backpacks, swords, shields, and daggers were collected and put into separate piles. Tyler found a pair of leather leggings and a buckskin shirt. Tyler glanced at Jimmy, who, unlike the others, was barefoot and wearing only thin pajamas.

Tyler had more reason to hate Jimmy than anyone. Back when Jimmy was still called Merlin and was the chairman of the wizards, he had gotten a terrible idea. Like all truly terrible ideas, it had seemed like a great idea right up until the moment he told someone else about it. He tried to bring Tyler in on his schemes. When Tyler refused to be a party to it, Jimmy kept him quiet by "ghosting" him. Tyler spent days invisible, insubstantial, and unable to communicate, which would have been bad enough if he also hadn't spent the entire time experiencing the sensations of starving, dying of thirst, suffocating, and having to go to the bathroom. The whole time he was suffering this, he could see his friends going on about their lives, wondering where he was. He was right there with them, suffering the torments of hell and knowing that it was Jimmy who did it to him.

Tyler cleared his throat. Jimmy looked up. Tyler threw him the clothing. Jimmy caught it clumsily. When he saw what he had, his face lit up.

He looked back to Tyler and said, "Thank you."

Tyler scowled and turned his attention away from Jimmy's gratitude and back to the more pleasant topic of corpse robbing.

Soon they were on the move again. Phillip, Tyler, and Gary wore furs and cloaks over their robes and street clothes. Jimmy wore the britches and shirt Tyler had found, along with some boots that the former owner no longer needed. All carried swords, shields, and daggers. The backpacks were used to carry the other useful items they'd looted, including a flint. Jimmy's boots were too loose, but he knew better than to complain. Nobody in this group would have much sympathy.

They had only been carrying weapons for less than an hour when they got their first opportunity to use them. The path up the mountain remained a narrow track with a sheer rock wall on the left side and a sickening plunge on the right. They rounded a corner and found a large mountain wolf blocking their path.

Phillip was walking in the lead and stopped in his tracks when he saw the wolf. It had dark gray fur, yellow eyes, and paws the size of catchers' mitts. It was one hundred pounds of tense muscle and anger. Their eyes locked for an instant; then the wolf leapt for Phillip's jugular.

Luckily, Phillip's luck being what it is, Gary was walking behind Phillip and was not paying attention. He walked into Phillip's back, causing Phillip to fall forward unexpectedly onto his hands and knees. Nobody was more surprised than the wolf. Instead of biting Phillip's throat, it landed clumsily on his back as he hunched over. Gary let out a startled yelp. The wolf quickly got its footing and leapt off Phillip's back, now trying for Gary's throat instead.

Gary instinctively shielded his face with his right arm, shrieking as he did so. Gary was grateful for the thick fur-covered hide that took the worst of the wolf's bite. Even with the hide, he felt like his arm was being crushed in a vise. The wolf's weight pulled him forward. Gary kept to his feet. As the wolf continued its vigorous assault on Gary's arm, Phillip came to his senses, stood up, and shoved the wolf's rear in the general direction of the cliff. Gary spun to his right, swinging the wolf out over the edge like some deranged carnival ride for animals. Gary barely managed to keep his footing, avoiding being pulled off the cliff to his death. The wolf kept his grip on his arm, so as Gary spun, the wolf swung around and hit a very startled Tyler in the side of the head.

Tyler was knocked sideways into the rock wall on his left. The wolf fell to the ground and struggled to regain its footing on the narrow path. It got all four paws underneath it just in time to receive one of Jimmy's too-large boots in the side of its head.

The wolf rolled sideways off the edge of the path. They watched as the wolf tumbled, then fell, then tumbled some more, then fell some more, then grew too distant to follow.

Gary said, "Wow. Good thing we have these swords."

They hiked in relative silence for the rest of that day. The path remained narrow, precarious, and littered with the occasional angry wolf. After the third wolf blocked their path and attacked Phillip, he insisted that it was someone else's turn to lead while he brought up the rear. The next wolf somehow attacked from behind, but by this point, Phillip had gotten the hang of waiting for them to leap, then pushing them off the cliff while they were in midair. All the others agreed: you wouldn't want to mess with Phillip if you were both standing on a cliff. He had become the master of death by shoving.

After a day that felt years long, the path widened into a stand of trees inhabiting a relatively horizontal spot on the side of the mountain. They decided to camp for the night. Jimmy was surprisingly adept at building the fire.

"Where'd you learn to do that?" Phillip asked.

Jimmy replied, "I spent thirty years living on a bicycle. It's not like it had a kitchen and central heat." He made a point of smiling as he said it. They had accepted his apology, but none of

the wizards had truly forgiven, and they certainly hadn't forgotten. There were certain things he could never do if he wanted to
ever regain their trust, and chief among them was that he could
never express any anger over their punishment of him.

Phillip and Jimmy tended to the fire, or, to be more precise,
Jimmy tended to the fire and Phillip kept an eye on Jimmy. Tyler
and Gary fought and killed another wolf, which had slunk out of
the underbrush and attacked Gary with no provocation, again,
leaping straight at Gary's throat. Gary shielded his face and fell
over backward with the wolf riding him to the ground. While
the wolf was distracted trying to kill Gary, Tyler came from the
side and skewered it clumsily with his sword.

Tyler shook his head. "These wolves. They all seem to attack
the same way."

Phillip said, "That's because they're all the same wolf. I suspected it on the trail, but now I'm sure. Todd just has one wolf,
and he keeps generating it over and over again. They all look
exactly the same, are the same size, and attack the same way.
They see you. They hunker down. They growl for a three count,
and they leap at your head. Then, if you time it right, you can just
shove them right off the mountain."

Gary looked down at the dead wolf and said, "Ah. Cool."

"Yeah," Tyler agreed. "Guess we shouldn't let this one go to
waste." Tyler reached down to grab the wolf's carcass and was
surprised when his hand went right through it. As they watched,
the wolf corpse slowly faded away into nothing, leaving behind a
small wrapped package marked "Wolf Jerky."

"Oh yeah," Tyler said. "Todd's a game designer."

"That's standard in later video games, is it?" Phillip asked. "In
games from my time, when things die, they just kind of explode."

"Yeah," Gary said, "In lots of our games stuff still explodes, but that doesn't make sense for a sword-and-sorcery game. It wouldn't seem natural to stab a wolf and have it explode."

"But fading out does seem natural?" Jimmy asked.

Tyler said, "Kinda. Not really. Look, the thing is, they learned fairly early on that players enjoyed killing stuff, but didn't enjoy being reminded that they had killed stuff. Also, it was easier on the computer if it didn't have to keep drawing all the guys you've killed. Having them disappear frees up the processor to render the stuff you haven't killed yet. Speaking of which, I'm hungry." Tyler opened the package of wolf jerky and tried a piece.

"How is it?" Phillip asked.

"Awful," Tyler said with his mouth full.

"Figures," Phillip said. "Give me some."

Gary asked, "If Todd's trying to punish us, why would he give us food?"

"Maybe he doesn't want us to starve to death too early into the quest," Phillip said through a mouthful of jerky. "Or, maybe he figures making it easy to get something awful to eat will guarantee that we'll eat something awful."

Tyler handed a piece to Gary and another to Jimmy, who looked at it and asked, "What if it's poisoned?"

Phillip said, "If he were going to poison us, he'd have poisoned the water, or just shot us with a dart. No, this is all about prolonging the suffering."

Jimmy shrugged and bit off a piece of the jerky.

Tyler said, "If we get too tired of the jerky I can try to hunt for something, but I doubt there are any real animals here, so I'm afraid it's jerky or nothing."

"You know how to hunt?" Jimmy asked.

"I used to go with my dad," he explained.

Gary said, "I didn't know black guys hunted."

Tyler laughed. "In Montana, we do."

The sky grew darker, the fire grew brighter, they sat, and, predictably, the conversation turned to Jeff.

"Guys," Gary asked, "what do you think the chances are that Todd was faking us out and Jeff's still alive?"

Jimmy said, "Low. Pretty much nonexistent. I mean, it's possible, but we have to assume he's gone. Even if we think he might be alive, we have to assume he's not. You heard Todd. He killed him to prove a point. It does him no good if he pops up later and says, 'I was just kidding.' No, we have to assume that he killed one of us and that he'd be happy to do it again."

"So he's really gone," Gary said.

Phillip said, "Yeah, I'm afraid so. But we have his memory."

Tyler said, "We have better than that. We have time travel. We can still go back and save him."

Phillip said, "I thought about this. There are ways that might be possible, but they all are dependent on one or all of us surviving, getting away from Todd, and getting our powers back."

Jimmy said, "I agree."

Phillip said, "I didn't ask."

"I know," Jimmy said. "Just saying, the way to save Jeff is to save ourselves."

"That's convenient for you," Tyler said.

Jimmy smiled, lifted a foot, and pointed to one of the larger blisters his ill-fitting boots had given him. "Tyler," he said, "there is no part of this situation that I would describe as 'convenient.'"

They were all bone-tired and had bellies full of wolf jerky. They'd have loved to have been able to say it tasted like chicken, but it did not. The wolf's final revenge was to make certain that you never forgot that you were eating wolf meat.

They slept in shifts, always having one man awake to keep watch. By "keep watch," they meant "kill wolves." Now that they all understood the timing, it was not that difficult. Spot the wolf, count to three, duck, and stab. They had it down to a science, and it was a good thing, because for every wolf they dispatched, a couple of hours later two wolves would appear. Fighting multiple wolves was not that much harder, because like ninjas in a bad kung-fu movie, they only attacked one at a time, hunkering in a group, looking vicious but waiting patiently for their turn to growl and leap while whoever was keeping watch went through the motions, muttering, "One, two, three, duck, stab. One, two, three, duck, stab."

At dawn, they all awoke just in time to help dispatch sixteen wolves, which was difficult even when you knew the secret, just because of the sheer stamina required. The fact that the area around their camp was littered with the jerky pouches left behind by fourteen former wolves did not help either.

As Tyler finished off the last of the wolves, Gary asked, "Does this mean that thirty-two wolves will be chasing us?"

"—duck, stab. Nah," Tyler said. "I'd bet they don't travel very far from their spawn point."

"Yeah," Phillip said. "At the rate they multiply, we'd be overrun by them before we got to our first task. No, I think they're just meant to keep us moving. Discourage us from staying in one place too long."

Jimmy said, "Or backtracking." He looked at the path from which they had come and shuddered. "I don't envy anyone who has to follow that path after us."

8.

Martin, Gwen, Brit the Younger, and Roy materialized. They had not known what situation they would be teleporting into, so they had attempted to prepare for anything. They wore rugged clothes and hiking boots. Roy and Martin wore their robes, hats, and staves. Martin had a thin, modern coat on under his robe. Roy's robe was a coat, so he was covered. Gwen and Brit wore jackets without any magical accoutrements. They looked like two couples on a double date to a Renaissance festival that only the men were interested in.

All were pitched forward on the balls of their feet. Martin and Roy brandished their staves menacingly. Martin held his like one would aim a rifle, the small bust of Santo out in front, showing any attackers which was the "business end." Roy held the bridge cue that he used as a staff like a batter waiting for a fat pitch. Gwen brandished her dual magic wands like ninja swords. Brit used no implement to channel her magic and merely held her hands in front of her body as if they were registered weapons.

When they'd fully materialized, they saw that they were high in the mountains. They could see the woods in front of them. A path led away, into the forest. The path started at the cliff face, about thirty yards ahead of them.

It took only an instant to realize that if the cliff face was in front of them, they were not standing on the cliff. They looked down, then shrieked and flailed, startled by the fact that they had materialized in midair. Then they yelped and flailed at the fact that they were not falling but seemed to be standing on some invisible surface. Then they silently flailed in an effort to maintain their balance, which had been thrown off by all of their previous flailing.

Once he had his equilibrium, Martin used his staff the way a blind person uses a cane, in an effort to see how far the surface that was supporting his weight extended.

"Huh," he said. "Feels solid enough. We just can't see it."

Hundreds of feet below them, a river wended its way through a landscape composed of jagged rocks. The rocks led to cliffs, which became mountains before terminating in the rough, forbidding peaks that made up the horizon. It was day, but the sun was still quite low, a hazy white disk in a battleship-gray sky. The only part of the landscape that looked even a little bit inviting was the stand of woods with the path in front of them, and it seemed to invite them to their doom. Really, none of them would have been inclined to move at all if not for the fact that they were suspended unnervingly in midair.

Roy said, "Welp, as great as this is, I think we should probably get moving." He held his staff aloft and said the magic word to trigger the Leadchurch shell program's flight subroutine: "Flugi."

Roy did not move.

He tried again. "Flugi, dammit!"

Martin reached into the pocket of his silver robe and pulled out his smartphone. He zipped through a couple of screens, then said, "Huh. Interesting. The programs are running, but they don't seem to work. I guess we're cut off from the signal."

Roy looked ruefully at Brit and said, "Heh. Well, you were right. You said it would be interesting for us to see if it works, and the kid is interested."

Brit said, "I'm as angry as you are. Brit the Elder said that, not me."

"Yeah," Roy replied, "but you're her, aren't you?"

"Not yet, I'm not," Brit the Younger said.

Roy started to respond, but he was distracted by four large and obviously full backpacks that materialized next to them. One of the backpacks had a note taped to its front. Martin leaned over (none of them were confident enough in the invisible surface on which they stood to walk just yet) and snatched up the note. He read it aloud. "Since your powers are not working, you'll need these supplies. Good luck! Signed, Brit, XOXO."

Roy said, "That was nice of her."

"Oh," Brit the Younger fumed, "when she does something *nice*, we're different people!"

"Is she good at recognizing sarcasm?" Roy asked. "Because you seem to have a problem with it."

Gwen told the others to stop bickering but was drowned out by a deafeningly loud voice that said, "Silence!"

They reflexively cried out in surprise and covered their ears as the voice echoed off the mountains.

Gwen asked, "Who said that?"

"I said silence," the voice repeated. It was so loud it made their clothing vibrate.

Brit muttered, "Yeah, we heard."

In front of them, a dim point of light flickered into existence, and as it radiated outward, an unkempt old man appeared. His hair and the rags he wore were filthy. His eyes conveyed much expression but looked as if they were not good for anything else. Like them, he appeared to stand in midair.

The old man said, "Soon, it will be dawn, and your quest will begin."

Gwen said, "Dawn's past. It's midmorning, I think. Might be evening. Which direction is north?"

The old man said, "Aye. You're going on a quest. A quest full of danger, and peril, and risk of life and limb."

"Did some other wizards come through here?" Martin asked.

Brit added, "Did you send them on a quest?"

The old man said, "First, you'll brave the dangers of Cardhu Pass. If you survive, you'll make your way to the cursed Mines of Mortlach. There, you will seek out Blandoch, head of the mining guild. The miners will give you a sample of a mystical ore called dailuaine. You will take this splendid rock many miles, to the town of Bowmore, where it will be used to craft a weapon fit for use in the final battle."

Martin said, "I'm pretty sure he's just a recording. Hey, are you a recording?"

The old man said, "Take a moment to prepare, adventurers, and be warned. On your journey, you will face death a thousand different ways."

"Yeah," Martin said. "He's a recording."

"Are you sure?" Roy asked. "Maybe you should ask again."

The old man gazed in their general direction for a moment, then said, "I can see you are men of valor. Which of you shall lead his fellows on this quest?"

Roy said, "Um, two of us aren't men."

Gwen said, "Thanks for pointing that out."

The old man continued to look at them. They looked back, then looked at each other.

The old man repeated, "I can see you are men of valor. Which of you shall lead his fellows on this quest?"

Gwen pointed to Brit and said, "She will."

The old man said, "Can you please repeat that?"

Gwen repeated, "She will."

The old man said, "Can you please repeat that?"

Brit said, "I will."

The old man said, "Can you please repeat that?"

Gwen said, "Brit will."

The old man said, "Can you please repeat that?"

Roy said, "You're not a man. He specified a man."

The old man said, "Can you please repeat that?"

Brit said, "I'm not sure he did."

The old man said, "Can you please repeat that?"

Roy said, "I will."

The old man said, "Can you please repeat that?"

Roy said, "Roy will."

The old man said, "Can you please repeat that?"

Brit said, "I guess you're not a man either."

The old man said, "Can you please repeat that?"

Martin said, "Gwen."

The old man said, "Can you please repeat that?"

Gwen said, "What?"

Martin said, "No, I was trying to make you the leader."

The old man said, "Can you please repeat that?"

Gwen said, "Oh, I see what you mean."

The old man said, "Can you please repeat that?"

Gwen said, "Martin."

Martin muttered, "I hate being picked last."

The old man said, "Can you please repeat that?"

They stood in silence, having run out of options. After a long moment, the old man said, "I can see you are men of valor. Which of you shall lead his fellows on this quest?"

Martin said, "Screw this."

The old man said, "Can you please repeat that?"

Martin glared at him, then started silently probing the invisible surface on which they stood with the tip of his staff. Once he was convinced that there was solid footing in front of him, Martin successfully took a step forward. Roy followed his lead, and the two started making their way to a position where they could pick up the backpacks.

The old man continued asking them who would be their leader, and they continued ignoring him, silently distributing the backpacks among themselves. They formed a kind of conga line. Gwen and Brit followed behind, taking care to follow in Martin's and Roy's footsteps exactly. Martin and Roy led them, using their staves to map the area ahead and to the sides, slowly navigating a path to solid, or at least visible, ground.

Once they were standing on a surface they could see, they did not waste a lot of time. They took a moment to gawk at the back of the old man, still hanging in midair, periodically asking the void to choose a leader. They made a quick survey of the contents of their backpacks. Brit the Elder had sent them energy bars, water filters, purification tablets, lighters, knives, some other basic camping equipment, and spare socks. In retrospect, it was now obvious why she had suggested that they all wear jeans, hiking boots, and coats.

It was easy to reach consensus on what their next move should be. There was only one path to take. They took it with minimum discussion.

As they walked, Martin thought aloud. "Clearly, this quest was deliberately set up by someone."

"Agreed," Brit said.

"And whoever set it up," Martin continued, "took Phillip, Jeff, Tyler, and Gary but left me and Roy behind."

"They also took Jimmy," Gwen reminded him.

"Yeah," Martin said. "Well, my point is, whoever it was, they took specific people they wanted, not just whoever was around."

Brit bit her lip while she thought for a moment, then said, "Hmm. That makes me wish we'd have thought to tell that old coot that one of them was our leader. It might have prompted the recording progress. We might have gotten more information."

"I'm kinda glad we didn't," Martin said. "For all we know, something awful might have happened. This way the program, whoever it was designed for, might not be working for us. We may just have an easier time than them now. Maybe we'll catch up faster."

They all reflected on this positive thought as they rounded a corner and found the remains of the party that had been killed by wolves. Unlike those they had come to rescue, they had not been warned that they would find this sickening scene, or that there were wolves around in the first place. All four of them separately experienced a moment of silent panic, thinking that it might be their friends. Soon it became obvious that this was a different group, partly because they had clearly been dead for several days and partly because when Roy went in for a closer look, the bodies disappeared, leaving swords and neatly folded clothing and other items behind. After a bit of debate, they took the swords, shields, daggers, and a few of the furs.

Soon after that the path left the woods and started snaking its way up and across the steep mountainside. They walked as fast as they could, keeping to the left side of the path, closer to the rock wall and a few inches farther from the cliff that formed the path's right edge.

Less than an hour later, their progress was blocked by two wolves, standing in single file. Martin was walking in the lead and froze when he saw the wolves.

The wolves looked identical but behaved quite differently. The wolf in back continued to stand upright, looking alert but uninterested. The wolf in front immediately sunk into a crouch, growled, then leapt for Martin's throat. Martin blocked with his staff. The wolf's jaws clamped onto the staff, and it fell back to the path. Martin and the wolf played tug of war with the staff for a few moments before Martin twisted the staff free of the wolf's grip. The wolf sprang for Martin's throat again. This time Martin attempted to block it with his arm and backhanded the wolf, which would have been really cool if it had been deliberate. The wolf's momentum carried it into Martin, covering his face with the dirty fur of its flank. The wolf rolled down Martin's front and fell to the ground, sprung back to its feet, and immediately got hit with the staff again, knocking it off the cliff.

The second wolf flattened, growled, and leapt for Martin's throat just as the first had. This time, instead of accidentally striking the wolf with his hand, Martin deliberately struck the wolf with his staff. Like his partner before him, the wolf fell to the ground. This time Martin kicked the wolf before it found its feet. The wolf scratched and clawed at the cliff edge as it went over and fell out of Martin's life forever.

Gwen said, "Wow."

Martin swelled a bit with pride.

Gwen continued. "Those wolves seemed really easy to kill."

Martin deflated. "Well, maybe I made it look easy."

"Maybe," Roy said. "It could be we were dazzled by your battle cry, 'ai-yi-yi.'"

"I did not yell 'ai-yi-yi,' did I?" Martin asked.

Roy said, "You did, but I'm not surprised you didn't notice it, what with you being in a berserker rage and all."

"I doubt those will be the last wolves we see," Brit said.

"Yup," Roy agreed. "And the next ones probably won't be so easy to kill. From now on we walk single file, and Martin and I should take the first and last spots."

Roy scooted sideways past Brit and started walking quickly up the trail. Brit gave chase.

"Hey, why is that?" Brit asked. "Why do you and Martin have to be in front and back?"

Gwen followed Brit, leaving Martin bringing up the rear.

"Hey, Roy," Brit said. "I asked you a question. Why do you or Martin have to be in front and back?"

Roy didn't answer. Brit asked again. When Roy failed to even acknowledge the question for a third time, Brit resorted to lightly shoving him.

"Hey, I asked you a question," she said.

Roy stopped walking and turned to face her. His expression said that he was trying to be patient but was not doing a very good job of it.

"You got a problem, young lady?"

"Yes, old man. You won't answer my question. Why do Gwen and I have to walk in between you and Martin?"

"It's pretty simple. We're on this narrow path. There are only two ways that a wolf can approach: in front of us and behind us, right? So it just makes sense, if you take even a second to think about it, to have the kid and me in those two spots."

"Why?" Brit asked. "Why does it make more sense to have you two be where the wolves might attack?"

Roy sighed. "Because you and Gwen are . . ."

Roy paused. He had gotten into this argument because he believed men were better at fighting, but the looks in Brit's and Gwen's eyes made him rethink that idea. Beyond them, Martin was bugging his eyes, gritting his teeth, waving both hands, and shaking his head no. Roy took a second to choose his next word carefully.

Roy said, "Ladies."

Martin winced. Gwen looked disappointed. Brit had taken on an expression of serene fury.

"So," Brit said, "you think you're better equipped to deal with wolves because you're gentlemen?"

Roy scowled and walked away, up the path. Brit gave chase.

"I must say," Brit shouted at Roy's back. "I simply cannot wait to watch our strapping he-man champion engage in the gentlemanly art of fisticuffs with those ill-mannered poodles! I bet he'll slap them silly until they apologize!"

Martin and Gwen watched them walk away, looked at each other, shook their heads, then followed.

9.

Jimmy took the lead when they left camp, but they made a point of rotating every hour or so to make sure that they all got their share of wolf murder. The path continued to cling to the side of the mountain. They had grown used to having a drop that meant certain death on their right. They were still terrified of falling, but they were accustomed to the terror.

They never reached a peak as such; they just realized that the path was now going downhill instead of up.

Slowly, chatter started to pick up as they walked. They had started walking in depressed silence, then angry silence, then resigned silence. When they started talking, they made depressed conversation, then angry conversation, then finally, resigned conversation.

Eventually the path led them down from the edge of the cliffs and onto a wooded hillside, which meant that their usual technique of heaving attacking wolves off cliffs would no longer work. Tyler tried it once out of sheer muscle memory. He body-slammed the wolf, which was satisfying but did not stop it from attacking again.

They camped that night, eating their customary dinner of wolf jerky. The next day they walked through sparse forest until the path led them to a sheer rock wall, with a massive carving set into its face. It was a statue, at least fifty feet tall, depicting a solidly built man standing with his legs apart. In one hand he held a pickaxe. In the other, a cartoonishly large gemstone. The statue's splayed legs framed a hole that reached far into the mountain. A small railroad track led out from the hole and terminated at a large pile of rock, next to an old wooden sledge that looked designed to be pulled by a mule.

Jimmy said, "Behold, the cursed Mines of Mortlach."

Phillip groaned.

Jimmy shrugged. "What? We're stuck in this thing. We might as well get into the spirit."

They approached the mine's entrance. Gary looked up at the statue and said, "They're trying a little too hard to make an impression, I think."

Tyler said, "You live in a cave shaped like a skull."

"Yes," Gary said, "a skull. A whole skeleton would be overkill. You have to show some restraint."

As they reached the entrance, they could see dim lights inside. They entered, instinctively bending over slightly even though the opening was more than tall enough to accommodate them. The inner chamber of the mine was surprisingly vast. As their eyes adjusted, they could see that there were dim lanterns placed randomly throughout the chamber.

As their eyes became more accustomed to the dark, they could make out the miners who were holding the lanterns. They were short but extremely stocky, with massive, bulging arms, stooped shoulders, and sad, grimy faces. If they had been presented as statues or paintings, they'd have been impressively realistic, but they were being presented as living, breathing people and looked unmistakably fake.

Between the miners who held lanterns were many other

miners who only held pickaxes. They stood not quite motionless and looked at their uninvited guests with an expression that was not quite hostility.

The miners looked at the wizards and said nothing.

The wizards looked at the miners and said nothing.

The whole situation seemed infused with a sense of foreboding. Everyone seemed worried that bad things might happen to whoever dared break the silence.

Jimmy turned to Phillip and mouthed, "May I?"

Phillip nodded, and made a shooing gesture with his hands.

Jimmy stepped forward, spread his arms, and said, "We mean no harm. We are travelers, fresh from traversing Cardhu Pass. We seek Blandoch, who we are told heads the mining guild. We have business to discuss."

A murmur spread throughout the miners. They seemed more excited than upset by what they heard. They parted like a curtain, revealing the back of the chamber. The rough rock wall held a chunky timber post-and-lintel structure that framed a passage that receded into the darkness. No doubt, this was the actual mine shaft.

Next to the shaft entrance sat a miner who looked similar to all the other miners, except that his body language reeked of depression. Also, his pickaxe was made of gold. He sat on the mine floor with his pickaxe in his lap and his head hung low. He glanced up toward the visitors without moving his head, and in a voice drenched in sorrow, he said, "I am Blandoch, but I have no business with you, nor anybody."

Jimmy said, "We have business with you, sir." Jimmy walked toward the moping wretch. He took a few steps, stopped, turned back to the rest of his party, and beckoned them to follow.

Phillip shrugged and followed Jimmy. Tyler and Gary followed Phillip.

The miners watched them silently as they walked the thirty feet or so to the back of the chamber. In its way, it felt like a longer trip than the walk that had brought them here.

They stood, looking down at the sulking form of Blandoch. He looked up at them and said, "State your business."

Jimmy said, "We seek the rare mineral dailuaine."

Phillip leaned toward Jimmy and whispered, "How do you remember all this stuff?"

Jimmy muttered, "It's a skill I work on. People tend to think better of you if you remember their names. Comes in handy for other things too. I could teach you."

Gary asked, "Hey, is that the stuff?" He pointed toward the ground, just inside the mouth of the mine shaft. There were several round boulders roughly the size of basketballs. They were a dull gray color that did not match the rock walls.

Jimmy said, "Let me handle this."

Blandoch said, "Aye, we have dailuaine. More than enough for your needs, but alas, we cannot get to it."

Tyler said, "He started that sentence with 'Aye,' but you hadn't asked a question. I think he's another recording."

"Yeah," Jimmy agreed. "I figured."

Gary had walked over to the strange rocks. "If this is it, we could just grab some and be on our way."

Phillip said, "Gary, please let us handle this."

With tremendous effort, Blandoch got up on his feet. With even more effort, he explained, "We cannot get you your dailuaine, for we are cursed. We are miners, but we cannot go into the mine without our beloved canary, Oban." Blandoch gestured to his right. The miners who had been watching moved aside to reveal a simple stone pedestal. There was nothing on the pedestal, but above it, carved into the rock, was a homey little sign that said "Oban."

Phillip asked, "What happened to your canary?"

Jimmy said, "Oban."

"Yes," Phillip said, "Oban. What happened to Oban?"

Blandoch said, "Without him, it is too dangerous to enter the mine."

Tyler said, "That's not really a curse. It's more of an equipment problem."

"They don't have to go into the mine," Gary said. "I think I have some right here. Look, it's not even that heavy!" Gary was hunched over with his legs spread wide, holding one of the gray boulders between his legs like a small child with a bowling ball. Jimmy, Phillip, and Tyler all glared at him until he dropped the boulder and stood up straight again.

Blandoch said, "He was taken from us."

Phillip said, "The bird."

"Oban," Jimmy corrected him.

"By an evil king," Blandoch explained, answering a question nobody had asked yet. "King Milburn the Mad. He and his vile viceroy, Flagler. They stole our beloved canary."

"Oban," Jimmy interjected.

"And took him to Castle Cragganmore," Blandoch said.

Tyler said, "Milburn the Mad and his vile viceroy took the canary to Castle Cragganmore. It appears our author is agog for alliteration."

Blandoch's face took on a look of amazement and childlike glee. He clapped his hands together. "Yes! Indeed! If you were to go to the castle and retrieve Oban, we would gladly give you all the dailuaine you could ever need!"

Phillip said, "Well, that seems settled, then. If you all would just tell us the way to this castle."

"Cragganmore," Jimmy said.

"Quite," Phillip said. "Please tell us the way to go . . . there."

The miners erupted into spontaneous cheering, followed by singing and a surprisingly well-choreographed dance number. Giant flagons of beer appeared as if from nowhere, seemingly for the purpose of spilling on the ground as they danced. Delicious-looking roasted drumsticks from some animal that was far too large to be a chicken, or even a turkey, also appeared but were waved in the air, rather than eaten.

Tyler said, "I figure they'll tell us the way when they're done celebrating."

"Yeah, probably," Jimmy agreed.

The miners enjoyed their preprogrammed celebration all through the night. The next morning the wizards were given fresh water and directions to Castle Cragganmore. Of course, the directions had consisted of pointing to one of the three paths that led away from the mine and saying "That one," but still, it saved the wizards some guesswork.

The mountains had given way to rolling hills, so the terrain itself no longer seemed to be trying to kill them. The downside of this was that instead of only having to watch in front of them and behind them for attacks from mountain wolves, now they had to watch in all directions for attacks from what the miners referred to as "hill wolves."

Hill wolves differed from mountain wolves in that they lived in the hills instead of the mountains. That was where the differences ended. They looked identical, attacked via the same pattern, and appeared with the same regularity. The only real difference from the wizards' point of view was that you couldn't just chuck them off a cliff, because there was no cliff. Hurling them down a hill only worked if you were standing at the top of the hill, and even then it only gave you a moment to regroup while the wolf ran back up the hill. Instead, they took to counting to three, then simply stabbing the wolves out of the air.

The path was wide and well trodden and began to parallel a large, fast-moving river. The river started to descend into a picturesque canyon, which seemed to have been carved by the river.

Phillip thought, *For the first time since this ridiculous quest began, we're almost having a nice time. Sure, we're trapped in a poorly designed death maze, at the mercy of a man who doesn't know what the word means, because he's both cruel and stupid, but the weather is nice and thanks to the river and its gorge, the hill wolves can only attack us from two directions again.*

Phillip was torn from his reverie by Tyler, who was pointing at the water and yelling, "River wolf!"

A wolf swam clumsily though the treacherous currents, dragged itself up onto land, growled for the traditional amount of time, then leapt for Tyler's throat, got stabbed, and hit the ground with a wet thud.

The river canyon twisted and turned through the landscape, and the path followed. The walls around the wizards grew steeper, and the blue sky above them narrowed to a blue slit visible beyond the canyon rim.

It was still broad daylight outside the canyon, but in the shadows down along the riverbank, it felt like dusk. They became aware that the canyon seemed to widen ahead of them. Soon, they saw that the course of the river had gently turned one direction, then bent back upon itself in a turn so sharp it almost created a full loop. The forces of gravity and erosion had worked together, most likely at Todd's direction, to form a giant bowl with steep rock walls easily a hundred feet tall. The river shot around the bottom of the bowl so quickly that it actually raked outward at an angle, like the surface of a whirlpool, before completing its right-hand turn and then taking a violent left, away from the bowl, and down the remainder of the canyon. The riverbed was littered with immense boulders that had no doubt fallen from the high walls around the bend. They poked up through the surface of the water, creating violent currents and making navigation of the river by boat impossible.

In the middle of these turbulent hairpin turns, the canyon's far wall narrowed into a teardrop-shaped spit of land that formed the inner bank of the bend. On this dry, stony outcropping, there was a castle so Gothic it might as well have been wearing black eyeliner. Buttresses supported larger buttresses, which supported arches, which supported stained-glass windows, balconies, gargoyles, and spires so numerous and packed together so tightly that there appeared to be no visible building at their source. From a distance, it looked like a black stone pincushion.

The castle's island narrowed to a knife's edge of stone. The path the wizards had been following led across this land bridge, but it offered little reassurance. The path was lined on both sides with rushing white water, heading in opposite directions. To fall from either side would mean certain death. Between this natural bridge and the castle stood a small army of large men; thus, making it safely across the bridge also meant certain death.

Tyler said, "That must be Castle Cragganmore."

"Are you sure?" Gary asked.

"We're on the path to Castle Cragganmore," Tyler explained, "and the path ends at that castle, so unless there's another smaller castle hiding inside that castle, yeah, I'm pretty sure."

The men backtracked, ducking around the corner to make themselves harder for any prying eyes from the castle to spot. They climbed as far up the canyon wall as they dared, in order to get a better view. They surveyed the situation and started to plan.

"I say we give up," Phillip said. "This is madness. Clearly Todd has set this up just so he can watch us all die horribly at the hands of those soldiers, or maybe, if he's very lucky, we'll fall into the river and be dashed on the rocks before we get within killing range. Either way, I say we refuse to move and make Todd come down here and show us the courtesy of killing us himself."

Gary said, "I don't think it's as hopeless as all that."

Phillip said, "Think again."

"No, seriously," Gary said, "look over there, guys." He pointed across the river, to the far canyon wall. Because the river had effectively cut a groove in the earth, the various strata formed by different layers of minerals were visible in cross section.

Tyler squinted and said, "What am I looking for? I see striations in the rock, but that's about all."

"Striations. Do you mean stripes?" Gary asked.

"Yeah," Tyler said. "I guess I do."

"Then why don't you just say that?" Gary asked.

"Because those kinds of stripes are called striations."

"Whatever," Gary said. "There are a couple of them that are bigger and flatter than the others. They make kind of a ledge, just wide enough that if we went sideways, one at a time, I think we could walk on them."

Jimmy said, "Yeah, I suppose, if we could find a way across the river, but what good would that do us? The castle is on this side of the river, not over there."

"Those soldiers aren't on that side of the river either," Gary said. "And if you look down there, where the river goes around the castle, you see all those boulders?"

Jimmy and Tyler said that they did.

"Some of them are pretty close together, aren't they? Almost close enough that someone could jump from rock to rock and make their way across the river."

Phillip said, "The whole way along the cliff we'd be sitting ducks. If they have any archers, they'll use us for target practice."

"So we wait for nightfall," Gary said. "It'll be clear tonight. There'll be plenty of moonlight for us to see by, but the soldiers won't be looking for us. They're guarding the path."

Phillip considered this for a moment, then said, "Okay, say we do scrabble along the cliff face in the dark of night, then successfully leap across the rapids. What then? How do we get the canary?"

Gary smiled. "We steal it. We go in like burglars, find where they're keeping the canary, take it, and get out the same way we got in."

Phillip looked over to Tyler and Jimmy. Jimmy was peering into the distance at the rocks, planning. Tyler was deep in thought, but there was a hint of a smile on his face. Phillip shook his head. "That's pretty optimistic, Gary. What makes you think we can pull this off?"

Gary smiled broadly. "I know something none of you know. Something that will help."

Tyler and Jimmy both turned and looked at Gary. Phillip was also waiting to hear what he would say next. Gary savored the moment, then said, "I know the stealth secret of the ninjas!"

Tyler turned to Phillip and said, "He really had me up until he said that last bit."

Gary said, "No! Really! Guys, we can do this! Tyler, you know I'm telling the truth. I've used the secret to sneak up on you. Remember that one time I stuck your hand in that bowl of warm water?"

Tyler said, "I was asleep."

"Yeah," Gary said, "and I didn't wake you up. That's gotta count for something."

Phillip turned to Tyler and asked, "Does that really work, the bowl of warm water thing?"

"Yeah," Tyler said. "If your goal is to make someone wake up with a wet hand, it works every time."

Gary said, "Look, I'll show you the secret, okay. I saw it on the Discovery Channel."

The other three agreed and stood respectfully while Gary explained his ancient stealth technique.

"Okay," Gary said. "Here's how the ninjas did it. They lowered their center of gravity—you don't quite crouch, but you bend your knees more than you normally would." He lowered his stance, slightly hunching his shoulders.

"Then, you extend your elbows and your wrists. This gives

you greater balance, and allows you to feel obstacles that you can't see." He spread his arms out wide and extended his hands in front of himself.

Gary said, "You start with your weight distributed evenly across the soles of both your feet. Now slowly shift your weight so that one foot is carrying the load, then slowly extend the other foot forward. As you do, try to keep your pelvis moving in a straight line without raising or dipping. Slowly shift your weight to the forward foot, then repeat the process until you reach your goal. Move silently. Silently. Silently."

Gary demonstrated, walking stealthily in a circle several times, muttering, "Silently."

Tyler asked, "Do we have to keep repeating 'silently' the whole time?"

"No," Gary said. "That's just part of the demonstration."

Phillip said, "Now we all know, gentlemen. The stealth secret of the ninjas was that they would sneak."

Gary ignored Phillip, focusing on Tyler and Jimmy. "Come on, guys. What do you say?"

Phillip said, "No, Gary. It's an interesting idea, but I'm afraid it's hopeless."

"So what, then?" Gary asked. "You're gonna give up?"

"No," Phillip answered. "A few minutes ago I was going to give up. Now I have given up."

Gary was aghast. "I can't believe this! You're really just going to wait here for Todd to show up and kill you?"

Phillip pointed to the castle in the distance. "It's better than going over there and killing myself for him."

"Really?! *Really?!*" Gary whined. "Man, I just don't get you. You can't just give up like this! Surely, it's gotta be better to die trying."

"Trying to do what?" Phillip asked. "Something dangerous and pointless for the amusement of someone who wants us to die anyway?"

"It's not pointless," Gary said. "Your way, either the river wolves will get us or Todd will pop up and take us out himself. Either way we die. My way, we will probably be killed, but there's a small chance that we might live, and I don't think that's pointless."

Phillip thought about this for a moment, then turned to Tyler and Jimmy and asked, "Do you two think this is a good idea?"

Tyler said, "No. It's a terrible idea. But, we're going to do it." Jimmy nodded agreement.

Phillip had expected that answer. For the most part, he even agreed with it. He was now objecting more out of momentum than because of any actual hope of winning the argument.

"So we go with Gary's plan, even though we'll almost certainly be killed?" Phillip asked.

Jimmy shrugged. "We'll most likely die either way. At least Gary's way won't be boring."

10.

They didn't have to backtrack far to find a part of the river that was narrow and boulder-strewn enough to work their way across. They spent the remaining time until nightfall eating wolf jerky, making sure anything they had that was reflective was covered, killing the occasional river wolf, and napping in the shade of the canyon walls.

When it was dark enough to launch their assault, they crossed the river. As they leapt from rock to rock, Phillip and Tyler found themselves on a boulder, surrounded by rapids, with Jimmy and Gary already across. It was the first chance they had to talk even semiprivately since the quest began, and they dawdled there, pretending to take a breather to capitalize on the opportunity.

Phillip said, "The boulders are just close enough together to make crossing the river possible, but dangerous. There coincidentally happens to be a side route to the castle that's just well hidden enough to be obvious. Doesn't this seem a little too easy?"

"Yeah," Tyler said. "I've been thinking about that. Two things. One: Todd is a game designer. Now, I know you mainly play stuff like *GORF* and *Choplifter*, but games get a lot more sophisticated later on. It's not unheard of for there to be more than one way to complete a mission. Could be that he deliberately made it so we could fight our way through the front door, or sneak around back."

Phillip said, "Yeah, that would explain it."

Tyler said, "Mm hmm. The other thing is that Todd went to a lot of trouble to make this quest. He wants to get maximum entertainment out of it. That means he wants us to survive, at least some of us, to the end. Also, he probably gave us the choice because he wants us to argue. He wants us at each other's throats."

Phillip laughed. "I wondered why you were being so nice to Jimmy."

"Yeah," Tyler said. "Until we get out of this, or he gets killed, I'm going out of my way to be civil, but make no mistake, I can't stand the sight of him. I certainly don't trust him. You?"

"You know I've disliked the bastard longer than anyone. But, in a weird way, I do trust him. I trust him to do what he thinks is best for him. Right now, he stands a better chance of surviving if we all stay alive to help him, so yeah, I trust him to help the group, for now. If, at the end of this, he's given a chance to sell us all out to save his own neck, I trust him to do that too."

Phillip and Tyler finally joined Jimmy and Gary on the far side of the river, and they were on their way. As predicted, there was a stratum of rock that extended from the one above it just far enough to make a path that was wide and flat enough to walk on, yet narrow and uneven enough to cause constant fear of falling into the river. As they progressed, the canyon got deeper and the river farther below them. By the time they reached the sweeping blind corner that marked the beginning of the natural bowl that protected Castle Cragganmore, the narrow path was easily fifty feet above the river's surface, and the steep rocky slope below left no doubt in the wizards' minds that if they did fall, they'd be far too injured to swim properly by the time they made it to the water. The rapids did not look swimmable anyway, so it didn't matter. Falling from the path meant death; whether you died from the fall or from drowning was an unimportant detail.

Luckily, the soldiers all held torches, and they all had been lit at dusk. From a distance the small army guarding the castle resembled the candles on an octogenarian's birthday cake. Clearly they would not be able to see the wizards, as their night vision would be ruined by the torches. Nor would they even be looking for invaders halfway up the cliff wall. Even if they did, they would not fear four men foolish enough to get themselves into such a predicament in the first place.

I gotta hand it to Gary, Phillip thought. *This plan is so idiotic, it kinda goes all the way around the horn to being smart.*

Slowly, they inched their way along the canyon wall. The path was still the same width, but the increased height and the darkness made it more precarious. The knowledge that falling would lead to death, either by being dashed on the rocks, drowning, or most likely, being dashed on the rocks *and* drowning, did not make the path feel wider.

After what seemed like an eternity, they were behind the castle. The physical structure of the castle was noticeable for its invisibility. The dull black stone swallowed the moonlight and starlight, reflecting almost nothing back. The light shed by the soldiers' torches was visible around and through the innumerable arches, buttresses, and complications of the castle's lower structure.

Higher up, light poured out from the castle's stained-glass windows. Phillip had never seen glass that better deserved to be referred to as "stained." The color palette ranged from dark red to light brown, with the occasional spot of sickly yellow as an accent.

When the wizards reached the very back of the castle, the cliff face roughened, creating a rock formation down to the riverbank that fell somewhere between being stairs and a ladder. The river itself was strewn with boulders spaced just far enough apart that it looked as if a person could just about kill himself trying to jump across.

Gary said, "Wow! What luck!"

Jimmy looked back at Phillip and Tyler and gave a brief smile, a smile that said, "I know it isn't luck, and I know you both know it too."

They carefully picked their way down the cliff. The river was a raging torrent of white water and deafening noise. Crossing the maelstrom was made all the more nerve-racking by the fact that every single boulder they touched on their way was slick with moisture and wobbled sickeningly, as if it could let go of the riverbed and be swept away at any moment.

Once they were on solid ground again, the men lay there, trying to catch their breaths and slow their heart rates. They were badly winded and soaked to the bone, both from the spray of the river and their own sweat.

When they were ready, the wizards set about finding a way into the castle. The only visible windows were the large, stained-glass monstrosities toward the top of the castle, but they found the castle's exterior surprisingly easy to scale. They climbed the smallest buttresses with little difficulty, and they were able to scale the larger buttress with ease. The final buttress was a piece of cake, and then it was a short trip over the back of a gargoyle, and they were standing on a ledge outside a stained-glass window.

They had discussed the possibility of having to break the window to enter, but they found that toward the bottom of the window there was a hinged panel that allowed them to crawl into the castle.

Once inside, they found themselves on a ledge approximately ten feet above an onyx-floored terrace that overlooked the interior of the castle. They dropped to the floor as quietly as they could. From where they crouched, they could see the floor in front of them, a curved railing, and a wall in the distance. From the way the railing sloped downward and the floor stopped, they could tell there were staircases leading downward to the right and the left.

Gary said, "I'll go take a look around." He started to rise but Phillip stopped him, grabbing his arm.

"Remember," Phillip said, "you don't have to whisper 'silently' while you're sneaking."

Gary said, "I know that. Jeez." He turned his back to the others, bit his lip, and skulked to the railing. He cautiously peeked through the balusters. He rose a bit to look over the top of the rail. He extended his head well out over the handrail and craned his neck one way, then the other. He stood up straight, turned to face the others, and shrugged.

After a moment's thought, he held up one finger as a suggestion that they wait; then he snuck to the staircase. He looked around, clearly saw nobody, and crept down the stairs.

Phillip followed, just far enough to watch Gary make his way down the stairs. Tyler and Jimmy both went to the handrail, and like Gary before them, they saw nobody. The hall was large, ornate, and empty. The room was a large circle. The wall opposite them was taken up mostly by the immense arched doorway that was being guarded on the other side by the torchbearing soldiers. Luckily, the door was closed. The wizards saw no reason to change that. The floor was mostly onyx, with soapstone and black granite. The lack of clear color contrast made it difficult to tell, but the floor was inlaid with the same pattern as the six stained-glass windows that circled the upper half of the chamber, except where the door was in the way.

Big decorative torches blazed away on every wall. There was no furniture. The inlaid pattern on the floor was marred only by two slightly raised platforms set a bit over halfway between the front and back walls. They were equidistant from each other and the sides of the circular room, like the eyes on a smiley face. On each platform there was a large lever.

Gary reached the bottom of the stairs. He held on to the banister with both hands and looked in every conceivable direction. He looked again. Then looked up to Phillip at the top of the stairs and to Tyler and Jimmy peering over the railing and raised his eyebrows, as if to say "What the heck?"

Gary tiptoed around the end of the banister, into the area immediately in front of the terrace. He took three steps, then glanced into the area beneath the terrace, jumped straight up in the air, and said, "NGAAAAH!"

Phillip, Tyler, and Jimmy all yelped, cringed, and withdrew several feet into the shadows. Gary leapt back and grasped the banister with both hands as if he were playing tag and the railing was "base."

For a moment, they all silently exchanged panicked eye contact, but nothing happened. Finally, Gary ventured to retrace his steps, more slowly this time, and to peek back into the area beneath the terrace.

Gary leaned to the side and peered with one eye into the place where he'd seen whatever had startled him.

The others remained silent, ready to defend themselves if possible, or more likely, flee.

Gary peered into the area they could not see.

The others held their breath.

Gary continued to look at whatever it was; then he waved.

Tyler and Jimmy glanced at each other quizzically.

Gary gritted his teeth, stood up, and in a loud voice said, "It's a mirror. Come on down, guys."

Phillip, Tyler, and Jimmy walked down the stairs. They still made an effort to be quiet, but if Gary's yelp hadn't drawn any attention, nothing they did would. When they reached the bottom of the stairs, they could see that immediately beneath the terrace they'd been standing on, the wall was decorated with a spiral design about twenty feet in diameter. It was made of individual slabs of polished stone and looked like a camera's aperture. On either side of the aperture were large decorative mirrors.

They were definitely the only people in the chamber, and looking around, it was clear that the only ways in or out were either the massive doors at the front of the room, the stone aperture at the back, or the stained-glass windows that ringed the upper portion of the wall.

Jimmy said, "It's a bit, I dunno, spare, isn't it?"

Phillip said, "Well, I'm afraid not everyone has the good taste to coat every available surface in their castle with fourteen-karat gold, like you did."

"That's not fair," Jimmy said. "It wasn't every surface. I didn't have the marble floors covered with gold foil. One must show some restraint. Besides, I notice none of you were offended enough to tear the castle down once I was gone."

Phillip said, "After all the work the citizens put into building the place, they'd have killed us if we tried to tear it down. We'd already been chased by one murderous mob that week and didn't want to do it again."

Jimmy chose to let the subject drop, as he was the one who had set the mob on them. He saw no way to win this argument.

Tyler was standing on one of the raised platforms. He took the lever in both hands and tried to pull it but couldn't make it budge.

"Hey, Gary," he said. "There are two levers. Let's try pulling both of them at the same time."

Gary mounted the other platform and grasped the lever.

Tyler said, "On three."

Gary nodded.

At the same instant Tyler said, "One," and Gary said, "Three." They both stopped.

Tyler repeated, "I said on three."

Gary said, "Sorry. I thought we'd count down."

"Well, what sense does that make?" Tyler asked. "If we go on three, then start with three, we'd pull the levers right away, then just count down to zero afterward. We might as well just say 'now' and pull the levers."

Jimmy said, "Why don't you do that?"

Tyler and Gary both looked at Jimmy, making it clear that his input was not required. Jimmy muttered an apology and looked to Phillip, who shook his head ruefully.

Gary said, "Whatever. Let's just do this."

Tyler counted to three; then they both pulled, and with the sound of an enormously heavy lid sliding off the world's largest toilet tank, the aperture in the wall spiraled open like the iris of an immense eye. Torches set into the walls beyond lit a stairway down into inky blackness. Phillip and Jimmy approached the opening. The air that rose to meet them smelled like centuries of decay. As Phillip and Jimmy started to cross the threshold into the passage below, Tyler and Gary let go of their levers so they could follow. As soon as they released them, the levers whipped back to their original positions like the throwing arms of synchronized catapults. The stone aperture slammed shut and would have taken Phillip's leg off if Jimmy hadn't yanked him out of harm's way.

Tyler said, "Huh. Sorry about that, Phillip. I guess Gary and I will wait here."

"I guess," Gary agreed.

Tyler grasped the handle again and said, "Okay, on three?"

Gary glared at him.

Tyler counted to three, the levers were pulled, and the aperture spun open again. Phillip and Jimmy approached the opening, keeping an eye on Tyler and Gary as they did.

Once they were safely beyond the opening, Phillip asked, "Will it be a problem for you two to hold the door open? I don't know how we'd get a signal to you that we're ready to come out, and we might be coming back out in a hurry."

Tyler said, "Shouldn't be a problem. What do you think, Gary?"

Gary said, "Sure, as long as you don't take too long."

Phillip and Jimmy walked down the stairs. The torches, set at regular intervals along both sides of the staircase, seemed to stretch into infinity. Thick cobwebs clung to the walls. A layer of dust so thick you could draw in it coated the steps. The torches cast large shadows that leapt and danced menacingly as the flames flickered.

Phillip said, "Gotta hand it to Todd. He did a good job of making this place seem ancient. I wonder how much time he spent just getting the cobwebs right."

Jimmy said, "Probably very little. If I had to guess, I'd say that he designed the castle, picked the location and period of history he wanted, then built this passage a few hundred years earlier. Why artificially age the place when it's just as easy to let it age on its own?"

Phillip was amazed. "All these years of time-travel experience, and that simply didn't occur to me."

Jimmy chuckled. "Yeah. You and I, we did the same thing. We learned how to time-travel and teleport, we found a new time and place to call home; then we called that good and pretty much stayed there. We made a nest for ourselves. Of course, you did a better job. I made a real hash of it."

"That's what you call it?" Phillip asked. "You lied, manipulated, accidentally killed an entire town, and tried to kill all the rest of us, and you say you 'made a hash of it.'"

"Yes," Jimmy said, "I do, because if I dwell on what I did for too long, I spiral into a depression that takes days to drag myself out of. Anyway, back to my original point: we used time travel as a simple means of transportation, but it can be much more. It can be a powerful tool, if you think about it."

Phillip looked sideways at Jimmy. "And you've thought about it?"

"While I was in exile, I spent thirty years traveling by foot and bicycle from Argentina to the Pacific Northwest. I had plenty of time to think."

Phillip said, "Wait just a minute, Jimmy. Considering what you did, I think thirty years of exile is pretty damned lenient. In fact—"

"Hey, no argument. I did not mean to suggest that I've been treated badly. Really, Phil, at the time I resisted, but in retrospect I'm nothing but grateful that you didn't just kill me and be done with it. I certainly gave you enough reason. I was just describing the situation, not blaming anyone but myself for it."

Phillip said, "Okay, then," but it didn't sound like it was okay. "You've never said that before."

Jimmy said, "We don't exactly talk much, which, again, I don't blame you for. Like you said, I killed a town. If the current manifestation of my punishment is that I'm a pariah, I'm still getting off pretty easy."

The two men walked in silence for several seconds before Jimmy decided to risk saying what was on his mind.

"By the way," he said, "I think I know that you and Tyler were talking about me back when we first crossed the river."

"You think so?" Phillip asked.

"Yes. It was your first chance to have a private conversation since the quest started, and I'm pretty sure you were discussing whether or not you could trust me."

Phillip nodded. "What do you think?"

Jimmy smiled. "There are a few answers to that question. I know that you can trust me, and I don't think you will. I think you were perfectly right to want to discuss it. I think that if I were in your place, I'd have a great deal of difficulty ever trusting me again. I think that if you did trust me, that I'd be extremely reticent to ever betray that trust unless I had a very good reason, which sounds bad, but if you think about it, that's the most you can really ever trust anyone. Lastly, I think that if I were you, I'd trust me to do what's best for me, and to that end, let me assure you, it's best for me to keep the three of you alive and happy. I have a much better chance of survival if I have you here to help me. Besides, when we return to Leadchurch and have to explain that Jeff is not coming back with us, I fully expect everyone to suspect that I had something to do with it no matter what you three say. Imagine if I came back without any of you."

Jimmy's analysis of the situation exactly matched Phillip's. Phillip didn't know how he felt about that. He didn't have long to dwell on it, because in the distance, they could see the end of what had looked like an endless line of torches and the entrance to some sort of very well lit chamber.

It was hard to know how far underground they were. The staircase had been several hundred yards long at least. They reached the landing and the passage widened into a large chamber that appeared to be shaped roughly like a cube. It was full of unusual items. They decided to investigate.

Set along the walls of the chamber were six large stone bowls, three to each side. Each bowl contained a roaring fire. Beside each bowl there was a large glass lens set in a bronze fitting, focusing the light from the fire in a specific direction.

In the center of the room, on a stone pedestal, there was a statue of a muscular warrior god. The statue had six overdeveloped arms, each wielding a dagger. The daggers had dull metal handles, but the blades were polished to a mirror finish. Also, the arms looked to be jointed at the shoulder so that they could swing through a specific range of motion.

On the far wall of the chamber there was an ornately carved stone door, covered with cryptic symbols that neither Phillip nor Jimmy recognized. Several feet in front of the door, on either side, there were three large stone cylinders set into the floor, six in total. The cylinders were also covered with cryptic markings. In front of each set of cylinders there was a handrail and a small mirror on a pole.

Phillip said, "I think it may be some kind of puzzle."

Phillip and Jimmy solved the puzzle, but only after quite a bit of trial and error and no small amount of frustration. When stone doors slowly opened, the two men were so relieved they nearly hugged. Their exuberance was muted by the fact that they could hear distant voices coming from the dim passage beyond the door.

They crept in as quietly as they could. The passage led to a treasure chamber. Heaped all around the walls were piles and piles of precious objects. There were sculptures of chariots, horses, mighty warriors, and beautiful women, ranging in size from about four inches to full size. There were artworks depicting horses, chariots, mighty warriors, and beautiful women hanging on the walls and resting on the floors, leaning against the piles of other glittering loot. There were ostentatious cloaks and boots, hewn from fine fabric and supple leather. Many of them bore pictograms of horses, chariots, mighty warriors, and beautiful women. They littered the floor, far too many for any one man to need. There were also crowns of various size and design, all distinct while remaining essentially the same. Despite the opulence, there were only two real pieces of furniture: a large, comfortable-looking throne and a stone stand for displaying the most precious possession of all, or at least the most entertaining to look at.

Phillip thought, *It's like a bachelor's apartment, dipped in gold.*

A gangly king sat on the throne, dressed in an oversized crown and ermine robes colored green and gold, similar to the robes Jimmy wore back when he called himself Merlin. The king was cackling with delight. His crown slid around on his too-narrow head as he rocked with laughter. As the king squirmed with delight, Phillip briefly caught a glimpse of his face and immediately recognized it as an unflattering caricature of Jimmy.

The object of the king's laughter was instantly clear. On the table opposite the throne rested a beautiful golden birdcage. Inside the cage, a canary that appeared to be made from hammered bronze and clockwork parts was waving its wings and swooning as if it might soon fall unconscious. In front of the table, a short, fat man in a sky-blue court-jester costume was leaning on the birdcage with his sweat-stained armpit looming menacingly directly over the poor creature's head. As the clockwork-canary choked and the king laughed, the jester stood straight, spun in place, and took a bow. Despite the too-prominent nose, the eyes being too close together, and the teeth being too far apart, the jester was clearly meant to be Phillip.

"More!" the king cried, pounding on the arms of his throne. "More!"

The jester bowed and said, "As you demand, your stuposity!"

The king clapped his hands with delight as the jester turned and regarded the canary, who could only be Oban, the canary the miners had lost. Oban had just stopped coughing and was catching its breath. The jester leaned forward, putting his face right up to the bars of the cage. Oban eyed him wearily. The jester opened his mouth and belched extravagantly right in Oban's face. The metal bird hacked and wheezed, much to the king's delight.

"Ugh," Phillip moaned. "It's just so lowbrow."

Through gritted teeth, Jimmy whispered, "We've gotta save the bird before that fool farts."

Phillip's hand went to his sword. He said, "You take the jester. I'll handle the king."

Jimmy said, "Done."

The two men rushed from the shadows, swords drawn, screaming bloody murder. Jimmy closed the gap between himself and the jester almost instantly. The jester didn't even have time to raise his hands before Jimmy brought the pommel of his sword down on the jester's skull, instantly knocking him unconscious. Jimmy turned triumphantly to show Phillip his handiwork but was struck speechless by what he saw.

The king had managed to rise from his throne and offer some resistance. Not enough, clearly, as the king's left hand and half of his forearm were lying on the stone floor, and Phillip's sword was buried deep in the king's ribcage, having gotten there by chopping through the royal trapezius and clavicle.

Phillip jerked at his sword, but it did not budge. The king slumped into his throne and fell backward as far as he could with Phillip's sword protruding from his back. Phillip raised a foot, braced it against the king's torso, and pulled his sword free. He turned around to face Jimmy, grinning from ear to ear.

He saw the jester, lying unconscious but alive on the ground, and the look on Jimmy's face, and said, "Oh, uh. Sorry. Look, it wasn't really you."

Jimmy said, "Yeah, I get it." He lifted the birdcage and said, "Come on, Oban, let's take you home." Oban fluttered happily, emitting a slight clanking noise.

As they left the treasure chamber, Phillip said, "He wasn't real."

"Yeah, whatever. I know."

"Would it help if I said I was sorry?"

Jimmy said, "Maybe, if I thought you meant it."

11.

When Phillip and Jimmy emerged from the stone aperture carrying Oban the mechanical canary, Tyler and Gary were deep in conversation. They had their backs turned and were holding the levers forward by leaning back on them.

Tyler said, "I give you that Kirk was more entertaining on his own to watch, but that's because he made more mistakes. When I said that Picard was the better captain, I meant that I'd rather serve on a ship under his command, because he was a better leader."

Gary shook his head. "Okay, Tyler, I just meant that Captain Kirk was better because he was more fun to watch, because that's all that matters. He's a fictional character. You're talking like you think he and Picard are real people, and that's kinda scary."

"Gary, I've heard you say some ridiculous, dishonest things," Tyler moaned, "but I never thought you'd stoop to that. I say Picard's the better captain, you disagree, and when I prove logically that I'm right, you act like I'm crazy to try to shame me into dropping it. Pathetic."

"Whatever you say, Tyler."

"Oh, that's even worse! Pretending to humor me because I'm irrational instead of just admitting you're wrong."

"Okay, Tyler. If you say so."

"Okay," Tyler said, "now you're starting to piss me off."

Phillip cleared his throat and said, "Um, guys, sorry to interrupt."

Gary turned, looking relieved. "Don't be. Is that the canary?"

Tyler said, "Hey, this isn't over."

Gary rolled his eyes. "Okay, Tyler, that's fine. Whatever you say."

Tyler pointed at Gary and started to say something, but Jimmy interrupted. "We'd better get going. We want to be long gone before the sun comes up and someone finds out that Phillip killed the king."

"Phillip killed a king?!" Gary asked.

Phillip said, "Yeah, I'd rather not talk about it."

"Don't be silly," Jimmy said. "It's all right. You should tell them all about it later. They'd probably think it was pretty cool, but now we really should get out of here."

They went up the steps to the window through which they'd come in. They might have been able to go out the front door and sneak away behind the soldiers' backs, but none of them liked the idea enough to even bring it up.

When they got outside, the night was crisp and quiet, save for the rushing of the water below. Surprisingly, the task of climbing down the buttresses was far more challenging than climbing up had been, partly because they were leading with their clumsy feet rather than their relatively dexterous hands and partly because the act of descending forced them to look down, which constantly reminded them of how much danger they were in.

Once they were back on the ground, they immediately left it again, leaping from rock to rock, crossing the river back the way they'd come. Again, it seemed much more difficult this time, since the slight downhill slant on the way to the castle was now an uphill slog, making all of the jumps more difficult. Also, the rocks seemed substantially less stable this time. They rocked more alarmingly as Gary, Jimmy (carrying Oban's cage), and Phillip leapt from one to the other so that at any given time each of them had a rock to themselves. Tyler went last, and by the time he reached the first rock it was shaking constantly and felt like it could let go at any second.

"Guys," he shouted, "I hate to rush you, but I kinda need you to move faster."

The others looked back, and seeing how much the boulder was trembling, did indeed hurry up. Phillip had barely vacated a stone when Tyler leapt for it. To everyone's horror, the boulder on which Tyler had been standing broke loose and swept away the instant his foot left it.

Tyler landed on all fours on the next boulder, which seemed to have been loosened by the others' passing. It was shuddering even more alarmingly than the first boulder.

Gary nearly screamed. "Don't worry, Ty! We'll get you out of this!"

Tyler scowled over his shoulder at the empty space where he had been standing. His thoughts went back to the first day of the quest and the crumbling rock bridge, and he calmed way down. He muttered, "Oh, man," then yelled, "Don't worry about it," but the others were already hastily scrambling from rock to rock to get him out of his predicament faster. When the next stone was vacant, Tyler made the leap, more in an effort to keep up than out of any sense of self-preservation. He threw himself across the gap between the rocks. The river raged beneath him and the stone that had just been supporting his weight fell away with the current and was gone before he landed.

Phillip watched the whole thing and saw that the boulder Tyler had landed on was also rocking dangerously. Phillip turned to Jimmy and Gary, shouting "Move! Move! We gotta go! He can't hold on much longer!"

Tyler yelled, "No, guys! Hold up! Be careful!" He watched miserably as they did neither of those things. Jimmy, already off balance carrying the large metal birdcage, misjudged a leap and barely made his landing. He teetered sickeningly on one foot, swinging his free leg and arm. Oban clanked and fluttered on his perch as Jimmy swung the cage out over the river, trying desperately to alter his center of gravity. Jimmy finally regained his balance and immediately fell into a crouch. Ahead of him, Gary was scrambling like a gecko, hurling himself to the next rock with abandon. He landed on all fours and nearly slid forward off the far side of the rock. Jimmy had only just regained his footing, but he leapt to the next rock without taking any time to judge the distance. Phillip followed suit, landing hard on his stomach when his shoes lost traction on the wet stone.

Tyler shouted, "Guys! Slow down! You're going to kill yourselves! I'm not in any more danger than you are!" He could see that it was useless. Phillip was now two boulders ahead and had scarcely heard him. Jimmy and Gary were too far away to hear a thing, especially since Gary had already jumped another gap and was nearly to the far bank of the river.

Tyler took his time, mentally measuring the distance to the next rock and gathering his strength before committing to the jump. When he landed on the now-shaking boulder, he looked back and saw that the boulder from which he had just leapt was gone, traveling downriver at great speed. Tyler looked ahead. Gary was on solid ground now, and even in the dark at this distance, Tyler could see from Gary's body language that he was deeply concerned.

As Tyler watched, Jimmy made the final leap to the relative safety of the riverbank, with a quick helping hand from Gary. Phillip threw himself onto the last stone, then forward to the waiting hands of Gary and Jimmy in one fluid movement. They all looked back at Tyler, who was standing five boulders back from them, looking nonchalant.

They were all yelling, but Tyler couldn't hear a word over the thunderous roar of the rapids. From their arm motions and general demeanor he suspected that they were beckoning him to keep trying, to come to them, to not give up. He couldn't help but smile. He knew that they would not be able to hear him, no matter how loud he yelled, so the only way he could communicate was through body language and actions.

Tyler stood tall. He moved slowly and deliberately. He stepped to the front of the boulder, taking care to maintain his balance as the rock shook beneath his feet. As gracefully as he could, he jumped to the next rock. He could tell from the terror on the others' faces that the boulder behind him was no longer there.

Without looking back, he took his time, judged his distances carefully, and casually jumped to the next rock. The others on the riverbank seemed apoplectic. His attempt to calm them by remaining calm himself clearly was not working. *Oh well*, he thought, *I'll keep at it. Maybe they'll get the hint, and if they don't, it'll be fun to watch them freak out.*

Tyler had two more jumps until dry land. He stood stock still, watching the others yelling themselves hoarse trying to encourage him forward. Tyler attempted to make eye contact with each of them, no mean feat in the low light; then he pointed at the unsteady boulder on which he was standing. He took a deep breath, then made the next leap. Without looking behind him, he flourished with his hands to show that he knew that it had washed away once he had moved on. Then he shrugged. Both Phillip and Jimmy stopped yelling. They looked at each other, then back to Tyler. Gary was still freaking out, but that didn't surprise Tyler. It wasn't that Gary wasn't smart. His brain was as good as anyone's. He just chose to use it sparingly.

Tyler made the next jump. One more and he'd be on the riverbank. Also, he was now within yelling distance of the others.

"Come on," Gary yelled. "Before the rock gives way!"

Tyler yelled back, "It's not going to. I could stand here for a year and the rock wouldn't budge."

Tyler made the final jump to the riverbank, then shouted, "Todd, that ignoramus, wanted us to hurry and risk our necks, but again, he was too lazy, or too stupid, or maybe he was lazy and stupid, but anyway, he didn't want to go to the trouble of timing things out and seeing how long we'd take to get across on our own, so instead of making the rocks wash away at a set interval, he just made them go whenever the last of us left them. That way, we panic and hurry without him having to bother to actually put in any effort! Isn't that right, Todd?!"

There was no visual sign of Todd's presence, but they heard a microphone click on, and Todd's voice said, "Yeah, well it worked for three out of four of you, didn't it?" They heard the microphone click off again.

They looked at the river. The boulders were gone, leaving nothing but a fast-moving torrent of liquid death.

Jimmy said, "The entire path across the river is gone."

Phillip said, "I guess it's a good thing we don't need to get back in there."

They clambered up the steep slope to the path that would lead them back away from the castle. They worked their way around the far canyon wall, the way they'd come in.

By the time morning broke, they were making their way out of the canyon, carrying Oban in his cage, stopping only to fight off pairs of wolves wherever they had killed a single wolf on the way in.

They were dead tired. None of them had slept much since they'd left the mine, but they kept moving. There were wolves to contend with and the paranoid suspicion that the small army they'd left at the castle might be following them.

Just before nightfall, they finally dragged themselves into the cursed Mines of Mortlach. The miners parted reverently as they approached, holding Oban's cage. The little mechanical canary was fluttering and singing with glee to see its home again.

They walked back into the dark interior of the mine, past the miners to Blandoch, the head of the mining guild. Blandoch's face was a picture of delight. Tears of joy filled his eyes as he took Oban's cage from Phillip's hands and placed it back on the stone plinth where it clearly belonged. Oban seemed to fly a loop-the-loop in his cage. A mighty cheer rose up from the miners. It all would have been quite moving if they hadn't known that it was part of an elaborate death trap designed by a murderous idiot.

Blandoch looked as if his heart might burst watching Oban tweet and flutter on his perch. After a long, blissful moment, he turned back to the wizards. "You've lived up to your part of the bargain. You've returned our beloved friend Oban to his rightful home, and now that he is back"—Blandoch turned to the miners and spread his arms wide, raising his voice—"we miners can mine again!"

A raucous cheer went up from the miners and echoed deafeningly off the stone walls.

When the cheer had died, Blandoch turned back to the wizards and said, "Now it is time for us to fulfill our half of the bargain. You came looking for dailuaine, did you not?"

Phillip said, "We did."

Blandoch said, "And you will have it." He leaned down to pick up his golden pickaxe in one hand and removed a lantern from its spike, holding it aloft with his other hand.

"Now that Oban is back," he said, "I can go mine it for you."

Blandoch walked toward the mine entrance at the rear of the chamber.

Gary asked, "Aren't you going to take the bird?"

Jimmy said, "Don't sweat it."

"No, wait," Gary said. "The whole point of having a canary in a mine is to take it with you to tell you if the air is bad."

"I'm sure he knows what he's doing," Jimmy said.

"No," Gary replied, "I don't think he does. Or maybe Todd doesn't."

Blandoch reached the mine entrance. He paused for a moment before stepping into the darkened shaft. He held his lantern forward, then took a single step into the mine. He looked at the ceiling and walls of the mine, clearly looking for something. His eyes came to rest on a round rock, about the size of a bowling ball. It was a dull gray color that did not match the cave walls and was one of several such rocks that littered the wall of the mine.

Gary said, "No."

Blandoch said, "Ah, let's see here." He sat down his lantern and swung his pickaxe once, lightly tapping the rock, making a little sound and no discernable difference whatsoever. Blandoch leaned his pickaxe against the wall and lifted the dailuaine with both hands.

"What?! But," Gary sputtered. "I told you all that that was the stuff, and you didn't listen!"

Tyler, Phillip, and Jimmy watched Blandoch go about his work in silence.

"And none of you are listening now either," Gary said.

"I'm sorry, Gary," Phillip said. "Were you saying something?"

Gary said, "Yes! I was saying—"

Phillip held up one finger. "Hold on a sec, Gary. I think Blandoch's about to say something."

Blandoch approached, carrying the lumpy sphere of dailuaine with great effort, despite his beefy miner's arms. He held it up for the wizards to see. "Gentlemen, you have done us a great service this day, and it is our honor to present you with this dailuaine."

"Which we could have just taken!" Gary cried.

"What do you mean?" Tyler asked.

Gary said, "Last time we were here, getting fed all that mumbo jumbo about castles and canaries—"

"Ooh," Tyler said. "That sounds like a tabletop role-playing game. *Castles and Canaries.*"

"Marketed toward little girls," Jimmy said.

Phillip added, "Or parents who are trying to keep violent games away from their kids. Do parents still do that in your time, Tyler?"

"A few," Tyler said, "but most of them gave up when NERF started making guns."

"Shut up!" Gary shouted. "I told you all that was the rock we wanted."

Tyler said, "Jeez, sorry, Gary. We just tend to tune you out sometimes, because so much of what you say is nonsense."

Gary said, "Was that meant to be an apology? You should listen to me. Sometimes I'm right, like when I pointed right at that rock and told you all that it was the rock we needed. I even picked it up."

"Oh, good," Phillip said. "Then you should be able to carry it."

12.

Phillip, Tyler, Gary, and Jimmy got as much sleep as they could with the miners celebrating all through the night. The next morning the miners gave them a breakfast that consisted of drinkable water and dry meat. They experimented with carrying the dailuaine and quickly realized that none of them was strong enough to carry it very far alone, nor were any of them patient enough to carry it with another person for long. They tried rolling it, but it was so heavy and its surface so uneven that it was unsteerable, and still killed your lower back in the process.

The miners offered to let them use their mule sledge to transport the heavy chunk of dailuaine that was their prize. The sledge was a heavy wooden flatbed with runners instead of wheels, but it was better than nothing. The wizards thanked the miners profusely.

Eventually, it dawned on the wizards that the miners did not have a mule to pull the sledge and that the wizards themselves would have to take turns. They still thanked the miners but noticeably less profusely.

While they lashed the rock to the sledge, Jimmy noticed that Phillip had been unusually quiet that morning. Jimmy said, "You seem down."

Phillip said, "What? Uh, yeah, I guess so. I was just thinking. I wish Martin were here."

"Really? I mean, I know you two are friends, but I'd have thought you'd be thinking about being with Brit."

"Oh, I am. I wish Martin were here instead of me. He enjoys this kind of thing more than I do. And then I'd be somewhere else, with Brit."

The mine entrance, with its immense carved façade, sat in a large dusty clearing at the base of a cliff. The woods surrounded the clearing, and there were only three paths that led away. One was the way they had come. One was the path that terminated at the castle. The wizards were not surprised to hear that the third would lead them to the next stop in their quest, a town called Bowmore, where the dailuaine would be crafted into a weapon of some sort.

Blandoch told them, "The path will take you through Edradour Forest. So you will no longer have to fear the mountain wolves, or the river wolves."

Phillip leaned to his companions and muttered, "Wait for it."

Blandoch said, "Only the tree wolves will trouble you on your journey."

Once the dailuaine was secured, Jimmy volunteered to take the first shift of manning the rope and pulling the sledge. The entire journey, Jimmy had been first to volunteer for any unpleasant duty. The others knew that it was a transparent attempt to make them think better of him. They also knew it was working, if only a little bit.

With renewed energy and grunts of exertion, the four men left the mines and disappeared down the forested path to Bowmore.

+⧓==⧓+

Five minutes later, Brit strode wearily into the clearing, followed by Martin, Gwen, and Roy bringing up the rear. Brit stopped, stretching her back and looking up at the wall carving of the miner with the cartoonishly large gem.

"This must be the mine we were told about."

"Finally," said Martin. The others muttered in agreement. It had been days of difficult travel. They had faced harsh weather, treacherous terrain, constant danger, and wolf jerky. Until the day before, the only relatively flat and hospitable ground they saw was swarming with over thirty wolves, which was odd, since the wolves usually attacked in pairs.

As Martin removed the cap from a bottle of water and lifted it to his face, he said, "I wish we had some way of knowing how far behind the others we are."

They took a moment to have a drink of water and catch their breath. Then, without needing to discuss it, they approached the cave entrance. From a distance, it seemed pitch dark inside. As they drew nearer, they saw faint points of light inside. When they reached the opening, they saw that the lights were lanterns held by bedraggled-looking miners.

Roy asked, "Are you miners? Is this your mine?"

The miners all moved to the sides of the chamber, allowing an unobstructed view of the back wall and the dark, ominous entrance to the mine itself.

Roy turned to the others and said, "These are the miners. This is their mine."

Brit said, "Thanks for that, Roy." She turned to the miners and said, "Who's in charge here?"

All of the miners turned to look at a miserable-looking figure at the back of the room. He was slumped down on the floor, hanging his head and cradling a solid-gold pickaxe in his lap. Next to him, on a stone pedestal, there was a large birdcage. The miner on the floor briefly looked up at the visitors and said, "I am Blandoch, but I have no business with you, nor anybody."

Brit and Roy walked over to him. Gwen and Martin followed.

Roy said, "Blandoch, I'm Roy. We were told to come to you for some rare mineral."

Blandoch glanced up at her and said, "State your business."

Brit said, "He did. We're here for a mineral. Dalvaline, or something like that."

Blandoch said, "Aye, we have dailuaine. More than enough for your needs, but alas, we cannot get to it."

Roy chuckled. "Really, Brit? Dalvaline? It sounds like an off-brand motor oil."

Brit scowled. "Oh, but dailuaine is much better."

"Speaking of which," Roy said, "I'm pretty sure this guy's just an automaton, like that first guy we met."

"Or this bird," Martin said. He had walked over to the stone pedestal and was peering into the birdcage. Inside the cage, a metal canary was peering back at Martin with his head cocked to the side, and chirping.

"It's made out of clock parts! It's really cool. Kinda steampunk."

Blandoch rose to his feet, exhaling from the exertion. He said, "We cannot get you your dailuaine, for we are cursed. We are miners, but we cannot go into the mine without our beloved canary, Oban." Blandoch pointed to the pedestal, where Oban sat, chirping in his cage.

Martin said, "Well, this must be Oban."

Gwen said, "But it can't be Oban."

Martin said, "He pointed right at the bird and he said 'Oban.' That seems like pretty good evidence that the bird is Oban."

Gwen said, "But the fact that this bird is here seems like even better evidence that he isn't Oban."

Brit said, "Yeah, but there is a sign carved into the wall over the cage that says 'Oban,' so I think that clinches it."

Gwen's eyes got wide. "Maybe," she said, "the others have already been through here and retrieved the bird. Then, when we arrived, the program reset, but the bird stayed."

"That's some pretty shoddy programming," Roy said.

Brit shrugged. "It was made by the same guy who made all the wolves look the same, wait in line to attack, and leap after three seconds."

Roy said, "I suppose he never expected a second raiding party to come through."

Brit smiled. "And the fact that he's not fixing the error suggests that he doesn't know we're here."

Blandoch said, "Without him, it is too dangerous to enter the mine."

Martin looked at Blandoch, looked at Oban, then picked up the birdcage and thrust it toward the miner.

"Here," Martin said. "Here he is."

Blandoch did not seem to hear. "He was taken from us," he explained, "by an evil king, King Milburn the Mad. He and his vile viceroy, Flagler. They stole our beloved canary and took him to Castle Cragganmore."

"And I'm giving him back to you," Martin said, pressing the cage to Blandoch's chest.

Blandoch made no move to take the cage, but a smile brightened his face. He looked at Martin through the cage and said,

"Yes! Indeed! If you were to go to the castle and retrieve Oban, we would gladly give you all the dailuaine you could ever need!"

Roy said, "No dice, kid. Looks like we have to go out to this castle, wherever that is, to trigger the next event."

Brit said, "Yeah. I agree."

Roy said, "That's good, since I'm right."

The miners started singing, dancing, and enjoying a celebratory feast, all of which they did poorly because they tried to do it all at the same time.

Roy said, "And the miners agree with me too."

13.

After a day of dragging the rock along the forest path, the four men all agreed that the sledge and rope made the task much easier. Unfortunately, the task of dragging a heavy rock was arduous enough that "much easier" still meant "really hard."

They each took turns dragging the sledge, leaning forward into the loop of rope that rode under their arms or over a shoulder, depending on which option seemed less unbearable at the moment.

The sledge was made of heavy oak and was sturdily constructed. Being a sledge, it had no wheels, just a smooth underside that helped reduce its friction. On level, even ground, it made pulling the dense ball of ore much easier, but on uneven terrain, or when walking up an incline, it was just more weight to drag.

When the path through the woods grew narrow, they had to take great care not to catch the sides of the sledge on a root or tree limb. If the sledge did get caught, it would come to an instant halt, causing whoever was pulling it to also stop as if he'd walked straight into a brick wall. It was more embarrassing than it was painful, and it was pretty damned painful.

The men also agreed that the woods were quite nice and that hiking through them might be rather pleasant if they had a choice, but they did not. Unfortunately, human nature dictated that anything, no matter how pleasant it is, can become hateful if you feel you must do it. Just ask anyone who's ever entered a pie-eating contest.

Any illusion that they were on a pleasant nature walk was also shattered by the periodic attacks of the tree wolves. Even though they'd been warned of the tree wolves' existence, the first attack had come as a surprise. After they dispatched the wolf, Gary said, "I knew they were called tree wolves, but I thought that just meant that they lived, you know, out here among the trees. Not up in the trees. Do wolves climb trees?"

"Not usually," Tyler said, "and I don't think these wolves are doing any climbing. I think they're just appearing in the trees when we approach. And, before you ask, no, they don't usually do that either."

They went on like that for the rest of the day, one of them pulling, the other three scanning the trees and listening for growling noises from above. That night, as was their new routine, Jimmy scavenged for edible plants. His years living as a vagabond in Central and South America had proved to be a treasure trove of useful information.

"Thanks for the berries," Tyler said grudgingly.

"Don't mention it," Jimmy said. "It's nice to be able to pull my weight. When I was in Colombia, I was doing some odd jobs, and I spent a pretty sizeable chunk of my pay on an old book about the edible flora of the Americas. It was the best money I ever spent, and a pretty exciting read. The writing was awfully dry, but the chance of not starving to death made it a page-turner. I did have a mishap with some berries that gave me the winds, but luckily it was the middle of summer and I didn't have regular access to a shower, so my normal odors were strong enough that nobody noticed a difference."

Phillip said, "Speaking of which, I would point out that you're not smelling too good these days, but I suspect I'm not smelling much better."

Tyler smiled, and said, "I can confirm those suspicions."

Phillip bent his head down and sniffed his fur cloak, then winced. He thought a moment, then cupped his hand to his mouth to smell his own breath. He winced even more. He looked at his companions and said, "Gentlemen, we've gone to pot."

Gary said, "Well, it's not like we've had a real chance to clean up. I'm just grateful that my beard is past the itchy stage."

Tyler and Jimmy murmured in agreement.

Phillip nodded. "Yeah, you're right. We're all in the same disgusting boat, and the only person who's going to see us like this is Todd. I certainly don't care about his opinion. It just bugs me that these cloaks and leggings we're wearing smelled better when we got them, by looting them from corpses."

The next day they continued taking turns, one man pulling the sledge while the others fended off tree wolves. One bit of wolf-related drama occurred when a tree wolf sprang from the limbs above and landed directly on Phillip's back, clinging to the black fur cloak he had been wearing since the beginning of their quest. It clamped its jaws onto his shoulder, and while it did not break the skin through the thick layer of leather and fur, if given enough time it might well have broken some bone. It did not get the chance, as Tyler and Jimmy both leapt to Phillip's aid, stabbing the tree wolf and killing it while it still clung to Phillip's back. Phillip was quite grateful.

He was less grateful an hour later when two wolves sprang from the spot on his cloak where the previous wolf had died and attacked him.

After a few moments of frantic fighting, cursing, and laughing, the wolves were dead, and conversation turned to Phillip's cloak.

Tyler said, "You know you have to ditch that cloak, right?"

Phillip said, "I dunno."

Jimmy, grunting with exertion from pulling the sledge, said, "He's right, Phillip. The cloak has to go. The sooner the better. In an hour, it'll be four wolves."

"No, wait," Phillip said, "the first wolf was killed on my back, but the next two wolves weren't on my back when we got 'em, so now the cloak is fine."

Gary looked puzzled, and said, "You know, I'm not sure if he's right or not. All the times we've stuck around long enough for the wolves to come back more than once, it's been dark, or there have been too many to keep track of. I don't know if they come from the spot where the last wolf died, or where the first wolf died."

"Yeah," Tyler agreed, "we haven't done a proper scientific study of it. I suppose we could."

Jimmy diverted a bit of energy from pulling to say, "But do we really want to do it right now . . . on Phillip's back?"

"Oh, come on, guys," Phillip said, clutching the edges of the cloak toward him like a security blanket. "It's cold."

Tyler nodded sympathetically. "Yes, and the cloak will keep you warm, especially with all the exertion of fighting off four wolves."

Phillip said, "The wolf died on the back of the cloak, right? What if I don't expose the back? What if I wear the cloak inside out for the next hour?"

Gary said, "That might work."

Jimmy grunted, "Or, you might end up with four wolves inside your cloak with you."

"Yeah," Phillip said. "That doesn't sound good."

Gary said, "Not for you, but it'd be fun to watch."

Phillip looked defeated, but he didn't remove the cloak.

Tyler said, "You know we're right."

"I know," Phillip admitted. "It's just—"

"I know, it's cold. Look, Gary and I can give you our wizard robes. You can put them on over yours. They aren't that thick, but with three of them, you should be okay," Tyler said.

"It's not just that," Phillip said. "I just . . . I really like this cloak. It's the coolest-looking piece of clothing I've ever owned. I'd never think of getting a black fur cloak, but now that I've worn one a while, I really like it."

After a moment's thought, Tyler said, "It's not a good look for you, Phillip."

"No?" Phillip asked.

"No," Tyler repeated.

Jimmy said, "It makes you look like some sort of man-sized rodent."

Phillip said, "Oh," and started taking the cloak off.

Gary said, "Yeah, Phillip. That cloak, what is it? It's like a Superman cape covered with bear fur."

Phillip paused in taking off the cloak and looked down at it again.

Tyler leaned over to Gary, and whispered through gritted teeth, "Great, Gary. Make it sound awesome."

Phillip removed the cloak and threw it to the ground. They stopped walking for a moment while Gary and Tyler rearranged their garments. They gave Phillip their wizard robes. Jimmy would have gladly offered his own robe if he'd had it, but he'd been pulled into this mess wearing only pajamas, so all of his clothes were what Jimmy liked to call "locally sourced." He liked to call it that because it sounded better than "stolen from the dead."

Neither Tyler's nor Gary's robes were particularly clean, so Phillip put them on over his own, which was none too fresh itself. They walked away, trying to put as much distance between themselves and Phillip's old cloak as possible.

Gary said, "Looking good, Phillip."

Phillip said, "Shut up."

"No, really," Gary said. "You're like a triple-wizard."

The day wore on, and wolves did not spontaneously leap out of Phillip's back, as the other members had feared (and kind of hoped) they would. They eventually settled into their normal routine, light conversation interspersed with periods of quiet contemplation and dreading of the night. They had all long since gotten over the idea that the nights would be pleasant in any way. As outdoorsmen they were unenthusiastic, ill equipped, and uncomfortable. Each night they would take turns, one of them watching for wolves, guarding the other three as they slept. In theory, it allowed for everyone to get the maximum amount of sleep possible, but in practice, it worked out to be three men lying on the cold, hard ground trying desperately to get to sleep while one man sat next to the fire and tried desperately to stay awake. Then, every two hours or so, the guard would switch, and everyone would be disturbed by the hushed sounds of two men trying not to disturb anyone.

Nothing wakes one up faster than the sound of someone tip-toeing and whispering, even when one expects it.

Especially when one expects it.

They were all playing their daily battle of wills where they each tried to not be the first one to suggest setting up camp for the night, when they saw it. A small trail of smoke was rising from the treetops in the distance.

It was a single, puffy, grayish line that rose straight up from the treetops before the wind caught it and smeared it into a hazier diagonal streak that faded into invisibility.

Phillip was about to speak, but Jimmy beat him to the punch, saying the exact word that Phillip had intended to say.

"Chimney."

Phillip knew that there was no guarantee there would be a cabin or, if there was, that they'd be welcomed by its owners. The entire quest had been created specifically to make them suffer, so the idea that Todd had created whatever was ahead as a nice little break did not seem likely. Knowing this did not slow Phillip's pace.

The path bent away from the smoke, then toward it, then away again before finally aiming them directly at it. In the distance, through the trees, at the end of the path, they could see some sort of dark mass directly below the column of smoke.

As they drew nearer, they could make out what looked like a porch.

Then they could make out movement on the porch.

Then they could tell that there were multiple people.

They hurried their pace.

When they got close enough to hear laughter and conversation coming from the porch, they all slowed down and listened intently, trying to figure out who and what they were going to find.

When they realized that the people on the porch were all young women who seemed to be in excellent spirits and excellent health, the men started walking casually toward the source of the feminine sounds.

Phillip and Jimmy stood extra straight. Jimmy placed one hand on the side of his gut. Phillip thrust his hands into the pockets of his jeans, causing the three robes he wore to flap open and spill back over his wrists in a manner he hoped might be described as Humphrey Bogart–esque. Tyler draped his right hand over the pommel of his sword. His mouth formed a sneering smile that said, "I know that you're happy I'm here." Gary leaned extra hard into the rope he used to pull the sledge, making sure to flex every arm muscle he knew of. They all cleared their throats, so that when the time came to speak to their new friends, their voices would be deep and rich.

This is what men call "acting casual."

The building was surprisingly large, two stories, with a porch that ran the whole width of the building, and a veranda on the second floor that mirrored the size of the porch. There were many windows, but there was still more light outside the building than in, so it was impossible to see inside. The front door was hanging open invitingly.

On the porch, three women were making pleasant conversation while they tended to their chores. All three of them had long hair, but in vaguely different styles and very different colors. One was blond, one brunette, and the third, predictably, had flaming red hair. They wore white, low-cut peasant blouses and rough, high-hemmed peasant skirts. The redhead was turned away from the men and was slowly churning butter, doing most of the work with her back. The brunette sat straddling a washtub, her strong, bare legs holding the tub steady while she looked down and scrubbed her garments in the warm, sudsy water. The blond stood between them, leaning against a post, knitting. She held her knitting just below her cleavage, slowly working the needles through the yarn. Her head was bowed, her eyes on her work. Her blond hair hid her eyes, but the men could see the tip of her button nose, and her lips slowly mouthing "Knit one, purl two. Knit one, purl two."

The redhead said something to the other two, both of whom giggled.

Jimmy cleared his throat and said, "Good evening, ladies."

The blond looked up from her knitting, fluttered her eyelashes, and smiled. Phillip got a good look at her face, and his blood ran cold.

The blond breathed, "Greetings, stout menfolk."

The brunette looked up from her laundry and smiled. She wrung out whatever garment she was cleaning in such a way as to squeeze her breasts together and forward. The redhead stopped working but stayed bent over forward and left her hands on the churn as she turned and smiled over her shoulder, saying "Welcome."

Tyler groaned.

Jimmy grimaced and said, "Please excuse us, one moment."

The three women watched them silently as the wizards retreated several steps to confer in hushed tones.

"Why do they all look like Gwen?" Tyler asked.

Jimmy said, "I don't know. Maybe he had a thing for Gwen."

Phillip said, "No, that's not it. The last time he saw her was years ago from his point of view. He'd have met plenty of women between then and now, and copying them would have been much easier than making a likeness of Gwen from memory. No, he set this up to torture us. Maybe he figures we all have a thing for Gwen. Gary, he was your apprentice. What do you think?"

Gary shrugged. "Yeah. I bet that's it. After all, we all did have the hots for her back then, didn't we?"

"Well, I don't know that I'd say that," Phillip said. "I mean, she's certainly an attractive young lady, but I've never really considered a romantic relationship with her."

"Yes," Jimmy agreed. "She was always a valued member of the community, and any man would be lucky to be in a relationship with her, certainly, but to say that we all had *the hots* for her isn't at all accurate."

Tyler nodded emphatically. "I mean, sure, if she were interested, there isn't a wizard in Leadchurch who wouldn't have been interested as well, but no, Gary, I don't think it's fair to imply that we were all just sitting around pining after Gwen."

Gary said, "Uh huh. Okay. Well, you all can tell yourselves whatever you want, but I'm pretty sure that Todd walked away thinking that we all had the hots for Gwen."

Tyler asked, "Well, what gave him that impression?"

Gary said, "I did, when I told him that we all had the hots for Gwen. In fact, I might have said those exact words, several times."

"Why would you tell him that?" Phillip whined.

"Because it's true. Be honest, Phillip. Not one of you denies that she's attractive. Not even just now. All you really said was that you weren't planning to act on it. Well, Martin and I did, and that's probably why we got further with her than any of you ever did."

"She turned you down," Tyler said.

"Yeah," Gary said. "But that's one step further than you got."

"Okay," Phillip said, attempting to get the conversation back on track. "We can discuss this later, or preferably not. Right now, Todd's clearly trying to use the three Gwens over there as bait."

"Yeah," Jimmy said. "I say we go ask some questions, see if we can figure out what the trap is."

After a silence that implied consent, Jimmy walked back toward the porch, the other three men following very close behind.

Jimmy cleared his throat again and said, "We've been walking for many days. It's been a long time since we've had a roof over our heads, or a hot meal."

The blond Gwen parted her cherry-red lips to speak but was interrupted by a distant, muffled voice from inside the building that said, "What's that? Who are you talking to out there?"

Here it comes, Phillip thought. *He lured us in close with the ladies; now we'll get surrounded by angry male relatives and we'll have to fight our way out.*

The blond kept her eyes locked on the men but tilted her head back over her shoulder and said, "Come see for yourself."

The door opened and another stunning young woman with Gwen's face emerged, this one with short, jet-black hair and features altered to look vaguely Asian.

Now that they were close, the wizards could see that while all four of the women looked similar enough to Gwen to be recognizable likenesses, none of them was quite right. One had cheekbones that were a little too pronounced. One had a jaw that was a little too square. One's eyes were a little too large. Like the miners and the wolves they'd been fighting off, the women were artificial creations, and permanent residents of the uncanny valley. They were just perfect enough to look totally wrong, but Phillip knew from experience that being struck or bitten by them felt perfectly convincing. There was no reason to believe that anything these Gwen clones chose to do wouldn't feel equally real. Phillip made note of this likelihood, then felt ashamed of himself for it.

"Oh," the new Gwen said. "Who are our handsome visitors?"

The blond, whose gaze had never left the men, said, "Warriors on a long journey. I expect they'll be looking for a place to rest."

The black-haired Gwen took stock of the men, then said, "I'll go prepare the guest beds, though I don't know how restful their night will be."

The other Gwens tittered and blushed as the black-haired Gwen disappeared into the house.

Jimmy said, "Please, ladies, we appreciate your offer, but we don't want to be any trouble."

The blond Gwen said, "Kind sirs, please don't embarrass us with talk of money."

Phillip noted that just like every other character in this ridiculous quest with whom they'd tried to talk, the responses didn't quite match what they had said. This was obviously because Todd had preprogrammed the characters' dialog without knowing, or caring, what the wizards he'd trapped would actually say.

The spokes-Gwen continued. "We insist that you stay with us. Please, you'd be doing us a favor. The four of us have lived alone here since we were small girls. We've been without any companionship since our father died, somehow."

Tyler turned to Phillip and mouthed, "Somehow?" Phillip waved him off.

"We have a great deal of delicious food, all of which has been cut into bite-sized morsels, perfect for hand-feeding. We'll happily share it. All we ask is your company. We have never had men visit before. We are very curious, and have many questions."

In spite of himself, Jimmy asked, "What kind of questions?"

The blond said, "And, of course, we'll give you shelter for the night. We have soft beds, satin sheets, silk pajamas, and a large variety of exotic lotions."

Gary stammered, "Ooh. That's . . . that's a lot of . . . smoothness."

Jimmy blurted, "Excuse me," and turned his back to the Gwens, walking back to where he thought they could not hear.

Jimmy said, "I stand by my position that this is a trap."

Phillip nodded. "Clearly."

"Yup," Tyler agreed.

Gary said, "Let's go in."

Phillip goggled at Gary and said, "It's a trap! Why on earth would you want to go in there?"

Gary said, "I'm curious. I want to see where this is going."

"Have you been listening?" Phillip asked. "Have you looked at those women? It's perfectly obvious where this is going."

They all glanced back at the women. The redhead and the brunette had gone back to slowly churning the butter and scrubbing the laundry. The blond was watching the men talk while absentmindedly putting the end of one of her knitting needles in her mouth.

"Yes," Gary said. "And I want to see it."

Jimmy spoke up. "Look, I agree it's a trap, but maybe we should go in."

Phillip let out a long groan, then said, "You desperate, lonely old—"

"No. Phillip, that's not . . . that's not why we should go in," Jimmy said. "Look, they have food. Food that isn't wolf jerky."

"Food that's probably poisoned," Phillip said.

"No," Tyler said. "If Todd wanted to just poison us, he'd have probably done it by now."

"Right," Jimmy agreed. "And they have a roof and a nice warm fire, and probably a place where we can get cleaned up."

Phillip said, "Oh, I don't doubt it. I'm sure the bathtub is the very center of their decor in there. That or a big bearskin rug."

"And we'll be able to figure out what their plan is," Tyler said.

"We know what their plan is," Phillip said. "Enough of it at least. Tyler, Jimmy, I expect this kind of thing out of Gary, but I can't believe that this is what's finally brought you two together. You really think this is the smart move, spending the evening with Zoot, Dingo, and Piglet there?"

Tyler muttered, "*Holy Grail*," then asked, "Piglet?"

Phillip said, "Yeah, she was one of the doctors who examined Michael Palin. The other was named Winston."

"Look," Jimmy said. "We know it's a trap, right? So that means we have the advantage. All we have to do is keep our eyes open and be ready for it when the trap springs."

Tyler added, "Besides, pretty much everything here is a trap. At least this one looks like fun."

Phillip knew he was defeated. "Okay, we'll go in. I guess there's no harm in having a look. There's only harm in Martin finding out about this later. Or even worse, Gwen."

14.

Roy was leaning heavily on the canyon wall, muttering to himself and looking ruefully around the corner at the fortifications of Castle Cragganmore. Brit and Gwen were leaning on the wall, looking ruefully at Roy.

Roy could see the castle, the soldiers in front of it, the raging river surrounding it, the steep canyon walls containing the river, and a third of the way up the canyon wall, he could see a lone figure emerging from behind the castle, making his way back toward his position.

"I can see Martin," Roy said. "Let's hope he found a back way into the castle, 'cause I don't like our chances in a frontal assault."

Gwen and Brit thanked him for the information, and Roy went back to analyzing the castle's defenses.

"Soldiers," Roy muttered. "Four groups, standing eight abreast, eight rows deep. Classic phalanx formation. They look well trained and in good condition. I don't see how we could possibly fight our way through them to the castle, even if we didn't have the women to worry about."

Gwen shook her head and laughed. Brit did not.

"What women are you worried about, Roy?" Brit asked. "I didn't see any standing in front of the castle. Do you think the soldiers' girlfriends are hiding inside the castle?"

Roy groaned.

Gwen said, "He thinks they're in there cooking dinner, and when he and Martin kill all the big, scary men, they'll come running out with their frying pans and rolling pins, and he and Martin will be defenseless, because they could never hit a lady."

Roy turned to face Brit and Gwen. He rubbed his face with his hand and said, "Look, girls . . . "

Brit and Gwen stared at him.

"Sorry. Gals," Roy tried.

Brit continued to stare. Gwen shook her head.

"Ladies?"

Gwen shook her head again.

Roy gritted his teeth and said, "Look, you two . . ."

Brit continued to stare, but Gwen subtly nodded her head.

"All I meant," Roy continued, "was that getting past those soldiers will be more difficult because we'll want to keep you safe. That's all, I assure you."

Brit smiled mirthlessly. "That's enough, I assure you."

Roy grimaced and turned his back to continue peering at the soldiers. He hoped this would end the argument. He was disappointed.

"What makes you think it's your duty to keep us safe?" Brit asked.

Roy said, "Hundreds of years of tradition."

Gwen said, "Roy, come on. The whole reason Brit and I are here is to try to help keep our male friends safe. Besides, haven't Brit and I proven that we're just as good at killing the wolves as you and Martin?"

Roy squinted at the soldiers in the distance. "Yeah, well, killing a man is very different from killing a wolf. Men are smarter."

Brit said, "I'm not so sure of that."

Roy scowled over his shoulder at her.

Brit cocked her head to the side and looked Roy in the eye. "I didn't mean to insult you. I didn't mind insulting you, but that's not the point I was trying to make. These wolves we've been fighting, they're not real wolves, right? They're all exactly the same. They always attack the same way. They show up in groups of two or more, attack one at a time, and die instantly, then dissolve, leaving behind some jerky. Then a while later, two wolves will pop up for every one we've killed. That's not natural wolf behavior, is it?"

"No," Roy admitted. "We've been through this. The wolves are artificial, set up as part of the quest."

"And so were the miners, and so are the soldiers," Brit said. "So I see no reason to believe that they'll be smarter or harder to kill than the wolves are."

Roy furrowed his brow and turned back to look at the soldiers. "They do all seem to be the same height and build. It's hard to tell from this distance, what with them all wearing armor, but they may be identical."

The prospect of having to hack and slash their way through all of those soldiers, even one at a time, gave them plenty to think about while Martin worked his way around the far cliff wall. Happily, he had stopped wearing his silver robe and hat. Unlike Roy's trench coat, Martin's robe was not practical attire for wilderness survival and would have made him far too visible. Since he had no powers here regardless of whether he wore his robes or not, that was three strikes. Instead, his robe was folded neatly in his backpack, in case they needed to use it as a blanket or a signal. When he was directly across the river from the others, they all headed back upstream to meet him at the narrow spot where he had crossed the river, leaping from rock to rock.

Martin rejoined them, sharing what he'd learned as they walked back toward the castle. It was not good news.

"There are no rocks at all on the far side of the castle."

Gwen asked, "Could we swim it?"

Martin shook his head. "No way. The current's way too fast. You could get into the water, and you might be able to keep your head above water, but by the time you swam to the other side of the river, you'd be half a mile downstream, and the banks look to be nothing but rock walls. You'd just leave a streak of claw marks if you tried to climb out."

"Okay," Roy said. "So we know they didn't get in that way."

"Yeah," Martin said, "but we aren't sure that they didn't try. There were footprints, lots of them, leading all the way around back, down to the riverbank and back up. If they didn't try to cross back there, they at least seriously considered it."

Brit said, "Well, I'm sure they thought about it, but they wouldn't have actually gotten into that river. They're not idiots."

After a moment, she corrected herself. "They're not all idiots."

After another moment, she said, "Of course they're all capable of idiocy, we all are, but they wouldn't risk their lives over it. Probably."

Roy said, "Getting down to brass tacks, we can't get in the back way, so the main road and through those soldiers is the only way we're going to get in there and get that canary."

"Which the miners already have," Martin added.

"Well," Roy said, "we'll see."

"We already saw," Martin said. "We all saw the canary. The miners already have it."

Brit said, "Yes, but we have to go through the motions to get credit for retrieving it so we can get our next instructions. Honestly, Martin, you know this."

"Yeah," Martin said. "I just wanted to hear someone say it out loud again. It's fun listening to intelligent people talk nonsense as if it's perfectly reasonable. Speaking of which, Roy, what's the plan once we get back to the castle?"

Roy said, "I figure you and I will leave the ladies back on the path, hidden around the corner; then we'll walk up to the soldiers, ask them to let us in, then fight our way through them if they don't."

Martin turned to Brit, smiling. "See? He said that as if it were perfectly reasonable. Isn't that amazing?"

Brit said, "Amazing. Roy, why do you think you should leave half of the team behind before you go into battle?"

Roy said, "Division of labor. We do our job, you do yours."

"And what, pray tell, is our job in this situation?"

Roy said, "I don't know. I'm not your boss. I'm not going to tell you what to do."

Brit said, "You're just going to tell us what not to do, and when not to do it, and where to stand while we don't do it."

Roy said, "You can look at it that way if you want to. I know I'm not trying to order you around. We'll discuss it later. Wait here."

Roy walked around the corner, into view of the soldiers guarding the castle entrance. Martin shared a meaningful look with Gwen, then nodded to Brit, who shook her head. Martin walked quickly to catch up with Roy.

They were walking along a couple hundred yards of narrow path on a precariously narrow strip of land, bordered on each side by raging torrents of water, toward a small army of heavily armed men. They had good reason to walk slowly.

"I swear," Roy muttered, "that girl's gonna drive me nuts."

Martin said, "I think the feeling's mutual."

Roy said, "I'm just trying to keep them safe. That's what a man does, isn't it? Try to keep the women and the children safe?"

Martin nodded. "Yes. Historically speaking, that's what men do."

"Then why are they fighting me?"

"Because they resent it. Historically speaking, that's what women do when you treat them like children."

"I'm not treating them like children. I'm treating them like ladies."

"Yeah," Martin said. "I noticed. You even keep calling them that. 'Ladies.' Sometimes even 'young ladies.'"

"So what's wrong with that?" Roy asked. "That's a compliment."

"Not coming from you."

"Why not?"

Martin sighed. "Because they think that you think you're better than them, so coming from you, 'ladies' is an insult, and 'young ladies' is a condescending insult."

"That's a bunch of hooey," Roy groaned.

Martin decided to try a different approach. "Have you ever had someone in a position of power over you call you a lady?"

"Yeah. My drill sergeant used to call us ladies all the time."

"Did he mean it as a compliment?"

"No, of course not, Martin, but that was different. We were—"

"Men, Roy? You find being called a lady insulting. How do you think it sounds when you call someone else one?"

"Okay," Roy said. "I get it. Everything I'm doing is wrong. What do you suggest?"

"You're overthinking this. Just treat them like equals."

Roy said, "I don't treat my equals well."

"Okay, yeah," Martin agreed. "Point taken. Look. Don't suck up to them or anything. It'll just seem insincere. Give them credit where it's due. Don't compliment them for no reason. Just try to stop insulting them for no reason."

They walked in silence. Martin thought, *Poor Roy. What a terrible situation he's gotten himself into.* A few steps later, Martin thought, *And I'm following him. Things aren't looking so good for me either, are they?*

Martin looked to the side, downriver. As he'd described earlier, the river got still narrower and faster, squeezing itself between two vertical rock walls before disappearing around a bend in the distance. To fall in the river off either side of the path would mean being swept down there to whatever waited around that bend. He shuddered at the thought.

They had closed half the distance to the soldiers, and it was already clear that they were indeed many copies of the same person. The same large, menacing, angry person.

Martin said, "Man, I hope this works."

"You hope what works?" Roy asked.

"Your plan," Martin explained.

Roy said, "I don't have a plan."

"Then why am I following you?" Martin asked.

"Because you don't have a plan either."

"Well," Martin said, looking at the looming soldiers, "I guess we still have a few seconds to come up with one."

They walked, both locked in thought as they closed the remaining gap between them and the motionless soldiers. At the last possible moment, Martin whispered, "Okay. I've got something. Follow my lead, and be ready to run."

Roy doubted that any of the great plans in military history had included the phrase "Be ready to run," but he didn't have any better ideas, which was all the more reason to be ready to run.

Martin strode purposefully toward the front row of soldiers, stopping barely two feet in front of one in the middle of the row. Martin looked the clone in the eye (having to look up at a fairly sharp angle to do so), and said, "We've come to enter the castle, free the canary, Oban is his name, I think, and then we'll be on our way."

The soldier looked down at Martin and said, "None shall pass."

Martin smirked over his shoulder at Roy, nodded, then turned back to the soldier. Martin set his jaw, gave the guard a look of steely determination, then kicked the guard in the crotch and shouted, "Run, Roy, run!"

Martin turned to sprint away and was surprised to see that Roy was already several steps ahead of him. Clearly, Roy had been ready to run. *Good to know he can follow directions*, Martin thought.

Roy shouted back over his shoulder, "Okay, what now?"

Martin glanced behind them and saw just enough to be sure they were being chased. "Keep running!" Martin yelled.

"That's your plan?!" Roy shrieked. "Keep running?!"

"Would you rather stop?" Martin asked.

Martin risked a longer look over his shoulder and was delighted by what he saw. "Good news! Like, eight of them are chasing us."

"That's good news?"

"Yes!" Martin gasped, beginning to run out of wind. "It means that when we get them over to where the girls are, we can gang up on them."

Roy wheezed, "Four of us ganging up on eight of them?"

"Yes. They're running identically, like the wolves do," Martin said between gulps of breath. "Odds are they'll take turns fighting. Just like the wolves. We won't."

"Yeah," Roy barked. "I get it. Hope the girls are ready."

Martin gasped, "Gwen knows me. She's probably . . . been ready for this . . . since we walked away."

The path widened; then a ridge formed to Martin and Roy's left that grew quickly into a canyon wall as they ran. They could see the point up ahead where the wall seemed to end, but actually turned left, hiding what was waiting around the bend. From a distance, Martin had seen the tops of Gwen's and Brit's heads as they looked around the corner, but as they got closer, the heads had vanished. Martin told Roy to take the corner wide. Roy waved a hand dismissively rather than wasting his breath saying "way ahead of you."

Roy shot past the corner of the canyon wall, almost to the edge of the path before turning left and continuing down the trail. Martin followed suit, and as he rounded the corner, he could see that Gwen was waiting with her back to the canyon wall and her sword poised like a baseball bat. Brit was beside her, slightly farther down the trail, holding her sword almost like a pitchfork.

Martin skidded to a stop, barely avoiding running into Roy, who had also slid to a disorganized halt. They looked back. For a panicked moment Martin thought that Gwen and Brit had misjudged how close behind them the soldiers were, but, as was often the case when Martin thought that Gwen had made a mistake, she had simply thought things through a little more fully than he had.

The eight soldiers were running in a single-file line. The first soldier ran straight past Gwen without ever seeing her. He did notice Brit, even before she ran him through with her sword. He let out a pained scream that harmonized sickeningly with the yelp of surprise that came from the second soldier in line as Gwen chopped him in half at the navel.

The two halves of the bisected soldier fell to the ground around the first soldier's feet as Brit pulled her sword from his gut. The first soldier fell to his knees among the parts of his comrade before slumping to the ground and being covered by the body of the third soldier in line, whom Gwen had nearly decapitated with her next swing. There was little blood and no gore, but the pile of dead fake soldier parts was still not a pretty sight.

Roy and Martin both made involuntary sounds. Roy's was one of shock and amazement, Martin's, delight, and more than a little pride. While the remaining soldiers rounded the corner and froze in horror at what remained of their three cohorts, Gwen and Brit fell back to Martin and Roy's position, emitting squeaky little sounds of surprise and disgust as they stepped around the body parts of the fallen.

"Well done!" Martin said.

Gwen said, "It wasn't that hard. The swords don't feel any resistance when you stab them, and they die after one hit."

Martin and Roy had recovered enough to have gotten their swords out. Brit and Gwen flanked them so that they presented a unified, sword-wielding front. The five remaining soldiers, who were still standing in single file, looked up from their fallen comrades. The soldier in front drew his sword, bent at the knees, stood sideways, and waved his sword menacingly. The four soldiers behind him did the same. They had the same posture and made the same motions at the same speed. The only thing that kept it from looking like a choreographed dance routine was that they all started the animation at slightly different times, so their sword waving was slightly out of sync.

The front soldier let out a triumphant "Ha-ha!" and lunged forward. His sword met Martin's, and the two froze there for a moment, locked in honorable combat, before both Brit and Roy stabbed the soldier with their swords. The soldier fell back, next to the remains of his fallen fellows, who were already beginning to fade and disappear, leaving their mostly unused weapons behind.

The next soldier in line said "Ha-ha!" and lunged for Martin, who parried his thrust and held him there while Roy stabbed him.

Brit said, "Rotate." Since they all (even Roy) had played volleyball, they knew instinctively to move around in a circle to allow everyone to see an equal amount of action and get an equal amount of rest. They had all taken a step just in time for the next soldier to yell "Ha-ha!" and lunge at Brit, who had taken over Martin's position. Gwen stabbed him, and as she withdrew her blade, Martin shoved him back onto the fading pile.

By the time the eighth soldier attacked, they had the process fairly fine-tuned.

They looked at the pile of carnage for a moment and briefly discussed any way they could improve the system. Then Martin said, "I'd better go get the next row headed this way. We have to get through all of them before this row regenerates twofold."

About an hour later, four very tired adventurers pushed open the doors of Castle Cragganmore. Their arms felt like spaghetti, and they were drenched with sweat, but they were alive, and the soldiers who had stood in their way were not.

They opened the doors wide enough to walk through, but the doors themselves were so large that they appeared to have only opened a crack. A thin shaft of daylight sliced through the darkness, paradoxically making it harder to see what was in the room, not easier. They pushed the doors closed again behind them, just in case the soldiers respawned in their original positions, rather than, like the wolves, where they'd been killed.

Once the doors were closed, their eyes could adjust to the light that filtered in through the stained-glass windows. There were large decorative torches on every wall, but as it was still day, they were not lit. There was more than enough light to see by; it just did not seem like it at first because everything visible was dark. Dark stone floors supporting dark stone walls beneath a dark stone ceiling, all illuminated by dark stained-glass windows.

The room was large and circular, with two symmetrical staircases leading to a nonsensically placed terrace at the back of the room. Beneath the terrace, there was a stone carving of what appeared to be a circular aperture, flanked by two large decorative mirrors. In the middle of the floor, two raised platforms held two levers.

Brit shook her head and said, "Look at this place."

Martin said, "I know!"

Brit smirked at him before sighing. "I've never understood why men think all you have to do to make something cool is to make it big and paint it black."

Martin said, "I've never understood why women think it's more complicated than that." They shared a small chuckle, then turned their attention to Roy, who was standing on one of the two small platforms in the middle of the room, pushing on the lever that seemed to be the platform's reason for existing.

"Hey, Martin," Roy said, "why don't you apply a little elbow grease to that other lever? Let's see if we can make something happen."

Brit silently walked toward the second lever.

Roy said, "I said—"

"My elbows are just as greasy as his," Brit said.

She stepped up onto the platform and grasped the lever with both hands.

Roy said, "On three?"

Brit replied, "That works."

Roy counted, and as he said "three," they both easily pushed their levers forward. The room filled with the sound of giant heavy stones sliding against each other as the stone aperture opened.

Brit and Roy made eye contact, and in unison started to release their levers, which instantly caused the portal to close. They quickly pushed their levers forward again, and the portal reopened.

Brit said, "Okay, I guess we're staying here. Gwen, Martin, you're up. I know you two haven't really been alone for a long time, but please, don't spend too much time in there making out."

Gwen and Martin approached the threshold and saw a stone staircase and a seemingly infinite row of torches stretching off into the distance. After a quick promise to not waste too much time, they started down the stairs.

After they'd gone far enough that they were sure they wouldn't be overheard, Gwen said, "We should try to get back to them as quickly as we can. Poor Brit. She can't be happy stuck up there with Roy."

Martin said, "Yeah, I don't think it's a picnic for Roy either."

"I thought you liked Brit."

"I do. I like her a lot, and I actually think Roy thinks quite a bit of her, but just shows it badly."

Gwen said, "He treats her like a weakling and bosses her around."

Martin smiled and said, "Like I said, *badly*."

"That's not badly," Gwen said. "That's oppositely, if that's even a word."

Martin attempted to let the topic drop. He was not successful.

After a few steps, Gwen said, "Seriously, Martin, you're saying that he treats Brit and me like idiots because he likes us?"

"That isn't quite what I was saying," Martin said, "but yes. He thinks he's being strong and protective. If he didn't think you both deserved protection and strength, he wouldn't bother."

"So he thinks he should treat us like precious porcelain figurines."

Martin shrugged. "I think he'd say he's trying to treat you like ladies."

Gwen looked at Martin in disbelief. "Martin, you agree with him, don't you?"

Martin stopped walking and turned to face Gwen. "Look, that's not a fair question, and you know it."

"Why not?" Gwen asked.

"Because you're asking for a yes-or-no answer to a multiple-choice question."

Gwen said, "This isn't the SAT, Martin."

Martin said, "I know. I did well on my SAT."

Gwen didn't laugh, or even smile, but she did noticeably relax, which was enough encouragement for Martin to continue.

"Look," he said, "you and I are from 2012. Brit's from the 1990s. Roy was born in something like 1930. Think about that for a minute."

Gwen said, "That doesn't justify his attitude."

"No," Martin said, "but it explains it. Gwen, I look at you and Brit and I see modern women. He looks at you and he sees creatures from the friggin' future. A future he can barely imagine. He came here from the seventies. Do you know how awful things were back then? The women Roy's friends would have considered crazy, hardcore feminists were demanding jobs. That's it. Jobs that weren't nursing, sewing, or food service. They weren't even demanding equal pay yet, because they wanted to be realistic."

Martin continued down the stairs. Gwen followed.

"So what are you telling me?" Gwen asked. "Brit and I should take his behavior as a compliment? Should we thank him for belittling us?"

"Not at all," Martin said. "I think you both have played things about right. What's that called when psychologists electrocute you when you do something wrong? Abhorrent conditioning, I think? Anyway, he won't learn that he's doing the wrong thing unless you two show him that he is, so I say keep up the good work. I'd just appreciate it if you try not to hate him. He's a grumpy old cuss, but he's not a bad guy. It's not that he doesn't respect you. He just respects you wrong."

At last, they reached the bottom of the stairs, and found themselves in a large room. The center of the room was a statue of a six-armed warrior. In his six hands he brandished six knives, the blades of which were polished to a mirror finish. On the far wall there was an intricately carved door that was covered with strange symbols. On each side of the door there were three stone cylinders, about the height of a man, which also held carved hieroglyphics, though much larger than the ones on the doors. In front of both sets of cylinders there was a rail holding a small mirror. Along the sides of the room, six braziers held six roaring fires, the light from which was focused by large lenses toward the statue in the middle of the room.

Gwen and Martin surveyed the scene silently for a moment; then Gwen said, "Puzzle."

"Obviously," Martin replied.

"I'll take the left side," Gwen said. "You take the right."

Martin said, "Cool," and they went about their work.

The statue stood in an exaggerated squat that looked fearsome and allowed people of normal human height to use its legs as a place to stand. Gwen and Martin climbed up on the statue's bent knees and started pulling on the arms, each of which were attached to the torso via a swivel joint at the shoulder. Each arm easily swung into position with a satisfying click, and the light from one of the braziers, focused by the lenses, reflected off the dagger blades to illuminate one of the symbols on the door. In short order, they had all six arms in position and six glyphs highlighted. They moved on to the cylinders, which turned smoothly but slowly. Martin spun the columns until the three symbols displayed on their fronts matched the three illuminated on the door closest to him. He turned to check on Gwen's progress and found her smirking at him with her arms crossed.

"You done?" he asked.

"Yup," she answered.

"Hmm," Martin said. "Then why isn't the door opening?" He pushed and pulled on the door. It didn't move.

"Are you done with your side?" Gwen asked.

Martin said, "Yeah."

"Are you sure?"

"Yes," Martin said, "I think." He looked at the cylinders. The markings matched. He thought for a moment, casting his eyes around the room.

"The mirror," Martin moaned. "I totally forgot about the mirror."

Martin stood between the cylinders and the mirror, then swung the mirror around so he was looking at the cylinders, and of course, when looked at this way the symbols were backward and in the wrong order. He spun the first cylinder until he found a glyph that was the reversed version of the symbol on the last cylinder. Gwen smiled, approvingly.

As he arranged the other two cylinders, Martin said, "I gotta admit, these puzzles are a lot more tiring when you're actually physically doing them, instead of sitting on your couch with a controller, watching Lara Croft do the work."

"*Tomb Raider*, huh?" Gwen said. "I preferred *Uncharted*."

"Well, I'm a dude, and Lara Croft is fun to look at."

"I'm a chick, and I feel the same way about Nathan Drake."

Martin shrugged and continued spinning the cylinders.

"And Victor Sullivan," Gwen continued.

Martin turned to face her, grinning. "Really? The old guy?"

"Yeah, why not? Age differences like that don't always bother women. Look at Phillip and Brit."

Martin said, "Brit's older than Phillip."

"Mentally," Gwen said. "Physically, she's much younger."

Martin said, "Age differences like that don't always bother men. Almost never, in fact."

Martin slid the last glyph into place, and the doors swung open on their own.

Gwen and Martin crept into the dark passage beyond the door. The only sound was the rustling of their own clothing. They could see a well-lit room waited at the end of the hall, but there was no source of light between there and where they were.

As they approached the light, their view of the room grew wider. They saw a fortune in gold and other assorted loot, piled and heaped in such large amounts that it couldn't help but look terribly fake. In the midst of the gold there was a throne. The arms of the throne and its backrest, seat cushion, and the floor around it were stained with blood, in such large amounts of it that it couldn't help but look terribly real.

Across from the throne there was a table, and on that table there was a familiar-looking ornate metal birdcage. Inside the birdcage there was an ornate metal bird, just like the one back at the mine, except this one was not moving, seemingly frozen in mid-flutter. It hung motionless in the air, beak open, wings outstretched.

On the floor just behind the table, there was the body of a portly man in a filthy jester costume, lying motionless, arms akimbo, and facedown on the floor with his head turned away. There was no sign of blood, gore, or decomposition of any kind, and he was clearly not a real person, but that only made the sight of him more disturbing.

Anyone involved in a healthy long-term romantic relationship can tell when their partner wants to leave a place. Usually the place in question is some place the other person does not want to leave: a party, a Broadway musical, or a sports bar with scantily clad waitresses. In this case, both Martin and Gwen were able to tell that neither of them felt like hanging around, so they simply walked in, grabbed the cage, and walked out again without ever having to discuss it.

Brit shifted her weight, adjusting her stance so that the lever's handle dug into a different part of her anatomy. Using her body weight to hold the door open didn't require a lot of strength, but it still had its cost. Early on she had been forced to make a choice. She could have a single, smallish bruise that went clear to the bone, or she could spread the damage around and end up with a less painful bruise that had more surface area.

Once she was confident with her new position, she turned her attention back to the conversation at hand.

"So," she asked, "about the SR-71, I understand that the friction of the speeds it flew caused so much expansion that the skin panels had to be made smaller than usual, and that at room temperature the whole plane had big honking panel gaps."

"Yup. If you looked too closely, it looked like we'd had the thing built by British Leyland." Roy was sitting on the floor, leaning back on his lever as if it were a backrest. "That's a car company that makes crummy cars."

"Yeah, I know," Brit said. "They did, anyway. They're long gone in my time."

"I'm not surprised. How's a young lady like you know about all this guy stuff?"

Brit chose to let the "young lady" bit slide, and instead focus on how she knew about "all this guy stuff."

"Roy," she said, "I love machines and engineering and problem solving. Before I found the file, I was going to be an architect. I know things."

Roy scoffed. "Well, now, I don't know what all you know, but I'll tell you something I know. Saying you were going to be something isn't the same as being that thing."

"What's that supposed to mean?" Brit asked, despite the fact that she knew exactly what it was supposed to mean.

"Just that reading about building things isn't the same as actually building things, that's all," Roy explained.

Brit said, "I built a city. An entire city. Atlantis. You've been there."

Roy said, "Yeah, about that. I've always been hazy on how that whole thing happened. When did you build Atlantis?"

Brit said, "About forty years from now."

Roy waved his hand dismissively. "Yeah, great, I know. We're all time travelers, great. What I'm asking is, to you, from your point of view, when did you build the city?"

"That's what I'm trying to tell you," Brit explained. "From my point of view the city will be built thirty-eight years from now."

Roy smiled. "Oh, so what you're saying is that you didn't build Atlantis. Brit the Elder did."

Brit said, "She's me!"

Roy said, "Not yet she isn't."

Brit said, "Besides, the city is based on my plans and ideas."

Roy said, "Ideas don't impress me as much as execution. Sorry, kid, but where I come from we judge people by what they've done, not what they say they'll do."

"I'm not telling you what I will do," Brit said. "I'm telling you what I will have done."

Roy mulled this over for a moment, then said, "Yeah, well, I don't know what to think of that."

Brit admitted, "Neither do I, most days."

The conversation might have continued, but they were distracted by the sound of footsteps echoing up the staircase behind them. Roy and Brit glanced at each other, silently confirming that they would enact the plan they had hatched shortly after they'd stopped actively pushing on the levers and had started leaning on them. Roy smiled, Brit nodded, and they both started arranging themselves as discussed.

Gwen and Martin walked up the stairs much more slowly than they had walked down. With each step, the light from the door at the top of the stairs grew brighter. The fact that there was light at all was reassuring, as it meant that Brit and Roy were still there to keep the door open.

As they reached the last few steps, and their heads rose above the level of the main chamber's floor, they could see Roy and Brit, doing their jobs. Roy was leaned over, holding the lever with both hands and bracing it with his shoulder. His knuckles were white with exertion. His feet struggled to find traction on the slick marble floor. Brit had spun around to the other side of her lever and was hanging from it by one elbow, using her other arm to keep herself from slipping.

Roy looked up, saw Martin and Gwen, and gasped. "Hurry up! We can't hold it forever!"

Both Gwen and Martin practically threw themselves through the portal, only taking care to not damage the birdcage with its frozen cargo in the process. They were barely free of the door when Roy rolled sideways off his lever, allowing it to spring back into its original position. Brit merely let go of her lever, falling to the ground in a panting heap.

Martin said, "Guys, we're sorry. We went as fast as we could."

Roy massaged his hands. Brit sat up, shoulders sagging, and limply held up a hand, signaling that a response would come when it was darned good and ready. After several heavy breaths, she said, "We know. We know. You did your best, I'm sure. A few times, I turned to Roy, and I said, 'We have to hold on. Martin and Gwen are counting on us.' Didn't I say that, Roy?"

"Yeah," Roy agreed. "I knew she was right, but it took you so long, I was sure something terrible had happened. All we could do was worry, and hold on as long as we could."

Martin said, "Oh, guys. We're sorry. It must have been terrible!"

"It was," Brit said. "Roy cried."

Roy instantly looked furious with Brit. Brit looked at him, innocently, and said, "Isn't that right, Roy?"

Through gritted teeth, Roy said, "I didn't think you were going to tell them that."

Gwen walked over to Roy and put a hand on his shoulder. "Oh, come on, Roy. It's all right. You have nothing to be ashamed of. I'm sure you cry all the time."

Roy looked up at Gwen and said, "Thanks for that."

Martin offered Brit a hand up, which she accepted. Once she was on her feet, Martin asked, "Why didn't you just lean back on the lever? It might have been easier than hanging from it."

Brit said, "Really, Martin? You're gonna second-guess us? You don't know what went on up here. You don't know what all we tried."

Martin quickly said, "You're right. I'm sorry."

Brit glared at him for a moment, then looked down at the birdcage, saying, "So, the bird was there."

Marin said, "Yeah, but he's not right." Martin held up the cage so Brit and Roy could get a good look. The metal bird was still frozen in place, hovering in midair above its perch, wings frozen midflight. Martin spun the cage around so they could see that the bird remained motionless in relation to the cage no matter how it moved.

"Weird," Roy said, summing the situation up nicely.

"Yeah," Gwen agreed. "And it wasn't the only thing that was a bit off. There was a jester down there who didn't seem to be dead or even really hurt. He was just lying perfectly still, face-down on the floor."

Brit said, "Yeah, that does seem like some kind of glitch. Any sign of what messed things up?"

Martin and Gwen exchanged a quick look; then Martin said, "Well, there was also a lot of blood down there."

"The jester's?" Roy asked.

"No," Gwen said. "It was on the other side of the room."

That silenced all conversation while they all thought seriously about whose blood it might have been.

Roy said, "Speaking of blood, we should get moving. Every second we stay here, the more likely that those soldiers have regenerated."

Martin pushed the immense doors open a crack and peeked through, fearing that he'd find a sea of soldiers all waiting their turn to attack him. Instead, the courtyard was empty. He pushed the door open far enough to poke his head out and look from side to side.

He saw nobody.

He pushed the doors open and walked out into the open air, followed by the others.

"Looks like they haven't regenerated," Martin said.

"At least they haven't regenerated here," Gwen side. "Two wolves usually respawn where one was killed, so if the soldiers did come back, there'll be twice as many of them around that corner." She pointed down the only path leading to or from the castle, which turned left in the distance and went behind the wall of the canyon, creating the natural hiding spot they had used earlier.

Martin said, "I'll sneak up there and see if the coast is clear. It's the least I can do after what we put you two through."

Martin jogged away. Roy said, "That's decent of him."

Brit said, "Well, I'm sure he feels terrible. He knows it had to be bad if it made a big strong man like you cry."

Roy grimaced and said, "Hmph."

Brit said, "Like a little girl."

Roy glared at her, then focused on the frozen bird in the cage he was holding. Gwen made eye contact with Brit. Brit shrugged.

Gwen continued her eye contact. Brit shrugged again.

Gwen raised her eyebrows. Brit blushed a bit and nearly laughed. Gwen nearly laughed too, and might have if not for the distant yelp and the sight of Martin running their way, pursued by sixteen regenerated soldiers.

15.

Gary walked into the cabin with the blond Gwen on his arm, cooing in his ear about how nice it was to have visitors. Behind him, the redhead entered holding Tyler's hand, gushing about how rough and manly it felt. The brunette Gwen entered walking backward, holding both of Jimmy's hands, leading him forward and gazing over every inch of him as if he were a priceless work of art.

Phillip followed them in, alone and grumpy.

Phillip had no sooner crossed the threshold than the black-haired Gwen appeared and clung to his side as if drawn there by magnets.

From the outside, the building had seemed like a normal medieval dwelling, larger than usual but of conventional design and made of predictable materials. Inside, it was a different story.

They entered a large room that looked as if a swinging bachelor from the late sixties had attempted to decorate his pad using materials he stole from a renaissance fair. The floor on which they stood formed an elevated ring around the perimeter of the room. Set into the middle of the floor was a sunken seating area, the kind of thing that used to be called a "conversation pit," although the silky pillows and cushions that lined the sofas and the floor made Phillip doubt that it had been designed with conversation in mind. Along one wall there was a bar with several bottles of no-doubt-intoxicating liquids ranging in color from perfectly clear to dark brown. On another wall there was a fireplace with a roaring fire and the mandatory bearskin rug. The third wall held a staircase leading upstairs and a series of pegs. Various garments hung from the pegs. At a glance, they seemed period accurate, but when Phillip looked for a moment, he saw that in addition to the expected fur and leather items, there were garments made of gauze, denim, plaid, and something that looked like shiny black plastic.

Gary, Tyler, and Jimmy allowed themselves to be led down into the pit, where they were gently placed into seats and gently fussed over.

Phillip said, "No thanks," and walked over to the fireplace instead. He immediately took off the multiple robes he'd been wearing in an unsuccessful attempt to stay warm. The black-haired Gwen took each filthy robe as if it were a treasure. Phillip crouched before the fire, warming his hands while the black-haired Gwen watched, waiting for him to remove more clothes.

Once everyone seemed comfortable, the blond Gwen drew back from Gary and said, "After your long journey, you must be terribly hungry."

Gary arched his eyebrows in a way he hoped was suave and said, "Yes. Very."

She drew her face closer to his and said, "I bet it's been a long time since you've had a good meal."

"It's been so long," Gary said. "So long."

The blond Gwen giggled and said, "Well, we'll be right back, and then you'll have as much food as you like." She and the other Gwens all stood up as if on cue and walked out of the room through a door next to the bar.

Phillip stood by the fire, looking at the other three men lying prone among the cushions, looking forlornly at the door through which the Gwens had just left. "You're pathetic," he said. "It's no wonder women don't respect men."

Tyler said, "Women don't respect men because we didn't respect them first. It's retaliation."

Gary added, "And we're not pathetic. We're just playing them, drawing them out, hoping they'll tip their hand."

Phillip said, "Yeah, I bet."

"Relax, Phillip," Jimmy said. "We're in complete control of the situation. We're not going to let it go any further than it already has. We've all got our guard up."

Phillip said, "Yeah, I can see that."

Tyler said, "Come on, Phil, you knew what we'd find in here. You knew it would be something like this."

"That's it, Tyler. Todd, if he's going to watch any part of this little misadventure he's cooked up for us, it'll be this. Anyway, Todd designed this whole scenario to be irresistibly seductive. Look around, you guys. We're standing in a sexist buffoon's idea of romance."

"And credit where it's due," Gary said. "I think what he came up with is pretty effective."

"Yeah," Phillip agreed, scowling. "That's why it angers me."

The door to the next room reopened, and the four Gwens returned, each carrying a lidded platter. Three settled in next to Jimmy, Tyler, and Gary. The one with black hair stood next to Phillip, brandishing her platter. She glanced down to her own cleavage, then looked up at Phillip expectantly and said, "Are you hungry?"

Phillip groaned, "I feel like I owe every woman on the planet an apology, including you." The artificial Gwen did not seem to understand the response.

Gary said, "Yes, he's hungry. We're all hungry."

In unison, the Gwens removed the lids from their platters to reveal grapes, cherries, bite-sized chunks of melon and pineapple, small cubes of cheese, and what appeared to be wood and brass medieval analogs of cans of aerosol whipped cream.

Phillip squeezed the bridge of his nose and said, "Oh, Lord."

"I know, right?" Gary said, almost giggling.

The blond, brunette, and redheaded Gwens each delicately picked up a morsel of food from their platters and slowly pushed them toward the men's mouths. Jimmy, Tyler, and Gary dutifully opened their mouths to receive their first bite. Phillip gently grasped the black-haired Gwen's wrist with one hand and took the piece of fruit with the other, popping it into his mouth.

The black-haired Gwen withdrew her hand and sucked the juice from her fingertips while looking deeply into Phillip's eyes.

Phillip looked away while he chewed his pineapple chunk. Without looking back, he asked her, "What's your name?"

The black-haired Gwen purred, "I'm the one with black hair."

"He didn't even bother to give them names," Phillip said, straining the words through gritted teeth. He sat down on the bearskin rug, sighing heavily. The one with black hair put down the platter and lowered herself to the floor as well, though she didn't sit on the rug so much as she stretched her legs out to one side, keeping them together but bent to accentuate the flare of her hips and the narrowness of her waist. Her torso remained upright, her weight supported by one hand while the other explored the surface of the rug. She slowly ran her fingers through the long fur, humming with pleasure.

"Hmmmmm," she said. "It feels so soft and warm on my skin."

"The skin of your hand?" Phillip asked.

She gave him a heavy-lidded look in the eyes and said, "Yes." She held her hand out to him.

Phillip shook his head, then picked up the platter of food from the floor and turned so he could eat it without looking at the black-haired Gwen. He said, to anyone who was listening, "I notice these simulations adapt a little better to our responses."

"Yeah," Tyler agreed. "He probably put more time into writing this part of the program."

"Yeah," Phillip said. "I bet he did. I'm sure this part of the quest has been rigorously tested."

Down in the seating area, the other men were thoroughly enjoying their meal. The blond Gwen had just placed a grape in Gary's mouth and was reaching for a cherry when he shook his head no and nodded toward the can of whipped cream. Blond Gwen smiled wickedly and picked up the can.

The can was made out of very small barrel staves, held together with small riveted brass hoops. The domed brass top was tipped with a nozzle that looked like carved ivory. She lifted the can and dispensed some whipped cream onto her index finger, which she offered to Gary. He accepted the offer. She started to put more of the whipped cream on her finger, but he again shook his head no, and opened his mouth wide. She aimed the nozzle at his mouth and fired. She was a tad overzealous, and whipped cream went all over Gary's face. He laughed.

"Oh, you poor dear," she said. "I guess we'll have to go get you cleaned up."

"Yes," Gary said. "That! We have to do that!"

The blond stood up and offered Gary her hand. He leapt to his feet and took her hand. He beamed down at Tyler and Jimmy.

"I'm going to go get cleaned," he said.

"So we heard," Jimmy said.

"Yes," Gary said. "You did hear it, right?"

"Yes, we did," Tyler agreed.

Gary said "Good" as the blond led him by the hand to the staircase. He glanced over and saw Phillip, sitting cross-legged on the bearskin rug, holding the platter of fruit chunks as if it were a paper plate at a summer barbecue, miserably eating while the black-haired Gwen watched his every move adoringly.

"Don't worry, Phillip," Gary said as he and the blond walked up the stairs. "I'll be vigilant. No detail will escape my notice."

Phillip muttered, "He's gonna get himself killed."

"Well, he's gonna get himself something," Tyler said, chewing a strawberry while the redheaded Gwen looked on adoringly. "Lighten up, Phillip. He's not a dummy."

Phillip stared at Tyler.

"Not as big a dummy as you think," Tyler said. "Besides, it's easy for you to take the high road here. You're the only one of us with a steady girlfriend."

Phillip said, "First of all, that shouldn't matter."

Tyler said, "But we all know it does."

"Secondly," Phillip continued, "Gary hits on every woman he meets, constantly."

"Yeah," Tyler said. "Do you think that means he has a lot of success?"

"That's a good point," Jimmy said, peeking around the side of the brunette Gwen's head to make eye contact with Phillip. "Do you really keep looking for something after you've found it?"

Phillip lapsed into a sullen silence, quietly munching his mixed fruit and cheese platter and trying not to listen to Jimmy and Tyler slurp and giggle their way through theirs.

After a few more chunks of fruit, Jimmy said, "Hey, Tyler, you wanna take your bath next?"

Of course Tyler did, but he was deeply suspicious of anything Jimmy did, especially if it seemed like an act of kindness. Tyler glared at Jimmy, then said, "Why? Why do you want me to? You trying to get me out of the room for some reason?"

Jimmy said, "No. I'm just trying to figure out the order. Honestly, Tyler, I know you don't trust me, but you're going to have to let me out of your sight, unless you want to watch me take my bath."

Tyler thought a moment, then said, "I've decided to trust you, for now."

Jimmy said "Splendid" and went back to allowing himself to be fed.

Phillip spent a moment contemplating his view of the back half of the brunette Gwen until he snapped out of it and averted his eyes. His gaze resettled, quite naturally, on his side view of the redheaded Gwen. Phillip physically turned his face away and found himself looking directly at the black-haired Gwen staring at him, smiling.

Phillip looked at the floor. "How are any of us going to face Gwen after this?"

Tyler said, "The same way we face every woman we've fantasized about but not had sex with."

"Which is a lot of them," Jimmy added.

Phillip looked up from the floor and watched Jimmy and Tyler enjoy their meal for a moment before saying, "This is a lot more than just a fantasy, Tyler."

"Yes," Tyler allowed, "but it's a lot less than sex."

Phillip said, "Yeah, for now." He glanced at the staircase. "For us."

"You're worried about Gary?" Tyler asked.

"Yes," Phillip answered.

"Well, don't be. He may act dumb sometimes, but I trust him. I promise you, Phillip. He's in complete control of the situation."

Upstairs, in the bathroom, Gary was in complete control of the situation. He had entered the room, seen the bathtub full of warm, soapy water, and had decided that the only prudent course of action was to immediately disrobe.

I'm supposed to be taking a bath, right? You don't do that in your clothes, he thought. *That would be crazy.*

He started removing his clothes, then turned to see if the blond Gwen was watching him undress. She was. As he continued to undress, he watched her watching him undress. As always happens whenever someone watches you do something you usually do alone, Gary was gripped with the uneasy feeling that he was undressing wrong, and that the false Gwen was judging him.

Get a grip, he thought. *You're taking off your pants. As long as you end up not wearing pants, you can't be doing it wrong.*

Despite his internal pep talk, the surveillance had him so unnerved that he did end up tugging at his pants as they pooled flaccidly around his ankles before realizing that in order to fully remove them he would have to lift at least one foot off the ground.

Gary got down to his underwear. They were the style commonly called "tighty-whities," though after having been worn for so long and while covering so much distance, they were no longer either white or tight. He knew they were not flattering, but he couldn't quite force himself to remove them.

He turned to gauge the blond Gwen's reaction to the sight of him mostly undressed. She did not scream and flee, which he took as a positive sign. She also did not disrobe herself, which he found less encouraging.

Okay. Fun is fun, Gary thought, *but I can't let this go any further.*

Gary slowly approached her. She did not retreat or look away.

I mean it, he told himself, *I can't let this go too much further.*

Soon he was kissing her, and she was kissing him back. He carefully started untying the laces of her peasant blouse. She made no move to stop him.

Gary thought, *Seriously, I can never let anyone know how far I'm letting this go.*

Gary stopped thinking. He felt her in his arms. He heard her breathing, heavy in his ear. He felt her fingernails digging into his back, her movements becoming jerky and uncoordinated. The sound of her breath took on a wet, panting quality.

In a deep, husky growl she said, "I'll gnaw the meat from your ribcage."

Gary said, "If that's what you're into, baby." He continued kissing her, moving down to the base of her neck when she started swinging her head a bit more violently than he would have liked. He was becoming dimly aware that she no longer seemed to be actively engaged in the project. He opened his eyes and looked at the shoulder he was kissing, and thought, *I'm pretty sure that wasn't mint green before.*

Gary drew back from the woman, holding her at arm's length to get a good look. Her flesh was green and wet. The centers of her eyes were white and her teeth were black, the opposite of how Gary usually liked it. Her cloud of blond hair had become slick, slimy, and matted.

I can make this work, he thought. He tried kissing her again, but his heart wasn't really in it. It was over.

She croaked, "You will suffer a thousand torments before this night is through."

Gary sighed. "Don't. Just . . . don't." He let go of her and looked around the room. The walls were decrepit and covered with mold. The inviting tub full of hot, clear water was now filthy and full of green slime.

Zombie Gwen stood where he left her, hissing and sputtering, but she made no move to attack.

He turned and took two steps to get back to his clothes, which still sat in a heap where he'd left them on the floor. He became aware of zombie Gwen closing in on him very rapidly. He stopped, whipping around to defend himself. She stopped just short of him, snarling threateningly but not making any move to actually harm him.

"You will beg me for mercy," she said. "Mercy you will not get."

Gary mumbled, "Yeah, I wish." Then, playing a hunch, he took one large step backward. She lurched forward exactly as far as he had, but no farther.

It's just like the bridge, and the river rocks, he thought. *Keep us moving, but don't actually kill us.*

Zombie Gwen slathered and snapped crazily at Gary, but she did not move any closer to him. He glared back at her while he slowly pulled his clothes back on.

When he was fully dressed, he walked back down the stairs with zombie Gwen following right behind, closely enough that he could hear her wet breathing and feel the wind from her repeated attempts to grab him but not close enough to actually make physical contact.

"Hey, guys," he said. "We were right. It's a trap."

As his head dipped below the ceiling of the first floor, he saw that the seductive decor of the room had been replaced with splintered rotten wood and moldering filth. Tyler and Jimmy were standing ankle deep in a pit of muck that had been the conversation pit. Standing next to them were two identical copies of the zombified Gwen that pursued Gary. The only difference was that instead of a matted slick of sickly blond hair, they had wet mops of red and brown hair falling limply from their scalps. They hissed and cursed and slobbered, but they remained roughly arm's length from Tyler and Jimmy and seemed rooted in place.

"Oh," Gary said. "You know."

"Yeah," Tyler said. "We kinda figured it out for ourselves."

"The first hint was when a piece of cantaloupe turned into maggots in my mouth," Jimmy said. "A thing like that tends to get your attention."

Phillip said, "At least you got some protein." He was standing in front of the long-dormant fireplace, on a rotted, moldy rug, next to a black-haired deadite who seemed to want to tear out his jugular with her teeth but could not quite bring herself to do it.

Tyler said, "Man, you don't have to act so happy about this."

Phillip said, "No, I don't have to, but I choose to. Really, guys, you didn't think this was going to have a happy ending, did you? With you settling down with your Gwen-shaped pleasure replicants and having kids?"

Gary ambled down the stairs, followed by his evil Gwen. "No," he said. "I didn't picture that, but I was hoping for a happy ending."

Tyler looked at the hellish effigy of Gwen nearest him. "You will beg me to let you die," she said.

"You're all talk," Tyler said. After a moment's thought, He continued, to the whole group, "Everything here is. I'm beginning to think that since Todd killed Jeff, the only real danger we've faced has been the danger we've put ourselves in. Walking on narrow ledges and playing with pointy weapons. I don't think the wolves would even kill us if we let them. They'd probably just chew on us without breaking the skin."

Gary said, "That still sounds irritating."

"Yeah," Tyler said, "but not deadly. That's Todd's game. He wants to keep us moving, but he also wants to keep us alive. I bet we could still spend the night in this house, no problem. We'd just have to trap the Gwens here in another room, hopefully one outside of hearing range."

Phillip surveyed the room and said, "I don't know. I mean, I think you're right, but this doesn't seem like a very pleasant place to spend the night."

"Yeah," Gary said. "It would have been before. I think things went sour when I tried to get my freak on."

"Not the first time that's happened," Phillip said. "Perhaps the fact that you call it 'getting your freak on' is part of the problem."

Tyler considered the red-haired zombie Gwen. "They're not really people. They're artificial characters, just like the miners and the wolves. I wonder, if we killed them, would two more pop up in their place, and would they be like these, or would the new ones revert to the way they were before?"

Jimmy said, "I have a better idea. They follow us, right? Why not hitch them up to the sledge? Then we could walk out in front, and they'd pull all the weight."

Without warning, a rectangle of light appeared on the wall and quickly resolved itself into a program window, showing the feed from Todd's webcam. The kitchen visible over his left shoulder was untidy. The living space to his right was no better. He looked tired, unshaven, and angry.

Todd said, "I figured you'd be scared when the ladies all putrefied. I honestly thought you had higher standards than this."

Gary said, "Glad to disappoint you."

Todd took a long sip from the straw of a large carbonated beverage, then said, "I hate you. All of you. I go to all this trouble to create a quest, and you jerks just can't wait to screw it up."

Gary said, "Todd, we didn't screw it up. You did. You made a death trap that won't actually kill us. Who does that?"

"It won't kill you yet, Gary," Todd said. "It will kill you. Make no mistake. I killed Jeff, and I will kill you too, just not yet. Right now I'm just prolonging the suffering."

"Well, that's more reason for us to not cooperate," Tyler said, folding his arms.

Todd looked down at the four of them and let out a long breath.

"Look," he said. "You're right. A lot of the stuff I've thrown at you so far has been designed to keep you moving without actually killing you. I saw that you were on to it on day one."

"When I told you that I was on to you," Tyler suggested.

Todd ignored him. "The wolves seemed to work okay, so I figured you'd forgotten, but the river rocks showed that you hadn't. I've been calibrating the later challenges to be more dangerous. I just hadn't gotten to the temptresses yet. Don't worry, from here on out, the dangers you face will be real. Actually, I guess you should worry."

"So you say," Jimmy said. "But why shouldn't we just assume that you're just saying that to scare us, and that you'll go right back to prolonging our agony?"

Todd leaned into the camera so that his face filled the entire window. "Because you idiots are getting on my nerves now, and I'm not really interested in prolonging my own agony. I plan to take a more active role in things from now on. I'm really looking forward to watching you die, one at a time, for my amusement. I'm getting impatient."

"Well, fine," Jimmy said. "We'll just get a good night's sleep in this house you've provided for us; then tomorrow we'll hitch your sisters here up to our sledge and we can all get on with it."

Todd smiled. "You're welcome to spend the night. In fact, let me make it a little cozier for you."

At the bottom of the window, the tops of Todd's hands moved a bit. The familiar sound of a computer keyboard filtered up. Fire flared from the corners of the room and raced along the edge of the floor as if following a trail of gasoline. The flames consumed the corners of the floor, leaving an ever-decreasing area in which the wizards could stand. The walls of the building began to creak and groan. The ceiling bowed downward alarmingly.

Phillip joined Tyler, Gary, and Jimmy in the middle of the room. The Gwens receded into the inferno and were engulfed. Waves of unbearable heat lashed the wizards. Tyler pointed toward the door and shouted, "Typical!"

The others saw that there was a narrow, flame-free path leading to the front door, which was open, offering a clear view of the cold night air outside.

"Gosh, Todd, I get the feeling you might want us to go outside," Tyler shouted at Todd, whose image was still leering at them from the wall.

Todd said, "You picked up on that, eh? Well, you'd better get to it. I can force you to move on with fire, or I could just fill the building with wolves. Ooh! Or, how's this idea grab you? Fire wolves! I'll have to work on that. In the meantime . . ."

As Todd's voice trailed off, the heat intensified. The flames leapt higher into the air and started to work their way up the walls. The wizards could feel their skin crisping, and they instinctively ran for the door.

Because of where he'd been standing when the flames appeared, Phillip was the last one in line as they dashed for the exit. Even as his feet were fleeing the heat, some part of Phillip's brain realized that he was also fleeing into the cold and that he didn't have his fur cloak or even his three robes to protect him from the chill. He noticed again that there were coat hooks on the wall next to the door. There were still garments hanging from the hooks. Since the cabin had transformed, they were now dusty and covered with cobwebs and mildew. A few of them were on fire, but the others seemed serviceable. He didn't have time to make a careful selection, so he snatched the two largest and least flaming objects as he fled through the door and out into the chill night air.

They stood a safe distance from the blazing cabin, panting and feeling grateful to be safe until Gary pointed toward the inferno and yelled, "The rock!" The heavy lump of dull gray dailuaine ore was where they'd left it, less than five feet from the porch, which meant that now it, and the very flammable wooden sledge that made it easier to transport, were less than five feet from the fire. As they watched, they could see smoke rising from the raw timbers of the sledge.

They ran back toward the fire. They pushed and heaved and attempted to smother the flames with curse words. Finally they got the sledge back to where they'd been, a safe distance from the fire, and panted from their exertion, grateful to be alive.

"Well," Jimmy heaved between breaths, "at least we won't have trouble keeping warm tonight."

The flaming cabin extinguished as suddenly as if someone had flipped a switch, because that's essentially what had happened.

Jimmy glanced at the sky and said, "Good one."

Phillip stumbled over to the two garments he'd rescued from the fire. He'd thrown them on the ground when they dashed back to save the sledge. Now he had time to shake the dirt out of them and see exactly what he had.

The larger and warmer-looking of the two items turned out to be a fur coat, a slinky, full-length silver-and-gray-striped ladies' fur that instantly tore at the shoulder seams when he put it on and would not close around his middle. On the plus side, the fur was thick, warm, and soft, with a high collar that would help keep his neck and ears from getting cold, and large cuffs that would help protect his hands. The others watched him test his range of motion, each gyration of his torso accompanied by a small tearing sound from the shoulder seams.

Tyler looked at the second item lying on the ground and asked, "What else did you get?"

Phillip lifted the garment and held it up in the moonlight. It was a tank top, made of shiny black plastic. It had surprising cutouts in obvious places.

Phillip said, "I don't believe it would fit."

Tyler said, "Thanks for not trying."

16.

Fighting their way through the reconstituted soldier corps had really taken a toll. Brit, Gwen, Roy, and Martin put what they thought was a safe distance between themselves and the spot where eventually twice as many soldiers would appear, then unanimously agreed to rest for the night. They took turns keeping watch and ended up sleeping well into the next day.

They still did not make great time, now being overtired from too much sleep. They covered about half the distance back to the mine, camped for the night again, and finally returned to the Mines of Mortlach late on the next day.

The miners fell into an awed silence as they entered the mine, Gwen in the lead, carrying the ornate birdcage holding the frozen mechanical bird. At first, they worried that the miners would see that something was wrong with Oban, but those fears died when they reached Blandoch, the head of the mining guild. He stood along the back wall, next to an identical birdcage in which an identical mechanical bird was whistling and fluttering joyfully.

Blandoch looked like a child on Christmas morning as he took the second cage from Gwen. He peered at the frozen bird inside. The other bird, in the cage that sat on the plinth, chirped happily, and Blandoch, never removing his eyes from the frozen canary, giggled with delight.

Blandoch placed the cage in his hands on the plinth, knocking the other birdcage on the ground in the process as if he did not see it. When the new cage was sitting on the plinth for which it was clearly designed, the Oban in the cage that had just clattered to the floor flew a neat loop-the-loop in its cage and landed back on his perch, which was impressive, as the cage was on its side and the perch was perpendicular to the ground.

The miners cheered. Blandoch stared delightedly at the frozen bird while the nonfrozen copy's tweets and chirps rose from the floor.

Blandoch turned to Gwen and the others and said, "You've lived up to your part of the bargain. You've returned our beloved friend Oban to his rightful home." Blandoch faced his fellow miners, spreading his arms wide and raising his voice. "And now that he is back, we miners can mine again!"

The miners cheered.

Blandoch turned back and in a quieter voice said, "Now it is time for us to fulfill our half of the bargain. You came looking for dailuaine, did you not?"

Martin said, "Yeah, I guess."

"And you will have it," Blandoch said. He leaned down and picked up his golden pickaxe, which was partially covered by Oban's cage. Lifting the axe sent the cage and its twittering occupant rolling across the floor. He grabbed a lantern that was hanging from a spike on the wall.

"Now that Oban is back," he said, "I can go mine it for you."

Blandoch walked toward the mine entrance at the rear of the chamber.

Roy said, "You forgot your bird."

Blandoch did not seem to hear him.

Roy continued. "Miners need canaries to tell them when there's too much CO_2."

"Yeah," Brit agreed.

"Then why isn't he taking the bird with him?"

Brit said, "Maybe because it's not a real bird."

"Or a real mine," Gwen added.

"Or a real miner," Martin said.

Blandoch got to the mine entrance, paused, then took a single step into the shaft. He looked at the ceiling and walls of the mine, then focused on a seemingly empty patch of ground.

Blandoch put down the lantern and swung the pickaxe downward. It stopped abruptly and rung as if it had struck something solid, although it had stopped in midair. He put down the pick, then mimed as if he were lifting something heavy and round with both hands. He carried the invisible sphere back and presented it to Gwen, saying, "Gentlemen, you have done us a great service this day, and it is our honor to present you with this dailuaine."

Gwen looked at the empty space between Blandoch's hands, then looked to her compatriots and shrugged. The three of them shrugged back, so she turned and put her hands out, accepting whatever it was that Blandoch was offering. Blandoch carefully placed the nothing in Gwen's arms, and she immediately let out a startled grunt and started shaking and sinking toward the ground.

"It weighs a ton," she said. "Help!"

Martin dove forward to help her carry her burden, but he could not see her burden and ended up jamming his fingers on the void, which caused him to yelp in pain and surprise. The force of Martin striking the invisible mass caused Gwen to lose control of it. It rolled out of her hands, away from Martin.

Gwen had not seen Roy lurching toward her on the other side to try to help her with her load. Because her load was invisible, she did not see it land directly on Roy's foot with an audible thud. Roy yelled and cursed and reached down with both hands and pushed whatever it was off his foot.

While Roy checked for broken toes, and Martin checked for broken fingers, Brit went to the spot where she estimated that a heavy, round object would stop rolling. She carefully explored the area with her foot until she found what she was looking for. She crouched down, felt the contours of the object, and when she was convinced that she knew where it was and what shape it was, Brit sat on it. She seemed to hover in an impossible squatting position.

Okay, Brit thought. *We've got something invisible that we're going to have to transport who knows how far. We have to do something to make it visible. Think, Brit. What is the most visible thing you know? Something you can't miss, something obnoxiously obvious.*

Brit thought for a moment before saying, "Martin, can I borrow your robe?"

17.

After more hiking through what the wizards had dubbed Falling Wolf Forest, the path led them to a town. A smattering of nearly identical buildings was the backdrop for a set of nearly identical peasants doing obviously repetitive things. A man whittled. A woman kneaded dough. A child ran in a circle for no apparent reason. It was all clearly designed to be just convincing enough to be boring. A stack of damp hay here, a chicken darting across the street there. A dilapidated oxcart tucked between two buildings. The wizards' eyes were drawn to the only interesting thing in the town, a blacksmith shop set in the center of the village like a jewel in a setting. It wasn't a workshop so much as a large open pen with a rough awning overhead and a metal sign out front that said "Ye Olde Towne Smithy." Beyond that, Phillip couldn't make out any detail. Just motion, flame, and rhythmic clanking noises.

It was Phillip's turn to drag the sledge, and he was good and tired of it. He didn't really mind so much, though, because he was also tired of not pulling the sledge at this point, so it made little difference. Phillip chose not to slow down and lose momentum. He knew that the next step in the quest was to have the cursed chunk of ore he was dragging fashioned into some sort of weapon, so he assumed that the blacksmith shop was his destination. He leaned forward, the taut rope wrapped over his shoulder, resting on his full-length fur vest. The collar stood high, warming his ears. The sleeves had long since fallen away and now were wrapped around his forearms like leg warmers on a dancer on the cover of a Jazzercise video.

Jimmy approached the woman who was endlessly kneading a large lump of bread dough and asked, "Pardon me, can you tell me, is this the town called Bowmore?" Jimmy held no illusions about having a real conversation or about his courtesy even being noticed. He was polite out of habit.

As with all of Todd's artificial creations, her response almost fit the question, but not quite. "How can ye not know where you are? This be the town of Bowmore."

Jimmy said, "Right, thanks" and moved on.

They reached the blacksmith's shop and left the sledge and its heavy cargo out front. They weren't particularly worried that anyone would try to steal it. Knowing how difficult it had been to get here, they would have enjoyed watching someone try.

Under the awning, there was a smoking black pile of bricks with a fiery hole in the front, like a New York City pizza oven, only much hotter and slightly dirtier. All around, laid out on metal racks, there were metal implements, all clearly used to form more metal implements. Every vertical surface was covered with handmade hasps, hinges, nails, hooks, and horseshoes. In the center of the room, a tall man with arms thicker than a normal man's legs was using tongs and brute force to bend a glowing metal bar.

Tyler took the lead in interacting with the blacksmith. He was over any pretense at playing along with the fantasy of this quest. They were not knights performing tasks to fulfill some prophecy. They were mice trapped in a poorly made maze, trying to find their way out as efficiently as possible. Pretending that this blacksmith was anything other than a preprogrammed puppet was a waste of time at best, and a source of entertainment for their tormenter at worst.

The blacksmith stopped hammering the glowing metal and turned his soot-covered face to look at Tyler.

"Greetings, stranger," the blacksmith said. "How does this day find you?"

Tyler said, "We got the rock," and pointed over his shoulder, toward the sledge that waited out front.

The blacksmith put down his soot-encrusted tools and walked to a soot-encrusted basin, which seemed to be full of a mixture of equal parts water and soot. He "washed" his hands and dried them on a soot-black towel, saying, "I am Inchgower, skilled blacksmith and crafter of fine weapons."

Tyler said, "We got the rock."

The blacksmith nodded as if listening intently, then said, "Aye, 'tis a long journey to be sure. I'm certain you didn't come all this way without good reason."

Tyler said, "We got the rock."

The blacksmith raised his eyebrows. "I see. You've come to the right place, but sadly, I cannot help you."

Tyler rolled his eyes and made the motion of a yakking mouth to Gary, then repeated, "We got the rock."

"I know all about the prophecy," the blacksmith explained, "but to make the weapon you need, I require certain raw materials, materials that have not been available for quite some time, I'm afraid."

Tyler glanced back at Phillip, who chuckled lightly. Tyler turned with a flourish, motioned toward the sledge with much fluttering of hands, bowed deeply, and said, "We got the rock."

Inchgower dropped the soot-soaked towel on the soot-covered floor and walked slowly past the wizards to the front of the shop. He gazed down in amazement at the dull gray lump of stone they had dragged all the way from the mine. "You have it," he said. "You managed to procure the dailuaine. I cannot believe it."

Gary said, "We got the rock."

"I can handle this, Gary," Tyler said.

Inchgower spread his massive arms wide, turned to face the wizards, and said, "Gentlemen, I will make you your weapon."

He stood there, almost motionless, cycling through some small subroutine designed to make him seem less statue-like while he waited for the next bit of stimulus to which he would respond.

Tyler looked back at the others, then looked at the cheerful, benevolent look on Inchgower's face. Tyler sighed. "What's the catch?"

Inchgower laughed and seized Tyler by the shoulders, shaking him slightly. "We will need bricks! Lots of bricks, my friends. Come with me—there are wheelbarrows out back."

Sometime later, and several hundred yards away, the wizards stood beside a massive clay pit. They had found a seemingly endless row of recently sun-dried bricks that were just irregular enough to make it painfully obvious that Todd had only created a few of them, then endlessly replicated those. Much like Chicken McNuggets, the slight variations only made them seem more identical.

"Fantastic," Phillip said. "Todd's going to try to work us to death."

Gary said, "Oh, I dunno. This might not be so bad. A little physical activity might be nice for a change."

"Nice for a change?" Phillip asked. "Doesn't hiking count as physical activity? Because it seems to me that's all we do anymore."

"That's my point," Gary said, stretching his back, limbering up. "We've been doing the same things over and over. Maybe this'll break up the monotony."

"Ah, I see," Phillip said. "Stacking and hauling bricks seems like a source of variety and mental stimulation to you."

"At least it'll work the upper body," Gary said, stretching his hamstrings. "We haven't really been doing all that much with our arms."

Tyler asked, "What about sledge dragging?"

"And wolf stabbing?" Jimmy added.

"Yeah, I see your point," Gary allowed, "but you have to admit, we've been working the same muscle groups over and over. This will give us a chance to hit some new ones. See my point?"

The other three made eye contact for a moment, silently reaching a consensus; then Phillip said, "No, we don't."

Gary exhaled. "Look, I'm just trying to keep a positive attitude. Is that okay with you?"

Again they silently took a vote. Again Phillip spoke for the group.

"No, it isn't."

They piled as many bricks as they dared into the two wheel-barrows and, as was now their custom, took turns maneuvering them back to Inchgower's shop.

Inchgower was waiting for them to arrive. He rubbed his hands together excitedly, generating a small cloud of soot in the process. "Good work. Well done. You can unload them right here." Inchgower pointed to a specific bare patch of ground and made it clear that he would not move again until all the bricks were unloaded.

No sooner had Jimmy placed the final brick on the stack than Inchgower sprang back to life, bustling around his shop, gathering certain tools he would need, and clearing work space in the middle of the floor. Inchgower rummaged through his tool rack, and when he turned to them, he had four shovels that had seemed to appear from nowhere. He said, "Now, we're ready for the clay."

Later, they returned from the clay pits, carrying well-used shovels and fully loaded wheelbarrows. Their arms, like their tools, were coated up to their shoulders in a thin gray coat of cracking clay.

"This stuff is gonna take forever to wash off," Tyler complained.

"Nah," Gary reassured him, "I bet it'll dry and most of it will crack off on its own. In the meantime, we'll all look like the Thing, and that's always cool."

"Yeah," Tyler said, "that's what the Thing was famous for, looking cool."

They hauled the wheelbarrows full of wet clay to the rear of Inchgower's shop. Predictably, Inchgower was waiting for them with vague praise and specific instructions.

They unloaded the clay in a sullen, exhausted manner, but they did it all the same. Inchgower stood almost motionless, pointing at the spot where they were piling the wet clay, waiting for them to finish. Jimmy was just about to gather the last shovelful from the wheelbarrow when he stopped. The others looked on, puzzled.

"Come on," Phillip said. "Let's get this over with."

"No," Jimmy said. "Let's not get this over with." He put down his shovel and sat in the shade for a moment. It did not take long for the others to get the idea. They rested for a while, ate some wolf jerky, explored the town a bit, and got a good night's sleep under the awning that formed the roof of Inchgower's shop; all the while, Inchgower stood silently, pointing to the clay pile, waiting for them to complete their task. When they were good and ready, they moved the last shovel of clay.

"Well done, lads," Inchgower said. "Now we can start making things."

Inchgower led them from the rear of his workshop to a spot out front and said, "We'll start by making a pile of bricks! Bring in the bricks, and I'll tell you how they should be stacked."

Tyler asked, "Why can't we just stack them behind the shop, where they already are? And already in a stack, for that matter."

He hadn't expected a real answer, but when Inchgower said, "There's a good lad," it was particularly unsatisfying.

Phillip reminded him of the real answer. "Because Todd designed this whole thing to irritate us, remember? He knows we didn't become wizards, or get into computers in the first place, because we love manual labor."

The wizards took their time, but they did as they were told. Each time they'd return from out back with an armload of bricks, Inchgower would talk them through the process of stacking them. Soon, they had a solid square base, three feet long and three feet wide, with the beginnings of walls that had small holes along the base.

"Splendid," Inchgower said. "Now one of you will bring some of the clay to my worktable, and the rest of you will continue building the walls. You should be able to keep going without instructions from here."

Jimmy, Gary, and Phillip spent a good long time stacking the heavy bricks, piling up the walls of whatever they were building. Inchgower instructed Tyler (most likely because he was standing closest to Inchgower at the time) to bring him some clay and place it on a worktable.

When the clay was on the table, Inchgower said, "More clay, please."

After several repetitions of this cycle, Inchgower thanked Tyler, then got to work. Work, in this case, meant moving his hands in a vague, repetitive manner so as to give the impression that something was getting accomplished without ever actually touching the clay. After a few seconds of this, the heap of clay disappeared and was replaced by some sort of vessel, like a crude pot made of soft clay, about eight inches across and a foot tall, with thick walls.

"If Todd can have all this crap done automatically," Gary asked, "why are we having to do any of this?"

Phillip said, "To go into detail about the things the black-smith has to do, the skilled labor, that would be extra work for Todd, so he glosses over it. The stuff that's extra work for us to do, the grunt labor, that's easy for him to just order us to do, so we're getting all that in exquisite detail."

When the brick structure was an almost perfect three-foot cube, Inchgower stopped construction. He put the pot he'd made, and a lid he'd quickly slapped together for it, in his forge fire and closed the metal door.

"We'll just let that harden for a while." He turned his back to them, poking around his tool rack. When he turned back around, he had four large hand scoops. "In the meantime, lads, we'll be needin' charcoal, and plenty of it."

Hours later, they returned from the surprisingly distant bonfire pit, dyed pitch-black with coal dust and pushing wheel-barrows piled high with chunks of charcoal.

They unloaded the charcoal, triggering Inchgower to tell them to pack clay around the walls of the cube but to leave the holes in the cube's bottom accessible.

Their arms had no strength left, so packing the wet clay onto the cube seemed to take forever. Their hands were caked with sweat, dust, clay, and soot, and they were too exhausted to care.

Inchgower removed the crude cylindrical pot from his forge and told the wizards to get a good night's sleep. "For tomorrow, you do battle."

Phillip said, "Yup, fair enough," as he settled into his bed-roll. After the half second his brain needed to process what he'd heard, he sat bolt upright and asked, "Wait, what? Do battle? We're not here to fight anything. We're here to make a weapon."

Inchgower nodded in inappropriate agreement. "In order to complete my work, I will need a bone from a wretched beast known to the villagers as Strathisla. It comes once a fortnight to eat a villager. We have been quite powerless to stop it. You will slay the monster for us. I will consider that my payment for all of my work."

Gary asked, "Your work? You've been working?" But being, essentially, a recording, Inchgower ignored him.

"When you have killed Strathisla, bring me one of the beast's bones so I can channel its strength into your weapon."

Inchgower smiled like a doctor telling a new father that he has a healthy baby. "Sleep well, for as fortune has it, Strathisla attacks tomorrow."

The wizards reacted like a new father who had expected the doctor to tell him that his wife had appendicitis.

18.

The next morning, shortly after dawn, Phillip, Jimmy, Gary, and Tyler were lined up across the road through Bowmore like gunslingers waiting for a long-overdue showdown, except that they had swords and had no idea who or what they'd be fighting.

The artificial villagers were locked into some sort of "acting terrified" subroutine. They would peek out the windows of the buildings, then emerge to sprint across the street, darting into a building on the other side of the street so they could peek out different windows.

"What do you think it will be?" Gary asked anyone who'd answer.

Phillip said, "Something with bones. That's all we know."

Gary considered this. "Well, that narrows it down a bit."

"Not really," Phillip said.

"Sure it does," Gary explained. "At least we know we won't be fighting a giant slug. That's good, at least."

"Giant slug? That's what you're worried about? A giant slug?"

Gary rolled his eyes. "Phillip, do you want to fight a giant slug?"

"No. You put it that way, I have to admit I don't want to fight a giant slug."

Gary said, "Good. Apology accepted."

Phillip started to react, but he saw both Jimmy and Tyler subtly shaking their heads and decided they were right.

They waited.

An old lady ran across the street.

The wind picked up.

A bird whistled in the distance.

A young boy ran across the street.

The wind gust died away.

Somewhere nearby, a cat hissed.

The old lady ran back across the street to where she started. A seam ripped open in the ground, and a dark blur shot out, grabbing the woman by the leg and dragging her underground before the seam reclosed.

They all looked at each other, then back at the empty patch of ground.

"Do you think that was it?" Gary asked.

The seam reopened, more slowly this time and with a terrible rumbling noise. From their point of view, the fissure in the ground looked like a black line that extended in opposite directions, curving away from the men and eventually reconnecting dozens of feet away. The broad, flat surface they had thought was solid ground lifted and tilted back. Beneath, supporting the road's weight, there was some sort of dark, movable mass. For what seemed like a long time, but was probably less than five seconds, Phillip struggled to make sense of what he was seeing. It looked like two large, broken umbrellas were fighting. Soon, his brain figured out what he was looking at, and he could not unrecognize it, no matter how badly he wanted to.

The spider was a little over ten feet tall and at least thirty feet across, with long, spindly legs and a body covered with thick black fur. It cast away the roof of its burrow as easily as a man in a sauna casts off his towel, and like the other men in the sauna, the wizards instantly wished it hadn't.

Phillip's mind was paralyzed with fear. Jimmy and Gary seemed equally speechless. Tyler was suffering no such problem.

"A giant spider?! Seriously?! Damn you, Todd, you idiot. Just when I think I couldn't respect you less, you go and pull this!"

The spider stopped moving, which would have been comforting if everything else, the villagers, the trees, the wind, everything, hadn't stopped as well. Silently, Todd's chat box blinked open in front of the spider, almost as if his unshaven face were the spider's.

Todd smirked down at them and said, "What's the matter, Tyler? Don't like spiders?"

"I got no problem with spiders, but I hate a cliché! Giant spiders are in everything! They've been done to death. If this is the best you could do, you shouldn't have bothered."

Todd looked genuinely confused and more than a little hurt. "But, it's a trap-door spider. Every time you see a giant spider, it's spinning a giant web. Nobody's done a giant trap-door spider. That's a new idea."

"Just because nobody's done it doesn't mean it's a new idea. It might just mean that it's a bad idea," Tyler explained. "Think about it! The blacksmith said that the monster comes every two weeks. Well, if it's a trap-door spider, that means it's here, hiding down there in its hole all the time."

Todd frowned. "I didn't think about that."

"You didn't think at all. You needed a monster, your brain

spit out the words 'big honkin' spider,' and you called it good. You gave no thought to the fact that it came to you so quickly because you've seen it a thousand times."

"Well, it's only been used so many times because it works so well," Todd said.

Tyler replied, "I've got two things to say about that. One: just because a giant spider might work in this case doesn't mean that something original wouldn't work as well or better. Two: a spider doesn't work in this case. Not at all! Because spiders *don't have bones!* We're supposed to bring back the monster's bones. You've given us a monster that has an exoskeleton! That's a hard outer shell, which means no bones!"

Todd smirked and shook his head. "What about octopuses? They don't have hard shells."

Tyler asked, "So what? Octopuses aren't spiders."

"Yeah, they are. They're the spiders of the sea."

"No, they aren't!"

"Huh? What?" Todd sputtered. "How are octopuses not spiders?"

"What do you mean, how are they not spiders? They're not spiders in the same way you're not a spider!" Tyler shrieked.

"But they've got eight legs," Todd explained. "'Octo' means eight. That's why Doctor Octopus has eight robot arms."

Tyler shook his fists and sprayed saliva as he shouted, "No! Doctor Octopus did not have eight robot arms! He had his normal four human limbs and four robot limbs! That equaled eight, like an octopus!"

"Or a spider," Todd said, thinking.

"Yes!"

"Because octopuses are part of the spider family."

"No, they aren't, and this whole conversation is pointless anyway because octopuses don't have bones either!"

Todd said, "Eight legs, no bones, but you're sure they aren't spiders."

Jimmy cleared his throat, then said, "Actually, marine biologists will tell you that octopuses have two legs and six arms."

Tyler said, "Let me handle this, Jimmy," without looking back.

Todd pinched the bridge of his nose and closed his eyes for a moment; then he said, "Look, okay, you have a point. Giant spiders have been done before, but that doesn't mean I'm not going to do something new with it."

"Like what?" Tyler asked.

"Maybe it'll attack you in a way you aren't expecting."

"It's a spider," Tyler said, flatly. "I'm pretty sure it'll involve webs and venom."

Todd smiled slyly and said, "Maybe."

"It's a spider!" Tyler was yelling again. "What else can it do?! Did you teach it kung fu?!"

Phillip leaned to Gary and said, "Ooh, a spider that knows kung fu. That'd actually be quite cool, wouldn't it? I wouldn't want to be on the receiving end of an eight-legged roundhouse kick."

Gary said, "Nah, man. Aren't you listening? Spiders have two legs and six arms."

Jimmy said, "That's octopuses."

Gary rolled his eyes. "And octopuses are the spiders of the sea. Come on, keep up, guys."

Jimmy was about to respond when he, Gary, and Phillip became aware that both Tyler and Todd were staring at them.

"Sorry," Jimmy said. "We'll discuss this later. Please, continue bickering."

Todd struck a conciliatory tone. "Tyler, I know that you don't think much of my quest. That's fine. You're entitled to your opinion. Complain all you want—just know that you're going to be complaining while you're completing the quest or dying in the process. No amount of whining will get you out of it. Right now, that means fighting my giant spider. And just to remind you, the spider can, and probably will, kill you. Remember, from here on in, as per your suggestion, everything can kill you."

Todd's chat window disappeared. The wind resumed blowing. The trees resumed swaying. Strathisla the giant spider resumed its climb out of the massive crater it had been using as its trap.

Tyler muttered, "How would it even dig such a large hole without the villagers noticing?"

"Tyler? Focus," Phillip said.

Tyler said, "You're right. Okay, guys. Don't let it bite you. Watch out for webs. Try to attack its eyes if its head gets close; otherwise go for the leg joints. Those are its weak spots."

"How do you know?" Gary asked.

"Because those are always the weak spots."

Phillip looked at the spider, and the spots where the leg segments met did seem thin and vulnerable. The eyes are universal weak spots no matter who or what you were fighting, so Tyler's advice seemed sound.

The spider was completely out in the open now. It slowly crept toward the wizards. They unsheathed their swords and readied themselves for action. As it loomed over them, Tyler said, "If it does kung fu, I'm going to be so pissed."

The spider planted all eight feet and leaned back, holding its body close to the ground as if preparing to leap forward, then froze.

The wizards held their ground, watching for the slightest movement.

The spider didn't seem to be in any hurry to move. The fur on its carapace ruffled and fluttered in the breeze. The thick black fur swayed, undulating like wheat in a field.

That's odd, Phillip thought, *it's not that windy. The breeze must be stronger over there.*

As they watched, the fur seemed to lengthen, growing spikier, like a time-lapse film in an ad for the Chia Pet; the fur seemed to spread up the spider's immense legs. It streamed off the spider's body, onto its legs. Only as the fur started to reach the ground did they see that it was never fur at all, just the legs of thousands of smaller spiders. They spread from the eight points where they made contact with the ground, swelling into a writhing black pool of horror.

The smaller spiders looked tiny gathered around the feet of Strathisla, but each one was about the size of a kitten, which would have been fine if they had been kittens, but they weren't. They were spiders, and as such, they had barely started advancing on the wizards before the wizards did the logical thing, which was to run in four separate directions, screaming four different random strings of curse words.

Gary reached the front door of the nearest hovel. He pushed, then pulled on the door with all of his strength, but it didn't budge. He turned around, pressing his back to the immovable door, and saw that the mass of smaller spiders had broken into four streams, each one chasing a wizard. Phillip had tried the door of a cottage across the street, with the same amount of success as Gary. Jimmy was climbing a tree. Tyler had run halfway back to the blacksmith shop before stopping and turning to survey the situation.

Gary called out, "Tyler! Does this always happen?"

Todd's voice filled the air. "Yeah, Tyler, does it?"

"Shut up," Tyler said. "Both of you."

Tyler instantly realized both that stopping was a mistake and that it was too late to undo the damage. The spiders were faster than he was and had nearly reached him by the time he'd stopped. He lurched to the left and then to the right, but the skittering mass swelled in whatever direction he moved, trying to flank him, and then advancing when he moved away from them. In trying unsuccessfully to pursue him, the spiders had managed to block him in on three sides. He ran a few more steps away from the mass, but looking at the ground as he ran, he could see that the spiders were advancing as a group, outpacing him on each side. Within a few more steps they had surrounded him. Tyler had no choice but to stop. He cast a desperate glance at the others, hoping they were in a position to help.

Gary had climbed the façade of the hut he'd tried to enter and was now standing on its roof, which would have been a brilliant move if spiders were bad at climbing walls. That not being the case, the spiders were advancing up the walls of the hut.

Phillip, uncharacteristically, was taking Gary's lead and had just made it to the roof of a hovel across the street. He stood up, looked down at the spiders climbing the wall behind him, and said, "Of course."

Jimmy had climbed a tree, which had worked out better in some ways, worse in others. The single, narrow tree trunk had limited how many spiders could chase him up the tree at once. It had also limited his obvious means of escape to one, the same narrow tree trunk that was now bulging with angry spiders. Jimmy had moved out to a thick lower limb. The central mass of the tree was alive with spiders, as if the tree were covered with thick, black, wriggling foliage. The spiders ventured out onto Jimmy's limb but stopped three feet short of his location.

Jimmy looked down at the closest spider, confused. He looked toward Phillip, stranded on his rooftop. Tyler looked to Phillip's location as well and saw that Phillip was standing in the center of a circle about six feet wide, a circle delineated by an ever-thickening mass of spiders. Tyler looked at Gary and found that he, too, was surrounded but unharmed.

Tyler realized that he probably should have been swarmed and devoured by now. He looked down. He was also standing in a clear circle. The fact that he was still alive didn't feel so much like a reprieve as a delay. He had no doubt that this was just a brief pause to let them be terrified before they were killed.

Tyler drew his sword.

Oh well, he thought. *At least the spiders aren't doing kung fu.*

Tyler heard a strange, low chittering sound come from the tangle of spiders at his feet. He looked down just in time to see a single spider spring free from the rest and fly directly toward his face. He killed it in midair with a single chop of his sword and readied himself to feel the other spiders cover him.

It did not happen.

Tyler looked down at the spiders and again heard the queer, low chattering, this time to his right. He spun, looked down, and saw a single spider in the group pressed down as if ready to leap. It sprang for Tyler's face. He dispatched it as he had the first. Scowling, Tyler scanned the spiders, listening for the sound again. It was difficult over the sound of the other guys' yelling, but Tyler focused on the spiders. He heard the sound, spun 180 degrees, and saw what he had both hoped and feared he would see: a single spider, surrounded by hundreds of its seemingly passive brethren, hunched down, preparing to strike alone.

He dispatched it easily, then shouted to the others, "Relax. The hack used the same stupid AI as he did for the wolves."

"We know!" Phillip shrieked. "Behind you! Now!"

Tyler had made it three-quarters of the way to the blacksmith shop before stopping and getting surrounded. He had pivoted and was standing with his left side toward the shop and his right toward the others. He glanced back to his right and saw Phillip, Gary, and Jimmy, all stuck in high places, surrounded by kitten-sized spiders on an otherwise empty street. He spun 180 degrees just in time to see Strathisla, the building-sized spider, shooting a web his way.

The sensation was like having someone dump a cooler full of Gatorade on you, only instead of being cold, it's sticky, and instead of meaning that you've won a game, it means that you're about to be eaten.

In an instant Tyler's legs were glued together, his left arm was cemented across his belly, and his right arm, which he'd used to shield his face, was now stuck immovably to his forehead. He wriggled, hopped, then fell over backward. The smaller spiders scattered to get out of his way, maintaining their respectful distance. None of them made the sound that signaled an imminent attack. It seemed that Strathisla had licked him, and as such, had claimed him.

The others watched Tyler squirming helplessly in the dirt and Strathisla slowly advancing in on him. Jimmy looked back to the central mass of the tree just in time to swat down an attacking spider. The tree, save for the branch on which he was stranded, was a living mass of arachnids. There was no way to crawl through them, and even if he could, Tyler would be dead before he even made it to the trunk of the tree, let alone the ground. Another spider chittered and sprang for Jimmy's face. He cut it in half with his sword and watched as the parts fell to the ground.

The empty ground, about ten feet beneath him.

Jimmy, he chastised himself, *I thought you were supposed to be smart.*

Jimmy hung from the branch by one arm, bringing himself a few feet from the ground. He let go of the tree and hit the ground running. If he'd looked back, he'd have seen the spiders cascading out of the tree like a black, hairy waterfall, but he didn't look back.

Tyler's vision was severely limited, blocked mostly by his own right arm. His field of view had been reduced to an irregular peephole formed by the crook of his elbow and the right side of his nose. He could see his body, covered with webbing, his feet gummed together beyond that, and beyond his feet, Strathisla advancing toward him. The smaller spiders parted, clearing a path to Tyler. He struggled, attempting to propel himself away from the immense spider, but squirming with all his might he only managed to move a few inches. He chose not to give Todd the satisfaction.

He thought, *So this is it. The end.*

He saw the spider slowly closing on him. He couldn't tell if it was being cautious or savoring the moment, but he didn't really think it mattered.

Killed fighting against a tired cliché. I guess there's some satisfaction in that for a writer. Not as much as there'd be in defeating the cliché, but you can't have everything.

Strathisla was close now; all he could see was the underside of its abdomen as it loomed over him. Tyler felt the spider lift him from the ground. His view of the world became a blur of blue and brown as it spun him, wrapping him with webbing. He felt nauseated. He pressed his eyes shut and braced himself. He knew in a second his vision would be completely blocked by webbing. After that, he didn't know what would come next, but he knew it wouldn't be pleasant. Would he get bitten and killed by venom? Would he suffocate, trapped like a mummy in the spider's web? Would he be left helpless to die of thirst, unable to free himself? Maybe Strathisla and the smaller spiders would simply devour him alive.

What happened was that he fell to the ground, landing square on his back.

Tyler opened his eyes. His field of view was even smaller, the bottom half being occluded by webbing. At first he saw a blurred, spinning field of black, but Strathisla took an awkward step back, allowing Tyler to see that the spider was missing a leg and had abandoned him to instead fight off the person who had removed that leg: Jimmy.

Jimmy yelled and cursed and whooped at the giant spider, obviously attempting to draw its attention. One would have thought that Strathisla's severed leg lying at Jimmy's feet would be enough, but Jimmy wasn't taking any chances.

Jimmy poked toward Strathisla's face with his sword while lunging backward like a man in his sixties imitating an Olympic fencer, which is exactly who Jimmy was and what he was doing. The smaller spiders that had chased him up the tree were now streaming in to surround him. Jimmy suspected they wouldn't attack him now that he had Strathisla's attention. Strathisla seemed to take precedence. Jimmy saw the spiders closing in around him, took one last mad swipe at Strathisla, damaging the lowest joint on its front-right leg, and took off sprinting in the one direction that wasn't quite closed off by arachnids. He had almost waited too long. As it was, he had to leap between a few blank patches of ground like a child on a patterned carpet trying to avoid stepping in the red-hot lava.

Jimmy peeked back over his shoulder just long enough to see that the massive spider was following him. Now he just had to think of something to do with it.

As if on cue, Phillip shouted, "Bring it here!"

Phillip had seen Jimmy's dismount from the tree. It gave him an idea. The spiders were maintaining a given distance from him. What if he moved? More to the point, what if he moved to the corner of the roof? On flat ground he could never leap over the spiders. There were just too many. If he could get to the corner of the cottage, though, half the spiders would be clinging to the side like Jimmy's spiders had been clinging to the tree. Then he might be able to jump off the building to the clean ground below. Then he would probably sprain his ankle, fall to the ground, and be surrounded by the spiders again, but it was something to do, and if he managed not to injure himself, he could help save Tyler.

It hadn't come to that. By the time Phillip worked this out and made his way to the edge, pausing a couple of times to fight off the attacking single-file spiders, Jimmy had taken one of Strathisla's legs, and now Strathisla planned to take Jimmy's life.

Phillip got Jimmy's attention, and Jimmy ran straight toward Phillip's position. Phillip glanced at Gary. What he saw was more encouraging than he'd hoped. Gary had clearly watched Phillip and understood what he was doing. Gary was standing at the front edge of the roof he'd claimed, and nodded when he saw Phillip look his way.

Jimmy led Strathisla directly beneath Phillip's perch, followed by a black wave of spiders. Now that their leader was injured, they were all attempting to help it, or kill Jimmy. Either way, they were leaving Tyler alone.

Phillip watched the spider's approach carefully. It was having a great deal of difficulty walking straight. Jimmy had cut off the lower two-thirds of one of its right legs and had injured one joint on another. Phillip pictured his trajectory in his mind's eye, adjusted his grip on his sword, holding it like a small oar; then, when the moment was right, he acted.

Phillip didn't leap so much as fall feetfirst while spinning 180 degrees. He landed on his rear, just to the right of the spider's center, with his feet extending down between Strathisla's right-third and right-rear legs. As he slid down the spider's side, his sword, driven by his momentum, pushed one of Strathisla's remaining right legs into Phillip, then, with a little effort, sheared it off.

Phillip fell to the ground, rolling to absorb the force. The leg flopped forward and tangled with the two remaining working legs on that side.

Strathisla's substantial weight was now supported unevenly, by four functioning legs on one side and one and a half legs on the other. It staggered and spun in a panic. Phillip crawled and scrambled through the forest of lurching legs, emerging to stand next to Jimmy. Now, together, they yelled and cursed and jabbed at the spider with their swords while the sea of smaller spiders advanced; then the two men took off running, Strathisla chasing them as best it could.

Strathisla's difficulty in turning to the left made leading it in front of Gary's shed a bit difficult, but they managed it.

Gary considered trying to impale and kill the spider outright in one blow but decided it was too risky when they already had a plan that was working. Instead, he again followed Phillip's lead, bouncing off the spider's back before falling to the ground, followed by the spider's last fully intact right leg, then the spider itself.

The right side of Strathisla's body rested on the ground, its four pristine left legs struggling to lift the spider, and its one damaged front leg lamely scratching at the ground, unable to even come close to supporting its share of the huge body's weight.

Gary looked to Phillip and Jimmy and asked, "You got this?" Then he sprinted to go de-web Tyler before Phillip was done saying "Yeah."

Tyler's instructions to attack at the leg joints had worked out pretty well, so Phillip and Jimmy followed his second directive, to go for the eyes as another weak point. It was a grisly but effective technique. It wasn't long before Strathisla stopped thrashing and started twitching.

The smaller spiders had followed the action in an orderly manner and kept their distance during the battle with Strathisla, but the instant the large spider seemed to die they flew into some sort of blind panic. They chittered, they ran in circles, they climbed over one another, piling up to four spiders deep in places. They didn't attack Phillip or Jimmy. The men were like two bewildered palm trees on an island amid a violent sea. Then, all at once, the smaller spiders stopped moving, chittering, or even holding their bodies off the ground. They all fell, as a unit, silently, to the ground.

Phillip gently poked at one of the small spiders with his foot. The spider's limp legs dragged behind as Phillip's boot pushed its torso along the ground. It was like kicking an extremely disturbing stuffed animal.

Phillip said, "It's dead."

Tyler said, "Not dead enough." Gary had cut him free, and he was unharmed physically, but he seemed shaken. He'd probably have spider-themed nightmares for years to come, but that was a problem for later.

Gary said, "You ever see a horror movie where the monster was dead the first time it looked dead? No, the spider's not dead yet. It's still got at least one more round in it."

Jimmy looked at Strathisla's face, slack and lifeless, with the handles of his and Phillip's swords protruding from its eyes like toothpicks stuck in two extremely unappetizing olives. "I dunno," he said. "Looks pretty dead to me."

Tyler said, "Gary's right, it doesn't matter. Try this. You two killed it, right? Phillip, you announce that it's dead; then you and Jimmy turn your back and start to walk away."

Phillip shrugged and said, "It is dead." He and Jimmy theatrically turned their backs to the hulking corpse and started walking away, through the sea of foot-sized spiders. Jimmy patted Phillip on the back and said, "Good job, killing that thing."

Phillip replied, "Nice touch."

The spiders through which they were wading suddenly started moving, parting around their feet, leaving the customary clear zone around the two. Behind them they heard a low, rasping noise and then the sound of giant spider feet scraping and clawing at the ground. They turned and saw that, as Tyler had predicted, Strathisla was still alive, and madder than ever.

Of course, it was still missing three and a half legs, and both of its eyes were out of commission as well, so it could do little more than thrash around and sound angry, but still, it was unnerving.

Jimmy said, "Oh, let me get that." He stepped forward, grabbed the handle of his sword, which was protruding from Strathisla's left eye, and twisted it clockwise, ninety degrees.

Strathisla fell limp, as if Jimmy's sword were an off switch, which, in a sense, it was.

The smaller spiders again fell dead, but this time, instead of just lying there, they slowly faded from view. Jimmy and Phillip pulled their swords from Strathisla's head, then watched as the giant spider's remains slowly dissolved away, leaving behind nothing but an immense spider-shaped skeleton.

Gary said, "Okay, yeah. Now it's dead enough."

"Take a good look, guys," Tyler said. "We're the first people in history to ever see a spider's skeleton, because they don't exist! Hear that, Todd?!"

Strathisla's legs were recognizable. Its skull was essentially a smaller, whiter version of its original head. The central mass of the spider's body, where its legs had been connected, was a tangle of small, stout bones, just complex enough to be bewildering but far too simple to actually function. Its abdomen, which on spiders is a large, bulbous appendage behind the legs, was a hollow, round cage of gracefully curving bones.

"Why are there ribs where its butt should be?" Gary asked.

"Because Todd's an idiot," Tyler answered.

On the skeleton's back, at the center of where the legs were connected, one bone stood out from all the others. It didn't seem to be attached to the other bones or to serve any structural purpose. Also, it was glowing.

Gary pointed to the bone and said, "Tyler, would you like to do the honors?"

Tyler scowled and said, "Just get it over with." He turned and walked toward the blacksmith shop. Gary pulled the bone from Strathisla's back, and the rest of the skeleton faded away into nothingness.

They followed Tyler to the shop. Once there, they decided to give it to Inchgower right away, for fear that if they didn't, two Strathislas might regenerate. The blacksmith took the bone. Suddenly every artificial villager in town was there, celebrating with the exact same celebratory song and dance the miners had used when they got their bird back. The villagers built a bonfire and made food. Surprisingly, Inchgower threw Strathisla's bone into the fire. Phillip, Gary, and Jimmy mostly sat and watched the artificial people enjoy their artificial celebration. Tyler excused himself and went to sit alone for a while and think.

That night they put down their bedrolls on Inchgower's floor, as they had before. When the wizards woke up, they were delighted to see Inchgower standing next to the heavy ball of dailuaine ore.

Thank God, Phillip thought. *After all that manual labor and spider fighting, now he'll actually get on to making the weapon, whatever it is.*

As the wizards got up from their bedrolls, Phillip felt an unfamiliar jabbing sensation from the pocket of his jeans. He put his hand in and by touch alone he instantly recognized that there was a ballpoint pen in his pocket. It had not been there when he went to bed.

Phillip surreptitiously pulled out the pen and found a sheet of paper, a page torn from a small notepad, wrapped around the barrel of the pen. Keeping the pen concealed, he made a quick visual survey of the room. Inchgower was standing almost motionless, as was his custom. Jimmy and Gary were rolling up their bedding. Tyler was also putting away his bedding, but he was looking at Phillip as he did it. His manner was so aggressively nonchalant that it couldn't help but get Phillip's attention. Their eyes locked. Tyler glanced quickly toward Phillip's pocket. Phillip nodded, then moved his right hand in such a way as to demonstrate that he was concealing the pen. Tyler immediately turned his attention to his bedding as if nothing had happened.

In the process of rolling up his own bedding, Phillip found a means of concealing and reading the note Tyler had passed. It said:

Todd is probably watching and listening. After we make the weapon, next stop is "Chasm of Certain Doom." We need a plan.

—T

Phillip knew that Tyler was right on all counts, but he didn't have the foggiest idea what to do about it.

Inchgower directed the wizards to remove the chunk of rock from the sledge and bring it into the shop. The rock was heavy enough that one man could carry it with great difficulty, two could move it with some exertion, and three or more could move it with little effort and a great deal of bickering.

When they got the dailuaine into the shop, Inchgower told them to place it on the floor. He turned his back to the wizards and started rummaging around his tools.

"All right," Gary said. "Now's when things start to happen."

Inchgower turned and started handing the wizards hammers and chisels.

"Yes," Phillip said. "Things are happening. Terrible things."

Inchgower pointed to the dailuaine and said, "Now you break the ore into chunks, about an inch square. You see, once I've worked the dailuaine, it will be one of the hardest materials known to man, but in its natural state, it is not as tough."

Phillip knelt down next to the gray chunk of rock. He placed the sharp edge of the chisel on the rock's surface, carefully aimed his hammer blow, and brought the hammer down with all of his might on the chisel. He felt a painful jolt of force run through the bones of his hand and arm. The rebounding hammer nearly hit him in the face. He examined the spot where his chisel had bit into the rock. He could barely make out a scratch.

Inchgower continued. "Of course, it's one of the toughest forms of raw ore in the world as well, but not quite as strong as it will be when it's been worked."

The four of them pounded the rock like prisoners in a cartoon from the 1950s. After most of a day of hammering and chiseling, and cursing Todd's name, the dailuaine was finally reduced to large-bore rubble.

Inchgower gathered the rubble and put it in the pot he had made the day before, which had now hardened. He threw in the burnt spider bone, which crumbled like a dirt clod in his hands. He instructed the wizards to lay down two bricks in the middle of the floor of the brick cube. While they did that, he put a few more items into the pot: an unidentifiable powder and a piece of broken glass. He placed the lid on the pot and put the pot inside the cube.

As the wizards stood, watching Inchgower do the work for a change, Tyler felt something touch one of his hands. He nearly looked down, but then he recognized the sensation as that of a pen being placed in his hand. He took the pen, noted that it had paper rolled around it, and then carefully slid the whole thing into his pocket. After a five count, he ventured a surreptitious glance at Phillip, who nodded.

Soon, it was time to get back to work. While Inchgower supervised via his usual method, standing silently and pointing, the wizards packed the rest of the charcoal into the cube. When the pot was completely buried, the remaining bricks were used to put a domed roof on the structure, and the remaining clay was packed in around the bricks for insulation.

Again they chose to rest for a bit before they covered the last brick with clay, which would cause Inchgower to issue more commands. They sat for a moment and looked at what they'd made.

"Man," Gary said. "That is some kind of ugly."

He wasn't wrong. The unevenness of their amateur brick-laying was not helped by the thick coating of lumpy clay they'd heaped inexpertly on its surface.

"It doesn't have to be pretty," Tyler said. "It just has to be hot. It's a furnace. The charcoal will burn, and the bricks will trap and intensify the heat and melt the ore."

"Makes sense," Phillip said. "What was the deal with the spider bone and the glass?"

Tyler said, "I don't know about the glass, but the bone was to add carbon. There was a time that sword makers would use the bones of their enemies. They thought it would imbue the finished sword with the fallen warrior's might."

Gary said, "So whatever he makes us, it will have the might of a spider."

"A fake spider," Tyler corrected him. "But it seemed to work. The carbon made the finished weapon harder—they just thought it was magic."

"How do you know this stuff?" Gary asked.

"Research. I write fantasy novels. You need to know this kind of stuff. Besides, this is the easiest possible thing to research. Anyone who's been to colonial Williamsburg or watched PBS on a lazy Saturday afternoon has been told this. Todd and I just took notes. I just hope he didn't take notes too well."

Jimmy asked, "Why? What happens next?"

"He lights the charcoal, and it burns for hours while it melts the rocks."

"Sounds hot and boring," Jimmy said.

Tyler said, "If we're lucky."

"What if we're not lucky?"

Tyler stood up and said, "Let's see." He scooped up a handful of clay and slapped it onto the last corner of exposed brick.

Inchgower said, "Well done, lads. Now I'll light the fire and as the charcoal burns down the ore will melt and change into pure, hardened dailuaine."

Gary nodded and mumbled, "Hmm. Okay."

Tyler muttered, "Wait for it."

Inchgower turned to his tool rack, rummaged for a moment, and turned back to them with four large hand-operated bellows in his arms. "And you will use these to pump air into the fire, making it burn hot enough to melt the metal."

Tyler said, "Yup. That's what I was afraid of."

"Yes, all four of you," Inchgower beamed, answering a question Todd had expected them to ask.

Tyler said, "The oxygen, it intensifies the fire."

Inchgower answered a second anticipated but unasked question. "Yes, the entire time."

Tyler said, "I think they usually have people alternate pumping. That way, no one person gets totally exhausted. Everyone stays just exhausted enough."

Inchgower said, "About six hours," answering a question nobody had asked because they feared the answer.

Tyler turned to Jimmy and said, "If it's any consolation, it'll be hot and boring, so you weren't wrong."

19.

Everyone agreed that the task of lugging a heavy chunk of rock was not made easier by having the rock in question also be invisible. Luckily, Brit solved the problem by wrapping it in Martin's silver-sequined wizard robe. Now, instead of looking like empty space, the ore looked like a poorly made disco ball.

The problem of the dailuaine's invisibility was solved easily. The problem of the sledge's invisibility was left unsolved, because they never even knew it had existed. Nobody had ever offered Phillip's party the use of the sledge. They just saw it and chose to use it. Nobody offered the sledge to Brit's party, and they didn't see it (Martin tripped on it at one point but chalked it up to his own clumsiness), so they didn't know it was an option.

They spent some time puzzling over how they would transport the boulder. It was heavy, and its round shape offered no convenient handholds, forcing the carriers to hold its mass out, away from their center of gravity. Gwen and Brit were both in fine shape, but neither of them would be described as large and muscular. Roy was well beyond his physical prime, and Martin was more the fast, wiry type, physically more suited to fleeing than to fighting, preferably doing either without carrying freight.

They discussed balancing the dailuaine on a cushion on their heads, but they decided against it on the grounds that it seemed like a terrible idea.

After a bit of debate, Brit and Gwen asked Martin and Roy if they could borrow their wizard staves. Gwen pawed through her backpack and came out with the sewing kit that Brit the Elder had supplied, presumably for mending clothes and stitching up wounds.

Brit and Gwen silently unwrapped the dailuaine. Brit sat on it to help everyone remember where it was. Gwen tore Martin's robe into two parts.

Martin knew that his robe had been pretty much superfluous ever since they'd arrived. It didn't serve any real purpose here, where he had no powers and where high visibility wasn't always desirable. Martin had worn it under his warm jacket, but he'd done so mainly out of affection for Gwen, who had made the robe in the first place. Still, it gave him a nasty jolt to see it destroyed, even if it was Gwen who was destroying it.

Gwen looked up from her work and said, "Don't worry. I'll make you a new one. A nicer one."

Roy said, "Yeah. Maybe the new one will be gold instead of silver."

"Nah," Martin said. "Gold's too flashy. I'd stick with silver, but maybe the new one can have big shoulder pads and lapels, like a zoot suit."

"Sure thing," Gwen said.

A little time and some industrious whipstitching later, the dailuaine was rewrapped in part of Martin's former robe. The bust of Santo and the head of the bridge cue were placed in a backpack for safekeeping. The rest of the robe was sewn into a rough sling three layers thick, strung between the two staffs, allowing any two relatively able-bodied adults to easily carry the heavy lump of rock as if it were Cleopatra.

Roy whistled, and said, "Well done, ladies."

Brit said, "Thanks, Roy."

Roy said, "Martin and I'll take the first shift carrying the rock."

Brit said, "I know."

With that, they were on their way. If actually carrying the weight of the rig Brit and Gwen made had done anything to dampen Roy's enthusiasm, he didn't let on.

"It's not just a good idea," Roy said. "It's really well executed too. It feels solid. If anything's going to give out, it'll be my pool cue, but we can cross that bridge when we come to it."

Brit said, "Thanks. I agree."

Roy was walking in front, holding the poles on his shoulders as he walked forward. Martin was bringing up the rear, with no choice but to look at the dailuaine and at the back of Roy's head.

Good work, Roy, Martin thought. *You were genuinely complimentary without being condescending. Now drop it.*

Roy said, "I shouldn't be surprised that it's well made. I mean, it's mainly sewn together."

Brit said, "Yeah?"

Martin thought, *No, Roy, stop now.*

"Are you saying it figures we'd be good at sewing because we're women?" Brit asked.

"No," Roy said. "Not at all. I've known plenty of women who wouldn't know what to do with a needle and thread."

Brit said, "And I'm sure you've known plenty of men who could sew."

Roy said, "Not really, but that's not my point. I shouldn't be surprised at the quality of the work because Gwen did it."

Martin nodded.

Roy continued. "And she's a seamstress."

Martin shook his head.

Gwen said, "I'm a designer, but I see what you mean. I do all my own sewing. I know you meant it as a compliment."

Roy said, "Good. I'm glad. I really do respect it. It's a highly technical skill."

"Thank you," Gwen said.

"Did you know," Roy forged on, "that the space suits for the Gemini and Apollo missions were mostly made by women?"

"No, I didn't," Brit said.

"Yeah, at a bra factory, which figures."

Martin and Gwen winced at each other. Brit remained silent. Roy kept talking.

"They had experience in sewing together multiple layers of synthetic fabrics."

Brit nodded and said, "Huh."

Roy said, "And, they had nimble little fingers that—"

"Roy," Brit interrupted, "I'm not offended."

Roy said, "Good."

Brit continued. "So, this would be a good time to stop talking."

Roy cranked his head around to look at Gwen and Martin. The looks on their faces told him that Brit was right.

Roy stopped talking. When Brit smirked at him, he knew he'd made the right decision.

They walked until nightfall, taking bearer-duty in shifts, with the two non-load-bearing members of the team fending off the occasional tree wolf. At first the height differential between Martin, the tallest of the men, and Brit, the shortest of the ladies, made carrying the litter awkward, but soon enough they got the hang of it.

Early the next day, Martin was walking in the lead. Brit and Gwen were carrying the litter, and Roy was walking well behind, watching for wolves and fighting the urge to offer to take one of the women's places.

From her place at the rear of the litter, Gwen heard Brit mutter, "It's no good."

"What?" Gwen asked quietly, hoping to keep Martin and Roy from hearing. "What's no good?"

Brit had been lost in thought, but snapped out of it, glanced back over her shoulder quickly, and said, "What? Oh, sorry, Gwen. It's nothing."

"So, nothing's no good," Gwen said. "Splendid. That certainly makes sense."

Brit said, "Oh, I don't want to make a big deal. I'm just worried about Phillip."

Gwen said, "Yeah?"

"And the others," Brit added hastily.

Gwen smiled. "Brit, you and Phillip are very close. You only really know Tyler, Jeff, and Gary through him, and none of us like Jimmy. It's only natural that you're more worried about something bad happening to Phillip."

Brit shook her head. "That's not it. I mean, yes, I'm very worried in general that something awful is going to happen to him. Them. That's not what I'm worried about right now. Right now I'm concerned that they're probably moving too fast."

"Really?"

"Yeah. Think about it. The wolves seem to attack in groups of at least two, right? And always in even numbers."

"Yes, I guess."

"And if we kill a number of wolves, then hang around long enough, twice as many wolves appear from where those wolves died, right?"

"Yeah? I think it's to give us incentive to keep moving."

"Exactly," Brit said. "I don't think Phillip and the boys have been getting attacked by two wolves. I think they've been attacked by single wolves, and we've been getting two wolves because we're behind them. If that's true, they have five people, not four, fighting half as many wolves and soldiers as we are. They have to be moving faster than us."

Gwen said, "Yeah, makes sense."

"So, unless we start thinking of ways to speed things up, the only way we'll catch up to them is for something to happen that brings them to a stop, and if that happens, I'm not sure I want to catch up to them."

Not long after that, Martin yelled back to the group, "Whoa, hold up. We found something."

Brit and Gwen put down the litter, and they and Roy walked up to Martin, who was hunkered down on one knee, looking into the middle distance at something that seemed to puzzle him greatly. Gwen followed his gaze, and the breath caught in her throat. A hundred feet or so ahead, four wolves were standing in front of a dark shape that was lying in the middle of the road.

Roy muttered, "Oh, no."

Martin said, "I know what you're thinking, but I'm pretty sure it's not a person. It's too small."

"Then what is it?" Brit asked.

Martin said, "Part of a person, maybe? I doubt it, though. There are only four wolves. It'd take some doing, but any of us could take out four of these stupid wolves single-handedly."

After a moment's quiet contemplation, Martin said, "I'm going to go get a closer look."

Gwen said, "It could be a trap."

"I dunno," Martin said. "Four angry wolves and a dark lump—that's not very good bait."

Roy said, "It's good enough that you want to get a closer look."

"I'll be careful. Besides, it's in the middle of our path. We kinda have no choice."

Martin crept, sword drawn, toward the wolves. They made no move to intercept him, but they never took their eyes off him either.

Martin slowed his approach. The wolves watched.

Martin was as close as he felt he could get without triggering the wolves' attack. He stood tall and leaned one way, then another, trying to see what the dark form was that they were guarding. He turned back to look at his companions, who were still standing in the path where he'd been.

Martin shouted, "I still can't tell what it is!"

"Thanks for the update!" Gwen shouted back.

Martin looked at the wolves. He knew there was only one way he was going to figure this out. He held his sword in front of himself and boldly stepped forward.

As expected, one of the wolves growled, then leapt for his throat. Martin took the wolf out with little trouble and dispatched the next three wolves in turn. Once they were all gone, he approached the dark shape, afraid of what he might find.

As the others approached, Martin poked at the shape with his sword. He nudged it harder. By the time they reached him, he was lifting it with his sword point. He reached out a hand, pulling the dark mass closer to his face, and after inspecting it for a second, he turned to the others and said, "It's a cloak. Some kind of fur. Bear, I think."

Gwen took it from him and held it at arm's length. "Ugh," she said. "It's awful."

Martin said, "It might not look like much, but I bet it's powerful."

"Its smell certainly is," Brit said, wrinkling her nose.

Martin took the cloak back, handling it as if it were priceless. "Don't let looks and smells fool you. This is important."

Roy said, "Kid, it's just a dirty old hide. That's all."

"No, think about it, guys! We're on an epic quest! It's a dumb epic quest, but still, it's an epic quest, and we've found an ancient-looking garment out in the middle of nowhere, being guarded by vicious animals. I'm telling you, this is important. We're supposed to do something with it."

"Yes," Brit said. "Ignore it and leave it where it is."

"I can't believe you all are against me on this. It's not practical to waste any resource in our position, and it's a fur. I thought women liked furs."

Roy said, "It's smelly and beat to hell, and we have all the coats we need. We have no use for it."

Brit added, "And some women like nice furs, but we're not them, and that's not one. Besides, it's not so much the fur they like; it's the fact that their guy was willing to spend that much money on something completely impractical to try to make them happy. The same thing with diamonds and roses. The same cannot be said of filthy bear pelts you find laying on the ground."

Gwen said, "And even if that were a nice fur, which it is not, it wouldn't really be something Brit or I cared about. Fur is murder."

"Especially that one," Brit said, "since we watched you kill four wolves to get it."

Martin rolled his eyes. "Oh, come on! We all know they aren't real wolves."

"And that's probably not a real bear pelt," Roy added.

"Which is all the more reason to get rid of it," Brit said.

Martin sneered at them. "I'm telling you, this thing is important. I'm keeping it, and it will eventually do something cool and you'll all be glad I grabbed it. You'll see." He draped the pelt over his shoulders with a flourish and took off down the path. The others shared a smile; then Roy took his turn carrying the litter with Gwen and they all followed.

An hour later, eight wolves sprung from the fur while Martin was wearing it. Roy and Brit dropped the litter due to their excessive laughter. Afterward, they apologized to Martin and admitted that the fur had done something cool and that they were glad he had grabbed it.

20.

The raw ore was in the crucible. The furnace was built, filled with charcoal, and sealed. Inchgower lit the coals and instructed the wizards to place the business ends of their bellows onto the holes at the base of the furnace, one on each side so as not to crowd each other. The wizards did as he said, but knowing what was going to come next, Tyler made sure everyone had used the restroom before they plugged the last bellows into its hole.

As predicted, the instant the bellows were in place, Inchgower said, "All right, lads, now the easy part. All you have to do is pump your bellows, one at a time so that there's a steady flow of air into the fire for the next six hours."

Tyler said, "I fear that does mean six hours straight with no break."

Inchgower said, "Yes, the whole six hours, nonstop."

Tyler said, "He was expecting the question."

Inchgower said, "I'm afraid so. Any more questions?"

Tyler said, "We didn't have any questions."

Inchgower said, "Good, then it's time to start pumping. Off you go."

As they each took their stations, Tyler muttered, "If I get my hands on Todd, I'll kill him, if just for subjecting us to this crappy workmanship."

"On the bright side," Phillip said, "your arms will be in good shape for it."

The actual business of pumping the bellows worked out to be very much like a large, polite, slow game of Hungry Hungry Hippos, wherein each player simply took turns eating a marble. Each man pumped his bellows in turn, and the action traveled around the furnace at a steady pace.

The first hour passed in grim silence, each man trying hard not to say, or even think about, how much they were not enjoying pumping the bellows.

During the second hour they tried to play I Spy, but it did not go well. They got off to a bad start when Gary said he spied something that started with a *B* and eventually revealed that it was "blacksmithing tools." When the others complained that since they were in a blacksmith shop, he had, in his first turn, used up virtually everything in the room, he merely said, "Then I guess I win."

They tried playing a game Phillip invented, which he called Desert Island Todd. The rules were simple. Imagine you were going to be exiled to a desert island with Todd, and list the three items you would bring along to beat and torture Todd with. Points were given for inventiveness, and for nonlethality, because they were better than Todd and because killing Todd would just end his torment.

Jimmy ended up winning but at a terrible cost. His three picks were a towel, orange juice, and toothpaste. He had been further into the future than any of the others at that point, so he had to explain the concept of waterboarding. Once they understood that, he did not have to explain why he felt it would be even more unpleasant if you made Todd brush his teeth first, then used orange juice instead of water.

They all agreed that this was the worst torture any of them had dreamed up yet, but instead of laughing and taking his next turn, Tyler went silent. Hearing Jimmy discussing inflicting hypothetical suffering on Todd had been a potent reminder of the time, not that long ago, when Jimmy had inflicted all too real suffering on Tyler.

Tyler didn't say what was bothering him, but everybody knew, and nobody knew what to say.

Finally, inevitably, it was Jimmy who broke the silence. He didn't know what to say either, but he knew that saying anything, even the wrong thing, would be better than saying nothing.

"Tyler," Jimmy said. "I've stopped saying I'm sorry every time I see you, but that doesn't mean I've stopped being sorry."

"Yeah," Tyler said. "That makes it all okay, doesn't it?"

"No, of course it doesn't. There's nothing I can say or do that will ever make any of it okay, but I'm not going to stop trying. Look, when we get out of this, I'll let you ghost me for just as long as I ghosted you."

"Great," Tyler said. "Fantastic, except that we both know I would never do that to you."

"And hopefully you know I would never do that to you again."

"Yeah, I know. It's the again that's the problem. There's a whole lot of stuff that I'd never do that you'd never do again. The thing that really burns me up is that I'd never get away without being punished, like you did."

Jimmy didn't want to argue with Tyler, but he had to. He couldn't let the idea that he hadn't been punished at all go unchallenged.

"Tyler, you can argue that the punishment didn't fit the crime, but you can't claim that there was no punishment."

Tyler said, "Spare me. We've all heard all about it. 'Wah wah, I had to ride a bicycle.' Big whoop."

"For thirty years," Jimmy said. "Thirty years with no money, no friends, no family, in Central and South America in the eighties. I was in constant danger."

"You poor baby. All you did was kill a town and you had to endure the world's longest backpacking trip. That's really a fitting punishment."

"You assume my punishment is over. It isn't. It won't be as long as I'm alive."

Tyler said, "Oh, please."

"Again, you can make the case that it's not enough punishment, but I've spent the last three years as a total pariah, and I don't see that ending anytime soon, or ever."

"Is that supposed to make us feel guilty?" Tyler asked.

"No, but I'd hope you'd feel some empathy. I made this bed, and I will lie in it, but it'd be nice if occasionally someone mentioned that it's not a very nice bed, that's all."

"Well, it's not going to happen."

"Yeah," Jimmy said, "I've come to realize that. That's the pillow on the bed I've made."

Tyler chose not to respond to that. Jimmy chose not to add anything further. Phillip and Gary chose to continue pretending that they weren't there. Tyler had said a few things that they had been thinking, and Jimmy had said a few things that they would need to think about.

After some sullen, silent bellows-pumping, Tyler said, "Jimmy, can I ask you a question?"

Jimmy answered, "Anything." This was his reflexive answer to that question. In the past, he had often followed it by thinking,

You can ask me anything you want, so I'm not lying. It doesn't mean I'll answer you.

Tyler asked, "After everything you did, did you honestly expect us to forgive and forget?"

Jimmy looked around the room and saw that while they were all working their bellows in perfect rhythm, the other three men were all staring at him, waiting to hear his answer.

Jimmy said, "The short answer is no. Of course not. I neither expected nor really hoped that any of you would forgive and forget. There's no forgiving what I did, and if you forgot it, you'd be fools."

"Then why'd you bother to come back?" Tyler asked, sounding more irritated than curious.

"Because of the third option. You can't forgive what I did, and none of us, especially me, should ever forget that I'm capable of what I did, but I needed to show you all, *us* all, that I won't ever do it again."

Tyler asked, "And how are you going to do that?"

Jimmy answered, "I thought not doing it would be enough. I was wrong. Now I wish I knew."

Phillip chose this moment to participate. "You want us to trust you. It's not possible. There's no way to prove that you're not going to do something. Trust is a person believing that someone won't do any of the thousands of awful things that any of us can do to each other. You got everyone to trust you; then you betrayed everyone's trust, repeatedly and in the worst possible ways. Even if you do want to be trustworthy again, how can we ever trust you?"

"So you're saying there's no way."

"Jimmy, there's always a way, but sometimes the way to success is worse than just admitting failure. The only way to convince us that you won't betray us again is to live the rest of your life without betraying us again. If you can do that, those of us who outlive you will be forced to stand at your grave and say, 'He never betrayed us again. He changed. He was trustworthy after all.'"

Jimmy thought a moment, then said, "So you're telling me that the only way to convince you all that I'm not going to betray you is to spend the rest of forever not betraying you."

"Pretty much," Phillip said.

"I'll get right on that," Jimmy said, sourly.

They pumped their bellows in silence well into the evening, each of them lost in his own thoughts. At long last Inchgower returned, carrying a large, rough, vaguely rectangular blob of hardened sand in his arms. It had the approximate proportions of a shoebox, only larger and more poorly made. He placed it on the floor.

"Okay, lads," the blacksmith shouted. "Pull out your bellows. You've pumped long enough."

They removed their bellows. Inchgower got down on all fours and peered into one of the holes into which they had been blowing air. A bright orange light illuminated his face in the darkened shop as he squinted into the hole. He stood up, slapping his thighs to brush the dust off the soot.

"Good work, lads. Well done."

He turned his back, rummaging around his tool rack. When he turned back to face the furnace, he was holding a large sledgehammer. With one smooth swing, he struck the flat side of the furnace. A spiderweb of cracks radiated from the point of impact, revealing the glowing, fiery interior as the cool, dull exterior shattered and crumbled. It was beautiful, and like many beautiful things, it was also more than a little terrifying.

The wizards saw the furnace crack open and spill coals across the floor like a fire-piñata. They felt a wave of searing heat wash over their backs as they yelped and fled for the far corners of the room, where they would at least be burned slightly later than if they had stayed put. Only when they were in position, cringing and as far away as possible, did they dare to look back at the source of all the heat.

The cracked walls and collapsed roof of the brick-and-clay furnace seemed to shimmer when viewed through the intense heat. Around the ruined base of the furnace, coals were heaped like gold coins around a sleeping dragon. Now exposed to ample oxygen, the coals were already beginning to turn a dull white instead of their original radiant orange, but the center of the pile still glowed.

Inchgower put down his hammer. He made a show of looking weary, and acting as if the heat was causing him discomfort, but he was standing less than four feet from the core. Several of the coals had rolled down the slope of the larger pile and came to a rest right next to his boots. If he had been a real person, he'd either have fled with the wizards or he'd have been screaming.

He shielded his eyes and said, "Ooh. A bit toasty."

He placed his hammer back on the tool rack and lifted a large set of tongs built with an accordion-like set of joints so that they would lengthen as he closed them. He extended the tongs, then used them to knock the cooling crust off the top of the coal pile, exposing the glowing orange core and releasing fresh, rippling waves of heat. With a bit of work, he exposed the top of the sealed clay pot at the center of the fire, the crucible.

He used the tongs to lift the crucible out of the fire. Gary gasped. "That thing weighs a ton, and he has no leverage. He must be strong as a bull."

"He's not real," Phillip reminded him.

Gary said, "Yeah, well, that just makes it all the more impressive."

Phillip said, "Not really."

Inchgower placed the glowing orange crucible on the dirt floor. He produced a mallet and a chisel and knelt down. He placed the steel chisel along the seam of the crucible's lid and tapped it with the mallet, protecting himself from the intense heat via the time-honored method of squinting, panting, and saying "hot hot hot hot hot" as quickly as he could.

The lid separated cleanly from the crucible and fell to the floor. Using the tongs, Inchgower lifted the radiant crucible over the rough sand mold he had placed on the floor. Carefully, he positioned the crucible over a hole in the top of the rectangular mass. He tipped the crucible, and for a moment it looked like he was pouring out a cup full of sun. A thin stream of pure light and heat streamed from the crucible into the hole. He tipped the crucible farther. The stream grew thicker. He lifted the crucible while maintaining the pour, like a bartender trying to make you think you're getting more than your allotted two ounces of vodka.

The crucible ran dry. Inchgower discarded the tongs and empty crucible and sat on the dirt floor, listening to the mold as it cooled.

"We don't want to hear a pinging noise," he said.

"This is weird," Gary said.

"I thought we'd established that long ago," Phillip replied.

"No, not the whole situation. This part in particular. I mean, up until now Todd hasn't wasted a lot of time on the specifics. The mines were one big cave with the ore we needed right at the threshold. The castle was essentially a big fancy lobby for the secret passage. Everything's been really broad and simplistic until this blacksmith shop. Now suddenly he's wallowing in detail. Why?"

Phillip said, "Probably because this part calls for a lot of manual labor, and he's trying to make us miserable."

Tyler added, "And, I suspect he might have dwelt on this a bit because he just thinks blacksmithing is cool."

Inchgower leapt to his feet and declared, "The dailuaine is cooling, lads. We've purified and toughened it, but we also need it to harden. Time for the quench. Remove the lid from the oil barrel."

Inchgower pointed at a metal cylinder with a wooden lid, which stood just outside, in front of the shop. Jimmy removed the lid, revealing the smooth, black surface of the oil inside. Inchgower grasped his sledgehammer and swung it over his head, bringing it down on the mold, which split open, then crumbled. The shape inside the mold, whatever it was, was glowing too brightly to look at for long. All they could tell was that it was something large and hot.

Inchgower again used the tongs and, with a noticeable but unrealistically small amount of effort, lifted the glowing mass into the air and lowered it into the oil. The air was filled with a deafening hiss, as if someone had stepped on God's pet snake. The surface of the oil burst into tall orange flickering tongues of flames, which disappeared when whatever it was Inchgower was making disappeared beneath the surface. After a moment of tense silence, Inchgower pulled the tongs back out of the oil. When the object breached the surface, it again burst into flames, but this time the flames persisted as Inchgower held the burning mass high in the air like a torch, pushing back the night.

"Yeah," Tyler said. "Todd definitely thinks blacksmithing is cool."

"Not period accurate, though, is it?" Phillip asked. "They can't have had big barrels of crude oil just sitting around in this time period, could they?"

Tyler said, "I think it's actually motor oil, and no, they didn't. If I remember correctly, back then they used either water or urine."

"Huh," Jimmy said. "It must have been a hard decision for Todd. Use oil, which is inaccurate but looks really cool, or have the blacksmith pee on it, which doesn't look nearly as cool but would have forced us all to breath pee steam."

Gary said, "I bet if he had used pee, he'd have named the blacksmith Calvin."

Inchgower bellowed, "Behold, lads, the fruits of your labors!" He brought the huge ball of fire down closer to his face and demonstrated an unrealistic amount of lung capacity by blowing out the fire with one breath. He swung the tongs toward the wizards. The dull metal mass was no longer glowing, but it was still putting out an alarming amount of heat. Smoke rose from its surface in wispy streams.

Even in the dark, through the heat and the smoke, the object they had made was instantly recognizable.

"An anvil?" Phillip cried. "That's the amazing weapon we've been making? An anvil? What are we going to do with that? Drop it on someone? Are we meant to go fight a giant roadrunner?"

Jimmy muttered, "They're more effective against coyotes."

"Quiet, you," Phillip said, scowling.

Inchgower laughed. "Gentlemen, you misunderstand. This is not the weapon."

Tyler thought, *For once the dialog tracks pretty well. Then again, Todd didn't have to be a genius to figure out what we'd be saying at this point.*

Inchgower continued. "Dailuaine is far too heavy to make an effective weapon, but it is the only metal hard enough to be used in the forming of Lagavulin steel, which makes excellent weapons, and of which I have an ample supply, and have had all along."

The wizards groaned.

"Sleep well, friends. For tomorrow we start work on the weapon. It will take a great deal of work. Luckily, I have you here to man the hammers."

The sound of the wizards' continued groaning was drowned out by laughter. Todd's chat window appeared, floating in the air behind Inchgower.

"I thought you'd like that," Todd said, grinning sickeningly. "Oh, and thanks for the pee-steam idea. Luckily, I still have time to incorporate it into the next part."

21.

Gwen was walking in the lead and was the first to notice the line of smoke in the distance. It rose straight up from the treetops, then followed the wind toward the horizon, dissipating as it went. They all agreed that the smoke probably meant that there was a campfire and, most likely, people in their path, which might mean comfort, or might mean danger. Most likely, it would mean one of those things followed by the other, but they didn't know what the order would be and couldn't know until they got there.

When they finally drew within sight of the cabin, they were not surprised to see the front porch populated by three women in stereotypical wench costumes, engaged in stereotypical wench activities: churning butter, washing clothes, knitting, and gossiping in high-pitched, giggly voices. They were surprised that the cabin seemed to have suffered a fire, which had left it badly charred but intact structurally.

Rather than having one member of the group break off and act as a spokesman, all four of them approached the cabin, Martin and Brit carrying the sequin-shrouded lump of ore with them.

Gwen was still in the lead and took the initiative to speak first. She smiled and said, "Hello."

One of the women on the porch looked up from her knitting, tossing her mane of blond hair back and smiling with parted lips before saying, "Hello, stout menfolk!"

Gwen listened to her greeting, looked at her face, her body, and her general demeanor, and said, "Son of a bitch!"

Of course, Gwen recognized her own features instantly, even though they'd been transplanted onto another person with very different hair, clothes, mannerisms, and measurements. She also recognized them on the brunette woman who was wringing out clothing provocatively and the redhead who said "Welcome" while churning butter in a manner that made provocation itself look demure.

Brit said, "They all look like you."

Gwen said, "I noticed."

After taking a moment to watch the wenches writhe and flutter and make prolonged eye contact with anything that would hold still, Martin said, "They don't act like you, though."

Gwen said, "Damned right."

Roy groaned, "Gwen, kiddo, I'm sorry. I feel like I owe you an apology just for seeing this."

She told Roy not to worry about it, then gave Martin a look that would have decalcified his spine if he'd been looking at her. The real her, at least. She shook her head and said, "I don't get it. Why do they look like me?"

Brit said, "Whoever made this quest must have had reason to think that one or all of the guys was attracted to you."

It only took an instant to remember that one of the guys Brit was referring to was Phillip, with whom Brit had been in a fairly serious relationship for three years.

Gwen said, "Oh, Brit, I'm sure Phillip isn't—"

"Gwen, I'm pretty sure he is," Brit interrupted, laughing, "and I'm okay with it. You're cute. Him thinking you're attractive just means that he has good taste. We haven't discussed it, and I don't believe he'd ever act on it, but if he told me he didn't think you were attractive, I'd be worried because he was lying to me."

Gwen smiled and said, "Thanks."

Martin, still looking at the false Gwens on the porch, said, "I think you're attractive."

Gwen scowled and said, "Yeah, thanks."

"Well, what do you want to do?" Roy asked.

Gwen said, "I want to get out of here and forget that I ever saw this, but what I'm going to do is go talk to me and see if we can figure out what's going on."

Martin said, "You don't have to do it. I could."

Gwen said, "No, I have to do it, so you can't."

Gwen stepped toward the cabin and asked, "Okay, what's your deal?"

The fake Gwen with the blond hair and the knitting needles licked her lips slightly and started to speak but was interrupted by a voice from inside the cabin, asking who she was talking to. The blond replied, "Come see for yourself."

The door swung open, and another slightly imperfect Gwen clone emerged, this one with straight black hair and a tight silk dress. The new Gwen cast her gaze over the real Gwen and her friends and said, "Oh, who are our handsome visitors?"

The blond said, "Warriors on a long journey. I expect they'll be looking for a place to rest."

The black-haired Gwen said, "I'll go prepare the guest beds, though I don't know how restful their night will be."

Gwen turned to look at her compatriots. Roy had turned his back, actively avoiding looking at the fake Gwens. Martin was looking more than enough for both of them. Brit tried her hardest to be reassuring. She said, "I know how this looks, but I'm sure the guys behaved in a perfectly honorable manner."

The blond Gwen said, "Kind sirs, please don't embarrass us with talk of money." Real Gwen whipped around to look at her as if she'd heard a gunshot.

"We insist that you stay with us," the blond said. "Please, you'd be doing us a favor. The four of us have lived alone here since we were small girls. We've been without any companionship since our father died, somehow. We have a great deal of delicious food, all of which has been cut into bite-sized morsels, perfect for hand-feeding. We'll happily share it. All we ask is your company. We have never had men visit before. We are very curious, and have many questions."

"Not as many as I do, sister," Gwen muttered.

Oblivious, the blond said, "And, of course, we'll give you shelter for the night. We have soft beds, satin sheets, silk pajamas, and a large variety of exotic lotions."

Gwen frowned. "And that answers a lot of them."

She looked at the blond copy of herself, sitting there coyly with the end of her knitting needle in her mouth. Gwen's gaze followed the needle down to the actual knitting, which appeared to be underwear. *That just seems incredibly itchy*, she thought. She chose not to look at the redhead churning butter and instead turned her attention to the brunette doing laundry. She glanced at the actual clothes being laundered. What she saw did not make her happy.

Gwen turned again to look at her friends. She considered asking them what they wanted to do, but she was certain she didn't want to know. Instead, she said, "We're moving on. Now."

None of the others were dumb or insensitive enough to argue, or even to look back as the cabin grew smaller in the distance behind them and eventually disappeared into the woods, and into Martin's memories.

Later, with no warning or discussion, Gwen turned to Martin and said, "Don't tell me you found them attractive." It was more a command than a question.

Martin didn't know what to say. She had told him what not to say, but excluding one possible reply didn't narrow things down very much.

"Did you?" Gwen asked, pressing the issue.

Marvelous, Martin thought. *She tells me what not to say, then gives me an opportunity not to say it. If I lie, she'll know it, and telling someone what they want to hear does you no good if they know you're lying.*

Martin gaped and stammered for a moment. He became painfully aware that Brit and Roy were silent, listening to how this would play out.

Martin said, "Gwen, do you understand that there's no right answer to that? You've asked me the Kobayashi Maru of questions. There's no possible way to answer that won't make you mad."

Gwen said, "That's not a no."

Martin replied, "It's not a yes either. Let's be clear on that. Think about it. What can I possibly say? 'No, I was not attracted to those four provocatively dressed women who looked exactly like you. They disgusted me to my very core.' That's no good."

Gwen said nothing.

"Gwen, they looked like you, and they acted like female characters from an old James Bond movie. Of course that's going to get my attention. But I'd rather have one of you than all four of them."

Gwen half-smiled for half a second, then went back to frowning, just less intensely.

When it was clear that the storm had passed, Brit asked, "Did any of you happen to recognize the clothes the one on the end was washing?"

Gwen said, "Of course I did. I made them." She saw the confused look on Martin's face and continued. "Wizard robes. I recognized Phillip's and Tyler's. There was something black that might have been Gary's, but the colors of the other two are pretty distinct."

"What does that mean?" Martin asked. "Are they dead?"

"Not necessarily," Gwen said. "Not yet. All it means is that they made it at least this far, and that they took off their robes."

22.

Later, Phillip, Tyler, Gary, and Jimmy all agreed that breathing in the pee steam was unpleasant but that it had been an unnecessary embellishment. Gilding the lily, if you will. Every other aspect of the weapon-crafting process had been so acutely unpleasant that by the time they got to the quench, it seemed an anticlimax.

They say that blacksmithing is a lost art, but Phillip had begun to suspect that it wasn't lost—it had been deliberately discarded.

First, the billet of Lagavulin steel needed to be heated until it glowed cherry red, which meant more pumping on the bellows. Then it needed to be flattened, which meant all four of them hammering it like mad on Inchgower's new anvil. Of course, it would begin to cool as soon as it was pulled out of the fire, so it would need to be heated up again, which meant more pumping until it was hot enough to start hammering again.

After they had lathered, rinsed, and repeated enough times to lose count, the Lagavulin steel billet had transformed into a long, thin, flat blade, three inches wide and twelve feet long.

"Typical," Tyler said. "After all this mystery about the ultimate weapon, it's a sword. A really long sword. Todd has no imagination."

Gary said, "Yeah, but still, it's gonna be really cool when it's done."

Tyler was unconvinced. "Nobody'd be able to swing a blade that big."

"No one person," Gary said. "Maybe two people use it together."

"How?" Tyler asked. "Would they each hold the handle with both hands and discuss where they want to swing the sword?"

Gary said, "No, I was thinking there'd be a handle at each end. Like an old-timey lumberjack saw. We could run on either side of our enemies and cut them in half."

Inchgower donned thick protective gloves and lifted the blade over his head to look at it. He held the blade's center high overhead, the ends sagging to nearly waist height.

"Yes," the computer-generated blacksmith said. "It's a good blade."

"For a small helicopter, maybe," Phillip muttered.

"You've all been a fine help," Inchgower said, oblivious to Phillip's comment. "But the time for brute force is over. Shaping and forming the blade into an object of might and power will require skill and finesse. This will take every bit of knowledge I have about the exquisite art of metalwork."

Inchgower turned his back to the wizards. He held the center of the comically oversized blade over the fire. He let go of it, and it stayed, hovering in midair. Instantly, the entire length of the blade glowed orange from the heat. Inchgower moved his hands in a vaguely work-like manner and made sounds of extreme effort. The blade glowed even more brightly. It turned so that the thin edge of the blade was perpendicular to the floor. All of the sag went out of the blade now that its thicker dimension resisted the pull of gravity. The blade bent up into a U shape, then into a circle, seemingly of its own accord. The now-circular blade spun and twisted in the air, forming the shape of an orange glowing sphere. As it gyrated in space, its free ends contorted and fused together. The spinning slowed, then stopped, leaving a glowing orange circle hovering behind Inchgower, slowly burning its way into the wizards' retinas.

Inchgower grasped the burning circle and turned to face the wizards. In a voice trembling with awe, Inchgower said, "Gentlemen, look upon what we have wrought!"

Inchgower froze, clipping the end of the word "wrought," as if he had been startled. He placed the glowing hoop on the floor. His movements were more mechanical than usual.

Tyler groaned.

The blacksmith stood unnaturally straight, looked directly ahead with a blank expression, and said, "We've purified and toughened it, but we also need it to harden. Time for the quench."

"He didn't even bother to record fresh dialog," Tyler said. "He just grabbed the same sentence from earlier and slapped it in there."

The sound of Inchgower unzipping his fly in preparation for "the quench" was cartoonishly loud and out of place.

"But he went to the trouble to dig up the sound of a fly unzipping," Tyler whined. "That's just great. Never mind that there's no way a Dark Ages blacksmith would even have a zipper."

Inchgower attained a state of readiness to proceed with "the quench," then froze, as he tended to when waiting for the wizards to make the next move. After a profoundly uncomfortable moment, Inchgower repeated, "Time for the quench." Another long silence followed and ended with the phrase "Time for the quench."

Phillip sighed heavily, then said, "We all know what he wants. We're not going to move on until it happens. We might as well get it over with."

The wizards reluctantly prepared themselves, then waited for a signal as to who should start the quench. When Inchgower failed to make the first move, they all took a deep breath and got on with it.

The sizzling noise and the noxious cloud of steam pouring off the circular blade was actually kind of satisfying. The quench might have almost qualified as fun if Inchgower hadn't bellowed, "Take a good, deep breath, lads! You've earned it!"

The wizards all continued to hold their breath, shaking their heads and humming emphatic "nuh uhs." Inevitably, they all ran out of steam and started to run out of air. Inchgower seemed to have an endless supply of both and repeated, "Take a good, deep breath, lads! You've earned it!"

After a long, silent moment, Inchgower said, "Take a good, deep breath, lads! You've earned it!"

More silence followed, until Inchgower again said, "Take a good, deep breath, lads! You've earned it!"

Gary was the first to give in and breathe. Because he had pushed himself to the edge of asphyxia, he took a deep, gulping breath and immediately started coughing and moaning simultaneously. Between coughs, he managed to say, "Ngaah! I . . . taste it!"

The others had been on the edge of giving in and breathing anyway. Now they were laughing and breathing, and tasting, and yelling, and then laughing again.

Todd's window winked into existence. Todd looked haggard but quite pleased with himself. "We had to rush to work that in, but it was totally worth it. Thanks for the idea, guys."

"You recorded new dialog about how we should take a breath. Why didn't you record a new explanation for the quench while you were at it?" Tyler asked, indignant.

"This is an independent project that I'm bankrolling myself. Voice talent and studio time are both expensive. I ended up sending an intern with an iPhone mike to get the new lines, and he dropped the ball."

"So you just rolled with it as is," Tyler said. "Typical. It's the lack of consistency and attention to detail that makes this all seem so rinky-dink."

Todd said, "Shut up," and disappeared along with his vid window.

Inchgower bent in half at the waist, stooping in a manner that physics would never allow. He grasped the now fully quenched dull metal ring. He lifted it high over his head.

Gary groaned, "Ew, it's dripping."

Inchgower resumed the triumphant posture he had held before the quench, and resumed his previous speech. Tyler silently noted that he could hear the very end of the *t* from the word "wrought," where the speech had been edited.

"T! We have created a weapon of power, elegance, and beauty. A weapon of such unusual and inexplicable properties that most men cannot even comprehend it! Gentlemen, I give you the Möbius Blade!"

A point of bright light started at Inchgower's gloved hand and raced around the outer edge of the dull metal ring, leaving a highly polished, razor-sharp edge in its wake. The light made a full lap of the ring's outer edge, then completed a lap of the inner circumference. The blade gleamed in the light, a perfect circle except for a single kink near the blacksmith's hand where the blade had been twisted one half turn, creating a weaponized version of the popular grade-school brainteaser, the Möbius strip.

"It is at once the simplest and most complex weapon imaginable," Inchgower explained. "The blade has but one edge, but mysteriously, that edge is somehow twice the length of the blade itself."

"Just the thing if you want to kill M. C. Escher," Phillip said.

Inchgower continued. "The Möbius Blade is a weapon utterly refined. Anything that cannot be used to kill has been removed as deadweight."

Gary raised his hand and said, "There's no handle."

Jimmy said, "That's what he means."

"It is so deadly," Inchgower said, "that it presents a mortal danger to anyone who comes near it, even those who wield it." As if to drive this point home, a trickle of blood ran down Inchgower's arm, originating from his palm, where the blade had cut through his heavy gloves and then into his hand.

Phillip said, "Wow, that's something."

"I'm glad you find it interesting," Jimmy said, "because we're going to have to think of some way to carry that thing to whatever the next stop is, then, presumably, use it in battle."

Inchgower lowered the Möbius Blade so that it hovered parallel to the floor, supported entirely by the blacksmith's powerful forearm and wrist.

"Take it," Inchgower commanded. "Take the Möbius Blade. Carry it to the Chasm of Certain Doom and meet your destiny."

Gary muttered, "That just couldn't sound less promising."

"But go with care, for it lies beyond a mighty desert known as the Scapa. You must transport the blade through the Scapa without damaging it. The edge is as fragile as it is deadly. You may take with you as much water as you can carry, but it will only help you ward off the thirst. It will be no protection against the sand wolves, nor the dreaded elemental that lies in your path."

"Elemental?" Jimmy asked. "What's an elemental?"

Inchgower said, "The well, as you know, is out back. Now take the blade. Your destiny awaits."

Inchgower froze, waiting for the next trigger, which suited the wizards just fine. They were in no hurry to get their hands anywhere near the Möbius Blade. They took the opportunity to examine it. From a distance, the blade looked like a polished metal ring, about four feet across with a single twist taking up about a quarter of its circumference. They were told that it was deadly, but from a distance it didn't look all that menacing.

When they got closer, close enough to actually touch the blade, the danger seemed like an actual physical presence. The thin, cold Lagavulin steel (whatever that meant) was honed to an edge so sharp that just looking at it made you fear that you were cutting your eyes. Every childhood memory of mishaps with kitchen knives and paper cutters was called instantly to mind. Every parental warning about scissors and gardening implements rang in their ears. Every safety film about shop equipment, every surprisingly graphic warning sticker slapped on the side of a deli slicer, it all flooded to mind, beseeching them to not get anywhere near that awful thing.

"Well, we have to take the blade from him somehow," Phillip said. "Things aren't going to progress until we all accept it."

Jimmy said, "I say we support the blade from underneath, with our palms up. Then we bow our fingers back so we don't get them anywhere near the edges."

"Edge," Tyler corrected him. "A Möbius strip only has one edge. If you follow it with your finger, you'll see that it follows the entire outside and inside of the ring without breaking."

"Sure," Jimmy said. "And I'll probably cut my finger off too. Anyway, three of us support it with our palms; then whoever gets the part with the twist can put his hands above it and use his fingers to pinch the sides."

"Side," Tyler said. "A Möbius strip only has one side too. If you drove a Hot Wheels car along—"

"I don't care," Jimmy said. "I just want to take it off Bluto's hands and put it down on the floor with minimal blood loss, okay?"

Tyler said, "Sorry. You're right. It's just that this is the first halfway cool idea Todd has had."

Phillip said, "I'm sure the fact that you think so makes him very happy."

"Ooh, yeah, okay. I'll shut up," Tyler blurted.

Phillip, Jimmy, and Gary placed their hands under the blade, making sure that the side of the blade rested on the meaty parts of their palms. This was the most convex part of their hands, but the blade was also perilously close to their wrists. Tyler pinched the blade from above. As soon as his fingers made contact with the blade, Inchgower let go.

"Good fortune on your journey, lads," the blacksmith said, resting his soot-covered hands on his soot-covered hips. "I've enjoyed your company, but now our time together is at an end."

He stood there, silently watching the nervous wizards holding the Möbius Blade.

Gary said, "I think he wants us to leave."

"And we will," Phillip said. "Just not yet."

The blade was surprisingly light, especially when its weight was spread out across four people. It also felt utterly ridged, as if they couldn't bend it at all even if they tried, which they absolutely, categorically were not going to do. They carefully lowered it to the ground. Tyler easily let go of his portion of the blade; then he ran around sticking rocks, chunks of wood, anything he could find under the blade so that it would be supported up off the floor and the others could get their hands out from under it without losing any skin.

Inchgower repeated, "Good fortune on your journey, lads. I've enjoyed your company, but now our time together is at an end."

"Great," Phillip said. "Now we get to listen to that every minute or so. A nice little reminder that we're no longer welcome here."

"So we ignore him," Jimmy said. "It'll serve as a nice little reminder to Todd that we'll move on when we're damn good and ready."

Gary scouted around the village looking unsuccessfully for something to help them carry the blade. Unfortunately, they had dismantled their sledge and used it to stoke the fire that, ironically, had helped make the very thing they now wanted to drag on the sledge.

The others experimented with various means of transporting the blade. They tried Inchgower's tongs, but there was only one pair, regular human muscles couldn't muster anywhere near enough leverage to lift the blade, and the metal tongs couldn't get enough traction on the metal blade to effectively drag it. Besides, they'd been told they would need the blade to be in good condition when they got to the Chasm of Certain Doom.

They tried suspending the blade from loops of rope, which turned out to be a fairly effective means of cutting rope into small chunks.

They tried wrapping the blade in rags and discovered that rags were easier to cut than ropes.

In a moment of desperation, they discussed rolling the blade, propelling it with a stick like a kid in the background in an episode of *Little House on the Prairie*. That idea was scrapped because the twist in the blade would make it lurch unpredictably, and because the idea was insane to begin with.

They decided to get some sleep, hoping a better idea would occur to them by morning. They found a place to sleep that was far enough away that Inchgower's continued reminders that their time together was at an end would not disturb them.

The next morning, as Jimmy got up from his bedroll, he felt something in his hip pocket, which had been empty when he went to bed. He explored the pocket with his hand and quickly recognized that the intruder was a plastic pen with a sheet of paper wrapped around it. Jimmy looked at his fellow adventurers. Tyler and Gary were going about their business, but Phillip was glancing in his direction.

Jimmy made eye contact with Phillip and slowly withdrew his hand from his pocket. Phillip seemed satisfied and went back to putting his bedding away. After an interval of time Jimmy had calculated to not be suspicious, he announced that he was going to go void his bowels. He didn't usually proclaim his intent to defecate so proudly, but he figured it was the most effective way possible to ensure that Todd would not want to watch him.

Once he was out in the woods alone, Jimmy unrolled the note.

This is good, he thought. *Phillip wants to conspire and he came to me. That shows some trust. I'm making progress.*

He still held the note close to his chest and made an effort to conceal his actions, in case he had misjudged Todd's proclivities. Jimmy read:

> Todd is probably watching and listening. After we make the weapon, next stop is "Chasm of Certain Doom." We need a plan.
>
> —T

> Agreed. Ideas?
>
> —P

> My 1st idea was to ask you. That was a dead end. 2nd idea, ask Gary?
>
> —T

> T, no need for snark. G, how about it. Any ideas?
>
> —P

> You two want a sneaky plan and you haven't asked J? Dumb.
>
> —G

> J?
>
> —P

Jimmy shook his head as he rolled the note around the pen and stowed them both in his pocket.

The wizards gathered as much water as they could, compared ideas as to how to transport the blade, and agreed that the best method they had was carefully, with lots of rags wrapped around their hands, while shouting instructions and insults at each other. They also agreed that this was a bitter disappointment.

They followed the path out of town, which was not marked, but there were only two paths in or out of town, so they chose the path that had not brought them in. The path was wide, more of a road, really, and was mostly downhill, but the going was slow, and they rotated their place in formation often. They positioned the blade so that the twisted portion was at the front, so whoever carried that portion could support it with one hand while walking almost fully forward, watching the path ahead for obstacles and wolves. The two supporting the sides of the blade walked sideways, more to control the blade than to support its weight. The man at the back had the easiest job, in that he got to walk straight ahead, but he also had the most dangerous job. His view of the path was obscured by the blade and his fellow blade carriers, and if there was a mishap, the others might lose a finger, while he could very well get decapitated or cut in half.

It did not take long for the lush forest, with its evergreen trees, thick undergrowth, and abundant tree wolves, to start thinning. They knew soon it would give way to some form of desert, which meant a bleak landscape, no shade, and, they'd been warned, sand wolves.

"What was that other thing he warned us about?" Phillip asked, walking sideways, both hands supporting the shining blade.

Jimmy, who was in the lead position, looked back and said, "He called it the 'dreaded elemental,' whatever that means."

Gary, bringing up the rear, yelped, "Eyes forward!"

Tyler said, "An elemental is a fairly common type of monster in fantasy stories and D&D adventures. They're supposed to be made of one of the four elements: earth, wind, fire, or water. It's almost always fire, because why wouldn't it be?"

"Maybe it'll be the fifth element," Gary said. "The supreme being."

Tyler saw the confusion on Phillip's face and explained, "It's from a movie." Tyler affected a high-pitched voice and a foreign accent and said to Gary, "Leeloo Dallas. Multipass." He turned back to Phillip and said, "In the movie, the fifth element was a beautiful woman who wore nothing but suspenders and an ACE bandage. We will not be so lucky."

Phillip said, "Marvelous. What else do we know about it?"

Jimmy glanced back. "He said 'the dreaded elemental,' so we know that it's an elemental, and we know that it is dreaded."

"Eyes forward!" Gary shouted.

"The dreaded elemental," Phillip said, bitterly. "Doesn't tell us much. We already know it's dreaded. We're the ones dreading it."

Jimmy shouted back, without turning his head, "Sorry I keep turning around, Gary. I'm not doing it on purpose."

Gary said, "Yeah, I know. Just try to remember, okay? Seriously, guys. I don't know how much of this I can take."

Phillip thought, *I don't know how much of this any of us will be able to take. I just wish there had been a better way to carry this cursed thing. Of course there wasn't, though. Todd's too clever for that.*

Phillip mulled that last part over a bit. *Todd's too clever. That doesn't sound right. Maybe . . .*

He considered suggesting that they put the blade down and run back to town to see if there was something they had overlooked, but dismissed the thought. *No, if there'd been something there we could have used, we'd have remembered it. We're too smart to have missed anything.*

Phillip mulled that over and thought, *That doesn't sound quite right either.*

23.

"Looks like there's a town around the bend," Roy shouted back to the rest of his group. Gwen was carrying the front of the litter. She nodded back over her shoulder to Martin at the back of the litter and said, "Town ahead."

Martin said, "Got it." He lifted the poles from his shoulders and turned to look at Brit. She nodded, sending the clear message that she'd heard, so he put the weight back on his shoulders without saying anything.

During the hike from the home of what Martin had learned not to ever call "the Gwenches," they had taken to having the person walking in the lead keep a bit of distance out ahead of the rest of the group. That way they could warn of any obstacles in their path, and often, if they were attacked by tree wolves, the lead had them dealt with before the rest of the group caught up.

Roy waited for the others. He felt it would be better if they entered the town together.

"This would be Bowmore, I think," Gwen said. "We're supposed to make the dailuaine into some kind of weapon here, if I remember right."

They entered the small town cautiously, Roy still in the lead. There were unconvincing citizens ambling aimlessly around the street. A clearly artificial old woman appeared to be making bread. There was some sort of motion in a shop up ahead.

Roy approached the woman, who was repetitively kneading her dough.

"Hello," Roy said.

The woman said, "How can ye not know where you are? This be the town of Bowmore."

Roy walked back to the group, who had heard the exchange and needed no explanation. Roy squinted into the distance and said, "I guess we head to the shop."

Gwen said, "Probably a blacksmith. Makes sense."

As they walked through the empty streets of the fake town, Martin saw that tucked between two of the huts, there was an old oxcart. He pointed and said, "We could have used that."

Brit glanced at the cart and said, "We don't have anything to pull it, but yeah, I bet a couple of people could make good headway on level ground. Oh well, we'll see if we end up having to carry anything out of here. That might come in handy."

When they reached the shop, Gwen and Martin heaved the heavy litter to the ground with an air of finality.

The shop was an open-air affair, with an awning to keep the weather off and a fence to keep the pedestrians out. There was a forge that looked like a pile of bricks, and a blacksmith, who also looked like a pile of bricks. There were various nails, horseshoes, hammers, and other products or tools of the blacksmithing trade strewn around the shop. The blacksmith was using his tools to assert his will over a glowing bar of metal, fresh from the forge.

Brit stepped toward the blacksmith and said, "Hi."

The blacksmith turned and said, "Greetings, stranger. How does this day find you?"

Brit shrugged and said, "Eh."

The blacksmith put down his work. He walked over to a basin of stagnant water, where he washed, or at least rinsed, his hands. Then he introduced himself. "I am Inchgower, skilled blacksmith and crafter of fine weapons."

Brit said, "Uh huh."

The blacksmith listened intently, nodding and stroking his chin. After a stretch of awkward silence, he said, "Aye, 'tis a long journey to be sure. I'm certain you didn't come all this way without good reason."

Brit made a "hurry it up" motion with her hand and said, "Uh huh."

Inchgower spread his hands apologetically. "I see. You've come to the right place, but sadly, I cannot help you."

Martin said, "No?"

"I know all about the prophecy," the blacksmith explained, "but to make the weapon you need, I require certain raw materials, materials that have not been available for quite some time, I'm afraid."

Brit pointed at the litter, with the invisible chunk of rock, wrapped in Martin's old robe. She stood there silently for a moment before Roy said, "I guess they do just wait for a verbal cue before continuing."

A look of amazement filled the blacksmith's face. He dropped the rag he'd been holding and staggered to the gate, where he looked down at the round lump that could really have been anything, wrapped in a bolt of dirty, sequined cloth.

"You have it." He gasped. "You managed to procure the dailuaine. I cannot believe it."

Brit said, "Uh huh."

Inchgower looked delighted. He said, "Gentlemen, I will make you your weapon."

Brit turned to Gwen and motioned for her to take a turn. Gwen bowed slightly to her, then said, "Yeah?"

The blacksmith turned to face Gwen, bolted forward three steps, seized her by the shoulders, and said, "We will need bricks! Lots of bricks, my friends. Come with me—there are wheelbarrows out back."

Brit cringed. "Yeesh, sorry about that, Gwen. I didn't know he'd do that."

Inchgower let go of Gwen and strode purposefully out the rear of the shop.

Martin said, "I think he's waiting for us to go get the wheelbarrows."

"Let him wait," Roy said, rubbing his hands together. He glanced at Brit and said, "That went really well, didn't it?" She smiled and nodded.

Roy turned to Martin and Gwen and said, "Just to make sure we're all on the same page here, at each stop in this stupid quest, we're supposed to do something, right? But at the last stop, with all the Gwens, we didn't, did we?"

"No. No, we did not," Martin said.

"Right," Brit said, taking over from Roy. "So, when the blacksmith started into his subroutine, it proved that we don't actually have to do any of this crap, which is good, because we need to catch up to the others. Now we know we can."

The whole point of coming here had been to meet up with their friends and offer them assistance. It had weighed on all of their minds that they didn't feel like they were making any progress in catching up to the first group. Of course, due to the other group's extended stay with Inchgower, they had gained a great deal of ground, but they had no way of knowing that.

"So you're saying we should just move on?" Martin said.

"Unless you like the idea of staying here and gathering bricks," Roy answered.

Martin said, "No, but he's supposed to make us a weapon. What if later we need it, whatever it is, to move forward?"

Roy turned to Brit and said, "The boy makes a good point."

Brit said, "Yeah, but if we stay here and do whatever it is we're supposed to, it'll be that much harder to catch up with the others. If, on the other hand, we skip this and make tracks as fast as we can, and catch up, they'll probably have the weapon, and we won't need ours."

"What if we never catch up?" Martin asked.

"Then we can backtrack and get the weapon, because if that happens, we have much bigger problems than making good time. Look, I know that leaving without whatever we're supposed to get here is taking a chance, but we have to stay focused on what our real goals are. We didn't come here to experience this quest. We came here to help our friends, and we aren't accomplishing that by following at a distance. We need to catch up to them."

Martin raised both hands, signaling partial defeat. "I'm not arguing with that. I'm just trying to think ahead for once, and I don't want us to get stuck here because we don't have some object we need later."

Brit smiled. "No, you're right. That's a good point, but we need to catch up, and that won't happen unless we start taking some risks. Besides, Martin, this isn't really much of a risk. We know we won't get stuck here because if we did, Brit the Elder wouldn't be in Atlantis right now. She'd be here with us. Of course, she might still be here with us right now, and we get her out so she can be in Atlantis now too, but even if that's the case, we still get out, because if we have the ability to get her out, that suggests we can get ourselves out as well."

Martin said, "I can't argue with that. Or even follow it, really."

Roy said, "Good. I say we look around the place, see if there's anything we can use, then get on our way."

Gwen found the water pump and refilled their bottles. Aside from that, there was little of any use, or so it seemed at first. When they regrouped to leave, and got a good look at the path out of town, Roy asked everyone to wait for a moment. The path was nice and wide. The ground was dry and solid. They'd been walking downhill for most of their journey, and the terrain didn't give them reason to expect a change.

"I think I have an idea," Roy said. "I know we need to get a move on, but like the lady says, it's time to take some risks, and this might be worth it."

Roy turned and walked back toward town. Martin followed, asking Roy for details. As the men disappeared around the side of the blacksmith shop, Gwen heard Roy ask, "Did kids still play with Radio Flyer wagons when you were a boy?"

Martin answered, "Yeah, big red plastic things, right?"

Brit stared down the path, as if trying to peer into the future. She muttered some words that were largely unintelligible. Gwen picked out "enough water" and "wolf jerky to eat." Brit stopped mumbling when she became aware that Gwen was smirking at her.

"Why are you smirking at me?" Brit asked.

"Was I?" Gwen asked, smirking.

"Yes. You still are."

Gwen said, "You must really be worried about Phillip."

Brit said, "And that's why you're smiling. You know, Gwen, I can see why Martin finds you confusing."

"You must be really worried about Phillip, because when people are really, deeply concerned, their true thoughts tend to come out."

"And?"

"And," Gwen said, "you're using the fact that Brit the Elder is back in Atlantis as proof that we can get out of here without whatever it is we were supposed to make at this stop."

Brit saw what Gwen was getting at. When Brit first traveled to the distant past and found the version of Atlantis she'd imagined building already there waiting for her—along with another woman who looked exactly like her, and claimed to be her from the future and to have built the city she'd wanted to build as a gift for her—Brit's natural first reaction had been to become very, very confused. Her natural second reaction was to be deeply suspicious of the second Brit. As time went on, and the other her seemed to remember everything she said, did, or thought, and did or claimed to have done everything Brit aspired to, Brit's natural third reaction was to wallow in resignation and resentment, and that's exactly what she did for years, until Phillip came along.

Phillip had two core beliefs: that the 1980s were the pinnacle of human culture and that people can always change their destiny. Brit liked his second core belief so much that she was willing to ignore how obviously wrong his first core belief was.

Phillip had looked at the massive pile of convincing evidence that Brit the Elder was Brit the Younger's future, and he said, "Nah." He immediately constructed an elaborate theory for how Brit the Elder was a projection, created in real time, based on estimates of the possible outcomes of Brit the Younger's actions. Thus, Brit the Elder wasn't living Brit the Younger's future; Brit the Younger was altering Brit the Elder's present. Brit, both Brits, oddly, loved him for that.

Since the day she'd met Phillip, Brit the Younger had refused to be pinned down on the issue of whether Brit the Elder was in fact her. If Phillip was around, she'd sit in silence, smiling, as he explained that she was not. If Brit the Elder was present, Brit the Younger would sit in silence, sulking, while the Elder explained that she was. If both Phillip and the Elder were in the room when the question came up, everybody else would sit in silence and watch the always-entertaining debate that would ensue.

Now neither of them was present. Brit was on her own, and Gwen had clearly been paying attention, waiting for her to take a position on the Brit the Elder question.

"It's just interesting to know that when it comes down to it, you believe Brit the Elder is you," Gwen said.

"Eh." Brit shrugged. "When it suits me."

"What's that supposed to mean?" Gwen asked.

Brit was not displeased to see that Gwen's smirk was gone. "Look, when that person you all call Brit the Elder is pretending to be humble and gracious while accepting praise and credit for my ideas, I tell myself that she can't possibly be me, because I'd never do that to someone."

Gwen said, "I can understand that."

"But that's not what's happening right now, is it? Right now, I'm wearing a warm coat she warned me to bring, carrying a backpack she sent, drinking from water bottles she provided. That's her being helpful. That's her doing something right."

Gwen nodded. "And you want to believe you would do that in her place."

"No," Brit said. "If she's just me in the future, that means I'm the one who helped us, and I like that. She steals my credit all the time. This is a way I can take some of hers."

24.

"What do you guys picture when you hear the word 'desert'?" Phillip asked.

"Sand dunes," Tyler said. "A sea of stark, clean, undulating sand dunes receding endlessly into the horizon under a clear blue sky."

They walked for a moment; then Phillip asked, "You're thinking about the movie *Dune* now, aren't you, Tyler?"

"Yes. Yes I am."

Jimmy said, "I picture salt flats, like Bonneville. Just a flat, lifeless plain. No landmarks. No features. Nothing but salt and sand and heat."

Gary said, "I picture an island with some ferns and a single palm tree. And before you say anything, yes, I know that's not right. That's pretty much the opposite of a desert, but when I was a kid, they always called that a 'desert island' and it just stuck with me, okay?"

Jimmy said, "That's fine, Gary. Everybody has that kind of stuff. When you think of a punk rocker, you probably picture a leather jacket and a Mohawk, but two of the biggest punk bands were the Talking Heads and Blondie."

"My point is," Phillip said, "when you hear the word 'desert,' nobody pictures this."

"No," Tyler agreed. "It might qualify as a desert, but they should probably call it a wasteland."

The path down the foothills and out of the woods had been wide and mostly downhill before terminating in the desert they'd been told was called the Scapa, and as Phillip had said, the Scapa was not what they were expecting.

They expected to find sand, but they found dirt. Gritty, dark red dirt. They expected a near-total lack of life, maybe punctuated with the occasional cactus, but they found plentiful tumbleweeds and occasional glimpses of tiny, fast-moving rodents. They expected to find no water, but it clearly had rained at some point in the recent past. They would occasionally pass a patch of damp ground, or a puddle of liquid that, if you were being a stickler, you would have to admit was water, but only someone who wanted to die or was desperate to live would dare drink it.

In short, where most deserts were hostile to life, the Scapa was merely passive-aggressive. Where the Sahara seemed to scream at people to stay away, the Scapa told them, "You want to live here? Go ahead! Fine by me. I've given you everything you need—plants, animals, water. Flourish, why don't you?"

Rather than being perfectly flat, or covered with treacherous but beautiful dunes, the landscape was made up of rolling hills that were just steep enough to be irritating to walk up and treacherous to walk down and just flat enough to be boring. The wizards had to put in effort and watch their step, but only because they were hand-carrying an object that had been designed solely for the purpose of cutting their hands.

One advantage of the gently rolling landscape and the scratchy, skeletal nature of the sagebrush was that they could see the sand wolves coming a mile away. Or at least they would have if the sand wolf simulation subroutine had been more realistic. As it was, they could see the sand wolves render out of thin air from yards away. When a sand wolf appeared, whoever was carrying the twisted portion of the Möbius Blade would let go and dispatch the wolf. Much like they had with the sledge, they took turns fending off wolves, and settled into a nice routine, which experience had taught them is exactly when things go wrong.

Phillip was on wolf duty, pinching the twisted portion of the Möbius Blade off to his side with his hand while walking forward. The others concentrated on their footing and on not getting their hands cut off. As Phillip watched the landscape ahead for attackers and obstacles, he saw something that he did not yet know would eventually qualify as both.

They had not been in the Scapa all that long, but their slowed pace and the monotony of the landscape made it feel much longer. As they crested a low hill, just like the hundreds before, Phillip saw in the distance, directly in their path, a mound of some sort that stood out from the others. In a landscape of gentle hills and equally gentle valleys, like a vast, two-dimensional sine wave, this one small bump seemed to erupt from the ground. It was one hill made of dirt in a sea of hills made of dirt, and yet it looked out of place.

Phillip told the others to stop for a moment. The others asked why. He explained, "There's a hill."

Phillip didn't blame them for not being impressed with his answer. He explained further, "It's weird." Again Phillip couldn't blame them for not being impressed.

The others did stop, and he pointed out the offending pile of soil, and they finally agreed that it looked wrong. They all kept an eye on it as they walked. Thus, in a barren landscape with only one thing that made them nervous, the wizards walked directly toward that one thing.

They were about fifty feet from the offending lump and Phillip was contemplating which side they should pass it on when the pile of dirt made the question moot by standing up.

At first Phillip was the only one who saw the hill moving, as the others were preoccupied with carrying the Möbius Blade. When the hill moved, Phillip got startled and yelled and jumped a bit, which startled the others, making them jump quite a bit and yell at Phillip. Then they saw what had startled him, and they all yelled at that.

The mound had stirred, then lifted off the ground, supported by two short, thick columns of soil. Its central mass was a thick, bulbous lump of dirt and gravel that sprouted two gnarled arms and a flattened lump that approximated a head. Scrub grass, sagebrush, and formerly buried roots sprouted from the thing's surface like body hair. It stood eight feet tall, much taller than any of the wizards, yet managed to seem short and stubby.

The creature's eyes were defined by their absence. Two dark pits marked the place on the head where eyes would normally be. As it looked down at the wizards, they were given the contradictory impressions that they were being watched and that nobody was home.

As the creature started to move, wispy clouds of dust rose from its joints, trailing behind it like a vapor trail as it lumbered toward the wizards.

The beast started slow but was clearly picking up speed, and there were only about fifty feet between it and the wizards, who set a world speed record for carefully putting something down.

The instant the Möbius Blade was resting on the ground, they scattered.

The creature pursued the nearest wizard, which in this case was Phillip, who did the natural thing and kept running.

When the others realized this, they stopped running and watched.

"Seriously? A dirt monster?" Gary said, catching his breath.

Tyler replied, "I'm guessing that's the elemental we were warned about. Earth is an element."

Phillip's luxurious full-fur vest bounced with each step and flapped behind him as he fled from the elemental. The creature was hunched over, swinging its arms from side to side as it ran, leading with its flattened head and dead eyes. It had attained its top speed, which was surprisingly slow but still slightly faster than Phillip's top speed.

"Run!" Jimmy shouted. "It's gaining on you!"

Phillip ventured a panicky glance over his shoulder at the thing chasing him.

"Don't look at it!" Jimmy shouted. "Run!"

Phillip would have glared at Jimmy, but instead he tripped on some sagebrush and slid to a halt on his face. He scrambled back up to his feet just in time to have the elemental head-butt him with tremendous force between the shoulder blades, sending him flying and causing him to once again slide to a stop on his face.

The elemental was moving slowly, having imparted all of its momentum to Phillip. It restarted its pursuit before Phillip had even touched the ground, but the beast was not a sprinter, and Phillip had enough time to roll to his right, operating mostly on instinct. After pushing off the ground, he brought up his arms to protect his head. His right upper arm collided with the elemental's wrist as the creature, unable to turn its bulk at speed, trundled past. Phillip felt the impact and was sure it had done serious damage, but felt no pain. The elemental, being made of dirt, was not so fortunate. Its fist broke cleanly from its arm. When it hit the ground, the severed fist exploded into a cloud of dust and a pile of loose gravel and dirt.

The elemental jogged to a halt and looked at the crumbling stump where its hand had been. It waddled to the spot where its hand had disintegrated. The cloud of dust created when the severed hand hit the ground had not dissipated as one would expect, but had remained in place, and now seemed to actually become thicker and more tangible. Phillip saw that individual grains of soil were lifting off the ground, as if supported by a strong wind that blew out of the earth itself. By the time the elemental reached the point of impact, all of the debris was airborne. It wafted toward the creature's shattered forearm and re-formed into a fist as the beast watched with its dull, expressionless face.

The elemental rotated its wrist and seemed satisfied. Clearly, it had no need of articulated fingers. Confirming that it was again fully functional, it turned its attention back to Phillip, taking the first slow steps that would soon become a full gallop.

Phillip crawled backward, away from the creature, and felt a sudden jolt of blinding pain from his upper arm. He had not realized it was even injured before, but now he was sure it was broken. He rolled on his side, cradling his arm, which actually made it hurt worse.

Looking down, past his broken arm and flailing, kicking legs, Phillip could see the dirt elemental coming his way, picking up speed. He knew that even if he did manage to regain his feet, he'd do it just in time to get knocked down again. His conscious mind didn't have enough time to come up with a plan. His animal instincts told him to roll into a ball and hope it would be over quickly. Phillip decided to call that "Plan B" and was starting to struggle to his feet when a Gary-shaped blur streaked into view, sword drawn, and hacked off one of the creature's arms.

The dirt elemental skidded to a halt, showering the still-prone Phillip with dust and gravel. Slowly, it turned its back on Phillip, then walked over to the ruined remains of its severed arm. The few bits still recognizable as a former limb disintegrated into rubble, drifted into the air, then consolidated back into a functional arm.

The dirt elemental glanced at Phillip, who was still trying to stand without jostling his arm. It looked as if it might finish Phillip off, but was distracted by Gary, who was jumping up and down and shouting insults in an attempt to get the creature's attention.

It worked. The creature looked at Gary, then started moving his way. Gary, naturally, fled.

Gary ran in a wide curve, looping around toward Tyler and Jimmy. The creature followed. The creature was slightly faster than Gary in a straight line, but because of its much larger mass, it had a hard time managing turns, which slowed it down just enough for Gary to maintain his lead.

When they saw that Gary was leading the creature back toward them, Tyler and Jimmy each ran in opposite directions, causing Gary, then the creature, to run between them harmlessly.

"What are you doing?" Tyler asked as Gary ran past.

"I'm bringing it over here, so you can get it off me," Gary shouted.

"That's no good," Tyler yelled to the now-distant Gary, who was still leading the creature in a wide arc.

"Why not?"

"Because then it'd be chasing me," Tyler replied.

Jimmy added, "Yeah, then I'd have to get it off him, and you'd have to get it off me. It's not a long-term solution."

Gary's cursing sounded distant and weak to Jimmy and Tyler. Phillip had made it to his feet by this time and was slowly walking toward them. He looked pale and shaken. Tyler told him to stay on his feet just in case but to keep his distance until they figured out what to do with the dirt monster.

Jimmy watched a moment, then said, in a distracted voice, "It's just chasing him. It's not trying to cut him off, or throw anything at him. It's just chasing."

Tyler nodded. "You're surprised it's not very bright? It was made by Todd. How smart can it be?"

Jimmy drew his sword and glanced at Tyler, who glanced back and drew his own sword. Jimmy nodded, then called out to Gary.

"Okay, we're ready this time! Lead him back here and run between us!"

Gary didn't say anything, but he immediately changed course, turning sharply toward Tyler and Jimmy. The elemental was not able to turn as sharply and swung wide behind Gary, like a water skier slewing out behind the towboat.

Gary made a beeline for Tyler and Jimmy. The creature continued making a beeline for Gary.

Tyler and Jimmy stood motionless as Gary ran between them. As expected, the beast paid them no attention, continuing to home in on Gary. As it went past, Jimmy and Tyler both swung their swords. If they had been more coordinated as a team, they might have discussed whether they should swing for different parts of the creature's anatomy, but they weren't, so they both swung for the legs, neatly severing them from the elemental's torso.

The legs fell and tumbled and shattered as they hit the ground. The torso, arms, and head continued to move forward, carried by their own momentum. The creature swung its arms wildly, as if trying to regain its balance, but it had no legs to balance on. What served as the dirt elemental's pelvis hit the ground first and crumbled into nothing as the mass of the creature's torso rolled forward. After a bit more flailing and rolling, all that was left was a mess and a cloud of dust, which really is all there ever was to begin with.

Tyler and Jimmy stood, looking down at their handiwork. Gary jogged up to join them.

"Good work, guys," Gary said. "Your plan worked."

"Plan?" Tyler asked. "That wasn't the plan. That was improvising. The plan was to knock you down and see if the elemental would trip over you, but I lost my nerve."

They shared a chuckle, but it was short-lived. Nobody had to point out that the dust cloud was not dissipating. Soon, it began coalescing into the familiar form of the dirt elemental, lying facedown on the ground.

Tyler looked to Phillip, who was still a good distance away. Tyler held up a hand, telling Phillip to keep his distance. Phillip did not need to be told this.

The elemental slowly lifted itself to its feet. It did not speak, but its body language said that it was not happy. Jimmy, Tyler, and Gary took off running in three different directions, forcing the creature to decide which of them to chase.

It chose Jimmy.

Jimmy looked back over his shoulder and yelled, "See, Gary, a short-term solution!"

Tyler sprinted to the top of the nearest mound, hoping he could see something, anything that might be of use. If not, they'd let the elemental chase Jimmy for a minute or so, chop it to bits, then start the whole process over again.

Tyler shielded his eyes with his hand and muttered, "Thought I saw, as we walked here . . ."

Tyler saw what he was looking for and yelled, "Jimmy! Jimmy!"

When he was sure Jimmy was looking his way, he pointed back the way they'd come from and yelled, "Puddle!"

Jimmy ran the direction Tyler had indicated, as did Tyler and Gary. They didn't know what would happen, but they wanted to see it.

Tyler tried to guide Jimmy toward the puddle, yelling, "Left! More to your left! No, not that far! Right!"

Jimmy missed the puddle but got close enough to get a good look. It was large for a puddle but far too small to be a pond. It was a ten-foot-wide amorphous blob of filthy-looking water that had either burbled up from the sickly ground or had fallen in the last rain and refused to penetrate any farther into this awful piece of land. It was surrounded by a three-foot moat of gummy-looking mud. Jimmy was glad he'd missed it, because he was half-sure that if he'd set one foot in the actual moistened area of the puddle, he'd have come to an instant stop and been helpless to escape from the dirt elemental.

When Jimmy was beyond the puddle, he made a quick forty-five-degree turn in the direction of the puddle. He thought that if he was lucky, the elemental would try to cut the corner and get stuck in the mud. He didn't dare slow down to look, but he didn't have to. Tyler and Gary's disappointed groans told him he had not been successful. He cursed himself, remembering that the stupid creature cornered like a tank. Expecting it to suddenly cut a corner more sharply than he had was a silly mistake.

Jimmy ran as fast as he could in a straight line for a bit, then turned widely and lined up on a direct path for the puddle. He deliberately slowed, allowing the creature to close the gap. Jimmy ran as near as he dared to the mud bordering the puddle, then dodged to the left. He heard a splash, and Tyler and Gary cheering, and saw a lump of mud about the size of a watermelon fly past him to his right and splatter on the ground. As Jimmy slid to a stop, a second lump fell to the ground from a much higher, slower trajectory.

Jimmy turned, hoping to see the monster stuck in the mud, and was disappointed. The elemental had made it to the other side of the puddle, and was down on its hands and knees, as if it had simply tripped on its way through the puddle, and now would get up, angrier than before. Jimmy couldn't figure out why Tyler and Gary sounded so happy. Even Phillip seemed to be yelling congratulations while sitting on the ground, cradling his injured arm.

It was only when the elemental tried to get to its feet again and failed that Jimmy realized why everyone was so delighted. The beast would not be able to get back on his feet because the two large blobs of mud that had gone flying were its feet. Clearly, they had quickly soaked up water on contact, then had become heavy enough to go flying when the beast kicked its feet forward to take a step.

Jimmy's eyes darted to the nearest foot, now just a blob of dark, wet mud on the ground. Jimmy expected to see it crumbling apart and drifting toward the dirt elemental, ready to resume its duties as a foot. Instead he saw the blob of mud stirring slightly and spreading out as it settled.

"It can't re-form," he yelled to the others. "The mud is too heavy! Lead it back into the puddle!"

The elemental was crawling toward Jimmy. Tyler sprinted toward it and used his sword to hack off one of the creature's arms, causing it to do an undignified face-plant. Of course, the creature's arm was bone dry and took little time to reattach itself to the beast's torso, but the object was to get the creature's attention. Tyler had accomplished that handily. The elemental turned away from Jimmy and crawled away in pursuit of Tyler, who had run around to the far side of the puddle.

Later, when they discussed the day's events, they would theorize that the dry earth that made up the elemental's body was very loosely packed, and thus the normal capillary action that drew the moisture up into the mass of dirt was accelerated. Whatever the cause, when the creature's right hand went into the puddle, the dirt that constituted its arm immediately darkened all the way past its elbow.

The left hand followed the right hand into the water; then the right was lifted to reach forward and continue crawling toward Tyler. As the right arm pitched forward, the sodden blob that had been the creature's hand flew straight up in the air and landed next to the creature, making a large, muddy splash. The creature pondered the soggy stump where its right hand had been. Then its left hand, still submerged in the foot-deep puddle, disintegrated. Since one-third of the creature's weight was resting on a hand that now no longer existed, the dirt elemental fell face-first into the water.

All of the still-exposed parts of the dirt elemental darkened and softened. It rolled onto its back, revealing the damage the moisture had done. It thrashed with its mangled limbs, flinging bits of itself all over the countryside as it struggled to get free. Eventually it stopped trying to get out of the puddle because it had become the puddle. What had been a still body of fetid liquid was now a viscous slick of dark, gummy mud. The force that allowed the creature to re-form when dry was strong enough to keep the mud bubbling and churning but did not seem strong enough to let it rise and be a threat again.

Gary crouched next to the edge of the mud patch, stuck the end of his sword in the mud, and said, "Whatever particulate-matter simulation he was using to make it clearly wasn't calibrated for the weight of the mud—just loose, dry dirt. I don't think it's going to give us any more trouble."

A tendril of mud started to climb Gary's sword, making its way toward his hand with surprising speed. Gary shrieked and jerked the sword out of the mud, flinging bits of muck far away. The beast was dispersed and subdued, but it wasn't dead. It was only a matter of time before it re-formed.

After he'd composed himself, Gary said, "All the same, I think we should keep moving."

Before they could move on, there was the issue of Phillip's arm. There was no doubt in anyone's mind that it was broken. The question was, how badly?

They looked at the affected region. They poked at it and listened to the volume and ferocity of Phillip's complaints. Then, falling back on all of their combined experience in the medical profession (none), they determined that it was a clean break in one place. They hoped.

They asked Phillip if it hurt. He said, "Yes," which did not surprise them. Phillip asked if there was anything they could to for the pain. They said, "No," which did not surprise him.

In the end they cut some excess fur from the hem of Phillip's increasingly ratty mink coat and made him the world's most glamorous sling. Normally this would have been difficult since every genuine fur coat is also a leather coat, and leather isn't famous for being easy to cut. Luckily, they had the Möbius Blade, which sliced through the leather as if it were tissue paper.

"Glad the Möbius Blade is so sharp," Tyler said, quickly following with "Man, there's a sentence I didn't expect to say."

Jimmy said, "I don't think it's possible for a blade to be this sharp on its own. I'm betting he used the file to alter the edge. Maybe the molecules along the edge instantly sever certain bonds in any other molecules they touch. Todd has played around with that kind of thing before."

"Really? When?" Tyler asked.

"Before he came to us. I found out all about it while I was working my way back. He killed a man by negating all of the molecular bonds in his body. Reduced him to a puddle of goo. The mess was horrendous. That's how I think the blade works.

Even if I'm wrong, it's a pretty good idea. We should remember it for when we get out of this."

From thin air somewhere above them, Todd's voice called out, "Good guess, Merlin. Sorry, you go by Jimmy these days. Anyway, right on the nose! Glad you approve. It took a lot of tweaking to get it right. At first it affected any molecules it touched, so the blade kept tearing itself apart. I made the effect directional. It only cuts things that hit it head on, which fixed the cutting-itself-to-bits problem, but then I found that if I dropped the prototype just right, it would cut all the way to the center of the earth."

"How'd you learn that?"

"I dropped it just right and it cut all the way to the center of the earth. At least I assume so. The hole closed itself back up. Anyway, I see what you mean, it might be useful for you"— Todd laughed—"*when* you get out of this. Especially Phillip. He looks great."

Phillip told Todd what he thought of his opinion, but Todd had either left or decided not to answer.

They fitted Phillip's new fur sling; then Jimmy helped Phillip to his feet, saying, "All right, Phillip, upsy-daisy. We'll handle carrying the blade. You just take the lead and keep an eye out for wolves."

Phillip asked Tyler and Gary if they agreed. They did, vigorously. He shrugged, winced in pain, then watched while the others lifted the Möbius Blade. When they had the blade in hand, Phillip resumed the path to the Chasm of Certain Doom. The others followed. Tyler and Jimmy exchanged an uncertain look.

"Hey," Gary said, "what was that?"

Tyler said, "What?"

"What was that look?" Gary asked.

"Nothing," Tyler said. "There was no look. Shut up."

Without turning, or even slowing down, Phillip said, "Don't worry about it, Gary. It just meant that Jimmy and Tyler aren't sure how long I'm going to last with a broken arm."

"Oh," Gary said. "Okay."

25.

"Brake!" Roy bellowed.

"I'm braking! I'm braking!" Martin called back, pulling with all of his weight on the metal bar that now protruded through the bed of the cart, just in front of the rear axle. Martin pulled hard on the bar, bracing his feet on the rear wall of the cart's bed and hanging off the back of the cart in his desperation to slow it down. Sparks showered the sides of the path as the metal rims of the rear wheels ground against the metal pads on Roy's "improved" brakes.

Martin knew that if his hands slipped, or the bar broke, he'd fall backward into the cart's wake and watch, helplessly choking on dust, as the cart careened away without any brakes, save for the emergency brake Brit, Roy, and Gwen had cooked up. They'd explained how it worked to him. He suspected falling backward out of the cart was the safer option.

At the front of the cart, Roy had both hands full wrestling the tiller he had connected to the front wheels. Modern people are accustomed to vehicles with power or at least rack-and-pinion steering. This cart was never designed to be steered from the driver's seat, and the basic geometry of the axle put Roy at a mechanical disadvantage.

Roy stopped shouting for more brakes while he guided the cart around a turn, barely managing to keep all four wheels on the ground. The path ahead was fairly straight, so he ventured a look at his passengers.

Gwen and Brit were in the middle of the cart, between the driver's bench and the brakeman's position. They were both holding on to the sides of the cart, crouched as if prepared to jump over the side at the slightest provocation but moving only when necessary to either shift their weight to the inside of a corner or to dodge any of the loose items rolling around in the back of the cart. It had been decided that they should bring along some tools and lumber to repair the cart, should it break before they ran out of hill. They had stacked their supplies carefully in the center of the bed, an arrangement that had lasted until the first sharp turn.

Both Gwen and Brit were wide-eyed, their mouths agape. Somehow, even with the wind and the rattling and the grinding drowning them out, Roy could tell that Gwen was screaming, but Brit was laughing.

"How're you two doing?" he asked.

Gwen shrieked, "I'm terrified!"

"Fear means you're making progress," Roy yelled.

Roy turned back to the path ahead just in time to almost not make the next turn.

"Relax," Brit said, between laughing jags. "We aren't really going that fast. I think we're doing something like twenty miles an hour. It just feels much faster because the vehicle is fundamentally unsound."

"Why didn't you say so to begin with?" Gwen asked.

"Say what," Brit asked, "that the vehicle was unsound? I did. All three of us did. We discussed at length that we'd have to try to keep things slow and be ready to bail out because this cart was never designed to be used this way. You just weren't there. You were outside, working on the emergency brake."

When Brit had proposed her idea for the last-ditch emergency brake, Roy had actually laughed out loud, not because it was ridiculous but because there was no reason it couldn't work, despite being ridiculous. He and Brit brainstormed the elements necessary to make it work and determined that the handiwork of someone who knew how to work with fabric was called for. Gwen took the sewing kit Brit the Elder had sent, Roy's trench coat for material, and some general instructions for what she would make. Then she found a quiet, pleasant spot under a tree to do her work. As such, she had not been privy to any of the later design conversations.

At one point, Brit had decided to take a break from the hammering and the bending, and Martin's incessant humming of the theme from *The A-Team*, to check on Gwen's progress.

"How's it going?" Brit asked, sitting on the shady ground next to Gwen.

"Well, I think," Gwen answered.

Brit nodded. "Will it work?"

"The emergency brake?" Gwen asked. "Yeah, I think it might, if we're going straight. If we're turning, no way."

"Yeah," Brit said. "That is one design flaw, but it's better than nothing."

Gwen said, "The good news is that this old trench coat is made out of good, strong material. It was a shame to cut it up."

"At least he has the coat Brit the Elder sent for him, so he'll stay warm and dry. We'll get Roy a new trench when this is all over. You can make him one if you want, or we could just zip back to the twenty-first century and buy him one."

Gwen shook her head. "No, we'll want to go to the twentieth century. Better craftsmanship then."

"Ah yes," Brit said. "Those skilled lady seamstresses with their nimble little woman hands."

Gwen chuckled lightly. "He's getting better. He's still kind of weird around us, but he's treating us like useful members of the team now."

Brit smiled. "I knew he'd come around eventually. The smart ones usually do."

"I suppose. I just wish he would relax," Gwen said, squinting at her stitching.

"Well," Brit sighed, "the awkwardness is partly our fault."

Gwen looked up from her sewing and squinted at Brit.

"Not women in general," Brit clarified. "Us, specifically, and in this one situation."

Brit could tell by the continued intensity of Gwen's squint that more clarification was needed.

"I'm just saying that I think, in the long run, Atlantis might have been a mistake. It made sense at the time. Early history was generally hostile toward women—more so the further back you went. Adding magical powers to the mix certainly didn't simplify things. When we started traveling through time, it seemed smart to create a separate place where women could go to be in charge of their own destinies, and be treated with the respect they deserved."

"Made sense to me," Gwen said. "That's why I moved there."

Brit said, "Yeah, but I think you had it right the first time, when you were living among the male time travelers, interacting with them. Proving your worth. I made Atlantis. It was my idea, and it was constructed by Brit the Elder, who is me, probably.

Anyway, by keeping women separate from men I've doomed women to being non-players in the men's stories. The male wizards can't see women as their equals because they never really interact with women who are their equals, aside from the very rare woman of equal or greater status who gets involved."

"Like you and me," Gwen said.

"Exactly. It's no wonder they treat strong, independent women as oddities. We are oddities in their world, and I'm the one who made it that way. It wasn't my intention, but that's what happened."

Gwen thought about this for a moment, then said, "Okay, say you're right. What do we do about it?"

Brit said, "Well, we can't fix the past."

"We're time travelers," Gwen reminded her.

"Yes, and as you've seen, all that really means is that we can mess up the past, not fix it."

"True."

"We can't fix the past, but we can improve things going forward. I'm going to make sure that the sorceresses of Atlantis mix and integrate with the other wizard communities in the future, and I'm going to try to remember this lesson and not make the same mistake again."

"Should you find yourself in a position to create another society from your imagination again," Gwen said.

"Yeah," Brit said. "If it comes up."

In the distance, Martin emerged from the blacksmith shop and called out, "Hey, guys, if you've got a sec, Roy and I would like your opinion about something."

Brit and Gwen listened to Roy and Martin's disagreement and offered their opinions. Discussion ensued, and consensus was reached. This process was repeated many times. They all worked hard, the men doing more than half of the grunt labor and the women doing more than half of the irritating, fiddly work. When it was done, they rested. The next morning they set out in the cart, which they'd heavily modified into what was possibly the world's first four-person all-terrain soapbox derby car.

It was almost certainly a mistake, but it was a mistake they'd made together.

The cart rattled down the winding path. They were moving fast. Fast enough to feel that they'd be seriously injured if the cart fell apart but slow enough that they all doubted whether they'd catch up to the others before that happened.

Roy yelled to his passengers "Lean right!" and threw the tiller all the way to the left, slamming the cart into a hard right turn. Gwen, who was sitting on the right side of the cart to begin with, pushed her weight into the side of the cart's bed as hard as she dared, fearing that the ancient wood might fail to support her weight. Brit scurried from her position in the left side of the bed to Gwen's side, using her body weight as ballast to help keep the inside wheels of the cart on the ground as they maneuvered through the turn.

Martin was putting most of his weight into the brake lever. His feet lost traction as they careened around the corner, causing him to fall out the back of the cart. He still had a firm grip on the brake handle, and now that his full weight was bearing down on the lever, the cart's speed slowed noticeably. They were really designed to be parking brakes, not to slow a vehicle already in motion. Roy and Brit had beefed them up as well as they could, but they all knew the brakes wouldn't last forever.

Roy yelled, "Good work," while Martin struggled to get his feet back into the cart.

Looking down at his sneakers as they scrambled against the back of the cart, a sudden streak of gray in his peripheral vision caught Martin's attention. Once he got both feet back on the cart he ventured a quick look at the path behind and saw that there were four wolves chasing them. He quickly theorized that they must have spawned at the same speed they would if the group walked by, but since they were rolling past at many times their walking speed the wolves didn't really spring into action until the cart was well past. That meant that the longer they rolled down this hill, the more wolves would gather behind them and the more important it would be to keep rolling.

Martin saw that the wolves were gaining on them. He eased off the brakes.

They were out of the turn and back on a relatively straight bit of path. Brit crawled back to her side of the cart.

"At this rate," she yelled to anyone who was listening, "we should catch up to the others in no time."

"Hell," Roy said, "I half-expect to crash into them."

26.

Phillip had always been a morning person, but Todd's quest was helping him get over that. It had shown him that what he had always perceived as the "promise of a new day" could also be taken as a threat.

Phillip sat up, grudgingly admitting to himself that he was awake. The night air had been frigid. The ground was lumpy with rocks. His bedroll and all the bits of him that were exposed were covered with cold, clammy dew, part of the Scapa's ongoing attempt to give life just enough of a foothold to keep suffering.

His arm hurt like hell, there was no denying that. This had been his first attempt to sleep with a broken arm and in a sling, and it had not gone well. He would have been willing to bet that he hadn't slept at all if not for two things: he did not remember seeing the sunrise, and somehow the pen with the note wrapped around it had found its way into his sling without him knowing it.

Taking care not to look down at the note, Phillip mimed using his good hand to adjust his sling while slowly unrolling the note into the hand of his broken arm. It had all of the hastily scribbled messages he'd remembered. At the bottom, in Jimmy's neat script, there was the single word "over" and an arrow.

Phillip flipped the scrap of paper over, rolled his eyes, and read Jimmy's contribution.

Gentlemen,

I'm sure you know the game "Rock, Paper, Scissors." Two players each pick whether to play rock, paper, or scissors, as each choice beats one of the others and is beaten by the third. People think it's a game of chance, but they're wrong. The key to winning is to get good at predicting what your opponent is likely to choose.

Todd thinks he's clever, but he isn't. Someone who makes no pretense at being clever will just do what you expect them to do. Someone who's truly clever is unpredictable. Someone who thinks they are clever will do the opposite of what you expect them to do.

Also, in Rock, Paper, Scissors, if you watch your opponent's hand, they'll often make their hand signal a fraction of a second before they should, giving you the advantage.

Todd wants to kill us, but he thinks he's clever, so he'll try to do it cleverly, so he'll try to trick us into killing ourselves. I say our best plan is to keep our eyes open for him to tip his hand, and if he tells us to do something, we do the opposite.

—J

Phillip looked up from the note, grimacing. *Brilliant*, he thought. *Keep our eyes open and don't do what he tells us. We certainly couldn't have come up with that. Of course, we didn't come up with that. The best plan we came up with was to ask Jimmy, wasn't it?*

Phillip's grimace did not fade. He hunched over, as if fighting back the pain from his arm, and in the limited free space at the bottom of the page, he wrote:

T, any more paper?

—P

After their customary breakfast of wolf jerky and grumbling, they got under way. Phillip continued to walk in the lead while the others followed, taking great care in transporting the Möbius Blade without losing any digits or blood. None of them grumbled about Phillip not helping with the blade, partly because they wouldn't want to trade places with him, since that would mean walking through the desert with a freshly broken arm, and partly because they all understood that having someone who was in some way impaired try to help bear the blade would be a grave danger to the other bearers. The last thing any of them wanted to hear was any of the others saying "Oops."

The low, undulating hills of the Scapa continued, though Phillip thought they were beginning to flatten out a bit. When you spend a long time in the same environment, your mind starts noticing even the slightest variation—just ask anyone who's ever driven across Texas. The monotony of the same rolling hills, punctuated with the occasional attack from what was essentially the same wolf, was taking a toll on all of their minds. So much so, that when there was something genuinely of interest to look at, they took it for an optical illusion at first.

As he crested a hill, Phillip saw in the distance what appeared to be a few spots of a slightly different shade of very dark brown, which in the Scapa constituted scenery. Many steps later, as they crested another hill, it became obvious that the discoloration was a continuous line running parallel to the horizon, a very long way away.

The more they walked, and the more hills they summited, the

more definite the line became. Phillip had been debating whether to say anything to the others. He suspected they were too focused on their footing and trying not to decapitate each other to have noticed the unusual geography of the path ahead. The decision to tell the others came quickly when Phillip finally realized what he was looking at.

Phillip said, "Better hold up, guys. Chasm."

The others stopped. "I'm sorry," Jimmy said. "What?"

"See that line up ahead?" Phillip asked, pointing with his good arm. "I've been watching it for a while. I figure it's the far rim of a canyon, or a valley, or—"

"Or a chasm," Tyler finished for him.

Gary swallowed hard and said, "The Chasm of Certain Doom."

"Yes," Tyler said. "Thanks for spelling that out. I'd worried that this would be some other, less dependable doom chasm before we got the Chasm of Certain Doom. The Chasm of Possible Doom. Something like that."

Gary muttered, "Yeah, sorry."

"The big cartoony gulp was a nice touch," Tyler continued. "It's a shame we don't have a spooky organ to play, or a big metal sheet to make some fake thunder every time you say that."

Gary mumbled, "I said I'm sorry."

Phillip peeled his eyes away from the chasm in the distance to look back at his cohorts. "Okay, guys. There's no need to argue."

Now Gary raised his voice. "I'm not arguing! I'm apologizing and getting insulted! That's not arguing, is it? Is it, Phillip?"

"You're arguing now."

"Well, now, yeah, over the idea that I was arguing. But I wasn't arguing then, when you accused me of arguing."

"Okay," Phillip said. "I get it."

"I don't even know why I was apologizing. All I said was that it was the Chasm of Certain Doom."

They were all startled out of their bickering by the deafening noise of an eerie organ and fake-sounding thunder.

Tyler looked toward the heavens and said, "Well done. That was fast work."

No chat window opened, but they heard the click of a microphone opening up; then Todd's voice said, "Thank you."

27.

Gwen didn't like it. Not at all.

She didn't like the idea when she heard it. She didn't like the amount of time and effort it had taken to put the idea into practice. She didn't like the jeopardy Martin had volunteered to endure to make the idea work.

Of course, she had stated all of these objections before they put it to a vote, and she'd still been outvoted.

She didn't like that either.

She peered around the wooden barrier at the dust cloud in the distance and said, "This is a bad idea."

Brit exchanged a knowing look with Roy and said, "Maybe so, but it's the bad idea we're going with. Sorry."

Brit, like Gwen, was sitting in the bed of the wagon, which was stationary on top of a rise, well into the charmless scrub desert they didn't know was called the Scapa. After the hill gave out, Roy managed to keep the cart rolling for a surprisingly long time on momentum alone, but still, they were eventually forced to abandon it and continue on foot.

They had been delighted to find their friends' footprints, clearly visible and easy to follow. They couldn't understand why the others seemed to be walking in a regular formation, or why there were only four sets of footprints. They decided that one of them must have been injured and the others were carrying him, which only strengthened their resolve to catch up as soon as possible.

They were less delighted when the trail led them to a peculiar-looking mound that suddenly sprang to life and chased them all around the desert. The only time it got close enough to hurt any of them was when it nearly head-butted Roy in the back.

Roy was aware of its attack and leapt at the last second, wrapping his arms around the creature's neck. His plan was to cling to the creature and attack its face while it stumbled to a stop. To everyone's surprise, the creature did not stop. It continued running forward while Roy hung around its neck like an albatross. The beast's running stride was not smooth, and it was not long before Roy lost his grip. He threw himself to the side as he fell and avoided being trampled.

The monster twisted slightly in the direction Roy had gone, then stopped, scanned its field of view, caught sight of Gwen, and started chasing her with the exact same speed, body language, and intensity it had when it chased Roy.

Eventually they stopped the walking pile of dirt by leading it into a fetid little bog they found and surrounding it while running laps of the bog. The creature didn't know whom to chase, so it just spun around in circles, stirring itself into the water as it slowly melted into loose, watery mud. They knew this was a temporary reprieve. The slop was clearly already trying to re-form into some sort of a shape that would dry out and continue the chase, but it looked like that would take quite some time.

They split up and searched the area, looking for the continuation of their friends' trail, or at least Martin and Gwen did. Gwen found the trail resolving itself from the frenzied, chaotic tracks left from the dust creature's pursuit of both parties. She was a bit unnerved that instead of the familiar tight, four-person formation, the trail was now a recognizable pattern of three people walking in formation and a fourth walking alone.

Gwen called out to the others. Martin was off on his own, looking for the trail Gwen had found. Brit and Roy were talking. Gwen didn't know what they were saying, but when they heard her say that she'd found the trail, they both smiled in a way that made her nervous. They were the smiles of two people who were sure they knew what to do, and that the first step would be talking you into it.

Gwen was right. They were sure that they knew what to do, and they were right: they did have to talk Martin and Gwen into it. They never fully convinced Gwen, but by then she was outvoted.

Counterintuitively, instead of following the trail, they backtracked to where they'd left the cart. They spent the minimum time possible repositioning the cart and making modifications, using all of the tools and scrap wood they'd brought and cannibalizing the sides of the cart in the process.

The cart was now a heavily modified flatbed. There was still a small bench by the tiller. Roy sat there, waiting to spring into action. Brit sat cross-legged on the floor of the cart, thinking through the next several hours and trying to hide her excitement. Gwen sat at the back, next to (but not touching) the hastily braced wooden wall that they'd constructed and nailed to the back of the cart.

Gwen peered around the wall again and said, "This is crazy. We're making a mistake."

Roy said, "Oh, come on, Gwen. This isn't a mistake."

"But you agree it's crazy?"

Roy shrugged. "Oh, I dunno. Back when I worked at Lockheed, half the stuff we came up with sounded crazy at first, and most of it was. Some of it actually worked, though. That stuff made it into the planes. We ended up with aircraft that could do things no one else's planes could. Yeah, Brit's plan sounds crazy, but I believe it'll work. Remember, you live in a city made of diamond. That sounds crazy. That was her idea."

Brit smiled. Gwen did not. "Even if the idea might work—"

"It will," Brit interrupted.

"Even if it might," Gwen continued, "are we sure about this barrier? I'm not even allowed to lean against it. How can it possibly hold?"

Roy said, "I told you, it's not designed to take force from this direction. If you want to get out and lean on it from the other direction, it'll hold all day. You could lean a car's weight on the other side, no problem. I had to prioritize where the stress loads would be. We had limited time and materials."

Gwen looked at Brit and asked, "Does that make sense to you?"

Without hesitation, Brit said, "Yes. It does. And even if it didn't, you heard the man. He was an aeronautical engineer at the Lockheed Skunk Works. He has real-world, non-magical engineering experience. Even if I didn't think he was right, I'd defer to his judgment."

Roy said, "Thank you."

Brit said, "It's the truth."

Gwen said, "I liked you both more when you liked each other less." She jumped down off the cart and walked around to the other side of the barrier to look again at what they'd done.

The sides of the cart and most of the spare wood had been

used to make a large, heavy plate, which was affixed to the back of the cart. It was like someone had taken the tailgate off their pickup truck and replaced it with a tabletop from IKEA. What spare wood remained was used to make thick braces that extended from the plank to the bed of the cart at forty-five-degree angles. Gwen hated to admit it, but it looked as if a great deal of force would be needed to push the barrier over from behind the cart. Of course, if you pushed from inside the cart, the only thing holding the plank on was the grip of the nails, thus the no-leaning rule.

One thin plank, similar to a two-by-four, leaned against the back of the cart, forming a very narrow ramp to the ground. The plank itself was studded with small strips of wood. They were nailed in at regular intervals all the way up the height of the plank. These were the only parts of the whole apparatus that had been designed and carried out by Martin, and as usual, they were the most seemingly haphazard parts, and Martin was absolutely convinced that they would work.

Thinking of Martin caused Gwen to look again at the column of dust headed their way. It was much closer now. Clearly, it was making better time than anyone had anticipated. Gwen watched, and saw a small human figure, running over the top of a hill, followed by a much larger figure, running slightly faster. The larger figure nearly caught the smaller, but at the last second the smaller one made a sharp turn, causing the larger to overshoot, stop running, and look around. The smaller figure stopped and bent over, breathing heavily and keeping an eye on the larger figure. The larger figure finally caught sight of the smaller and attempted to give chase. The smaller leapt out of his way, causing another full stop and confused scan. They repeated this a few times, until the smaller figure felt ready to continue; then the smaller figure took off on a dead run straight for the cart.

"Okay, get ready," Gwen said. "Martin's bringing it this way."

Brit said, "Great! Gwen, please remove the wheel chocks. We're go."

Gwen muttered, "If Martin gets hurt, *you're* going to be go." She did as she was told and removed the rocks that were wedging the wheels in place. With that done, she hoisted herself back up onto the flatbed of the cart. Roy sat facing forward on the driver's bench, holding the tiller with both hands as if he expected it to try to wrench itself free from his grip.

Brit stood, grasping the brake lever and peeking over the plank at Martin and the dirt monster's approach in the distance.

Brit said, "Roy, I'm going to try to give you a countdown from five, just like we discussed."

Roy said, "Roger!"

In the distance, Martin shouted, "Get ready! We're here!"

Everybody's enjoying this but me, Gwen thought. *That means either they're all wrong or I am. Funny, I can't see how either of those ideas should cheer me up at all.*

Gwen settled on the flatbed, one hand gripping the side of the driver's bench. The other held the cord that controlled her emergency brake. If things went according to plan, the brake wouldn't be needed. If they didn't, the entire cart would probably disintegrate, making the emergency brake superfluous. It didn't matter. She'd made the stupid thing, and she was going to be ready if the time came to use it.

Brit said, "Five. Four. Three."

Gwen heard an impact as Martin's foot hit the lone plank that acted as a combination ramp and springboard. She saw his hands grasp the top edge of the shield.

"Two."

Martin's feet scrabbled against the toeholds he'd installed.

"One."

Martin launched himself over the top like he was vaulting a fence. For a seemingly endless moment he hung in midair above the cart; then he started to descend. His legs and pelvis had just fallen lower than the back of the shield when Brit said "Impact," and the dirt monster rammed into the back of the cart.

The shield bucked and creaked, and the cart shot forward.

Martin, not being on the cart but rather hovering over it, did not move at all until the top edge of the shield hit him in the lower back. His head, arms, and torso rolled backward, and for an instant it seemed like he might fall over the shield and land on the dirt beast's back, but instead he balanced, teetering painfully on the splintery top edge of the shield, all of his weight resting on his lower back. He glanced down and saw that the beast was still running, chasing him, and the cart along with him, but that the collision had imparted so much of the beast's momentum into the cart that it was now rolling several feet in front of the creature. Martin knew from experience that the creature would accelerate, and even if it didn't, the cart was rolling downhill now but would be going up the next hill soon. The creature would hit them again, and if he was still balancing like a human teeter-totter when that happened, he would fall off the cart, and instead of him and his friends using the creature to push their cart across the desert, his friends would use the cart as bleachers to watch as Martin was trampled to death by Mr. Topsoil.

The idea of being stomped on by dirt amused Martin but not enough to make it happen.

Martin grabbed the top of the shield with both hands and pulled, moving his center of gravity forward and scraping the rough wood across his tender lower back. He rolled forward, catching one of the angled braces between the legs. He tumbled to the bed of the cart, landing in a heap at the base of the brake lever. Brit was forced to alter her surfer's stance to keep him from taking her feet out from under her. Unfortunately, the beast struck the shield again while she was shifting her balance, and both she and Martin fell back onto the shield, which squeaked and groaned at the sudden load striking it from a direction it was never meant to be struck.

"Brakes!" Roy shouted. "Brakes!" He was fighting the tiller with both hands, trying to avoid rocks and keep the cart from overturning.

Brit and Martin both attempted to crawl forward to the brake handle, but the cart reached a trough between two hills, slowed, and the monster struck the shield a third time, pushing them both back and knocking the wind out of them. Gwen let go of the emergency brake cord, knowing that using it in this situation would be disastrous. She threw herself toward the brake lever, pushing it back with both hands. The cart slowed.

The hope was that if they slowed the cart enough, they might be able to get the beast to maintain constant contact with the shield. Then they could use its endless energy and enthusiasm for chasing to power them forward.

That was the hope. The reality was that Gwen shoved the brake lever as hard as she could, and it slowed the cart enough that instead of sustaining a tremendous blow every few seconds, it sustained a hard blow roughly every second.

"More brakes," Roy yelled, struggling to keep the cart upright. "I think I can start turning this thing around, but we're going to need more brakes."

"I'm trying," Gwen yelled back, pushing with all her might on the brake lever, eyes squeezed shut with effort. No matter how hard she pushed, the lever didn't seem to move any farther than it already had.

Martin got to his feet and joined Gwen, but Brit said, "It's no good. This is as slow as we're going to get. We should have beefed up the brakes more."

Roy said, "Okay, that's a design flaw. We can make this work as is, but we'll remember the problem for Mark Two."

"Yeah," Gwen shouted. "'Cause we're totally going to do this again someday."

28.

Phillip lost any doubt that the chasm ahead was the Chasm of Certain Doom when the straight-line route they'd been walking slowly changed to a marked path, paved with what appeared to be bones. Phillip was convinced, but that didn't stop the chasm from trying to convince him further. The closer they got to the chasm, the louder it seemed to shout "Certain Doom."

After the path of bones, the next sign was the odor. They made a game of trying to describe what it smelled like, and settled on "somebody cooking rotten eggs and broccoli in a microwave."

A while later, they started hearing the sound. At first they thought it was a waterfall, but it was way too uneven. When they finally drew close enough to actually look down into the chasm, they saw what the noise was, but by then they were too distracted by the final, clinching proof that this was the Chasm of Certain Doom: the sight of it.

The chasm was deep. Grand Canyon deep. It was easily a mile to the bottom and at least four miles across. The canyon walls dropped at an alarming angle to the dark recesses of the canyon floor.

It was midday, and the sun was directly overhead, yet it was dark down there. It was as if the light from the sun could get to the bottom of the chasm but it didn't want to. Phillip couldn't blame it.

They would have been looking down into a featureless, black morass if it wasn't for the light cast by the river at the bottom of the chasm, which, instead of water, flowed with glowing lava.

The four men stood at the edge of the chasm, looking down, joylessly.

"That wouldn't work," Tyler said. "A river of lava wouldn't cut a chasm like this. If anything, it would add rock."

Nobody bothered to agree or disagree. Whether the chasm made any sense or not, it was there, and they'd have to deal with it.

Foul-smelling wind blew up from the interior, strong enough to make the remaining tail on Phillip's abused fur coat flap like a plastic pennant. Waves of heat and thick, dark smoke radiated from the lava, obscuring geological features that, ironically, were only visible because of the light the lava also emitted. What little they could see, they wished they couldn't. The flowing torrent of liquid rock flowed around islands of jagged stones and knifelike spires of glistening black rock.

They had no idea how they would traverse the bottom of the chasm, but they knew how they would get down there to try. The bone path had led them directly to the cliff, where it made a ninety-degree turn to the left and started a zigzagging path down the wall. The path was narrow. It made the single-file path they'd taken over Cardhu Pass seem like a freeway in comparison.

Gary asked, "So, what do we do?"

If he'd been looking at Phillip, the question would have been straightforward enough, but he looked squarely at Jimmy as he asked. The note containing Jimmy's thoughts on their predicament had fully made the rounds, and nobody had any objections, or at least any better ideas. He had asked what they would do, but by directing it to Jimmy, in essence, he had said, "I know what we're supposed to do, but what are we really going to do?"

Jimmy got the message loud and clear. He peered down at the path. He looked along the cliff's edge to the left as far as his eye could see, then did the same to the right. He looked at the path behind them, for anything that might be of use. All he saw was desert, and a tiny dust devil way far off in the distance. Nothing of any use there.

He turned to Phillip, who had been studying the situation as well. Phillip shrugged.

Jimmy said, "We go down the path, Gary. I don't see any other choice."

They spent quite a bit of time trying to figure out how they would carry the blade on such a narrow path. Their standard method of splitting the load (and the danger) between three of them would not work. They briefly considered just throwing it down like a Frisbee and retrieving what was left of it when they reached the bottom, but they remembered Inchgower's admonition that the blade must still be in good shape when they arrived. The idea of reaching the bottom of the chasm only to have some fictional character refuse to recognize the blade was not appealing. Climbing back up the cliff, walking back through the desert, going through all that with the blacksmith and the pumping and the spider again—none of them wanted that.

They tried the path and found that the only way it could be traversed practically was to walk sideways, leaning back, as if they were walking on a high-rise building's window ledge.

They ended up having three men scuttle side by side. The man in front and the man in back would pinch the circular blade, supporting as much weight as they could but mainly adding control and stability. The man in the middle would hold his well-wrapped hand flat, at just about throat height. The blade would rest on this hand where the blade twisted. He had to hold it at throat height because if he held it any lower, the other two men could not assist him without crawling.

The plan worked well until they reached the first switchback. Coordinating a turn for three people carrying something is complex enough, but the path was so narrow and steep that simply maneuvering the blade around the corner was out of the question. Instead, each switchback would cause a tense ballet. Everyone, even Phillip with his one good arm, would help move the blade through the switchback with a great deal of effort and insults. All were aware that to touch the blade's cutting edge meant pain at best, and slow painful death at worst. (Quick, painless death was somewhere in the middle.) There were countless switchbacks between the cliff's edge and the canyon floor, and before long they had perfected their switchback technique, and their insults.

The descent was tedious, terrifying, and irritating, a unique combination that Todd had mastered. The only moments of levity during the entire trip to the canyon floor came when they were attacked by a cliff wolf.

They had been descending for less than a half hour when the wolf appeared. Like the desert, the cliff offered no cover to hide the fact that the wolf was materializing out of thin air. Phillip saw it first and called out "Wolf," as was the protocol. He prepared to fend it off with his one good arm, which would be difficult while walking sideways and clinging to a cliff, but he'd find a way. The others were carrying that cursed blade, and Phillip needed to do his part.

As with every other wolf on every other part of their journey, the wolf spawned somewhere just off the path, then scanned for someone to attack. Unlike every other wolf on every other part of their journey, this wolf materialized on the side of a sheer cliff. It did materialize over part of the path, but it fell with enough force that it didn't so much land on the path as bounce off it.

First the wolf didn't exist; then it was falling; then it was bouncing; then it was falling again for quite some time; then it didn't exist.

If it had been a real wolf, it wouldn't have struck them funny, but it wasn't a real wolf, and it did strike them funny. Very much so. It helped that the wolves were so poorly designed and programmed. There was no barking or yelping or attempts to stay on the path, just an angry wolf snarling all the way to the canyon floor.

Wolves "attacked" several more times while they were on the cliff, and it never stopped being funny. Even the last time, when they were near the bottom and the wolf survived the fall and ran back up the path to attack. Something about watching the wolf come all the way back up to where it had materialized in the first place made it that much funnier.

By the time they reached the canyon floor they had lost all track of time. They agreed it had been hours, but none would venture a guess how many. It was dark, but they were at the bottom of the Chasm of Certain Doom. It was going to be dark down here. They had seen with their own eyes that even at midday it was dark. Acrid fumes from the river of molten rock obscured the sky. They knew it was late, but they didn't know how late.

What they did know was that they needed to rest. The trip down had been strenuous in every way imaginable.

They bedded down on the forsaken hunk of rock where the path ended. It was broad and flat and surrounded with moving liquid rock. The flow was just close enough to be uncomfortably warm without quite starting to burn. On the bright side, no campfire was necessary. Also, the bare patch of solid ground was littered with wolf jerky from all of the cliff wolves that had fallen to their deaths.

Tyler volunteered for the first wolf watch while the others got some rest. Later, Tyler woke Jimmy. Gary relieved Jimmy; then Tyler took another turn. Everyone knew that Phillip needed more rest and that he would deny this if asked, so they simply chose to not give him the chance.

There had been the usual escalating wolf attacks while they slept. They had all gotten pretty good at sleeping through the sound of a man fending off multiple wolves. They certainly didn't bother to wake each other over something as petty as anything less than eight wolves. That's why Tyler was the only one who heard a horrible crashing sound coming from the cliff above.

They all heard Tyler scream, which caused their lizard brains to take over. They scurried in every direction before even waking up enough to wonder why. They instinctively split their attention between making sure they didn't jump into the lava and looking behind them to see what they were getting away from.

They all heard the horrific crashing noise and saw what made it, and suddenly they were wide awake.

29.

They had only been driving across the desert on their dirt monster–powered oxcart for an hour before Martin's rendition of the chorus of "A Horse with No Name" stopped being even slightly amusing.

Of course, it took him another hour to actually stop, but they all knew that irritating everyone else is half the fun of singing.

Brit was steering. They had not been going for long when they realized that both steering and braking were far too taxing for any one person to do single-handed without relief. Swapping out the brake position was easy enough, but changing drivers was tricky. The vehicle was not going to stop, or even slow down.

The monster was pushing them just as Brit had predicted and would probably continue to until they either wanted to stop or screwed up. Watching the creature chase, then briefly carry Roy had given her the idea. She saw that the creature's programming was simple.

If the target is in front of you, chase it. If the target's no longer in front of you, acquire target.

She recognized instantly that if they could stay in front of the beast forever, it would chase them forever, possibly pushing them forward, at its top running speed, in theory, forever.

The dirt creature's top running speed turned out to be about fifteen miles per hour, which felt plenty fast. In a car, that would be "cruising around a parking lot looking for a space" speed. In a slightly modified oxcart with no sides, crossing an unpaved, hill-infested desert in the middle of the night with no headlights, pushed forward by a hulking creature that would stomp you into a puddle of ooze if you fell off, it was more than fast enough.

Luckily, the sky was clear and the moon was out. Also, the trail of footprints they had started following had become a relatively well-marked path. It was just narrow enough for the cart to straddle it, and it was paved with some white, reflective, gravel-like material. Brit didn't think it was rock, but she wasn't going to try to stop the cart to identify it. Whatever the stuff was, it shone in the moonlight and made it much easier to follow Phillip's party.

That was how she thought of it. Phillip's party. The others were here to rescue their friends and Jimmy. She was here to rescue Phillip and his friends, and Jimmy. She and Phillip had been a couple for years, but Phillip's circle of friends was still her circle of acquaintances.

That doesn't seem healthy, she thought. *It also doesn't seem like Phillip's fault.*

Brit had only been driving for an hour, but she was about ready to let someone else take over. Her arms ached and her nerves were fried.

Roy was on the brakes, releasing them as the cart went up hills and applying them as it coasted down, trying to keep steady contact with the dirt creature's head. The hills and valleys were small, regular, and gentle enough that they had spent some time debating whether you can call an illness seasickness if you got it on dry land. In the end, none of them could agree whether it was seasickness or not, but all agreed that talking about it was not making it better.

Martin and Gwen were huddled together in the middle of the cart, resting. Not sleeping. None of them made any pretense at sleeping. The cart was not a relaxing place to be.

If someone had asked Brit, she'd have sworn that she was concentrating on the path directly ahead, following the path, and trying to avoid any obstacles in their way. That's what she thought she was doing, but subconsciously she was occasionally scanning the entire area ahead. She kept not seeing anything worth noting, so her brain kept erasing the useless information her eyes had gathered. That's how people get to work with no memory of having driven there.

Then, with no warning, Brit thought she saw something. It wasn't really an object. It was more of a discoloration. A vast swath of the desert ahead of them just seemed to be a different color. The moon was putting out just enough light to let her see that something was there but not enough to tell her what it was.

Whatever it was, it was large. As she crested a hill she saw that it seemed to stretch across her entire field of view. It was miles wide. She still couldn't make out any features, just a line, parallel to the horizon, where the ground's color just changed, and another, closer line where it abruptly changed back. At the far line, the ground's color lightened and continued to get brighter, bit by bit, until the nearer line.

What is that? she thought. *I know I should recognize that.*

She stared at it, and she stared at it, and she stared at it, and then finally, she saw it.

Sometimes, when a song is playing on a car stereo that's turned way down, you'll only hear the drums and part of the bass, and you'll think, *I've never heard this song before. What is this?* Then you'll turn the volume up and listen, confused, for a few seconds before realizing it's a song you know well and have memorized. All at once the song snaps into clarity and you can't believe that you didn't recognize it in the first place.

Brit felt silly for not recognizing instantly that the thing before them was a vast, deep canyon, but she didn't beat herself up about it. She was far too busy turning the cart as hard as she dared and yelling for Martin and Gwen to shift their weight to the cart's inside edge.

The outside wheels left the paved path and plowed through the dirt. The inside wheels spun freely in midair. Martin and Gwen perched on the upper edge of the cart, weighing it down and preparing to jump off if need be.

Brit cursed herself for not seeing the canyon earlier. The wheels of the cart came within a few feet of the cliff as they careened past. Running parallel to the canyon, Brit straightened the cart out in an attempt to keep from turning it over and casting all of them into oblivion.

Roy, oblivious to the danger, shouted, "Don't turn so sharp! You'll lose our motor!"

"That's what I'm trying to do!" Brit replied.

"Why?!" Roy asked.

Brit grunted, "Can't explain! We need to stop!"

Roy said, "Oh, then you'll have to turn sharper." He looked back at the "motor". The creature's poor maneuverability had caused it to drift to the right side of the shield, but it corrected this, found the center again, and was still pushing. Just beyond the dirt creature, Roy saw a vast, yawning emptiness, the bottom of which glowed with fire. He yelped like a startled child, gripped the brake handle tighter, and yelled, "Okay, I see why we need to stop. Just remember to turn left."

Brit said, "I know that. But turning's no good. We're going too fast. We can't turn sharp enough to lose it."

Brit was busy trying to steer. Gwen and Martin were trying to hold on to the side of the cart bed and looked as if they were thinking about jumping. Roy had a good grip, a good view, and a moment to think. He yelled to Brit, "Try a diminishing radius."

Brit instantly understood what he meant. She yelled, "Hold on," and pushed the tiller to the right. The cart rattled and groaned. The inside wheels stayed on the ground, but only just. Roy tried to help by jamming his full weight into the brakes. He had been babying them, but now he knew it was all or nothing. The cart had reached the end of its usefulness, and he could save the people he was with, or he could save the brakes. It was an easy choice. He peered over the shield and saw that the creature had drifted to the right.

Brit slowly pushed the tiller a little farther to the right. Martin and Gwen held on, white knuckled, to the inside edge of the cart bed, but the force of the turn was pulling them toward the other side. Brit pushed the tiller farther still. Now the left wheels were in the air. Brit feared they would break under the strain. Roy was clinging to the brake lever like a sea captain clinging to the mast in a typhoon. Martin and Gwen looked like they were hanging from the edge of a roof, not lying on the bed of a cart.

Roy yelled, "A little more, Brit!" He continued leaning hard into the brakes, but he heard and felt a snap; then the lever went limp. He didn't know what had broken, but the brakes were out of commission.

Brit gritted her teeth and pushed the tiller just a hair farther. There was a scraping noise from the shield, and the cart had no power. Brit heard heavy footsteps recede to her right, but she

was far more concerned about the cart, which was still teetering on two wheels in the middle of a tight turn and now had no
forward impetus.

It teetered for an instant. Brit swung the tiller back past
the center, and the cart fell heavily back onto four wheels and
coasted forward on its own momentum.

Brit closed her eyes and let out a relieved sigh. She drew in a
lungful of air, opened her eyes, then shrieked, "Brakes!"

They had come out of the turn aimed almost directly at the
edge of the canyon. They had lost some speed, but they were still
rolling fast enough that jumping off the cart into the darkness in
a rocky desert was an unappealing prospect.

Roy saw what Brit saw, and yelled, "No brakes! Turn!"

Gwen lurched for the middle of the cart, shouting, "No!
Keep straight! Straight!"

Brit immediately knew what Gwen meant, and did as she
was told, steering directly for the cliff. Gwen grabbed a stick that
was tied to a cord that disappeared between the floorboards of
the cart. She yanked the cord hard.

Beneath the cart, the cord was tied to a second cord, which
was threaded through some small notches in the cart's frame.
The second cord terminated on both ends at identical, folded
bundles of the tough fabric of Roy's former trench coat. The
bundles were square and tied up like little gift-wrapped presents. When Gwen pulled the cord, the bows holding the bundles untied. The bundles unfolded into long strips of material
six feet long and five inches wide. The free ends were weighted
with lead. The other ends were nailed into the frame of the cart
and reinforced. The bundles were positioned in front of the rear

wheels. Because the cart was going perfectly straight, when the fabric hit the ground it was drawn beneath the rear wheels. The fabric pulled tight. The wheels stopped turning. The cart made a sound like it had been hit with a wrecking ball, but the wheels pressed the fabric onto the ground and the cart came to a stop.

Brit said, "That could have been worse." The cart was on solid ground. The cliff was still at least ten feet away. She turned around and smiled at Gwen, who was crouched in the bed of the cart with the ripcord in her hand and a relieved look on her face. Martin laughed.

Roy said, "I knew it would work," in a tone of voice that said otherwise, then looked back over the shield behind them. That's when he saw the dirt beast rapidly approaching.

Roy shouted, "Jump! Jump now!" Then he led by example, diving off the cart.

Gwen and Brit leapt off the cart, landing hard on the desert floor. Gwen looked back to the cart and saw Martin standing as if preparing to jump, but not moving. His right leg twitched rhythmically as he watched the dirt beast closing in. Martin only waited a moment longer than the others, three seconds at most, but they were three very important seconds.

Some of the earth elemental's targets had scattered, but one was still directly ahead. The algorithm that governed its actions saw no need to recalculate. It continued running straight ahead at full speed.

Martin held the shield-wall to brace himself, then glanced to the cliff edge. He waited approximately one half of one second, then jumped. The elemental struck at an angle, spinning the cart slightly while shoving it forward. The impact was substantial, and the cart lurched forward with surprising speed. The front wheels of the cart had already crossed into thin air by the time Martin's feet had left the cart. He didn't allow for this sudden forward speed when he calculated his trajectory and found himself flying through the air sideways, toward the cliff's edge. He landed on solid ground but desperately clawed at the soil with his hands while his feet swung out into the abyss.

The dirt creature noted Martin's jump and attempted to change its course, but it was far too late. Instead of simply following the cart over the edge, it veered off as if attempting to pass the cart as they both went over the edge and were swallowed by the darkness.

Brit, Gwen, and Roy were still too stunned to move. They were panicked from the close call, confused from Martin not jumping with them, impressed at his quick thinking, alarmed at his nearly going off the cliff anyway, delighted when Martin's plan worked, and relieved when he came to a stop safe and sound. Now they were standing there with all of those emotions still swimming in their systems. In the distance, there was a dull, quiet crashing noise as Martin pulled himself to the safety of solid ground and bellowed, "My name is James Tiberius Kirk!"

Only Gwen got the joke, but that was enough for Martin.

The others advanced on Martin, making sure he was really okay. Then they looked over the edge into the canyon below. The floor was alive with flowing rivulets of lava. They branched off of one another, flowed away and around seemingly random dark shapes that were only visible for their failure to emit light, then reconnected to continue flowing down the ravine. They knew

that what was left of the cart and what was left of the dirt creature were down there somewhere, but even with the light from
the lava, it was impossible to know where in this light, and at
this distance.

Gwen said, "Roy, not one crack about women drivers, okay?"

Roy said, "Of course not. One just saved my life."

30.

Jimmy asked, "Was that the earth elemental?"

Phillip said, "I'm not sure."

Whatever it was, it had fallen out of the night with almost no warning, along with what appeared to be a large heap of wood and metal. The wood and metal landed frighteningly close to where they'd been sleeping. The other thing landed on the edge of the lava flow and exploded into a cloud of dust.

There was a dark spot where it had landed, and for a moment, that spot was vaguely man-shaped, but half of it was on the surface of the slowly flowing lava, and the man shape grew disconnected and deformed. The dust floated, suspended in the air, then began to move, as if propelled by a strong breeze toward the dark spot drifting away in the river of rock. The dust coalesced into a cloud, which compressed into a form and hardened into the earth elemental, which immediately sank to the waist and began melting into the lava.

The elemental faced the wizards and moved its arms as if it were walking toward them, but with each passing instant more of it was consumed into the flow. It would have been tempting to think the creature was merely partially submerged, but the dark brown slick that was spreading out from where its body met the surface of the flow told a different story. The slick grew redder and brighter the farther away from the creature it got until finally it was just more molten rock. The elemental's head was the only part still visible by the time it was pulled around a bend and out of the wizards' view.

"Yup," Tyler said. "That was the earth elemental."

"To think, it re-formed and chased us all this way," Jimmy said.

"Yeah, it seems crazy," Phillip said, "but that's the only logical explanation."

"Doesn't explain this, though," Tyler said, turning his attention to the mangled pile of scrap lumber that had accompanied the elemental back into their lives.

After a brief examination, Phillip said, "Looks like it was a cart, maybe?"

Tyler said, "The cart must have gotten hung up on the elemental at some point between here and where we left it."

"No," Jimmy said, "no, if there'd been a cart between here and the bog where we fought Pigpen, we'd have seen it."

"Yeah," Gary said. "The last cart like that we saw was in Bowmore."

Tyler said, "Yeah. Wait, what?" Tyler closed his eyes and sighed. "Oh man, he's right. There was a cart in Bowmore. It was the first thing we passed on the way into town."

Phillip and Jimmy both closed their eyes, trying hard to remember, and regretting it deeply when they did.

"Why didn't any of us remember that until now?" Phillip asked.

"Never mind that," Jimmy said, looking at Gary. "Why didn't you mention it back when we were looking for a way to carry the blade? You clearly remembered the cart just fine."

"Well, I thought about it," Gary said. "But I realized we couldn't use it."

"Why not?"

Gary shook his head as if the answer were obvious. "It was an oxcart. Jimmy, do you have an ox?"

The other three men groaned in unison, like a barbershop quartet whose tenor just called in sick.

Tyler said, "Gary, just because it's meant to be pulled by an ox doesn't mean we need an ox. We could have put the blade in it and pushed it ourselves."

Gary looked at the others, wheels turning in his head. A look of comprehension flickered across his face. "Wow." He gasped.

"Yeah," Tyler said.

Gary whispered, "I didn't realize . . ."

Tyler nodded. "See it now, do you?"

"Yes," Gary said. "You guys really think I'm an idiot, don't you? Of course I considered putting the blade in the back and pushing it. That was the first thing that crossed my mind. Then I thought about it for five seconds and I saw what a bad idea it was."

Tyler said, "I don't know about that."

"Then let me explain. First off, that cart weighed a ton. It was meant for horses or oxes or something to pull, not four out-of-shape guys. It wouldn't have been like pushing a stalled Toyota in a parking lot. We're talking about wooden wheels on rocky terrain. Second, did you look at the path we were going to be traveling? From where we stood at the time, it looked like it was going to be mostly downhill, so we couldn't pull from the front or push it from behind. We'd have had to pull on it from behind to keep it from going out of control, and that would have been really hard."

"Well, maybe we could have ridden it down the hill," Phillip offered in a quiet voice.

Gary shook his head. "That's just dumb. We'd have crashed and broken our necks, even if we didn't have the magic cuts-through-everything blade in the cart with us. Hell, I wouldn't be surprised if Todd left it there for us as a trap, hoping we'd pull a *Calvin and Hobbes* and kill ourselves."

Jimmy said, "We could have rigged up some brakes or something."

Gary rolled his eyes. "It had a kind of parking brake thing, but it wouldn't have stopped the cart if it had any speed. We'd have had to improve the brakes, and none of us have the know-how to do that sort of thing. No, I see now that I should have mentioned it to you guys, but it wouldn't have changed anything. Now, are we gonna stand here questioning every decision I've ever made, or since we're all awake now, shall we get on with it?"

Five minutes later they were on the move. As with every other part of the quest, the terrain forced them to go a certain direction. In this case, the spot where they'd slept was surrounded on one side by a sheer cliff and on two sides by an impassable expanse of hot orange lava emitting smoke so thick you couldn't see halfway across the flow, let alone the far bank. The only options were to either climb back up the cliff wall or follow the land along the lava flow's bank for as long as it lasted.

It didn't last long. They walked "upriver" for less than ten minutes before they rounded a bend. Shortly before the bank disappeared, it was connected to one of the rocky islands in the middle of the flow by a thin, precarious bridge, as if the lava had eroded straight through a large boulder, leaving two islands and a thin tendril of rock between them. Beyond that island there were many more islands, piles of dangerous, sharp rocks surrounded by dangerous molten rock. The islands were

just different enough from one another to seem essentially inter-
changeable. Each island was connected to at least one other by
a rocky bridge, but many of the islands seemed to be dead ends.
They were sure that this was the only way forward, but toward
what?

They stood and gaped for a moment. Jimmy said, "What
could create something like this?"

Tyler shook his head. "Some guy who wants to make a
maze."

Phillip crossed the first bridge. It narrowed to only a foot
wide in the middle, which would seem easy enough to balance
on when you're walking on the ground, but suspended over
a moving stream of foul-smelling fiery death, it might as well
have been a tightrope. Tyler, Gary, and Jimmy took turns, two
of them carrying the blade across the lava. Like spreading your
arms, carrying the blade actually made balancing easier, if more
terrifying. Phillip's right arm was still in a sling. He had to trust
his inner ear to keep him out of the lava.

After two hours of balancing on narrow bridges while
breathing in mystery fumes and roasting from beneath, they
reached the far side of the flow. Resting against the black canyon
wall, looking back the way they'd came, they couldn't see the far
side where they'd started. They had intended to stop and take a
breather, but the air quality did not encourage breathing. They
had all wrapped whatever fabric they could spare around their
noses and mouths, and their inhalation had created black soot
stains over their mouths and nostrils. Phillip hated the idea that
if not for the torn bit of T-shirt fabric stretched over his face, all
of that would be in his lungs. He tried not to think about all the
stuff that had made it through the T-shirt.

They followed solid land for as far as they could and soon found themselves at the source of the lava. The canyon walls towered over their heads, extended out in front of them, and met at a single point. Beneath that point, a crease where the walls merged ran down to a fountain, spewing wild gouts of lava from beneath the surface of the earth. Viscous, orange blobs of hot liquid minerals spurted from the orifice as if the planet's artery had been severed. The sustained roar was low and loud enough that they felt it in their ribcages. The lower part of the spray merged with the existing lava to form the source of the flow they'd been following. The upper portions of the plume hardened and cooled in midair, then rained down, landing with enough force to crack open on the rocks or make small splashes in the lava flow.

Some trick of convection caused a steady wind to blow out, away from the fountain of rock, pushing all the fumes and particulate debris away from this part of the canyon to collect in a thick cloud downstream. The very cloud they had just walked through.

The flow started fairly high on the canyon wall, then split around a large, almost perfectly circular expanse of flat, bare rock big enough to serve as parking space for several buses. The lava flow rejoined itself and continued down the canyon from that point, and there were several more of the rocky islands connected by bridges that all seemed to lead to the large, round island. Also, because of some quirk in the way sunlight filtered down past the surrounding walls and pierced into the shade at the bottom of the chasm, there was a sort of natural spotlight shining in the center of the flat, rocky expanse.

"I may be reading too much into this," Phillip said, "but I think Todd wants us to go over there."

"Yes," Jimmy said, "that's what Todd wants." Jimmy nodded to Phillip, then to Tyler and Gary. The closest thing they had to a plan was the simple rule "Don't do what Todd wants," but up until this point they'd had little choice. They had to complete the quest because it was their only hope of getting out alive. Now the quest was all but complete, and they all suspected that Todd would try to kill them anyway. This was their chance. As soon as they saw any opportunity to mess up Todd's plan they would spring into action, unless that was what Todd told them to do.

They stood and scanned the area, examining their goal, the path forward, the ground on which they stood, the canyon walls, and the sky above. Finally, Jimmy sighed and said, "I think we have to go over there. I don't see a choice."

They navigated across the islands and the narrow bridges to the broad, flat stage. The smoldering fumes seemed to darken and intensify, making the single spot of light stand out even more. They stood along the edge of the stone disk for a long time, looking for the trap they knew was there somewhere.

Jimmy held up a single finger, telling the others to wait a moment before they proceeded, which seemed odd to Phillip, as none of them had indicated any intention of doing anything.

Jimmy let go of the blade, leaving it in the hands of Tyler and Gary, and took one large step forward. Nothing happened.

Jimmy took another step, with no result.

Jimmy lifted his leg to take another step, and suddenly the air was filled with the same defining voice that had ordered them to be silent when the quest began.

"You have done well," the voice said. "And now you shall be rewarded. Bring the Möbius Blade into the light, and the identity of the chosen one will be revealed!"

Jimmy strolled up to the edge of the spotlight but did not step into it. Instead, he turned to the others and motioned them forward.

There was no need to say that anyone smelled a trap. They were all quite used to the idea that they lived in a trap. This was just the trigger that would spring the trap. The others all moved forward but stopped well short of the spotlight's edge.

Phillip said, "He wants us to bring the Möbius Blade into the light."

Jimmy looked at Phillip, who mimed (as best as he could with one arm in a sling) the act of tossing something heavy. Jimmy turned and looked to Tyler, who nodded. Gary smiled broadly enough for it to be obvious despite the fabric stretched over his face, and started to pull the blade from Tyler, but Jimmy stopped him and took the blade himself.

Jimmy handled the blade easily. It wasn't heavy, just appallingly dangerous. He told the others to stand back, but they stood directly behind him, so close that their feet were almost touching.

Jimmy held the deadly metal hoop in front of him and mentally rehearsed his toss. He closed his eyes and breathed as deeply as he could without coughing.

Jimmy opened his eyes, drew back, and gently lobbed the Möbius Blade into the light.

The blade coasted into the center of the spotlight, then landed flat on the stone surface with a harsh clang.

The wizards crouched and huddled together, waiting for whatever would happen. Their heads swiveled and their eyes darted in every direction, looking for the inevitable attack.

They searched frantically for their impending doom; then they searched in a more confused manner. Slowly, they rose from their collective crouch.

Phillip said, "Huh." Then, the rocky surface beneath them shattered, and they all fell into the darkness beneath, leaving the Möbius Blade alone and unattended in the center of the spotlight.

31.

They only fell ten feet or so, but that was quite far enough. They landed on another stone surface, this one set at an angle, causing them to tumble over one another as they slid down the incline. Phillip cried out in pain as his weight came down on his broken arm. The tumbling naturally ground to a halt as the incline decreased. The wizards found themselves battered and disoriented in almost complete darkness.

Phillip groaned, "Is everybody all right?"

Tyler said, "Yeah."

Gary said, "I'm okay."

Jimmy said, "I'm fine."

Todd said, "Never better!"

The thick, velvety darkness was replaced with harsh, glaring light, which, for an instant, made it no easier to see but caused physical discomfort that the darkness had not.

Their eyes adjusted to the light, but it made little difference. They couldn't see anything because there didn't seem to be anything to see. A featureless white void stretched out in all directions. Phillip would have thought he'd gone blind if he hadn't been able to see Tyler, Gary, and Jimmy all shielding their eyes, searching for some landmark to give them a frame of reference. Gary seemed to see something. He was looking up at an angle and seemed shocked. The others followed his gaze.

Hanging in the distance, they saw what appeared to be a rectangular hole floating in empty, white space. Inside that hole, there appeared to be a room. The side walls were stylishly unfinished concrete. The back of the chamber was a rich, dark woodgrain wall that extended halfway across the width of the room. From their angle, looking up into the room, they could see the ceiling was white plaster with exposed beams. They couldn't see most of the area beyond the half wall, but they could see the tops of light-colored kitchen cabinets.

In the center of the rectangular portal there was a table. On that table there was a computer, positioned with its back to the opening, its cheap metal rear plate and dusty tangle of wires on display for all to see. Sitting there, using the computer, was Todd. He leaned around the monitor, looked down at the wizards, and said, "One sec, guys. Be right with you."

Seeing Todd, and the room he'd been tormenting them from in person, had helped both their eyes and their minds adjust to their surroundings. They were not floating in some trackless, mystical void. They were standing in a large, flattened bowl made of polished limestone. They could see where the curve of the floor rose and warped to meet the curved walls without a sharp line. The wall then bent inward to form a ceiling, clearly the underside of the flat rock they had fallen through. Now that he knew where to look, Phillip could see the broken hole and the trail of debris, soot, and, to be honest, filth they had tracked down as they slid to their current position.

Todd's room also was not suspended in space or being viewed through some magical portal. It was simply built into the wall high up where the floor had curved to be more or less vertical.

Todd rose from his computer. He lifted a bag from the floor and slung it over his shoulder, then lifted a tablet computer from the table. His hand hovered over the screen, and he said, "Stay right where you are, guys. Don't move a muscle."

All at once, they realized they were standing at the lowest point of the bowl, in the exact center of the room, the most predictable and exposed place they could stand. They scattered in all directions as Todd jabbed a finger at the screen of his tablet.

Todd disappeared from his room and reappeared in the center of the white chamber, exactly where the wizards had all been standing before they dove for cover. It was the first time in this whole ordeal that they'd actually been in the same place as Todd. His hair was short and combed forward. He wore a polo shirt that was tighter than necessary, made of a material that was shinier than necessary. His jeans had crossed the line from being rugged, casual pants to being denim tights. His sneakers were safety orange, and his shoulder bag was cartoonishly large so it could accommodate the extra-large sneaker-company logo printed on its flap. Like many middle-aged men, Todd was dressing like he thought cool young people dressed. That's why cool young people change their looks so often. Because if they don't, they'll eventually end up dressing like an aging dork.

Todd said, "Yeah, do the opposite of what Todd wants. Good plan. Caused me a bit of extra trouble. I had to move the spotlight ten feet back. It's not much, but it's all the victory you're going to get, I'm afraid."

Jimmy looked uncertainly at the others and found them all looking at him.

"He was on to us," Jimmy said.

"Yes," Phillip said, looking Jimmy in the eye, not blinking. "So it would appear."

Jimmy asked, "What are you saying, Phillip?"

Todd said, "Oh, come on, Jimmy. You know full well what they're thinking, and as usual, they're wrong. Guys, don't be stupid. Jimmy's not working with me. I'm not dumb enough to trust him. I saw the little love notes you were passing back and forth. I've been watching you the whole time."

"Even when we went to the bathroom?" Tyler asked, grimacing.

"Especially when we went to the bathroom," Gary said. "I bet it was the highlight of his day. He's probably edited together a greatest-hits reel."

"Shut up," Todd snapped. He took a moment to compose himself, then continued. "Yes, I've been watching you the whole time. Even when I was sleeping or away from the computer, you were being recorded so I could scan what I missed for anything interesting. I have a bit of a backlog. Gotta admit, I've been a little inattentive the last couple of days. I got some sleep and a shower, and I've been busy making sure all this was ready."

"All what's ready?" Gary asked.

"You'll see. But first, you were supposed to bring something, weren't you? Where is it?" Todd feigned confusion. The other men just stared at him, thoroughly unimpressed.

Todd smiled and pointed to the hole in the roof. "You left it up there, didn't you? Well, I could make you go back and get it. It would be fun to watch you jerks try to climb up there, but I think we should just get this over with."

Phillip said, "I agree."

"Really?" Todd said, raising an eyebrow. "I'll ask again in a few minutes. If you're still alive, I suspect you'll have changed your mind."

Todd looked down at his tablet and poked at the screen a few times. He casually strolled up out of the center of the room while a glinting silver streak plunged down through the hole in the ceiling and into the very spot he had been standing. The Möbius Blade stopped abruptly, vibrating and slowly spinning as it hovered in the center of the room.

Tyler, Gary, and Jimmy instinctively seemed to gather near Phillip, who was standing opposite Todd. The Möbius Blade floated between them like a poorly designed conference table.

Todd said, "There. All of the pieces are in place." He stopped, then held up a finger.

"One sec, guys. I forgot to trigger something." He jabbed his finger at the tablet again. The lights dimmed, except for a greenish light that came from under Todd's feet, giving him a sinister appearance. When he spoke again, his voice was deeper, louder, and had a noticeable amount of reverb.

Todd cleared his throat, then started again. "All the pieces are in place. The time is at hand. You have traveled far and suffered much, and now . . . your reward." Todd spread his arms wide. One hand was turned toward the sky. The other held his tablet like it was half of the Ten Commandments. He lifted his face to the heavens and bellowed, "Who will live? Who will die? We will find out now. The identity of the chosen one, the man who will be free, will be revealed." Todd held his pose of exaltation, then, without lowering his head, peeked at his audience, all of whom were slouching and glaring.

Todd shrugged and tapped his tablet. The lights and his voice reverted to normal. He said, "Yeah, okay. It's me."

Phillip shook his head. Jimmy guffawed. Gary actually smiled, because he knew how Tyler would respond.

"What do you mean, it's you?" Tyler spat.

Todd said, "Tyler, sentences don't get any simpler. It's two one-syllable words. It's me. It is me. I am it. I, the guy speaking to you, am the chosen one."

Tyler snarled, "But . . . explain to me how it makes any sense for you to be the chosen one."

Todd smiled. "You want to know how it make sense? Me being the chosen one is the only answer that could make sense."

"Why?!"

Now Todd actually laughed. "Because I chose. I got to choose who would be the chosen one, so naturally, I chose myself."

"You created a prophecy foretelling the coming of you. What the hell kind of prophecy is that?"

"A self-fulfilling prophecy," Todd said. "I am the self-chosen one, as I promised me I would be in my self-fulfilling prophecy."

Tyler looked to his friends, but the looks he got in return were more resigned irritation than support. He turned his attention back to Todd. "Look, this stupid quest of yours is, essentially, a story you've thought up. In the first chapter, you told us that we would come here and discover the identity of the chosen one. Well, aside from spying on us as we go to the bathroom, you haven't actually arrived as a real character in your story until just now, and you can't have the chosen one promised in the first chapter be a new character you introduce in the last chapter!"

Todd looked at the floor and frowned. He seemed to be mulling Tyler's words. Finally, he said, "Yes I can. It's my story. I can do anything I want. For example, there's nothing to stop me from doing this."

Todd pressed a button on the screen of his tablet, and the wizards found that they couldn't move. They were conscious. They could breathe, blink, move their eyes and their tongues, but they couldn't open their mouths or move their limbs. Any attempt to do so met with instant and insurmountable resistance.

Todd laughed. "Come on, guys, you can't be surprised. This is the trick that got me banished in the first place, isn't it?" He waited for the answer that he knew would not come, then asked again. "Isn't it?! Isn't doing this to that peasant the reason you all sent me back to my time to be humiliated and arrested? That's what you said at the time."

Todd waved his hand upward and the Möbius Blade lifted into the air and out of his way. He sneered at his captives as he stepped forward to get a better look at them.

"We all know that my macro wasn't why I was banished. It was just the excuse. You wanted to get rid of me from the moment I showed up. I know what it looks like when people want to be rid of me. My folks, the other kids at school, my coworkers at the mall, even my jailers wanted me gone. I was foolish to think you were any different. I thought I'd finally found people like me, people who would accept me. But what happened?"

He looked at the wizards, who were still grouped together, frozen in place. "It was just high school with wizard robes. You left me with the class clown to keep me busy while the most popular kid and the smartest kid decided what to do with me."

Phillip and Jimmy glanced at each other, trying to work out which one was which.

Todd continued. "Well, now I get to decide what to do with you, and I've had some time to think about it."

He looked down at his tablet and said, "First, let's move to higher ground."

He pressed some control on the tablet and they all, Todd included, floated into the air, then glided to a higher point in the dish, directly in front of the hole leading to Todd's room. As they flew through the air, they seemed to shuffle and rearrange themselves. They settled back down to the floor, but the force fields that held the wizards immobile also supported their weight. They seemed to be standing normally, but anyone who looked close would see that their feet were not conforming to the aggressively curved floor.

They were lined up like soldiers waiting for inspection. Tyler was on the left, then Jimmy, then Phillip, and Gary was on the end. Todd landed in front of them. He probably wanted to look imposing, but the slope of the floor meant that where he stood he was more than a full head shorter than they were. Beyond him the wizards could see the entire circular room with its concave floor spread out before them and the hole where they'd come in at the farthest point from where they stood.

"There we are," Todd said. "Everybody comfortable? Good. Most of my tweaking time these last couple of days has been spent readjusting the force fields to your new shapes. All this walking has made you lose some weight." He glanced at Phillip's midsection. "Not that much, but some."

He fumbled with his tablet some more, and the Möbius Blade

flew silently toward the group, stopping next to Tyler, hovering one foot above the floor as if it were simply joining the queue.

"Great," Todd said, clearly pleased with himself. "Now to set things in motion." He tapped the tablet and the blade's attitude changed so it hovered parallel with the curve of the floor. It started spinning and wobbled for an instant. The single twist in its contour that gave the blade its one side and one edge became a blur, making the blade seem even more dangerous than it was before. The blade slid like a hovercraft toward the lowest point of the room, the center. Todd turned to watch it go. Momentum carried it to the far edge of the room; then it started coming back. He turned back to his prisoners, satisfied that his plan was working.

The wizards' eyes were still locked on the deadly blade that was coming their way, but Todd was standing between it and them and did not seem concerned in the slightest.

"Are any of you familiar with Foucault's pendulum? Anyone? No?" He looked disappointed for a moment, then buried his face in his palm. While he was busy making a show of his disappointment, the blade returned but did not quite reach the point where it had started. It gained the same height it had before, but it seemed to stop slightly farther away from Tyler than its original starting point had been. After lingering for a split second, the blade started another journey across the room.

Todd looked up from his hand, smiling. "I forgot, you can't answer. I'll fix that." He noodled with his tablet, then said, "How about you, Tyler? You seem to know everything."

Tyler got back the use of his jaw but remained silent.

"What's the matter, Tyler? No answer?"

Tyler said, "Oh, sorry. Were you talking to me? I wasn't listening." His mouth and eyes were moving, but the rest of him remained motionless.

Todd smiled. "I just thought I'd give you the opportunity to explain Foucault's pendulum to your friends."

Tyler said, "Sure. There was this guy. His name was Foucault. He got himself a pendulum. They called it Foucault's pendulum."

There was a moment of heavy silence. The blade coasted to a stop, again, slightly farther away, then slid away again.

Todd's expression soured. "It would kill you to admit that I know something you don't."

Tyler said, "Not at all. I'm sure there are many things you know that I don't. I don't know what it's like to be held back a grade. I don't know where a guy would go to buy clothing that ill fitting and ugly. I don't know the phone number of the Hair Club for Men."

Tyler looked as pleased with himself as a person completely paralyzed except for his eyes and mouth could. The others laughed through their noses while looking at Todd's hairline.

Todd could make strategic parts of the custom-tailored force fields tighten at will, and he did so. The chortles took on a pained, alarmed quality. The blade returned again. He eased up, and any sound from his prisoners died away.

Now that he had regained control of the narrative, Todd explained. "Foucault's pendulum was invented by, as Tyler put it, a guy named Foucault. His was a heavy weight hanging from a rope, not a fiendishly deadly circular blade with only one side and only one edge, gliding frictionlessly through the air. It's a simple device. You start the pendulum swinging, and then you wait. You may have noticed . . ."

Todd paused while the blade again decelerated at the peak of its parabola, then sped away again.

"You may have noticed," Todd continued, "that it's actually getting further away from you, not coming back to its original resting place as you would expect. That's because the blade's angular momentum is interacting with the earth's rotation. It's essentially a giant clock. At this latitude, it'll take thirty-some hours to make a full rotation, but don't worry, I don't plan to make you wait that long. The other end of the blade's path should start sawing into you in a little over fifteen hours. It's a way you can actually see the rotation of the earth. Pretty cool, huh? I learned about it at the Exploratorium."

Tyler said, "You never mentioned that you had kids."

"I don't. I just like the Exploratorium."

He spent a full swing of the pendulum just watching his prisoners. They were as still as statues, but even with his back to the chamber, Todd could follow the blade's progress by following their eyes.

"So," Todd said, "before I retire to my room to watch TV and surf the Internet while we all wait for you to be sliced like deli meat, I'll do you all one last kindness. I'll give you back the ability to speak, so you can beg me for mercy."

Todd hit a button, and they felt the pressure holding their jaws shut relax. They worked their jaws around and flexed their tongues, but none of them spoke.

Todd said, "Go on. Beg."

Phillip said, "Well, we're not going to beg yet, are we? I mean, I understand that you're going for a 'Pit and the Pendulum' vibe—"

"Derivative," Tyler interrupted. "No originality."

Phillip continued. "But you've given us too long to wait. I mean, it's pointless to beg now. There's still too much time. We still have hope of thinking up a way out of this. You want to hear some groveling, wait fifteen hours. If we're still here, that's when the pleading should kick in."

Todd shut them up again, then thought for a moment. He glanced at the blade as it swung up next to Tyler, then slid away. Todd nodded and said, "Good point."

He fiddled with his tablet for a few seconds. The blade turned violently in the middle of its path. They didn't have long to judge the new trajectory. Gary had barely worked out that it was headed for his end of the line instead of Tyler's when he felt the blade bite into his left leg.

Todd made a show of carefully timing a button press, and the blade stopped moving. With his head frozen looking straight ahead, Gary could not look down, so he couldn't directly see what had happened to his leg directly. He could see a stream of blood starting on his left side and flowing in a thick, straight line down the clean white floor.

Todd said, "Ew, you're bleeding. One second. I'll fix that."

He poked, jabbed, and swiped his way through some screens on his tablet. He found what he was looking for and slid a single finger along the bottom of the screen. As he did so, Gary felt the force field just below his knee get tighter. Much tighter. The stream of blood slowed, and then stopped.

"There," Todd said. "That's better. Don't want you bleeding to death. Yet."

Todd smiled, fiddled a bit more, then said, "And we won't be needing this anymore." He made a few fast swiping gestures on the screen. Gary heard a quiet thud. The force field held him upright and immobile as he watched his own left shin, ankle, and foot, now no longer attached to the rest of him, slide down the steep incline of the floor, greased by a slick of his own blood as it made its way past Todd to the center of the room.

"Now that the danger seems a little more real to you," Todd said, "perhaps you'll be more in the mood to beg for your lives."

Todd again released their mouths back into their own control. He was immediately rewarded with a high-decibel torrent of threats, insults, and high-powered obscenities. He smiled serenely, letting their anger wash over him; then he pressed the button that silenced them again.

"I guess that means no. That's okay. There was nothing you could say that would've saved you anyway. You have no chance. You've had no chance from the moment the quest began. The instant you materialized on that peak, this outcome became inevitable. That's the whole point. I've put you through a long, irritating ordeal that can only end in failure and humiliation. Sound familiar? Sound like my training, maybe?"

Todd walked up the hill to approach Gary, taking care to avoid stepping in blood or touching the Möbius Blade, which was still hovering, motionless, just below what was left of Gary's left leg.

Todd came in close to Gary's face, looking up into his eyes. "In a minute, I'm gonna go up to my desk there and have a seat," he snarled. "Then I'll start the blade back up. It'll fly away, then it'll come back, and after a couple of round-trips, it'll take out your other leg, but this time there won't be a tourniquet. You'll stand here silently and watch yourself bleed to death. You, my trainer, who put most of his time and effort into teaching me fart jokes."

Todd lingered for a moment, savoring the look in Gary's eyes before moving on to Phillip.

"Then it'll be your turn," he said, studying Phillip's face as if it were a word-search puzzle. "Phillip, the self-appointed conscience of the group, who damned me with judgmental opinions nobody asked for." Todd's expression slipped from gloating to irritation. "Hey, Phillip! Look at me when I'm talking to you!"

It was true. Phillip's eyes were looking straight ahead at the far side of the chamber, but as soon as Todd mentioned it, his gaze snapped back to Todd.

"Good. That's better," Todd said. He stepped backward to address the whole group.

"Then, after watching you both bleed out, it's Jimmy's turn. Jimmy, a.k.a. Merlin, the man with the power to either save or condemn me. It didn't seem like a hard decision. Well, deciding to make you watch the others die wasn't a hard decision for me."

Todd looked at Tyler and snorted bitterly. "As for you, Tyler, I didn't really care about you at all. You and Jeff really only got dragged into this because I wanted a couple of disposable people, but you've managed to make yourself a real pain in the butt with your constant criticism and nitpicking. That's why you die last. I figured you'd appreciate the suspense, from a narrative point of . . ."

Todd trailed off, then quickly looked at all four of his captives' faces before shrieking, "Look at me! I'm talking to you! I'm telling you why I went to all this trouble to kill you! The least you can do is look at me!"

Of his four captives, not one had been looking at him. Gary, Jimmy, and Tyler all seemed to be looking off to their left, while

Phillip was rolling his eyes violently to the right. They all quickly looked back to Todd.

"Good. That's better. Anyway, so now, I'll—dammit! Look at me!"

They all had looked away. They all looked back as Todd demanded.

Todd carefully studied their eyes, but it's not possible to look multiple people in the eye at once. Every time his attention moved from one man to the next, he had the vague impression that everyone he was not looking at was also not looking at him.

"Fine," Todd spat. "If you want to go out acting childish, that's your call. Go ahead. Look wherever you want. I don't care. I suppose you think this is some sort of final act of defiance or something, but it's pointless. Nobody will ever know about it but me. It won't change anything. It won't save you. I've got you. You're done. Nothing can save you now."

Todd noticed that all four of his prisoners' eyes seemed to roll, in unison, from left to right. Their eyes locked on him at the very instant something heavy hit him in the back of the head. He hunched his shoulders, looked down, and put his hand to his head. On the floor at his feet, he saw a filthy boot. He spun to see where the boot had come from, and he saw Martin, accompanied by Gwen and Roy. They stood along the wall of the chamber in their road-worn, mud-spattered, soot-caked jackets and jeans.

Martin was wearing only one boot.

32.

Martin, Gwen, Roy, and Brit made their way down the cliff, across the lava flow to the far side of the ravine, and along the path upstream at a much faster pace than those they were following. Not carrying an item that was designed specifically to be almost impossible to carry made it much easier.

They came to the head of the flow, just in time to see a group of bedraggled men whom they all instantly recognized huddled together on a large, bare expanse of rock, preparing to toss some sort of hoop into a shaft of light. Martin considered calling out to them, but the constant thundering of the fire geyser would have drowned him out.

Their friends threw the hoop, which landed flat on the ground. They looked at it for a moment; then the rock beneath them opened up and swallowed them, leaving the hoop on the surface next to a hole.

Gwen, Brit, Martin, and Roy picked their way from island to island as quickly as they could without falling into the lava. They were about halfway to the hole when the shining metal hoop leapt into the air and streaked into the hole that had swallowed their friends.

They double-timed it across the lava flow, but even at twice their cautious pace they weren't moving that fast. It seemed to take forever to reach the side of the hole. When they looked down into it, they were puzzled by the sight of a polished white surface.

"We need to find out what's going on down there," Brit said.

"Yeah," Roy agreed, "but I wouldn't want to just stick my head in there. There's no way to tell what might happen."

Gwen said, "Agreed. It would be pretty foolish to just run up and stick our heads in that hole without taking any precautions. I guess it's a good thing Martin's already done exactly that. What do you see, Martin?"

Martin was lying on his belly, neck deep in the hole. He surfaced and turned back to report to the others.

"It's them! Some of them, at least. I definitely saw Phillip, Tyler, Gary, and Jimmy. I think Phillip might have seen me, but I'm not sure."

Roy asked, "Where's Jeff?"

Martin said, "Well, there's a fifth guy there. His back was to me, but I don't think it's Jeff. It doesn't look like Jeff, and whoever it is, he's got the guys lined up and is yelling at them about something. Also, that Hula-Hoop thing is whooshing around back and forth for some reason."

Gwen, Brit, and Roy looked at each other, puzzled, then dove to the ground to join Martin. They all hung their heads down into the hole for a few seconds, then pulled their heads out to discuss what they'd seen.

Roy said, "Yeah, that's not Jeff."

Martin asked, "Did you see Gary's leg?"

"What's left of it, you mean?" Brit said. "It was hard to miss. The trail of blood sort of drew the eye."

Gwen muttered, "He's gonna kill them, whoever he is. We have to get down there."

Brit said, "We can't just jump in. We need a plan."

"What do you have in mind?" Gwen asked.

"I don't know," Brit sputtered. "I haven't had any time to come up with a plan. I need a minute to think. Roy?"

Roy shook his head. "No, I don't know. I'm an engineer. Most of the job is taking your time and thinking things through. Gwen?"

Gwen said, "I'm a designer. Same thing. This is no good. We're all used to planning ahead."

They looked at each other, their expressions dripping with desperation. Finally, Brit sighed and said, "Martin, what do we do?"

Martin said, "Right. We jump in the hole."

"What?"

"Carefully," Martin said. "Sort of hang down and land on your feet. There's a room behind where they're standing. Did you see it?"

The others nodded, so Martin continued. "There is a computer on a table in that room. I figure whoever that guy is, he made all this. Brit, you're as clever as Roy, and you're better with computers, so you drop in first and sneak around to the left, try to get to that room. If you can access that computer, you might be able to transport us all out of here, or at least get our powers back. We'll drop in after you, cut right, and draw his attention away from you."

Brit said, "What if he sees me?"

Martin barely thought before saying, "Run to the left. Draw his attention. We'll drop in, sneak around to the right, and get to the computer."

Brit asked, "What if he sees all of us?"

Martin said, "He can't look in two directions at once."

Gwen said, "I don't think—"

"Don't think! Act!" Martin interrupted. "Time's a wasting."

Brit sat up and hung her legs into the hole but paused before she lowered herself in. She looked at Martin and asked, "Can I think while I'm acting?"

Martin said, "I don't recommend it. Just slows you down. In you go! We're right behind you."

Brit hung down by her hands. Her feet were still at least four feet from the floor. She studied the curve of the floor, let go of the rim, and dropped onto all fours. She made more noise than she would have liked, but the awful little man in the awful, ill-fitting clothes was too busy ranting and raving to hear. She glanced up to the others to let them know she was all right; then she immediately started sneaking around to her left.

She concentrated on being quiet, trying deliberately not to get caught up in whatever that lunatic who had Phillip and the others was saying. She definitely heard him tell Tyler that it had been a toss-up whether to kill him or Jeff, which made her breath catch. She didn't know Jeff well, but she felt bad for him, and terrible for the others who did know him well, especially Roy, who seemed to value him very much.

She heard the others dropping to the floor behind her. She had moved nearly a quarter of the way around the perimeter of the room and dared go no farther without some kind of distraction. She looked at Phillip. He hadn't moved—she suspected he *couldn't* move—but his eyes were locked on her. She gave Phillip her most reassuring fake smile, then looked to the rest of her team. Predictably, Martin was out in front with Gwen and then Roy behind him. She briefly wondered if Roy had heard what the lunatic had said about Jeff, and the look on his face told her he had. Martin was slowly approaching the stranger. Martin looked puzzled. He was probably trying to think of the best way to draw the man's attention.

Whoever he was, the man who had their friends was oblivious. He was far too engrossed in bellowing to care what was going on around him.

"Fine," the man said. "If you want to go out acting childish, that's your call. Go ahead. Look wherever you want. I don't care. I suppose you think this is some sort of final act of defiance or something, but it's pointless. Nobody will ever know about it but me. It won't change anything. It won't save you. I've got you. You're done. Nothing can save you now."

We didn't come all this way just to watch them die. We have to do something, Brit thought, *and we have to do it now.*

Brit detected motion, turned, and saw that Martin had removed his left boot and hurled it at the stranger. The boot struck him in the back of the head. He staggered forward, more startled than stunned. He shook his head to regain his senses, looked down to see what had hit him, and then turned to see where it had come from.

Before the stranger could recover from the shock, Martin chose to go on the attack. "Who the hell are you," Martin asked, "and what do you think you're doing?"

The stranger mumbled, "I'm sorry?" The interruption had clearly thrown him.

Martin didn't back down. "I didn't ask if you were sorry. I asked who you are and what you think you're doing. Now come on. Out with it. Chop chop." He snapped his fingers for emphasis.

The stranger looked around, stammering. Martin briefly made eye contact with Brit and tilted his head toward the computer. She remembered why she was there and resumed sneaking around the perimeter of the room. She took even more care to be silent now. Despite Martin's assurances, she knew that it was possible for the lunatic to see both Martin and her, and since they had no powers, they'd probably be at his mercy. Surprise was the only advantage they had, and Martin was using it to the best of his abilities.

"I'm Todd," the stranger stammered. "Who are you?"

"Don't change the subject, *Todd*." Martin said "Todd" as if it were an insult. "You've told us who you are; now explain what you're doing to those men."

They all knew that Martin couldn't keep this up forever. This Todd person would eventually remember that he had the advantage. Remembering what he was doing to "those men" brought it all back to him. His demeanor changed from quiet bewilderment to amused arrogance.

Todd sneered at Martin and said, "I am killing them. I am Todd, and I am killing these men. That answers both of your questions, doesn't it?"

Martin said, "Yes, *Todd*, it does."

"Well, good. I would ask who you are, but I already know. I did a little recon in Leadchurch when I was planning all this, so I know that you're Phillip's little pal Marvin."

"*Martin*," Martin corrected.

Todd said, "I don't care. The old guy is Roy, who will probably be pretty mad when he hears what I did to his surrogate-son figure Jeff." Todd inhaled deeply as he looked at Gwen. "Of course, I remember you quite well, Gwen."

Gwen said, "Yeah, we've seen how well you remember me."

Todd looked confused for a second, then said, "Oh, the roadhouse! You saw that. You aren't offended, are you? Come on. That just means I thought you were hot."

"Those things you made were nothing like me," Gwen said.

"That's how I saw you."

"Stop it!" Gwen shouted. "Stop seeing me that way!"

Todd turned to his captives as if they were a posse of friends who had just seen him get shot down in a bar. "Some chicks just don't know how to take a compliment."

Gwen said, "And some dudes don't know how to give one."

Brit froze dead in her tracks. She was almost to the corner of the hole in the wall where Todd's computer sat, but when Todd turned to look at his prisoners, the entire opening was in his field of view. Even when Todd turned his attention back to Martin and Gwen, Brit didn't dare get any closer. He could turn back at any time, and if he saw her, they were done. She looked to Roy and shrugged. He nodded slightly, understanding her predicament.

Todd looked at Martin and Gwen, but he talked to himself. "They must have followed their friends here. Applied the callout. The system would have automatically applied a dampening field and started them . . ."

Todd's eyes got wide. "You followed them all the way here. That means you did the quest too. You had to. It never occurred to me to look back behind these jerks. I mean, I knew they were dumb enough to let me trap them, but it never occurred to me that you might actually trap yourselves."

Todd laughed far longer than the situation called for, then said, "Well, I'm glad you did the quest just like them, because you're going to die just like them. I have powers here. You don't.

That means you're going to watch me kill your friends; then I'm going to do the same thing to you."

Roy stepped forward. "Not the same thing."

"What do you mean?" Todd asked.

"Jeff told me all about you," Roy explained. "He told me why you got banished, what you did to that poor peasant. From the looks of it, you're doing the same to the guys there."

"What is he doing?" Martin asked.

Roy said, "Phillip never told you? Gwen either?"

Gwen said, "It never came up, because I haven't thought about Todd once since the minute he left. Not once." She glared at Todd as she said this, wanting to make sure he understood. He winked at her.

Roy said, "For his macro he created, well . . . Jeff described it as bands of force fields, designed to exactly fit a specific peasant. Once the peasant's body was inside the force field, he would force the peasant to do anything he wanted. The bands would hold him immobile, or manipulate the poor bastard's limbs like a puppet."

"Wow," Martin said. "That's awful."

"Yeah, awfully labor intensive. The force bands have to fit perfectly. If there's even a quarter inch of space, the victim can struggle or slide out, and the whole thing is ruined. He has to take detailed measurements and tailor each force field to the intended victim, and that takes time."

Martin asked, "Couldn't he come up with code to automatically generate the force fields?"

Todd shook his head and opened his mouth to answer, but Roy interrupted. "If he was clever. Jeff has a couple of ideas about how it could be done, just as an intellectual exercise, of course. Like I said, Jeff is clever, Todd here isn't."

"Jeff isn't either," Todd spat. "Not anymore. He's dead. I killed him, in case my earlier hints were too subtle for you."

Roy said, "Nah, we're time travelers. Whatever you did, we'll think of a way to undo it."

"Not this," Todd said. "I made a point of it. I dropped him off a cliff; then I personally watched him fall all the way down until he crunched on the rocks. I can show you a video of it if you want." He motioned over his shoulder to the computer sitting in the opening to his quarters, not realizing that said computer was the most important object in the world as far as everyone else in the room was concerned.

Todd took a moment to savor the looks of fear and uncertainty on Martin's, Gwen's, and Roy's faces as they pondered Jeff's fate, then said, "Okay, you've got a point about the force fields. Of course, I could just jump back into the past, measure you all up for some force fields, then time-jump back, but I have a better idea."

Todd rummaged around in his shoulder bag for a moment, then pulled out a silver, two-handled game controller. Phillip, Gary, Jimmy, and Tyler recognized it instantly. So did Martin.

"Hey," Martin said, "a Wave Bird! I played a lot of *Double Dash* with one of those."

Todd said, "That was a good game."

"Yeah," Martin agreed. "*Mario Kart* never really got better."

Todd asked, "Did you ever actually try to use that stupid plastic steering wheel on the Wii?"

"Yeah, it was useless. I ended up using my old GameCube controllers anyway."

Todd smiled. "I'm glad you like my controller, because I'm going to use it to kill you."

Todd pressed the screen of his tablet with one of the free fingers of the hand that held the game controller. A glowing blue football-shaped jewel about a foot tall appeared above Phillip's head and hung there, spinning in midair.

Todd said, "You've played your share of games. I'm sure you recognize what that marker means. I've applied the control and melee combat algorithm from one of my company's games to your friends. See, my original idea was to play them through the entire quest myself, but I decided it would be easier just to watch them struggle. I left the code in the system anyway, because it was easier to just deactivate it than to fully remove it. It's a good thing I was lazy, because now I get to kill you three with your own friends. And, for a little extra fun, I think I'll give them their speech back. It should be funny to listen to them cry and beg while they murder you."

Todd pressed the tablet again, then turned it off and put it away. He waited a moment in silence, then turned to his captives, making Brit glad she had decided to hold still. When he looked at Martin, Todd turned, and Brit was standing directly behind him, but whether he was looking at Martin to one side or his bound captives on the other, all he'd need to do would be pivot a bit farther and he could easily catch her in his peripheral vision.

Todd said, "Well? They came all this way to rescue you. Don't you have anything to say?"

Phillip said, "Hi."

Martin said, "Hey."

Roy, Gwen, Tyler, Gary, and Jimmy all followed suit with quiet, monosyllabic greetings. Of course, they all had a great deal more they wanted to say, but not in front of Todd.

Todd looked back to his captives, causing yet another heart-stopping close call for Brit, and everyone else.

Todd said, "I don't think any of you appreciate the gravity of your situation. I'm about to force you all to fight to the death, and any of you who survives the battle will get the reward of being killed by me personally. One hour from now, you'll all be corpses, and I'll be seeing what's on TV."

Martin's mind was racing. Playing this low-key had clearly agitated Todd, but it also caused him to lose focus, nearly getting Brit spotted as he shifted his attention back and forth. Martin needed to get Todd to focus on him, and the easiest way to get attention is always to be unpleasant.

"No," Martin said as smugly as possible. "That's not how this is going to play out."

"Really?" Todd asked. "Why not?"

"Because you're gonna screw it up. We all know it. I'm sure you like to think you're this devious, calculating killer, but you're not. I don't know if it's that you're too dumb, or lack the backbone, or maybe your heart's not really in it. Really, probably all three. The point is, you'll screw this up just like you have every other part of this whole thing."

Tyler nearly voiced his agreement, but thought better of it. Brit was on the move again, and they all wanted Todd to keep his eyes on Martin.

Todd said, "I killed Jeff!"

"Yeah, your first mistake," Martin said. "Take out the most mild-mannered member of the group and keep the argumentative, immature, dangerous ones to play with. Brilliant."

"It was brilliant," Todd cried. "I made them all run around, risking their lives for my amusement, and it worked!"

"Only because you're easily amused," Martin said. It took all of his willpower not to look at Brit, who was now behind their friends. She had reached the corner of Todd's apartment and was trying to silently lift herself up onto the ledge. Martin needed to keep Todd focused on him.

"You're stupid, so everything you've made has been stupid, and the fact that you're happy with it is proof of its stupidity, or yours . . . or, really, both. Anyway, you can't kill us. You've already tried," Martin said. "There are only three of us, and we survived everything you threw at us. The mountain pass, the wolves that always attack in pairs, the army of soldiers in front of the castle, that enchanted cloak you left in our way that spawned eight wolves when I put it on . . . Why are you all laughing?"

Phillip, Jimmy, Gary, and Tyler were chuckling, in spite of themselves, but stopped abruptly when Todd turned to look at them. They were certain they had blown it, but behind them Brit had made it up onto the ledge and was ducking behind the computer desk. If Todd had looked directly toward her for even a second he'd have seen something was wrong, but he didn't. He glanced at his prisoners, then turned away smugly, happy that they'd stopped laughing when he looked at them.

Todd said, "You never caught on to what Tyler here did. None of that stuff was really meant to kill anyone. It could have, and it wouldn't have broken my heart, but none of it was supposed to be a hundred percent fatal. This next part is."

Todd pushed the left thumb stick of his controller forward. Phillip lurched forward with an awkward, zombielike gait. Tyler, Gary, and Jimmy walked beside him, shoulder to shoulder, parting to walk around Todd. Gary looked terrible, but his missing foot did not seem to impede his walking in the slightest. The ring-shaped cutting blade that had been hovering directly beneath Gary's severed leg remained firmly in place. Martin remembered that the force fields were supporting their weight and moving their limbs, meaning that they would be much stronger than normal, even without their powers.

They stopped, standing like a human barrier between their tormenter and their would-be rescuers.

"All righty, then," Todd muttered, fiddling with his controller. "Go into fight mode."

All four of the prisoners drew their swords. In unison they assumed a fighting stance, right feet forward, right hands holding their swords high in front of them. As Phillip's right arm extended, he let out a bloodcurdling shriek. The sling that had been cradling his arm was made of the same beige fur as his surprisingly fluffy coat and had blended in so well that Martin hadn't realized his arm was hurt. Phillip's arm reached forward with the same speed and force as the others. The sling stretched, then ripped. It would have been an impressive demonstration of strength if he hadn't been screaming bloody murder.

Phillip stood panting, holding his broken arm out ahead of himself. His makeshift sling was pinned to his forearm by the force field, but its broken straps dangled uselessly.

Todd lit up. "Hey, that gives me an idea!" He fumbled with his controller, and various parts of Phillip's body glowed until his left arm was selected. Todd rotated the right thumb stick, and Phillip's arm rotated, twisting his upper arm well past the point that a nonbroken arm could go. Phillip grimaced and shook, but he didn't cry out.

Todd said, "I think on G.I. Joe dolls they used to call that a 'kung fu grip.'" He looked at Martin, then Gwen, then Roy. He seemed genuinely surprised that none of them saw the humor in the situation. His face darkened.

Todd said, "Ugh, I'm tired of this. Let's get it over with."

Phillip's arm rotated back to normal and stopped glowing. A neon-blue line traced through the air from Phillip to Martin. The glowing blue jewel moved from Phillip to Gary, and a line extended from him to Gwen. Then the jewel leapt to Tyler, and a line connected him to Roy. Finally the jewel jumped to Jimmy, and after a moment of thought on Todd's part, a line went from Jimmy to Martin.

Martin said, "So I'm getting double-teamed. I'd be flattered, if your opinion meant anything to me."

Todd said, "Yak, yak, yak." The jewel went back to Phillip and all at once the four captives moved toward their designated targets. Jimmy, Tyler, and Gary took a straight path to their opponents, but Phillip was under Todd's direct control and weaved a bit on his way to Martin.

Brit was horrified that her friends were fighting her other friends but was delighted that the battle was taking place in front of Todd, giving him no reason to turn around and see her messing with his computer. The screen was dark, but the monitor's power light was flashing. She twisted the speaker's volume knob all the way down to nothing, then moved the mouse back and forth, hoping to wake the computer up.

This Todd guy seems like the type to either dumb things down to where even a child could handle it or keep everything convoluted and disorganized, she thought. *With any luck, there'll be one application running with a nice big button labeled "Restore powers."*

The black screen blinked, then resolved into a recognizable Windows desktop. The task bar was filled with the icons of minimized running programs, all with the same icon, a cartoon picture of a black computer screen. The left half of the desktop was a grid of program and document icons, each with a long nonsensical file name. They were lined up so tightly that they obscured most of the non-Disney-sanctioned drawing of Jessica Rabbit that Todd was using for a wallpaper image.

Todd only had direct control over one of his prisoners at a time. He started with Phillip. The others were all governed by the same poorly designed fighting algorithm that had controlled almost everything hostile since the quest started. This meant that Tyler and Gary had advanced on Gwen and Roy, stood motionless in a threatening pose for a moment, then each attacked their quarry with a single swing. Gary took a swing at Gwen while Tyler attacked Roy. Of course, Gwen and Roy could have killed them easily at that point, but they didn't want to. Instead, they blocked the blow with their own swords, then waited for the next attack, which always came from the same side, at the same speed, after the same amount of time.

I never knew there was such a thing as being "surprisingly predictable," Gwen thought.

Martin had both Phillip and Jimmy to contend with, but because Jimmy was also governed by the computer, he was waiting his turn while Phillip attacked. Phillip's swings were much less predictable, since they were being controlled by a real human being, but that human being was Todd, who was proving to be a bit of a button masher. Martin had his hands full fending off Phillip's flailing attacks.

Phillip was clearly in tremendous pain. Martin could only imagine that all of this movement with an unsupported broken arm would be excruciating. Martin tried to get Phillip's mind off the pain.

Martin said, "Nice mink you've got there, Zsa Zsa."

Phillip took a wild swing toward Martin's midsection, which Martin handily blocked.

"Is that you, Martin?" Phillip asked. "I didn't recognize you dressed like a person instead of the mirror ball at Studio 54."

Martin said, "God, you are old."

Phillip's body brought his sword down viciously with both hands. His mouth asked, "Would it have been less dated to say you usually dressed like the Silver Surfer?"

"Not by much," Martin said, holding Phillip's blade at bay. "It's good to see you in one piece, Phillip."

Phillip said, "You too, Martin. Try to stay that way."

Gwen's main challenge was not fighting off Gary's attacks but resisting the urge to offer him a seat and try to get him medical attention.

"You look like hell," she said, deflecting one of his sword thrusts.

Gary said, "Sounds about right. That's how I feel." His skin was pale. He was pouring sweat. He looked like he could pass out any second.

Gwen said, "Stay awake, Gary. I can tell you want to go to sleep, but don't. You lost some blood—you're probably in shock. You need to stay awake."

"I'll try," Gary said, swinging his sword toward Gwen's head. "But it ain't easy."

Gwen said, "I know." She raised her voice so Todd couldn't help but hear. "It just shows how poorly made this whole thing is, that you're having to struggle to stay awake while in the middle of a sword fight."

Todd continued mashing the buttons and staring intently at Phillip and Martin's fight but split his attention long enough to say, "Go ahead, Gary. Fall asleep. It won't make any difference. The force fields are doing the fighting. Get some sleep. Heck, don't bother waking up at all. Fine by me. Your corpse will keep fighting until Gwen gets tired and slips up."

Roy asked, "But if they're dead, won't they drop their swords?"

Todd said, "No, the force field's holding the sword. Even if they did drop it, I could still make them slap you to death with their limp corpse hands. That actually sounds pretty entertaining, now that I think about it. Huh. Maybe later, if this starts to get boring. I guess we'll just have to see where the evening takes us."

Brit tuned the rest of the world out as she sifted through applications and screens at breakneck speed. Her job was to end the fighting below, not pay attention to it. The faster she found a way to get their powers back, the sooner the fight would end.

Some of the active applications seemed to control aspects of the quest they'd been through; others governed things they hadn't seen, like a giant spider. Most of the windows were images of locations, like surveillance-cam footage of the path they'd taken. She could see the mine, the desert, the castle, but the majority of the images were live feeds of the inside of a cabin. Brit assumed that it was the roadhouse where the Gwen-shaped temptresses had tried to draw them in, seeing as the place was crawling with half-dressed Gwenches. Every angle of every room was covered, including the bathroom. Nothing happened in that place without Todd seeing it. Brit tucked this knowledge away to either protect Gwen from or torment Gwen with, depending on her mood at the time.

At last, Brit found what she'd been looking for, and what she saw made her heart soar, then plummet in quick succession.

It was clearly the application that was controlling the status of his various prisoners. While there was no big red "Restore" button, there was a pull-down menu marked "Dampening Field." She checked the options, and one was "Deactivate."

This was all good news.

The bad news was that the top of the window bore the headline "Merlin." Next to the various menus and statistics there was a rotating image of Jimmy, updating in real time to show what he was doing, and a map to show where he was doing it.

Brit allowed herself a few seconds to search for a menu that would switch to someone, anyone else, but none was obvious. She looked at the remaining running applications she had not yet checked. There was nothing to indicate what any of them did. She clicked on the next one and got another view of the bathroom in the Gwenches' cabin again. She minimized it and was back to Jimmy's page.

She could hear swords clashing and Todd gloating. She didn't shift her focus to listen to what he was saying. She didn't dare.

This wasn't the worst-case scenario. That would have been finding no way to give anyone their powers back, and the whole lot of them getting killed. This was the second-worst-case scenario. The only person she could restore power to at the moment was Jimmy, who was patiently waiting his turn to eviscerate Martin. Nobody trusted Jimmy, and "nobody" included Brit. Jimmy had killed people and proven himself untrustworthy. Now she was considering trusting him to save their lives.

She didn't know what to do, but she knew what she didn't want to do, and that was explain why someone died while she was hesitating when she had a way to save them.

She moved the mouse to the dampening-field menu and thought, *Phillip isn't going to like this.*

Gwen and Roy were getting tired, but they were still managing to fend off Tyler's and Gary's attacks. Martin, meanwhile, was having to work hard to battle Phillip, who was under Todd's direct control.

Normally, Martin would counterattack, but he had no wish to injure Phillip and knew that doing so wouldn't help anyway, so Martin was stuck playing defense. He tried to make up for this by pouring his extra energy into trash talk.

"You're done for, Todd," Martin said. "I've got your moves."

"Really?" Todd asked. "What are my moves then?"

"You keep trying the same two attacks in quick succession until you think I'm used to it; then you try a third. You think you're going to catch me off guard."

Todd said, "But not you. You're smart. You're paying far too much attention to Phillip's sword arm for that to ever work, aren't you?"

Martin said, "You know it."

Todd said, "Let's see if you're ready for this."

Phillip had been alternating between swinging at Martin's torso and his legs for a while. Martin was already watching for a changeup. His senses went on high alert. He watched Phillip's sword arm, waiting for some hint of where he would attack next. The arms did not move.

Phillip barked, "Martin!"

Martin looked up and saw that the spinning blue jewel that denoted who was under Todd's direct control was no longer hovering over Phillip.

In one smooth, coordinated motion Martin cringed, yelped, and spun 180 degrees. He saw that Jimmy was now under Todd's control. Jimmy held his sword in two hands like an axe and was bringing it straight down with all of his force directly toward Martin's head.

Time seemed to slow. Jimmy looked horrified. Martin was horrified. He tried to get his sword up to block, but he knew it would be too little, too late. He saw his own blade rising, and beyond it, Jimmy's expression changed from horror to shock. In the last instant, the momentum went out of his swing, and his elbows seemed to lose all strength. Jimmy's blade slowed and struck Martin's sword with greatly reduced force.

Jimmy's knees buckled. He dropped like a rag doll and landed on his butt, rolling backward on the slanted floor, but his face broke into a wide, delighted grin.

From the computer, Brit yelled, "Jimmy! You've got your powers!"

Todd let out an inarticulate cry of alarm and confusion but was drowned out by Tyler, still hacking away at Roy, shrieking, "No! Not Jimmy! Anyone but Jimmy!"

Roy moaned in such a way as to make it clear that he did not disagree.

Jimmy saw Gwen glancing wearily at him, distracting herself long enough for Gary to nick her left thigh. Martin was still cringing with his sword over his head. He was looking down at Jimmy with an odd combination of hope and fear. Behind him, Phillip was still in a holding pattern, waiting for his turn to attack. Phillip looked Jimmy in the eye and said, "Don't screw us."

Jimmy scowled, said, "Extraction: penthouse," and disappeared.

33.

Phillip and Tyler were stunned. Martin, Gwen, and Roy didn't have that luxury, since they still had to fend off the preprogrammed attacks of their friends. Phillip had come out of wait mode and swung on Martin immediately after Jimmy left the system. Gary seemed on the verge of passing out. Gwen slapped him as hard as she could between blocking his sword strikes, but if having his body attempt to kill a good friend wasn't enough to keep him awake, a few slaps didn't have much chance.

Todd allowed himself half a second to smile over Jimmy's departure, then turned his attention to the strange woman sitting at his computer.

"Stop that!" he shrieked.

Brit paid him no attention, focusing on moving through the remaining windows as fast as she could, looking for someone, *anyone* other than Jimmy to liberate.

If Todd had been thinking, he'd have used his powers to stop Brit. Or he might have teleported to the desk to stop her. Or he may have put his energy into sprinting there. It wasn't that far, after all.

Todd was not thinking.

Todd shouted, "Hey, get away from my stuff!" He moved with a strange gait that was half jogging, half jumping up and down waving his arms, trying to get Brit's attention.

"You! I said stop! Stop messing with my stuff!"

Roy, still fending off Tyler's blade, hissed, "You had to open your mouth. If you hadn't said that, he might have helped us."

"No," Tyler said. "If that was enough to put him off, he'd have found another excuse."

At the same time, Phillip asked Martin, "'Extraction: penthouse'? You know that spell?"

"No," Martin said, blocking a swing with arms that were clearly fatigued, "but I have other things to worry about right now."

Todd was standing at the entrance to his weird three-fourths of an apartment, yelling up at Brit. She was still ignoring him. She found a window that looked exactly like the screen that had restored Jimmy's powers; only this one featured Tyler. She scanned for the drop-down menu she'd used before.

Todd shouted, "Hey! Hey!" He stopped. The anger drained from his face. He said, "Hey," this time at himself. He followed the power cord from the back of the monitor down to the power strip under the desk, which was just below his eye level. He yanked the cord from its socket. The screen went dark before Brit could get the mouse to the proper menu. She cursed and looked under the desk.

Todd smiled at her as he pulled his tablet from his bag, turned it on, poked at the screen, and disappeared.

Brit heard a rustling behind her. She turned and saw Todd standing over her. He had his tablet in both hands and was wound up to swing it at her head like a wrestler with a metal folding chair.

The world seemed to go silent and still. Brit saw the look of murder in his eyes, saw the metal back of the tablet waiting to strike. She was distracted by the fleeting thought that she was going to die with an Apple logo pressed into her forehead, which pleased her a bit.

Brit lifted her left arm to shield her head and readied her right to punch Todd in the face once his tablet was clear of his head. She waited for a fraction of a second, anticipating the impact on her forearm. It didn't come.

He still hadn't swung. *Has he lost his nerve?* Brit wondered. *Is he toying with me?*

"Why don't you do it already?" Brit asked.

Todd remained still, his face a mask of rage and hatred, but a voice from above and behind Brit said, "He can't."

Brit stood. Todd remained frozen; only his eyes moved.

She turned and saw that the fighting had stopped. Phillip and Tyler seemed to have control of their movement back. Phillip cradled his broken arm with great care. Gary remained frozen like a statue, poised mid-thrust. Gwen, Martin, and Roy were all exhausted, but in one piece.

Brit asked, "What happened?"

None of the others spoke, but the voice, Jimmy's voice, said, "I've saved you. Surprising though that clearly is."

There was a terrible rumbling sound. The roof of the circular chamber shook. Cracks ran the ceiling's circumference; then the whole thing lifted into the air like an immense manhole cover. What had been a large room was now a hole in the ground. They looked up at the circular disk of rock that hung in the air above them. Below it, standing at the rim, was Jimmy. His hair and beard were neatly trimmed. He wore a slim black suit. Behind him, the lava fountain, the billowing clouds of smoke and soot, and the sullen, gray clouds were all frozen as if someone had paused the world. He waved his hand and the former roof flew away like a carelessly discarded Frisbee.

Jimmy took a single step. His stride was relaxed and casual. In that one step, he covered all the space between where he started, on the far rim of the crater, to where he landed, in what was left of Todd's office, next to Brit and Todd.

Jimmy brought his face in close to Todd's. "What do you think?" he asked. "How do you like my version of your macro? I haven't implemented it the same way, of course. There are differences. For instance, the force fields that hold you were created automatically when I targeted you, in real time." Jimmy motioned to Brit. "I could immobilize her in an instant, right now."

Jimmy smiled, glanced at Brit, saw the look on her face, then added, "But I won't. I wouldn't. That was just an example. You can relax."

Brit said, "Good," but she didn't relax. Jimmy shook his head.

He turned away from Todd and Brit. He looked down at the others. They were winded, wounded, and filthy, and not one of them seemed totally happy to see him. The only one who wasn't looking up at him wearily was Gary, whom he had deliberately left bound by Todd's force fields.

"Well, first things first," Jimmy said. He stretched out his arm toward Gary and said, "Quest extraction: Gary." Gary disappeared.

"Where did you send him?" Tyler demanded.

Jimmy closed his eyes and rubbed his temples. He opened his eyes and saw that Tyler was watching him like a hawk, ready to dodge at the slightest hint of trouble. Jimmy thought for a moment about how he must look, standing there with his fingers to his temples. He dropped his hands and said, "Oh, come on, who do you think I am, Magneto? I sent Gary to a doctor. Louiza, the doctor in Atlantis." He turned back to Brit. "She's good, right?"

Brit said, "Yeah, the best."

"Good," Jimmy said. "Right, that's what Brit the Elder said."

Brit the Younger said, "That's where you went? To Brit the Elder?"

"Yeah. Where else? Who would you go to for help?"

Brit chose not to answer that but said, "If you did anything to harm her—"

"She'd have seen it coming a mile away," Jimmy interrupted, "because you would find out right now that I'd done it and she'd have remembered that before I ever showed up. Come on, you gave me my powers back, but I didn't know how fully or what the best thing to do with them would be, so I went to future-you for help. Together we came up with a plan. Is that so hard to understand?"

Phillip asked, "Why didn't you just come right back the next instant, then?" He and the others had all limped closer to the edge of the apartment. "Why leave us here fighting?"

Jimmy smiled down at him, then said, "Showmanship."

Jimmy looked at the exhausted faces looking up at him and saw that his answer was insufficient. He sighed, then added, "And, if I'm being honest—"

Tyler snorted, "If."

"After your reaction to Brit here giving me my powers first, I wanted you all to appreciate my contribution a bit more. I knew I had to come back and help you, but I wanted you all to know that really, I didn't *have to*. Do you see what I'm saying? I couldn't just leave you all to die, but I could have."

"And we're glad you didn't," Roy said, "but you clearly weren't in a hurry. You took the time to go to the barber and get a new suit."

Jimmy said, "The suit's not new. I transported out, contacted Brit the Elder, let Eddie know what was going on; then, yes, I cleaned myself up. I was going to be working with a lady, and I didn't want to do it wearing leather pants and a fur cloak that I looted from a corpse before going on a two-week hike."

Roy was satisfied with the answer but not so much so that he actually said anything. Jimmy looked down at the group. They looked up at him as if he were on a stage. He asked, "Before I continue with the business of saving your skins, are there any more questions?"

Martin raised his hand.

Jimmy said, "Yes?"

"The trigger phrase you used to escape. 'Extraction: penthouse.' What is that? It's not any spell I've ever heard. It sure isn't one of the spells we're allowing you to use while you're on probation."

Jimmy sucked his teeth for a second, then said, "Yeah, I guess I should come clean about that. Remember three years ago when I told you that I had voluntarily stripped myself of all my powers? That wasn't true. I had taken the time to set up my own shell program you all didn't know about."

"So when you said you had no powers, you actually had all of your powers," Phillip said, unimpressed.

"No," Jimmy said. "Not at that time, but I've added to it since then."

"When?" Martin asked. "You haven't had access to any computers."

"In your time," Jimmy said. "I've been zipping back to modern times on a regular basis to work on my shell program."

"How often?" Roy asked.

"Once a week, and I'd stay there for a week. It's like I'm bicoastal, but with time. I've been splitting my time between Leadchurch and a condo I keep in the future. It's a good place to unwind and take a break from your constant suspicions."

"Our well-founded suspicions," Tyler said.

"But when were you doing this?" Martin asked. "We've been watching you twenty-four–seven."

Jimmy blushed slightly. "Not quite twenty-four-seven, Martin. None of you watched me when I went to the bathroom."

Todd, although held immobile, managed to make a muffled but unmistakably gleeful sound.

Jimmy looked to Todd and said, "Ah, yes, thanks for reminding me. Time to get back to business."

Jimmy stepped over to Todd, placed a hand on his shoulder, and said, "Extraction: penthouse."

Jimmy and Todd both disappeared. The room was silent for a moment; then Jimmy and Todd reappeared. Jimmy was wearing an entirely different beautifully tailored suit. Todd was no longer paralyzed, but he looked drawn and haggard. His clothes were rumpled and sweat stained. He looked as if he'd been to hell and back.

Gwen asked, "Where did you take him?"

Jimmy said, "I told you, my condo."

"What did you do to him?" Gwen persisted.

"I asked him some questions," Jimmy said. "And I waited until he decided to answer."

"He wouldn't give me food or water," Todd blurted. "And he wouldn't let me sleep!"

Jimmy smiled. "I said I waited, not that I waited patiently."

Phillip said, "Jimmy—"

"Oh, spare me, Phillip. He put us through the wringer; then he was going to slice us up like deli meat. Before you leap to judge me yet again, don't you think you should ask me what information I got from him?"

Phillip said, "Yeah, I guess."

Jimmy smiled down at Phillip.

Phillip looked up at Jimmy.

Jimmy tilted his head to the side, questioningly.

Phillip rolled his eyes.

Jimmy smiled a bit wider.

Phillip exhaled loudly, then said, "Okay. Fine. What information did you get from Todd?"

Jimmy said, "There. Thank you. Was that so hard?"

Phillip said, "Yes."

Jimmy said, "Splendid. I got the password to his encrypted hard drive. It's 'Hot Toddy.' You can see why he resisted telling me. Anyway, on the drive you'll find all the details of how he did all this, all the footage of the quest that he has gathered, and the exact telemetry of precisely how, when, and where Jeff died. If you're clever enough, you should be able to think of a way to save him. If you're not, the Brits almost certainly will be."

"Good," Roy said. "Well done, Jimmy."

Jimmy said, "Thank you! See, everyone! That's how it's done."

"Yeah, yeah," Roy said. "So, now what do we do with Hot Toddy over there?"

Jimmy looked at Todd and said, "*We* don't do anything with him. *We* don't have him. *I* have him, and *I* have to decide what to do with him. Todd, what do you think I should do with you? Should I send you back to prison where I found you, or should I strand you somewhere in the past?"

Todd glowered at Jimmy. "It doesn't matter. Lock me up wherever and however you like. I'll escape again like I did before, and when I do, you're all dead. No playing around this time, just the big dirt nap. All of you."

Jimmy said, "Ah, so it's the third option." He placed a hand on Todd's shoulder and said, "Execution: Todd."

Todd disappeared. No fanfare. No light show. He just blinked out of existence.

Brit recoiled in horror. Being that close when one person killed another in cold blood repulsed her to her core.

Jimmy held up his hands and said to Brit, "You're safe. I'm not going to hurt you, or anyone else. I knew you'd react like this. You, I mean, you as Brit the Elder, you were expecting me, but you didn't seem at all pleased to see me."

Gwen shouted, "You killed him!"

Jimmy turned back to the group, hands still raised. "Yes, I did. What was the alternative, Gwen? Leave him alive? That's what we did last time. That's what you all did with me. Are you happy with how either of those decisions worked out?"

"We don't do that, Jimmy!" Gwen cried. "We don't kill people!"

"That's pretty much what I was just saying, Gwen."

"We aren't murderers!"

"No," Jimmy said. "You're not. None of you are murderers."

Tyler asked, "And you are a murderer, Jimmy? Is that it?"

Jimmy laughed. "Tyler, that is one hell of a question for you, of all people, to ask me. Although in my defense, this is the first time I've deliberately killed. Rickard's Bend was an accident, and when I tried to kill the rest of you, I failed."

"Well, good for you," Tyler said. "I'm sure you're very proud."

"No. I'm not." Jimmy exhaled deeply. "This is the worst I've ever felt, but I did what I knew was right. I don't blame you for reacting this way, all of you, and I won't blame you for celebrating after my next trick."

"Why?" Tyler asked. "What are you going to do?"

Jimmy said, "You don't know? It was your suggestion, Tyler. I came back to you all because I wanted to somehow make amends for what I'd done, but you pointed out that there are some things that are just too bad to ever make up for."

"Like ghosting me," Tyler said.

"Well, yes, that," Jimmy said. "And accidentally killing an entire village of innocent people. You know, Tyler, I'm not the only one who has some selfishness issues to work through. Anyway, you told me your distrust runs so deep that the only way you all would ever accept that I truly have seen the error of my ways would be for me to go to my grave having never harmed any of you again."

Tyler said, "Yeah, that's about right."

Jimmy lifted his chin, striking what he calculated to be a noble pose. "That, friends, is what I intend to do."

Phillip said, "Your next trick is that you won't hurt us."

Martin mumbled, "Kind of an anticlimax."

"No," Jimmy said. "I'm going to deliberately end my existence. I will prove my good intentions and give all those I have wronged peace of mind by removing myself from the equation permanently."

A thick silence descended while everyone wrestled with the implications of what he'd just said. Finally, Phillip broke the silence, saying what everyone else was thinking.

"No, you won't."

Jimmy smiled benevolently. "Yes, Phillip, I will."

"This is the most transparent lie you've ever told."

Jimmy said, "Is not."

Phillip asked, "It's not transparent, or it's not a lie?"

Jimmy said, "Whichever."

Phillip said, "Jimmy, you're not going to kill yourself. You like yourself far too much for that. This is just a chance for you to get away from us, since it's clear we aren't going to give you what you want. It won't work anyway. We have the file, Jimmy. Go ahead, fake your own death. We can track you."

"You can try," Jimmy said, "and the file will tell you that I'm dead, but that won't satisfy you. You'll realize that I've had three years of unsupervised time, and that I could have used it to find a way to mask my entry in the file, making it appear that I'm deceased when I'm not. You can never be sure, one way or the other, so I suggest you don't look in the first place."

Jimmy looked down at the faces of the people he'd just saved and saw a sea of skepticism. He glanced at Brit, who was glaring at him with her arms folded.

Jimmy laughed. "You don't believe me, do you?"

Martin said, "No."

Jimmy laughed again. "So you see my point." He laughed alone yet again, then let out a heaving sigh. "Okay, look at it this way. There are three ways this situation can play out. The first option is that I'm telling the truth, and I am going to actually do it, in which case, you will never see me again."

Phillip said, "Go on."

Jimmy said, "The second is that you're right, and I am going to fake it. That might be a problem if I were bent on revenge, but I've had every chance to kill all of you several times over, and haven't. Clearly, this would just be a play to get out of your lives and get on with my own. In that case, if I do it right, you'll never see me again."

"And the third option?" Phillip asked.

Jimmy said, "It's the same as the second option, only I screw up and we bump into each other at some point in the future. If that happens, now instead of being mad at me for having tried and failed to kill all of you, you can be mad at me for having not really tried to kill myself."

Phillip said, "I think I can manage to be mad at you for both things."

Gwen said, "Jimmy, nobody wants you to kill yourself."

"Maybe not," Jimmy said, "but nobody wants me around either."

Phillip smirked. "You're really going to do this, aren't you?"

Jimmy went back into his practiced noble pose.

"Yes, I am."

Phillip smiled. "By 'do this,' I mean play out this ridiculous charade."

Jimmy pretended not to hear. He closed his eyes and held up

a hand to silence all argument and stop any movement. "Don't try to stop me."

Roy said, "We won't."

Jimmy put one hand over his heart and reached the other hand up toward the heavens. He parted his lips to speak, then said, "Oh, by the way, once I'm gone, just plug the monitor back in. Brit was just about to give Tyler his powers back when it was unplugged. It'll be easy for him to get the rest of you out of here."

Brit started to speak, but Jimmy held up a finger and shushed her. He resumed his death pose. He parted his lips again to speak, but Phillip interrupted.

"Jimmy," Phillip said. "I get what you're doing here, and I'm grateful to you for coming back to help us."

"If by 'help,' you mean 'save,'" Jimmy said.

"But," Phillip said, "if we should ever meet again, it won't be pleasant."

Jimmy said, "Believe me, I know that." Phillip and Jimmy shared a small chuckle; then Jimmy again stuck his death pose. He parted his lips, and uttered his final spell.

"Execute: A noble end . . ."

Everybody waited.

". . . for James Sadler . . ."

They all held their breath.

". . . who was known far and wide as . . ."

Phillip exhaled.

". . . Merlin . . ."

Everyone grew noticeably impatient.

Jimmy blurted, "At one time!"

A lightning bolt streaked down from the frozen sky, striking Jimmy and obliterating him in an instant.

When the shock had worn off and the smoke had cleared, the spot where Jimmy had been standing was not marked with the expected crater or scorch mark but rather with a tasteful tombstone that read, "James Sadler: He never betrayed us again."

34.

In downtown Reno, there was a high-rise hotel-casino that had somehow managed to go bankrupt. The new owners converted the building into luxury time-share condos and divided the top two floors into luxury penthouses. Jimmy materialized in one of these, the one he had purchased. It was the less expensive of the two, but it had what Jimmy believed was the best view in Reno, because it faced away from Reno and toward the mountains.

He bought the place new. It came fully furnished. The first thing he did was hire a decorator, and he gave her one instruction: "Make it look like it's not in Reno." As a result, he had a home full of expensive-looking, understated furniture; his designer got a nice fat payday; and the local secondhand shops were flooded with brand new furniture made mostly of mirrors, pleather, and gold electroplate.

Jimmy spent a moment enjoying the view. These transitional moments in life always left him feeling a bit wistful. He didn't think he would miss Leadchurch. He knew he wouldn't miss having everybody treat him like a monster. He had the sneaking suspicion that he might miss having people know that he was a monster. There was a certain amount of respect that came with the monstrousness. Nobody liked him in Leadchurch, but everybody was aware of his work.

Jimmy didn't know what he would do with the rest of his life, but he knew what the first step had to be. He took a deep breath, turned, and faced Todd, who was sitting comfortably in Jimmy's Eames lounge chair.

Todd said, "I love this chair."

"I thought you might."

Of course, Jimmy thought, *Tyler would consider putting that chair in a wealthy bachelor's penthouse a cliché*. The idea brought Jimmy more than a little pleasure.

"Did they buy it?" Todd asked.

"Well enough," Jimmy answered.

Jimmy sat down on the black leather couch opposite Todd, and the two men looked at each other for a few seconds, before Jimmy broke the silence.

"I sense you have questions, Todd."

Todd said, "I did everything you asked me to, didn't I? I gave you the password to my drive. I told you exactly where and when I killed Jeff. I showed you all my macros and I pretended you'd starved me to get me to talk."

Jimmy said, "Yes. Those are the things I asked you to do, and you did all of them."

"So why can't I move?" Todd asked.

Jimmy smiled. "I'll explain that in a minute, but first, I have a question for you. Todd, what have we learned?"

"What?"

"What have *you* learned," Jimmy clarified. "What has this experience taught you?"

Todd thought for a moment, then said, "Not to underestimate you and your buddies?"

AN UNWELCOME QUEST   411

Jimmy smiled broadly. "Todd, they aren't my buddies. They'd have been the first people to tell you that if you'd just asked. You do have a point, though, in a way. As a group they do have a talent for messing up plans, both other people's and their own."

Todd squinted at Jimmy. "What do you mean? They beat me."

"Yes, but not according to their plans. Heck, the main plan they live their lives by is to settle in and try to be left alone, but they behave in such a way as to make even that impossible. What else did you learn?"

Todd was silent. Jimmy shrugged and said, "Nothing? Fair enough. It's my turn anyway. Here's what I learned. There are some mistakes you can never make up for. There are things you do wrong that you can never make right. That doesn't mean you shouldn't try. You should, but if it becomes clear that you won't succeed, drop it. To force the issue just tortures the people you wronged in the first place. Once you've made your feelings clear, it's better to leave and get on with your life."

Jimmy studied Todd's face, looking for some hint of understanding.

"Take me, for example," Jimmy continued. "There are, in a sense, three of me. The Jimmy I was, the Jimmy I am today, and the Jimmy I want to be tomorrow. I can't change how the Jimmy I was behaved. I know how I want the Jimmy of tomorrow to act. I'm neither of those guys. I'm the Jimmy of today. But, theoretically, by behaving like I hope the Jimmy of tomorrow will act, I can make the Jimmy of today less like yesterday's Jimmy. See what I mean?"

Todd said, "I think so."

"You have to think about it?" Jimmy asked.

Todd said, "No?"

Jimmy leaned forward, just that much closer to Todd to drive his point just that much further home. "Past Jimmy," he explained, "would have taken someone like you, someone clever but not smart, and he would have lied and manipulated and used you for his own profit."

Jimmy studied Todd, who was immobile, save for his mouth and facial expressions, looking for some sign that he understood. Jimmy locked eyes with Todd and continued. "Future Jimmy, on the other hand, would have done what he said he was going to do. He'd have destroyed you quickly and humanely, because that was the only way to keep the people he had wronged safe from you, and because I want future Jimmy to be a man of his word."

"What's present Jimmy going to do?"

Jimmy said, "Present Jimmy isn't sure. It's one of life's little ironies. I tried to kill Phillip, Martin, and their friends, and I failed. Now I feel responsible for making sure nobody else kills them either. That said, I don't really like the idea of killing you. I told them I would erase you, and I still could. It would be instant and painless. I could also reinstate your magnetic field, send you back to The Facility, and send word to Miller and Murphy to make sure no computer is ever brought anywhere near you again. You'd most likely die of old age, after several more decades of solitary confinement and reading about video games."

"What do you think you're going to do?" Todd asked.

"I think I'm going to err on the side of mercy."

"Okay," Todd said. "Which of those options is the merciful one?"

Jimmy said, "I dunno. You tell me."

Todd looked out the window at the Sierra Nevada Mountains, thought for a while, then said, "I don't want to go back to prison."

Jimmy said, "Fair enough." He stood up, crossed the room, placed the palm of his hand on Todd's forehead like a faith healer, and said, "Execute: Todd disposition macro two."

Todd was gone. Jimmy spent a long time looking out the window, thinking about what he had done; then he turned around and walked into his office. His computer was just as he left it, juiced up and ready for work. Jimmy sat down, cracked his knuckles, and got on with his life.

35.

Jeff felt the ground beneath his feet threatening to give way. He saw the concerned faces of the others, Phillip, Gary, and Tyler. Even Jimmy seemed worried.

Jeff looked down. His heels and the balls of his feet were on the ground, but his toes hung out in midair over a sickening drop. He felt the ground shuddering and shifting under his weight. He looked back to his friends. They were farther away now. Jeff knew that they weren't moving. He was, and soon he would pick up quite a bit of speed.

I can't fly, he thought, *and I'm not invulnerable. I think this is it. At least I can go out with some class.*

Jeff felt the ground give way beneath him, and without consulting his brain, his mouth blurted out, "Crud."

Jeff was falling. The rock on which he had stood caught on a fissure in the cliff face, pivoted, and threw Jeff out into the clear, where he had a straight fall all the way down to the canyon floor. His mind was clogged with panic. Time seemed to slow to a crawl. Jeff was so fascinated by the sight of his own upcoming demise that he didn't even hear Roy's voice at first.

"Kid," Roy said. "Kid! You with me?"

Jeff said, "Whaaat?" His own voice sounded deep and slow to his ears, but Roy's voice sounded normal.

"Listen up, kid. We've slowed down time. Well, actually we've sped you up. We overclocked your brain as much as we dare. We got the trick from that doctor they have in Atlantis."

Jeff's mind felt as fast as ever, but his voice droned, "Whyyy?"

"We're going to get you out of this. Now, we need you to hold still."

"I'mmm faaallliinng!"

"Yeah, I know. You can't help that, but stop flapping your arms around."

"Youuu'd flaaap tooo . . ."

"Just cut it out," Roy snapped.

Jeff froze as best he could under the circumstances.

"Okay," Roy said. "That's good. Hold it just like that."

Jeff thought, *And of course, now my nose itches. Man, the ground's still coming up really fast, isn't it? Even slowed down to this pace, I wouldn't survive the impact. Actually, he said time wasn't slower, just my brain is sped up, so I'm still falling at the same speed and I'll hit with just as much force. I'm just getting more time to experience it. Fantastic.*

Jeff heard a female voice say, "Okay. We've scanned him. Rendering the simulation now."

Way down near the canyon floor Jeff saw a light source. He squinted into the wind. It was Todd's webcam window.

He's all lined up to watch me go splat, Jeff thought. *Bastard's got a front-row seat.*

The female voice said, "Ready!"

"Okay," Roy said. "Keep still just a second or two more. We need to time this right."

The ground was getting very close now. It took all of Jeff's willpower to keep from putting his arms out in front of himself, not that it would have helped.

Roy said, "Now!"

There was a flash and Jeff was awash in a sea of blinding light and bright colors. Time accelerated back to normal. Jeff's ears were filled with the rushing sound of wind. His eyes adjusted. He saw that it was a bright, sunny day, and he was many hundreds of feet above the ground. Green trees and rolling hills spread out beneath him. Directly below he saw a town and recognized it as Leadchurch.

This was all an improvement, but he was still falling.

As if on cue, Roy's voice said, "You have your powers back. You can start flying any time you like."

Jeff stopped himself, then hung suspended in the sky, catching his breath.

"Welcome back," Roy said. Jeff thought he could hear the traces of a smile in Roy's voice. "We're all over at Phillip's shop. Come by when you're ready to join us."

Jeff found a surprisingly large group of people waiting for him in the street in front of the shop. He'd expected Roy, and it made sense for Phillip, Tyler, and Gary to be there. He was happy to see Martin and Gwen as well, although he didn't know how they were involved in all this. What really surprised him was that the Brits were there, but upon seeing them, he suddenly realized the female voice that had been assisting Roy was probably one of theirs.

Jeff came to a landing and was greeted a bit more enthusiastically than he was prepared for.

Phillip asked, "So, what did you think of New Zealand?"

"Is that where we were?" Jeff asked.

Phillip said, "Turns out."

"Yeah," Jeff said. "What I saw of it, I didn't like so much."

As they all filed through Phillip's shop and upstairs to the rec room, Jeff said to Roy, "Thanks for saving me, but, why didn't you just yank me out of there?"

"We couldn't let Todd see that we'd rescued you," Roy explained. "We had to switch you with a copy."

"A copy?" Jeff asked. "Of me? We can copy people now?"

"Kinda. It was a computer-generated automaton. It's a trick we picked up from Todd's hard drive."

"I don't know why I was worried," Jeff said, chuckling. "We're time travelers. I should have known you all would find a way to save me."

"Not necessarily," Brit the Elder said. "If we hadn't been told the precise time and place that you'd been killed, we wouldn't have been able to intervene. We can't change an event we don't know about. If Todd had managed to kill you all without anybody knowing when and where, we would all be dead. It's something you all should keep in mind."

"But you don't have to keep it in mind?" Brit the Younger asked.

"The fact that I'm still here proves that I did keep it in mind, and that you did too, I suppose. Well done, dear."

Jeff looked around. The room looked much as he remembered it, except there were two large laptops on the coffee table with a microphone headset wired up and ready for use. He settled down in one of Phillip's lounge chairs. He sighed contentedly, then looked up at everyone else. None of them were sitting. They all stood in front of him, smiling down, unnervingly happy to see him. Looking at them now he saw that Phillip, Tyler, Gary, and Martin were all wearing new robes and hats. The colors were slightly different. The designs were fancier. The silver sequins on

Martin's robe were smaller and interspersed with what looked like rhinestones. Phillip's robe now incorporated some patches of black fur. Even Roy's trench coat and modified fedora were different.

"How long have I been gone?" Jeff asked.

"About a month and a half," Roy said.

Jeff said, "You took your time."

"We wanted to do it right," Roy answered. "There were animations to plot. It had to look absolutely convincing."

Jeff thought for a second, then said, "Fair enough. What did I miss?"

Phillip said, "I broke my arm."

Martin said, "Gwen has moved in with me."

Gary said, "I have a robot foot!" He lifted his leg and displayed the gleaming chrome appendage starting just below his knee. The metal toes clacked together as he wiggled them for effect.

"Huh," Jeff said. "A robot foot. That's the third-coolest possible cyborg body part."

"I know!" Gary said.

Gwen's expression soured. Martin leaned close and whispered, "What?"

Gwen said, "Third-coolest robot body part. You boys."

Martin said, "Yeah. Hand, eye, then foot. What's wrong with that?"

Gwen frowned. "Nothing," she said. "Never mind."

Gary continued. "It's a false construct, of course, not a real robot part, but still, it seems real, and it has three different looks: this one, a dragon's claw, or a normal human foot, but I never use that one."

"Why would you?" Jeff said.

"There's no reason to when you can have a robot foot," Gary agreed. "I keep fake skulls around just so I can stomp on them."

Jeff said, "Cool. Anything else happen?"

Martin said, "Well, Jimmy's dead."

"No, he isn't," Phillip added quickly.

Jeff asked, "How'd he die?"

Phillip said, "He didn't."

Martin answered, "He took his own life."

Phillip said, "Nobody really believes that."

Gwen stepped in. "He realized that we would never be able to truly forgive him, but we also couldn't let him run around free if we knew he was alive, so he made it look like he ended himself, but he may have just gone off to make a new life somewhere else."

"And we're just letting him go?" Jeff asked.

Phillip said, "We've looked at the file, and he appears to be dead. If he is still alive, we can't find him. Anyway, he was right. What he did was unforgivable, and we never would have trusted him again, but we have no concrete reason to believe he has or had any evil intent."

"I don't know," Jeff said. "I don't like the idea that he's still out there."

Martin said, "Yeah, I agree, but most of us don't really like the idea that he isn't still out there either."

"Look," Phillip said, "it doesn't matter. Jimmy didn't want to kill us, or else we'd be dead. He made it pretty clear that he doesn't want to spend any more time with us, and I know that none of us want to spend any more time with him. I'm confident that we'll never see Jimmy again."

Brit the Elder said, "Yes," which Phillip found quite encouraging, until she added, "You are totally confident of that, right now."

Phillip thought about what she might have meant by that, and deflated noticeably.

"And now," Brit the Elder said, "you're less confident."

ACKNOWLEDGMENTS

I'd like to thank my wife, Missy; my friends Steven Carlson, Allison DeCaro, Jen Yates, John Yates, Mark Yocom, Debbie Wolf, Mason Wolf, Rodney Sherwood, Leonard Phillips, Ric Schrader, David Pomerico; everybody at 47North; and the readers of my comic strip, *Basic Instructions*.

I'd also like to thank my aunt Donna, who gave me a Mexican worry doll, which I refused to carry because I was afraid I'd lose it, and my uncle Jim, who failed in his attempt to give me a work ethic, but he showed me what one looks like, and that was a start.

ABOUT THE AUTHOR

 Scott Meyer has worked as a radio personality and written for the video game industry. For a long period he made his living as a stand-up comedian, touring extensively throughout the United States and Canada. Scott eventually left the drudgery of professional entertainment for the glitz and glamour of the theme-park industry. He and his wife currently live in Orlando, Florida, where he produces his acclaimed comic strip, *Basic Instructions*.